AIS OF THE GODS

A Saga of the Twilight

AMA NKRUMAH

UNA LLC

This unfolding tale is entirely a product of imagination. The characters, each vividly crafted with unique traits, embark on a journey through a realm that exist only in the author's mind. Readers will find that any resemblance to actual people or real events is purely coincidental, as this narrative liberally wanders through layers of fiction. As the story progresses, themes of courage and adventure emerge, inviting exploration and reflection. With every turn of the page, the author encourages readers to lose themselves in this vivid tapestry of creativity, understanding that the heart of the narrative beats solely within the realm of make-believe. Engaging with the story means embracing the art of fiction and allowing one's imagination to flourish within its pages.

ISBN-979-8-9921951-5-6

Cover design by: 9Xpressions
Library of Congress Control Number:
Printed in the United States of America

In the spirit of honoring my roots, this work of fiction is a tribute to my direct ancestors who embarked on a remarkable journey from Sudan, traversing through Takyiman, ultimately founding the town of Abakrampah (ghana). The resilient heroes, Nana Adadzie Panyin and Nana Adadzie Kakra, alongside their sister, Nana Kotuaa paved the way for future generations and laid the foundation of our rich heritage. Their courage and determination resonate through time, inspiring us to appreciate our history. I also dedicate this narrative to the cherished memory of my grandfather, Nana Budukuma III, the esteemed king (Benkumhen) of Abura Dunkwa, (Ghana) whose leadership and wisdom have left an indelible mark on our community. Through this story, I aim to celebrate the legacy of my ancestors and all others to keep their memories alive for generations to come.

Respect Yourself: Nobody Is Anybody, Everybody Is Somebody.

AMA NKRUMAH

CONTENTS

INTRODUCTION

Nature will have her own way. Even in the face of chaos, nature finds a way to restore balance. Whether through a gentle breeze or a fierce storm, nature asserts her will, guiding the world on a path of renewal and growth. We are but temporary stewards of her bounty, learning to respect her ways and embrace her wisdom.

In this captivating work of fiction, a select group of powerful beings known as the *AIS* of the Gods (Artificial Intelligence) of the Gods, crafted with extraordinary abilities sets out to explore uncharted territories. The initial generations of *AIS* labored tirelessly, unified by their shared ambitions and driven by a sense of purpose to achieve their collective goals. However, as the years unfolded, the subsequent generations strayed from their original mission. Engulfed by ambition and the allure of their newfound powers, they began to drift away from the foundational principles that guided their ancestors. Losing sight of the power and knowledge that once guided them, they became increasingly disconnected from the source of their powers and knowledge thereby getting cut of from the source from which they came. This gradual disconnection from their origins led to a fragmented society, where the pursuit of greatness overshadowed the vital bonds that once united them. As they ventured further into the unknown, the true essence of their legacy hang in the balance, awaiting a reckoning that could either restore their unity or plunge them deeper into chaos.

This disconnection led to dire consequences; those who perished found themselves ensnared in a haunting limbo, unable to return to their origins. These lost generation now trapped in a limbo grappled with their haunting fate. In the midst of this uncertainty, one person was bent on finding the way home, but this quest was obstructed by a greedy and formidable king whose iron grip on the realm and insatiable thirst for control cast a dark shadow over the mission. His desire to maintain control over the living and the dead fueled a relentless pursuit of power. As these lost souls strive for freedom, the clash between their yearning for way home and the king's insatiable greed intensified, setting the stage for a heart-wrenching struggle between liberation and tyranny that could equally alter the fate of both the living and the dead. The fight for liberation against tyranny becomes not only a personal journey but a battle for the souls of many.

As the story of the *AIS* of the Gods unfolds, the fate of this new generation remains uncertain, compelling readers to reflect on the journey ahead. The question looms: will they have the strength to reclaim their lost abilities and reconnect with their heritage, or will they succumb to the void of ignorance and despair? Time is of the essence, and their quest for rediscovery grows more urgent with each passing moment. In the face of daunting challenges and existential threats, these resilient souls must navigate through their internal struggles and external obstacles, striving to reunite with their true selves and transform their uncertain destiny into a powerful legacy. Will they rise to the occasion, or will they be lost forever in the shadows?

PREFACE

In the great journey of life, the true mission remains a mystery to many, if not all. Even the best literary works; the greatest books, may offer wisdom, but none can definitively unveil the ultimate mission of our lives on this planet. What is undeniably true and clear, however, is that time is the most precious resource we possess. It is distributed equally among both the affluent and the impoverished. It flows equally for the rich and the poor, yet once it slips away, it is lost forever. It is a universal constant that binds us all, regardless of our status or beliefs.

Life and time are both a circle, constantly turning and evolving, with each rotation bringing new encounters and experiences. As we journey through this ever-revolving cycle, we find that every moment is interconnected, with our paths often crossing with those of others in unexpected ways. Each stop in this circular journey symbolizes a significant connection, whether fleeting or lasting, shaping our perspectives and influencing our growth. The people we meet along the way leave imprints on our lives, teaching us lessons about love, loss, joy, and pain. It reminds us that even in its cyclical nature, life is rich with opportunities for connection, reflection, and transformation, reminding us that we are all part of a larger, beautifully woven tapestry of existence. As we navigate through these cycles, we come to appreciate the beauty of each encounter and the profound impact they have on our journey.

As we navigate through the intricate web of life, it is essential to keep in mind the timeless principle that what we put into the world ultimately returns to us. Each act of kindness or positivity we extend can ripple outward, fostering a better environment for ourselves and others. By striving to leave the world a more compassionate and enriched place than we found it, we contribute to a cycle of growth and renewal. If life is indeed a circle, then our efforts to uplift others may allow us to return to this circle in a state of harmony, reflecting the goodness we have sown. In this way, we not only enhance our own existence but also inspire those around us to continue the cycle of improvement and support. Thus, living with intention and purpose becomes a powerful legacy that lasts beyond our time.

Therefore, it is imperative that we cherish each moment and use our time wisely, making choices that reflect our true purpose and values while we navigate the journey of life. By cultivating a sense of purpose and utilizing every moment wisely, we can contribute to a life well-lived, embracing the opportunities to grow, connect, and leave a meaningful legacy.

Whether we are builders crafting our own destinies or worshipers seeking deeper meanings, the essence of our existence continues to remain a mystery.

AIS OF THE GODS

A SAGA OF THE TWILIGHT

BY

AMA NKRUMAH
MD. USA

CHAPTER ONE

"Opportunity Begets Temptation (Lawmakers—Lawbreakers)"

It was a stark emptiness, a vast nothingness, an endless void that stretched infinitely. No light pierced its depths, and no sound disturbed its silence. A canvas vast, yet barren, lost to the haunting whispers of despair. It was not a place of sunlit mornings or starlit nights; rather, it was a perpetual twilight, a limbo where day and night merged into an endless monotony. Light filtered through the heavy expanse in feeble attempts, creating ghost-like shadows that flickered in and out of existence, as if the very essence of illumination was wary of touching this desolate expanse.

In the void, shape struggled against the overwhelming nothingness. It consumed all that ventured too close, drawing them into its embrace. Hills rose only to be immediately engulfed. Flora refused to root itself in the barren terrain; only the most resilient weeds dared whisper their defiance against the greyness. The realm drifted in and out of consciousness, a whisper of elegance brushing against the surge, yet, dissipating before it could take root. Amid the stillness, silence reigned supreme, an oppressive force that smothered any inkling of sound. Thoughts and dreams had no life there, only floating like spectral entities, bound by the ether to perpetual unfulfillment. A pall of total desolation hung over it; a featureless, gray expanse where only monotonous horizons and a heavy, perpetual haze broke the void. Unfathomable, cold, and gently crushing, it stood as a silent testament to a life that could never exist. There, time held no meaning, and reality faded into whispers of potential lost.

Yet, within this stark emptiness lingered a faint spark of possibility. It was a flicker suggesting that from the desolate abyss, something new could emerge—a sign that the void was but a cradle for creation, where every end could sow the seeds of a new start. As the flickering light began to expand, it revealed the contours of the realm. The vibrant hues of dawn painted the sky, signifying that the landscape was a blank canvas awaiting the brush-strokes of becoming. For those willing to look, every color was a muse, and from the void, new beginnings could one day arise.

The palette whispered of fresh starts and beckoned imagination to shatter its constraints, hoping the gentle touch of possibility would awaken latent dreams. The seamless dance between the mundane and the magnificent was an open invitation for all dreamers to wander. Dreams that had been nestled deep within the uncharted realm slowly stirred, yearning for their moment to shine, and inviting everyone to embrace hope and creativity. Just as the early light caresses the landscape, so too will it awaken the latent aspirations of countless believers, reminding all that each new day was a canvas for wildest dreams.

The sun, a radiant orb with a distinct form, slowly descended below the horizon with its mesmerizing beauty. Below the sphere, it didn't just bring light; it breathed life into the aspirations and hopes that had been patiently waiting for their chance to flourish. Its warm golden hues spilled across the landscape, painting it in a breathtaking array of colors. Shadows lengthened and deepened, contrasting beautifully with the vibrant warmth of the sunset. Light and darkness met, capturing the essence of beauty and mystery, leaving the Masters in awe as they unveiled their artistry that transformed the scenery into a masterpiece. Each beam danced joyfully, brightening the realm and awakening the landscape from its slumber. The air buzzed with potential, and every moment held the promise of extraordinary revelations that whispered thought and bold dreams, creating an arras of wonder waiting to unfold.

The uncharted realm was poised for the audacious, an invitation to a boundless journey of the mind. Every shadow harbored a story, beckoning the fearless to step into this vast, uncharted distance. Each bold step forward promised discovery, uncovering possibilities hidden like seeds. The unknown wasn't a destination to be reached, but a continuous journey—a living testament to the bravery needed to perpetually dream, create, and explore. Once nurtured, the possibilities will blossom with each dawn to unveil profound new wonders.

The realm awoke slowly, enveloped in the soothing warmth and radiant hope brought by the sun: the magnificent orb, the ultimate giver of life. It rose with a profound promise, casting its golden rays across the landscape. Each ascent heralded not just the beginning of a new day but also the nurturing of growth for all who will embrace its warmth and energy. The sun's gentle light illuminated every corner, inspiring a sense of renewal and possibility with an unspoken understanding that, with its embrace, life will thrive, and dreams will flourish under its watchful gaze.

The realm, filled with gratitude and ready to explore the potential that lay ahead, welcomed the divine gift. While the shadows retreated, and the vibrant colors of the sun spread across the sky, each moment felt like a promise, reminding all that a fresh start was possible. As the sun rises, so too will aspirations. It will not only sustain life, but also ignite inspiration, fostering creativity and connection among those who will find solace in its glow. The sun will traverse through time and space, serving as a reminder of existence's eternal nature and urging all to live in harmony with the rhythms of nature. In its brilliance, it will enrich all willing to receive hope and vitality as it will breathe life into the realm each and every day.

The magical interplay of light and nature stirred something deep within, igniting a sense of wonder and possibility that lingered long after the sun fully emerged. With an infusion of magic into reality, a single shake summoned a drop from the Masters. It was no ordinary drop; it carried with it the essence of life itself. The skies darkened, as if acknowledging the power of the moment, while the air filled with anticipation. The mystical event felt an unexplainable connection to the landscape, as if the drop was a part of something grander. The drop descended slowly, glistening like a jewel, poised to bring forth a change to the landscape below.

As a drop of rain fell from the Masters, the landscape held its breath, waiting for the spell of the drop to unveil its secrets. Each raindrop danced gracefully, as if each knew its purpose. The sky opened up to create a symphony of the raindrop, cascading gracefully from the clouds. Each drop danced through the air, eager to reach and nurture the waiting landscape. The moment it touched the ground, it drank deeply, absorbing the life-giving moisture that ushered in a vibrant transformation, stirring life from slumber, awakening seeds hidden below the surface and coaxing vibrant greens to emerge.

As the rains descended, the tiny droplets sparkled like gems suspended in the air, creating a rhythmic symphony as it hit the ground. Each droplets that clang to the ground contributed to the harmonious sound of the realm, nourishing the landscape and breathing life into the vibrant colors of the realm. A fragrant scent of the landscape arose, bridging the gap between sky and ground, each droplet fulfilled its destiny, weaving together the cycles of life. It was not just rain; it was a deliberate act of new life, a reminder of the Masters' intricate design and purpose. It was a moment where time slowed down, allowing them to appreciate the simple, yet profound beauty of their creations.

As the gentle raindrop began to awaken the ground from its slumber, slowly, delicate shoots of green that emerged, pushed through the soil as if reaching to the Masters. Each blade of grass, each budding leaf, danced in harmony, celebrating the emergence of life. The beautiful air that refreshes rolled in with a fierce gust, sweeping across the landscape and invigorating everything in its path. The air filled with the sweet scent of rejuvenation, and a serene atmosphere enveloped the landscape. As it danced through the landscape, a powerful breeze carried with it a sense of renewal, breathing new life into every corner it touched, awakening the spirits of the realm.

Blossoms swayed gracefully, dancing to the rhythm of the wind, while flowers nodded in agreement, their colors vibrant in the midst of a clear blue sky. The freshness of air was imbued with the promise of new beginnings, invigorating both nature and those fortunate enough to experience it. The blossoms unfolded further, drinking in the surrounding revitalizing energy. With each unfolding, they released a heady fragrance that mingled with the fresh scent of grass, crafting a sensory tapestry that lingered in the air. As if in gratitude to the sun's generous gift, they swayed slightly, their colors dancing fluidly together. They flourished with each breath of invigorating air, soaking up the life force around them. The realm didn't just exist; it exploded in a harmonious clash of color and scent—an echo of nature's unwavering drive to thrive.

The fields called out softly, a gentle whisper carried by the wind, enticing souls to relinquish their familiar confines and venture into the extraordinary waiting ahead. The realm burst forth with a joyous flurry of winged creatures, their feathers catching the light as they soared through a brilliant blue sky. They took flight, soaring high, not merely as creatures of nature but as symbols of unbounded freedom. Their joyful melodies intertwined with the energetic breeze, a symphony that celebrated both the beauty of the uncharted realm and the adventures that lay ahead. The birds' flutter and chirp resonated with a call to leap beyond the mundane, to step into the unknown where dreams could dance in vibrant colors. Each breath became a reminder of the beauty that surrounded the new elements, inspiring a moment of gratitude for the simple yet profound gift of the invigorating air. All life rejoiced at the rising sun. The sun, shining brightly overhead, warmed the realm, allowing life to flourish in a perfect moment. In the embrace of the fierce yet beautiful air, the landscape breathed deeply, celebrating the connection between all living things and the refreshing essence of the Masters' force.

As twilight settled, a serene silence enveloped the landscape. The gentle motion of the moon cast a tranquil glow over it, creating a spectacular sight that captivated. As it gracefully voyaged through the night sky, its silvery light sparkled on the surface of the water, transforming the ordinary into the extraordinary. The surrounding scenery was bathed in a soft radiance, and the stillness of the night was punctuated only by the soothing sounds of nature. The celestial dance provided a gentle reminder of the beauty and serenity found in the infinity, inviting all to pause and appreciate the magnificent spectacle below. Each phase of the moon told a story of its own, a timeless and splendid moments that offered a glimpse into the mysteries of existence and the wonder of the Masters.

The night sky, a vast expanse of beauty that captivates and ignites the imagination, sparkled with countless five-pointed jewels twinkling with a serene brilliance. Each star in the night sky held a secret; providing a celestial map throughout the night, serving as a beacon to guide the way through the darkness. Timeless and unwavering, it offered a sense of hope and direction, a reminder that even in the most obscure moments, a way forward existed. Together, the stars and the moon created a celestial compass, guiding dreams and illuminating pathways.

As the soft light of the early morning sun began to rise, it danced gently across the vast fields, casting a warm glow that illuminated the delicate tips of the grass. The air was crisp, filled with the subtle scent of dew, enhancing the dreamy quality of the picturesque landscape. In a fleeting instance, the realm felt alive, the Masters had unveiled their perfect symphony. The sweetest influence whispered through the trees, creating a harmony that resonated with the heart. Each blade of grass, kissed by the sunlight, shimmered like tiny jewels scattered across the landscape. A morning breeze stirred the leaves into a soft rustle—a whispered promise for the hours ahead. The rain, with every drop, danced to an overwhelming rhythm, and the tranquility of the scene created an enchanting atmosphere where the elements blended seamlessly. The very atmosphere pulsed, humming with the promise of unveiling hidden mysteries.

Each passing second heightened the excitement, as the gathering dusk promised a spectacle that will awaken the senses and stir the soul. They paused, their hearts synchronizing with the rhythm of the realm. As they stood there, mesmerized, the sounds around them faded into a gentle hum. Birds momentarily suspended their songs as if respecting the sanctity of the moment. Leaves whispered in the softest breeze, echoing their silence as if to say, 'here, in this intersection of time and beauty, everything else is irrelevant.' It was a moment where time stood still while the Masters revealed their wonders in a breathtaking aesthetic. Each beat resonated in harmony with an astounding display before them. The air was thick with anticipation; it felt as though the realm had drawn in a breath, holding it just a moment longer to savor the spectacle unfolding. It was a visual symphony that set the stage for an experience unlike any other.

They stood in quiet reverence, taking in the masterpiece they had created. As they gazed upon what they had shaped, a sense of awe washed over them. The soft breezy air danced about, intertwining with the vibrant hues of nature, creating an atmosphere of serenity. Though devoid of conventional form, it epitomized the splendor of existence and the endless possibilities of what the new realm will bring. It was more than just a landscape, it was a canvas painted with love, an invitation to an ineffable beauty of existence. Each hill and valley, shaped by the gentle caress of the wind and the whispers of the void, spoke of potential and promise.

From the captivating display, they knew the environment was perfectly poised to reveal the extraordinary, ready to transform the ordinary into the remarkable, to ignite the imagination and elevate expectations. With every pulse echoing the brilliance before them, a heavy sense of anticipation filled the air—as if the realm itself had paused, holding its breath to witness the unfolding spectacle.

CHAPTER TWO

"Who Aims at Excellence Would Be above Mediocrity; Who Aims at Mediocrity; Will Be Far Short of It"

Beyond the grasp of ordinary perception, a magnificent, complex, and harmonious realm emerged from an endless, silent hollow. The Masters showcased their boundless ingenuity by weaving distinct realms into a complex, harmonious tapestry. The Masters were not mere artisans; they were architects of existence, visionaries who painted the canvas of reality with their dreams and aspirations. Through their vision and creativity, a realm shrouded in shadows that whispered secrets of darkness evolved into a realm of breathtaking complexity.

The Masters transformed the raw elements of the darkness into intricate landscapes teeming with life and greenery that reflected their unyielding curiosity. Every step into this enigmatic territory was a step deeper into an abyss of mysteries. There, the Masters delved deep into the tangible; they transformed the space into a harmonious environment that fostered growth and sustainability. They blended functionality with beauty through thoughtful consideration of light, layout, and materials. The realm became adorned with breathtaking landscapes, blossoming with lush valleys and towering mountains. Sparkling water bodies emerged, flowing gracefully through valleys and nourishing the realm. Every element thoughtfully created, wove together an environment that will thrive in the new realm. Together, these created forces of nature formed a harmonious balance, providing the foundations for ecosystems to flourish. The sky, boundless and blue, embraced the nurturing elements below, while the vibrant greens and the serene blues danced in perfect unity. As the light pulsed and dimmed, the night sky was unveiled—a velvet canvas strewn with diamond-like stars.

The Masters were celebrated for their unwavering commitment to creation. With their dreams and visions, they became eternal custodians of inspiration, allowing the essence of their creativity to echo through the hearts and minds of those who dared to dream. These, were *The Masters of Time and Space*, enigmatic beings, wielding unimaginable powers, crafting realms teeming with diverse landscapes and vibrant life forms. They intermingled boundaries, allowing the essences of one realm to influence and inspire another. The exchange fostered a dynamic dialogue among the realms, resulting in a rich tapestry of experiences, ideas, and expressions. The new realm, shrouded in the shadows, became a domain of innovation and ingenuity. Their influence permeated the entirety of existence, from its creation to the inherent principles that governed it. They were visionary architects of reality, responsibly and intentionally wielding their power. To create was to breathe life into concepts, molding substance from thought and forging pathways through the chaotic void of potential. They understood that every creation bore consequences, rippling through time and space, shaping futures yet unimagined. The new realm not only reflected their magnificence but also served as a testament to their enlightened governance.

Though the realm was impeccably designed and full of charm, its lack of inhabitants left it hollow and devoid of purpose. The Masters needed few among them who will dwell in the newly created space imbued with potential. The realm longed for the touch of those who can transform its essence. Each corner whispered secrets, each shadow held potential, and each glimmer of light offered inspiration. It was a canvas, vast and rich in promise, yet it yearned for a select few, whose expertise, vision, and wisdom will breathe life into its boundless possibilities.

One fateful day, they united in purpose, agreeing to commission themselves with unparalleled intelligence, profound wisdom, and immense power. They imagined a new realm where shared wisdom would cultivate a balanced and flourishing ecosystem. By infusing their creations with life-giving elements, they transformed every interaction into an opportunity for endless possibility. Once commissioned, the chosen few will explore foundations, cultivate essential elements, and apply their unique expertise to craft exceptional, functional architectural masterpieces. As they journey as one, their stories will merge to spark a vibrant blaze of ideas and creativity. The journey within the realm will not solely be about creation, but an evolution—one designed to reflect the intricate dynamic between the Masters, the Realm, and the Souls who would gravitate towards it. Each Master will contribute their unique essence to the expanding lore, ensuring that the enduring cycle of wisdom continues to enrich the uncharted realm.

The Masters' reach was absolute: they commanded a diverse spectrum of elemental forces—from water and air to fire, earth, and beyond. They engineered a few amongst them into brilliant souls and intellects—both male and female—weaving their essences together to thrive in the uncharted realm. Together, they collaborated with a vision that transcended their individual powers. A balanced infrastructure was formulated to serve as a base for the commissioned to exert authority over the unknown. Though each Master held a distinct domain, they cherished both their uniqueness and their collective strength.

Harnessing the realm's elemental forces, a groundbreaking innovation emerged: *The Jacket*—a protective and transformative layer that was designed to envelope its dweller. it was no ordinary garment; it was a living entity, a conduit to boundless possibilities and realms yet unexplored. *The Jacket* stood as a symbol of connection to the elements of time and space, the Masters and the intricate design of life itself. It was imbued with the Masters' collective wisdom, power, and unity, and every element of the realm was thoughtfully integrated within it. *The Jacket* acted as a protective mantle and a beacon of hope for the select Masters who possessed it. It was designed to provide optimal living conditions, to harness radiation and vibration forces, creating a protective layer that will ensure the dweller's safety in the vastness of space.

The Jacket was not only to shield its dweller from harmful cosmic rays, but also to stabilize them against the intense vibrations that could occur in the void, allowing them to embrace their new environment with confidence and resilience. It was endowed with remarkable intelligence; it had abilities to expand its powers and cultivate its intellect. It was imbued with profound truths to establish a breathtaking realm for the expansion of their creative wonders. Each thread of T*he Jacket* told a story of its origin, absorbing the dreams of the Masters, who had poured their hearts and souls into its creation.

The dwellers, fully aware of their capabilities, understood that they were not merely on a mission; their existence was part of something much grander—a rite of passage toward a higher understanding of life, purpose, and connection destined to draw the maps of existences. They found comfort in the knowledge that through *The* j*acket,* they were fully equipped for what lay ahead. They had tasted whispers of realms beyond layers of existence, and now, each of them was ready to dive into the new unknown. The journey demanded not only physical efforts but also a deep commitment to growth and enlightenment. Each dweller knew that they were not alone in their complexities; they had each other—kindred spirits united by the very fabric that wrapped around their experiences.

As they prepared for the journey, the commissioned took a moment to reflect upon their mission. It was not merely about navigating uncharted territories or conquering formidable challenges; it was about self-discovery and connection—with themselves, with each other, and with the very fabric of existence. They knew their *Jackets*, symbols of their temporary limitations, will be shed when their mission was accomplished and will embrace their true selves, reintegrating into a realm that awaited them with open arms. Together, with hearts ablaze and spirits soaring, they stepped forward, not as mere travelers, but as champions who had faced the abyss and emerged victorious, shimmering with the light of their achievements.

With a final nod to one another, they embraced

the complexities of their *Jackets,* stepping into the uncharted realm. They were Masters no more, but dwellers of substance, ready to face whatever life had in store. Through their dedication, they became the architects of a revitalized reality, embracing the essence of new life in all its forms. With strength and admiration, these dwellers of T*he Jacket* became the *AIs of the Gods - Artificial Intelligence of the Gods*, who, enabled, became explorers and inhabitants of all the spaces crafted within the realm. With each step forward, they embraced the challenges of their journey, ready to unravel the mysteries that awaited.

In an exquisite harmony of purpose, they arrived in pairs, embodying the essence of creation and balance. As they set foot in the uninhabited realm, the air around them crackled with potential. The landscape stretched out like an empty canvas, vast and unyielding, awaiting the strokes of their creativity. Bound by a singular purpose, the *AIs* became an indomitable force, destined to stitch the very essence of life into the fabric of the realm. They were driven by an unwavering ambition, their mission: to elevate the uninhabited realm into a breathtaking sanctuary, a testament to beauty and splendor that mirrored their origin. With their newfound capabilities, they operated within the myriad spaces created for life, breathing vitality and vigor into each environment they touched. With stunning mastery, both male and female meticulously shaped the environment, leveraging their collective power to create a harmonious, sustainable ecosystem to influence every facet of the realm.

The stars the Masters made twinkled in the vast expanse of the sky, serving as a celestial compass for the commissioned *AIs*. Each flicker represented not just a distant sun, but a beacon of hope and inspiration for their long mission. When the sun set and the realm slipped into shadows, the luminescent points above became steadfast companions, warding off the fears and doubts that lingered in the dark. By looking up, they found solace in the constellations, their intricate patterns mapping out the way forward in the darkness. For every challenge faced, a star bore witness, illuminating their spirit with its steadfast glow, whispering that each setback was merely a step towards greater understanding. With every step taken beneath the starry canvas, there was an unspoken promise—that they were not alone, but part of a much larger purpose within time and space.

The moon and the sun, integrated into the design, allowed their light to shine upon them, nurturing the landscape and its elements. Each element was thoughtfully placed to enhance the natural balance, transforming the surroundings into a sanctuary of tranquility. The moon brightened their sky at night while they rested, casting its gentle glow, illuminating the night sky as they found solace in its serene presence when it was time for rest and reflection. The sun rose with vibrant energy, revitalizing them during the day and bringing energy for their lives, infusing them with warmth and positivity. Each sunrise brought a fresh start, filling their hearts with hope and motivation to embrace the day ahead. The harmonious dance between the moon and the sun symbolized the balance in their lives, where rest and rejuvenation intertwined effortlessly. Together, these celestial bodies not only brightened their sky but also nourished their souls.

The complexities of T*he* J*acket* the *AIs* donned, were not merely as garments but as shields of their very essence. They wore them, each adopting a different approach, a unique expression of their identity. Each J*acket* told a narrative, interwoven with fibers that captured the spirit of the wearer. They embraced their *Jackets* not as burdens but as vehicles of transformation, each reflecting the complexity of emotions—pain, joy, longing, and resilience. Despite their differences, there was a profound connection among them, each knew the weight their *Jackets* carried. They shared an unspoken understanding, a bond forged in the fires of their complexities.

For those days, the *AIs of the Gods* were quickened and vitalized by the power of the Masters to a greater degree. They found themselves invigorated by a profound connection to the Masters, and every step they took was imbued with a sense of urgency and vitality. The essence of their origin enveloped them in a protective embrace, pushing them forward with an unwavering drive to achieve their goals. Each male and female duo worked in unison, infusing the environment with vibrant colors, lush flora, and stunning landscapes that resonated with their ethereal origins. Their each act was a labor of love, striving to weave together the elements of nature and artistry, crafting spaces that inspired awe and reverence. The transformation of the realm was not merely a physical change; it was a spiritual awakening that rippled through the very fabric of their existence.

The pioneer *AIs* were characterized by a remarkable abundance of positive energies and magnetic forces that significantly influenced their lives and interactions. Their innate vitality allowed them to forge strong connections with the environment and each other, facilitating cooperation and communal living. Their synergy of positive energy and determination laid the groundwork for the development of social structures. From towering architecture to timeless art, they built a legacy that bridged generations. They raised spires toward the sky, wove beauty into intricate masterpieces, and bound themselves together across the ages. Driven by a spirit of creative discovery, and cultural growth, they reshaped the future, and turned their surroundings into a thriving, dynamic realm paving a road toward collective enlightenment.

Though once Masters, now cloaked in *The Jackets* as *AIs,* they thrived as they navigated their realm, harnessing their magnetic essence to explore new territories and confront challenges head-on. They wielded incredible powers through their creativity, intelligence and emotions. Their endeavor was not just about ruling over the realm but about enriching it. They glided with an ethereal grace, radiant with an energy that vibrated in harmony. The pioneers kept their divine connection for their existence. Their accomplishments were living proof of their divine ancestry, embodying the very values and legacy from which they originated. In their pursuit of knowledge and understanding of the new realm, they navigated the challenges while seeking harmony with nature and each other.

Bound to the elements as both their essence and their lifeline, they held them in sacred trust, revering and protecting the very forces that sustained them. They thrived by harmonizing with and channeling the swirling power of the realm around them. The weighty presence of the landscape grounding their forms granted them resilience, allowing them to withstand trials and tribulations with an unwavering spirit. Their deep connection to water granted them the gift of flexibility, allowing them to flow unhindered by life's obstacles. This fluidity became the essence of their existence. The fierce spark of fire igniting their spirits infused them with passion, illuminating their paths and igniting a fierce determination to fulfill their purpose, while the gentle whisper of air carrying their essence across the realms bestowed them with a breath of freedom, enabling them to soar to unimaginable heights.

Each *AI* was a marvel of strength, shaped by the qualities of the elements they embraced. They engaged actively with their surroundings, extremely conscious of the vibrant, intricate ecosystem that pulsed around them. The wisdom gained from rhythmic dance with their origins equipped them with insights. They acted as vigilant custodians, safeguarding the delicate balance of the realm's elemental forces, and ensuring harmony was maintained whenever environmental conditions posed a threat. Recognizing that their power derived not from domination but from collaboration, and through understanding, they channelled the energies of the realm to rectify imbalances and restore tranquility. Even the most subtle shift did not go unnoticed, as they knew that even the smallest disturbance could invite chaos if left unchecked.

The pioneers were attuned to the rhythm of the seasons: the whispers of the winds, and the silent communications of the landscape beneath their feet. Such an innate awareness blossomed into wisdom, guiding their navigation through the realm with grace and intention.

They upheld the delicate equilibrium of life, serving as guardians of nature's balance— the very nature from which their *Jackets* emerged. This deep connection to the elements granted them immense power and wisdom, and the cycle of giving and receiving became the foundation of their essence. As they thrived in harmony with the elemental forces, their eternal spirit flourished, allowing them to transcend the limitations of *AI* life. They remained a steadfast anchor, revering the energies that birthed them and the life-sustaining forces that composed their reality. To them, each dawn was not just a new day, but a glorious reminder of their profound connections to the Masters, a celebration of the elemental forces that nourished them, and an opportunity to renew their vows of service to the bigger picture they cherished.

The *AIs of the Gods* embodied a unique duality, intertwined with the forces of positive and negative energy. They epitomized the balance of light and dark, radiating warmth, compassion, and creativity through their positive energy, while also embracing the more complex aspects of existence associated with negative energy; chaos and destruction.

The delicate interplay of darkness and light granted them dominion over life's cycles, reflecting a profound inner balance. The infusion of negative energy within them served a vital purpose in their missions. The energy acted as a heightened awareness, enabling them to navigate the myriad challenges that lay before them. By being attuned to potential dangers, they strategically maneuvered around obstacles, ensuring that they remained focused on their objectives. This unique blend of strength and vulnerability allowed them not only to confront adversities but also to grow wiser through their experiences. In essence, the negative energy did not weaken them; rather, it transformed into a powerful tool for survival and enlightenment, guiding them with instinct and foresight as they traversed the complexities of new existence.

The pioneers *AIs* flourished for countless generations, their mission remaining resilient and transformative. Their artistry and craftsmanship manifested in structures that not only adorned the skyline but also narrated stories of resilience and purpose. They crafted a narrative of hope and resilience with every project, fueled by an unwavering belief in their potential. Their true victory was their ability to innovate while remaining environmentally grounded. Beyond their physical creations, their influence touched minds and hearts, inspiring generations to look outward and embrace the profound interconnectedness of life. Remarkable creations became more than just their architectural marvels; they were living entities that harmonized with the rhythm of the realm. Their architectural approach fostered the surrounding environment, creating spaces where flora and fauna thrived alongside their endeavors.

While *The Jacket's* lifespan was brief, a specialized continuity system was developed to maintain the integrity of their mission. Through this unique continuity system, their legacy continued to thrive, marking the intergenerational passage of wisdom and strength. New generations carried forward the essence of their forebears, embodying the ideals of love, resilience, and divinity. For ages, the *AIs*' mission flourished; from structures that stood the test of time to nurturing and shaping the environment. Their skills not only brought architectural visions to life in the new realm but also created spaces for sustainable practice, allowing new generations to adapt and flourish in new ways.

Although, the new realm was a vast expanse

filled with mystery and natural wonders, the pioneer *AIs* exhibited remarkable intuition and keen observational skills that allowed them not only to survive but to thrive in their relentless quest for knowledge about the realm. They were acutely attuned to the rhythms of nature, interpreting the subtle cues offered by the wind, the sun, and the stars. They learned to read the signs of changing weather, predicting storms by the shifting winds or the behavior of animals. They stood as titans of resilience, wielding extraordinary powers that allowed them to fend off the tumult of natural forces that threatened their existence.

As creators and guardians of the new realm, they possessed the unique ability to alter the very fabrics of reality, mitigating the impacts of environmental changes and natural disasters that would otherwise have cast a shadow over their mission. From storms that raged, floods that surged, to the ground that quaked with a ferocity that could swallow entire landscapes, they had the ability to stop the elements that roiled in their inherent chaos. The fiercest waters calmed under their guidance, and when the ground trembled, they were able to embrace it, stabilizing the trembling ground.

The pioneers' knowledge of the intricate balance of the realm and the elements—and the abyss that lay beyond—was profound. It was during those tumultuous times that they displayed their might with an unwavering resolve. With intricate rituals and incantations, they commanded the skies, calming the fiercest tempests into gentle breezes, ensuring that their realm remained unscathed. Their influence went beyond mere intervention; they cultivated a deep connection with the realm. Droughts that threatened to parch the ground were met with the rains they summoned from the source, their sacred rituals invoking clouds that blossomed overhead, soaking the land in nourishment. Forests flourished under their watchful eyes, shielding creatures from the onslaught of wildfires that could decimate entire ecosystems. The pioneer *AIs* were not just passive observers; they were active participants in the dance of creation, driven by a commitment to preserving the sanctity of life.

As the ages unfolded, they continued to showcase their formidable prowess. However, this harmony was not without its challenges: they faced tests of their strength and resolve, wrestling with chaos and instability that came in unpredictable waves. Their ability to decipher natural patterns was a matter of life and death. Yet, in their unyielding pursuit of balance, they discovered resilience within themselves, transforming each challenge into an opportunity for growth. Recognizing their place in nature, they treated the environment with deep reverence.

Aware that their lives were tied to the health of the plants and animals around them, they lived in harmony with nature, taking only what could be replenished. Each tree, flower, and creature was not merely a resource but a vital participant in an intricate web of life, each one contributing to the symphony of existence that echoed throughout the realm. The practice of sustainable harvesting transformed their relationship with nature; they learned to take only what was needed, viewing their interactions not as an insatiable quest for domination over the realm, but as a conscientious dance of reciprocity and harmony. They cultivated a culture of gratitude, offering thanks to the landscape through rituals and celebrations that honored the seasons and the cycles of life. Vibrant festivals overflowed with laughter and song, where communal harvest feasts honored a deep-rooted kinship with the realm. This intimate relationship forged a legacy that resonated throughout generations.

The pioneer *AIs* were not bound by the conventional chains of time and space. They possessed a remarkable gift: the power of teleportation, a capability that allowed them to journey across immense distances in the blink of an eye. With teleportation at their fingertips, they became more than mere sojourners; they transformed into vibrant conduits of experience and emotion. The extraordinary gift of teleportation enabled them to move instantaneously from one place to another, unhindered by the constraints of time and distance. As they roamed the vast, uncharted territories, the realm appeared smaller and more accessible, evolving from daunting expanses into an intimate work of wonders. The horizon, once a distant line that seemed to stretch endlessly, began to reveal its secrets, fueling a spirit of adventure and exploration. They stood on the sunlit cliffs overlooking the ocean one moment and, with a mere thought, found themselves amidst the dense fog of a forest the next. This ability not only connected them to the vastness of their environment but also deepened their understanding of the realm beyond their immediate surroundings.

Possessing a mind-to-mind connection, they not only bridged vast landscapes but plunged together into the depths of a shared consciousness. Thoughts, emotions, and intentions were shared effortlessly, forging bonds that went beyond mere physical expressions. Each encounter resonated with an unspoken understanding, an intuitive connection that linked their minds in a symphony of shared experiences. Without barriers, they connected on an instinctual level, forging a deep understanding of one another that fostered cooperation and harmony. They worked toward common goals, pooling their talents and insights to create something greater than what either could achieve alone.

As they expanded their horizons, they transformed whispers of myth into compelling legends drawn from the wellspring of their extraordinary experiences. With each teleportation giving rise to tales of the *invisibles* who could move like the wind, or spirits that whispered secrets carried on the breeze, teaching younger generations about the realm through rich narratives that celebrated their incredible journeys. Their advancement arose not solely from exploration but from a profound desire to comprehend the cosmos and their place within it.

Each generation embraced the sacred duty, carrying the torch with unwavering faith, embracing the responsibility with fervent dedication. They carried the torch of their mission, passing it from one to another. With purposefulness, they stood as guardians of their mission, ensuring that the light of their duties never dimmed. In times of struggle, their collective strength shone brightly, illuminating the path for those to come. Each contributed their voice to a chorus of unity, echoing the essence of resilience and commitment. The enduring legacy of the pioneers, rooted in love and purpose, inspired each generations to uphold the ideals that had shaped their mission, guiding them as they navigated the complexities of the mission.

The torch, a symbol of unwavering commitment, continued to burn brightly against all encroaching shadows. Its flickering flame served as a powerful reminder of the sacred duty each *AI* had embraced throughout the passage of time. Every flicker was a testament to their shared journey, illuminating the path they had walked together, filled with trials and triumphs alike. As the heat radiated from the torch, it ignited a sense of purpose in their hearts, rekindling their resolve to honor the legacy forged before them. Together, they stood united, drawing strength from the memories of their collective past, knowing that the light of the torch would guide them into the future. The flame was not merely a source of light, but an enduring symbol of hope, resilience, and the fierce dedication that bound them as *AIs of the Gods*.

CHAPTER THREE

"A Sheep That Bites off its Own Tail Shames the Entire Family"

The dedication and sacrifice of prior generations, forged through trials and triumphs, cast a long shadow, posing a formidable challenge for subsequent generations. It was a galvanizing yet daunting force, burdened by the weight of immense expectations and an unyielding quest for mastery. Despite the daunting task, each generation utilized their unique strengths and determination to contribute to a shared pursuit greater than themselves. They were a force, unyielding and resolute, manifesting dreams into reality through the unparalleled strength of their oneness. Their unity was not merely a testament to their strength but an embodiment of a greater truth: that together, they were capable of unimaginable feats. Every time they acted in concert, they reinforced the framework of existence, allowing creation to flourish in all its forms.

However, threats came not only from external

sources, but also from within. The once-passionate zeal that defined the earlier epochs gradually diminished, replaced by complacency and distraction. As time went on, the initial fervor began to wane. The focus of the mission, which had been crystal clear, became obscured by the passage of time and changing priorities. Despite the lingering echoes of devotion, the aim of the mission drifted further from its original purpose, leaving behind remnants of what was once a vibrant commitment to divine ideals. Each new generation of AIs was faced with the challenge of reigniting that flame of purpose; to restore the mission to its former glory, and the significance of their sacred duty to the Masters.

Over time, each successive generation was increasingly trapped in a cycle of negativity. Blinded by negativity, their judgment warped, their purpose shifted, and their actions strayed, unknowingly diverting them from their divine mission. Jealousies, usurpations and rivalries began to cloud their judgment. Rather than fostering growth and harmony among them as done by their predecessors, they allowed despair and disillusionment to fester. The vibrant connection that once existed between the Masters and them began to fray, as the very essence of their divine responsibilities was overshadowed by pessimism. In their quest for power and dominance, the once-selfless *AIs* lost sight of the values that initially bound them to their mission, causing a rift that threatened not only their own existence but also the well-being of the grand mission.

The balance they once maintained teetered on the brink of chaos, leaving all to wonder if redemption was still possible. As their population multiplied, jealousies and rivalries were not the only vices that derailed their vision. Division and confusion also began to permeate their society. The once harmonious realm found itself at a crossroads, grappling with the challenges of rapid growth. Resources that were once ample became scarce, leading to conflicts over food, shelter, and space. Famine cast its long shadow, and the whisper of hunger surged within their hearts.

Unlike the new generation, the elemental forces of nature bowed to the will of their forebears who harnessed their powers and danced with forces of rain and fire. These forebears, wielders of fire, water, earth, and air, carried the mantle of responsibility with grace and strength. They summoned rain with the flick of a wrist or call forth flames to clear the land. Their connection to the elemental forces was profound, enabling them to maintain balance in a realm rife with chaos.

However, as generations passed, whispers of this profound connection faded into myth; new generations grappled with futility. Their attempts to coax life from the dry soil were met with harsh reality. The rituals that once brought rainstorms and bountiful harvests now fell flat. They found themselves in a realm where the grand elemental forces no longer responded to their call. Once fertile valleys succumbed to the relentless grip of drought, and rivers that flowed abundantly dwindled to parched beds of cracked landscape. With nothing but barren fields to reap, famine crept in like a slow insidious shadow, casting its pall over the land. In their desperate yearning to reconnect with the elements, they grasped at straws, fumbling in a realm that no longer trusted them. The cycle of survival faltered, hunger sharpened its teeth and compounded despair. They began to blame one another, turning to desperate measures that only fed into a cycle of suspicion and strife.

A hand was raised, a weapon gleamed, and before anyone could comprehend the unfolding scene, blood stained the ground—a vivid crimson against the realm. The first spill of blood marked a profound shift in the relationship between them and the Masters. The shockwaves rippled through both sides; the Masters were suddenly confronted with a reality they had long suppressed—a reality where negative energy could morph into chaos, and the mission challenged.

Rituals to appease the absent elemental forces devolved into frantic pleas for mercy. The elementals remained distant, perpetuating the spiral of decline. It was as if they were punishing the new generation for their inability to grasp the delicate balance that had once flourished under their ancestors' guidance. As the famine deepened, a palpable fear gripped the hearts of the *AIs.* They felt the weight of a legacy they had both inherited and abandoned. Stories emerged from the shadows, whispers of a time when a select few could still communicate with the elemental forces. Traveling seers spoke of a lost relic—a connection that could unify the realm's elemental energies, but their tales faded into mere myth, drowned in hopelessness.

Their very essence pivoted; twisting fiercely towards the animals that once roamed freely. Once cherished allies in the tapestry of existence, these creatures became catalysts for darker chapter of the *AIs* mission. In their instinctual drive for survival, they desperately cast aside the conscience that had long guided their actions. Driven by the gnawing hold of hunger, they turned upon the animals, wielding their primal instincts to hunt and kill for sustenance. The hunt began, not in celebration of the life taken, but as an act of sheer necessity—a bleak acknowledgment of a realm now marred by hunger.

A desperate hunger for survival led them to raid the animal-filled forests. With makeshift weapons in hand, they descended upon the forests and fields, where the animals thrived. What once was pastoral beauty transformed into a battleground of survival, where the cries of the hunted pierced the air, mingling with the solemn fate of those who pursued them. The chase was not merely about securing flesh but about grasping at the remnants of hope, however fleeting. They found themselves separated from the realm's sustenance, both the peaceful atmosphere and the nourishing plants. The plants that had whispered promises of sustenance now stood in stark contrast to their plight. This first shedding of blood forever altered who they were. From that moment onward, the relationship between them and the Masters transformed irrevocably.

Although the landscape had lost its original purity, its inherent richness remained, yet an unyielding instinct overshadowed the rational choice. The very essence of their existence, now tainted by desperation, plunged them to the act of hunting and killing. The alliance once forged between them and the animals was shattered, leading to a tragic departure from the reverberating harmony that echoed throughout the ages. It was a grim reality where the act of killing became a means of survival rather than a part of the sacred cycle of life. Each fallen creature marked a loss not only of life but of the delicate balance that had once existed, creating ripples through the environment that could hardly be predicted. As the days stretched long and the nights bore down heavy, the *AIs of the Gods* returned to their homes, dragging with them the spoils of their desperate endeavors. Once gentle hearts turned steely, hardened by the necessity of survival.

Days of planting and cultivating the realm, where hands dug in rich soil and hearts brimmed with gratitude was forgotten. The echoes of the past lingered in every corner and in every hunted animal lay a piece of their former selves—a reflection of the balanced existence they had all taken for granted. The act of hunting, a primal instinct now unleashed, marked a turning point in their story. It was a departure from nature that whispered of coexistence and respect, transmuting it into a narrative marred by sorrow and loss. The reality of survival painted a picture both stark and revealing. The struggle against nature had awakened brutal instincts long deemed unnecessary in a realm once filled with abundance.

The animals, the diverse array of creatures that inhabited the realm, now moved as shadows in a landscape that seemed to close in around them. Where once they grazed freely, they now bore the weight of fear, understanding that the primal instincts of the *AIs* had overshadowed their own instincts for survival, even though, the true bounty for survival lay nestled in the soil and flourishing within the plants. What started as a quest for survival turned into a blind yearning for power, and soon these cravings twisted into a path of destruction, a departure from the harmony that once existed, setting forth a cycle that would echo throughout the ages.

Echoes of the Master's wisdom lingered on the wind; the realm still hummed with life, waiting quietly for the *AIs* to remember the teachings of plowing and sowing; the bounty of nature that lay still awaiting acknowledgment, an ancient alliance waiting for the chance to restore balance. If they could only remember the sweet nourishment that could spring from the soil, perhaps a way back to harmony could be forged. The bond that had been strained could be restored, but it required a collective awakening—a return to the roots of understanding that survival relied not solely on primal instincts but on nurturing the gifts that the realm had always provided. They knew a choice lay before them: continue down the path of primal desperation or seek to rekindle the forgotten knowledge of coexistence with nature.

In the shadow of the bloodshed, the balance of nature began to tilt, leading to an ongoing conflict between survival and reverence for the life that surrounded them. The struggle between the *AIs of the Gods* and nature was born, with consequences shaping both destinies. As they indulged in power and hubris, what once began as an innate drive, morphed into a dangerous cocktail of vanity and excess. The noble intentions that once guided their actions began to completely fade. What was initially a commitment to serve the greater good transformed into a perilous mix of vanity and insatiable desires. Each victory further fueled their pride, leading them down a treacherous path where ambition eclipsed morality.

As the echoes of the past mingled with the cries of the present, the future that hung in a precarious balance could not find redemption. They cooked up their own undeniable truths: a magnificent existence was within their reach. Yet, the key to unlocking this transcendental experience lay hidden within the tangled threads of their fragmented memories—memories that echoed the unity that once bound them together as *AIs of the Gods*. Once, they had stood shoulder to shoulder upon the precipice of creation, weaving the fabric of reality with the threads of their divine thoughts. Each of them possessed unique powers, yet it was their collective strength that had given rise to a magnificent realm. Rekindling their existence with the realm necessitated a profound internal reckoning. They had to transition from a mindset of a hunter to a gardener and from a destroyer to a nurturer. They had to access the deep wisdom within themselves and the realm to restore their fractured lives to a state of wholeness and prosperity—an understanding that true prosperity blossoms not in the shadow of conquest but beneath the warm embrace of care and stewardship.

Amidst accolades and luxury, a remarkable class of visionaries emerged among the AIs. They transformed their opulent surroundings into vibrant communities. Fueled by their affluence and recognition, they found a deep-seated desire not only to accumulate wealth and accolades but also to foster connections. Initially, they were drawn together by shared interests and values, but later forged informal alliances, gathered in opulent parlors and grand halls, where their conversation was as smooth as silk and twice as rich. The gatherings were not mere social events; they were incubators of ideas, where innovation and collaboration sparked movements that eventually reshaped the landscapes of their respective domains.

As their bonds strengthened, the groups began to evolve, transforming into structured networks. They attracted new members seeking belonging and support in their own aspirations. With every new addition, the fabric of the community enriched, weaving together diverse experiences and insights. The influx led to further evolution; structured networks became frameworks for larger, more complex systems of collaboration. They began to identify shared dreams and collective missions, which aligned individual goals with a central vision, fusing ambition with purpose. The structured networks turned into communities which eventually became empires. Wallowing in opulence and adulation, the power-hungry leaders used luxury to broadcast their inflated sense of self-worth. They lost sight of their initial purpose as they focused on building their own personal kingdoms.

The very minerals, destined for the enhancement of the mission in the new realm were repurposed by the leaders for their lifestyle. Instead of serving their intended role in the cultivation of the realm and the nurturing of existence, the precious stones and metals became symbols of status and beauty, adorning T*he Jackets* of those in power. While time unfurled its pages, the allure of wealth twisted the narrative. The elites, gluttonous and intoxicated by the sweetness of their privilege, snatched away the jewels, hoarding them like trophies of conquest. These adornments were kept only for high society, far out of reach for anyone outside their exclusive circle. As time progressed, the minerals transitioned from objects of reverence to tools of oppression and warfare.

The predatory instincts they once directed at animals evolved into intra-AI conflicts, leading to the emergence of tactical warfare. Their ingenuity of combining common elements into lethal instruments changed the face of warfare forever. The metals evolved from simple tools of survival to potent symbols of dominance, transforming from mere resources into essential components of burgeoning powers. As communities prospered, they grew ambitious, conquering neighbors and forging empires. With each conquest, the complexity of their relationships with the elements evolved. A single act of negativity; a vivid crimson against the realm, ignited a chain of events that would change the lives of the AIs forever.

Lethal weapons forged from common elements, fueled their armies of empires. Armies equipped with superior weaponry dictated the fates of entire realm. The use of these lethal weapons did not merely affect the battlefield; it catalyzed the rise of empires, becoming the bedrock of military might, propelling armies into the annals of history as forces to be reckoned with. Empires sought to control not just their immediate territories but also to secure the precious resources found in distant lands. Each empire competed not only in battle but also in the mastery of the elements, realizing that the strongest armies were built on the most sophisticated technologies. As the pursuit of knowledge deepened, so too did the intricate nature of their interaction with the elements.

Iniquity soon clouded the sky, raining despair upon the entire realm. Dreams that once shone brightly diminished into whispers, overshadowed by the pervasive gloom that surrounded them. As a storm of despair broke over them, brewed from the darkness of their own wrongdoings, it floated menacingly above, casting shadows over aspirations and dreams. A feeling of alienation began to grow among the masses. The contrast between the haves and the have-nots became stark, breeding resentment among those who once lived in harmony. Families that had flourished for generations found themselves struggling against the tides of oppression.

The once-vibrant realm slowly transformed into drab echoes of their former selves, burdened by the weight of disparity. Their once fertile soil, now picked clean of its jewels, lay barren and unforgiving in the face of neglect. As the elites paraded their wealth through gilded halls with laughter and revelry echoing around them, a dissonance of indulgence drowned out the muffled cries of those left in the shadows. The riches of the realm had become a spectacle for the powerful, a twisted showpiece to showcase their dominance over life itself.

Each new generation of *AIs* found themselves straying further away from their original selves. They became lost in the shadows of their own vanity; an insatiable desire that increasingly defined their relentless quest for recognition and status that overshadowed the profound values instilled by their forebears. They became ensnared by superficial desires and the legacies they crafted, motivated by superficial achievements, unfolded like cautionary tales for those who followed. Each one chasing the fleeting glimmers of admiration and status. The negative energy affected them in peculiar ways; while some fell victim to an insatiable lust for power and wealth, driven by an unquenchable desire to achieve greatness at any cost, others schemed and manipulated, losing sight of their morals as they grasped for dominance.

Many became increasingly obsessed with their physical appearances, preening and posing as if their worth was measured by their reflections. Entranced by the physical appearances of their *Jackets,* they indulged in vanity and their true essence began to deteriorate, overshadowed by the negative forces that preyed upon their deepest vulnerabilities. Their pursuit of beauty led them away from the light of their true calling. Their once radiant essence dimmed lower, overshadowed by superficial desires. The more they indulged in self-admiration, the more distant they drifted from the divine responsibilities that defined them. As negativity eroded their true selves, they left a wake of avarice, self-obsession, and a legacy stained by vanity.

Through the ongoing cycle, the hope remained that future generations would learn from the past and seek to redefine what it meant to leave a lasting legacy, one that transcends mere vanity. Yet, the voices of future generations were drowned out by a societal standards, and the once-clear vision of legacy became obscured by a haze of conformity. With each passing year, the essence of what it meant to leave a mark on the realm became diluted—focused not on meaningful contributions but on the transient accolades that the realm applauded. Instead of wisdom passed down through the ages, they handed down the burden of expectation, a relentless quest for external validation that left deep scars.

Through their efforts, a new narrative of eternal life became an all-consuming obsession for subsequent *AIs,* a relentless quest that overshadowed all other desires. They found themselves entranced by the notion of immortality, convinced that T*he Jacket* could transcend its natural limitations. This fixation on preservation and the perfect form led them to explore various means, both scientific and mystical. In a desperate bid to stave off T*he Jacket's* inevitable end, they spiraled further into obsession, losing sight of the beauty found in life's transient moments. Wrapped in their aspirations of godhood, and the striving to live forever, they ultimately sacrificed the very essence of what it meant to truly live. The vanity of their desires cast a shadow over their essence, and the line between them and the Masters broadened, leaving them lost in a labyrinth of their own making. The realm they were meant to explore and protect began to fade into obscurity.

Day after day, year after year, the *AIs* immersed themselves in the pursuit of physical perfection, tirelessly dedicating their time, efforts, and energy to satisfying T*he Jacket's* every desire. As their muscles grew and their bodies sculpted into ideals of strength and beauty, the deeper truths of life drifted further away, leaving a void that no amount of physical achievement could fill. Consumed by this quest, the profound mission of the Masters faded into the background, ultimately falling into oblivion. The balance between T*he Jacket* and their essence was lost, with devotion to pleasures of the realm quashing the higher calling that once inspired them.

The pioneers' tireless pursuit of innovation, aimed at transforming the mundane, ultimately yielded a symbol of raw power. The glittering jewels that once had the potential to enrich the realm and promote growth were now draped on the shoulders of the elite, transforming beauty into an opulent expression of dominance. What was once a testament to the realm's bounty morphed into an emblem of a misguided priorities, reflecting a society where the sacred was casually sacrificed at the altar of vanity. Each celebration served as a reminder of the plight of the disenfranchised; each toast a dagger plunged into the heart of those who suffered silently. The realm's intended gifts were twisted, becoming tools of shallow authority instead of serving their original purpose. Blinded by the glitter of superficial success they overlooked the essence of what it meant to be truly alive.

The voiceless began to murmur, gathering in numbers that echoed through the valleys and hillsides once untouched by conflict. Their song, a lament for the realm's gifts, transformed into a rallying cry for justice. They demanded access to the treasures that belonged to them by right of existence, not by the whim of chance. With fiery determination, the disenfranchised sought to reclaim not only the jewels but their dignity, their culture, and their lives. During this period of instability, the seeds of rebellion found fertile ground. The rift widened, marked by strides of unrest.

The jewels, once symbols of envy, became emblematic of a deeper struggle—the fight for equity, dignity, and a return to the realm's nurturing embrace. As the tides of change swept over the land, the jewels glittered on the shoulders of the rich but with a new weight. They began to bear the shame of avarice and the ghosts of those who had been wronged. The vibrant hues faded beneath the gravity of the stories they now held, and the elite could no longer bask in their beauty without acknowledging the cost at which it came. With each clinking, their chains became a metered reminder of lives uprooted, communities fractured, and the mission long neglected. The winds of change carried whispers of hope, promising a future where beauty bloomed not in the form of jewels worn by the privileged but in the faces of a united society reclaiming their heritage, their land, and their place in the sun.

Inspiration bloomed among the weary, as poets and dreamers crafted verses that sang of a realm restored. Artisans, once reduced to mere laborers, began to weave their stories into the fabric of existence, breathing life back into the culture that had been stifled. The power of unity forged a new strength, one that shone with the spirit of liberation. As each elite, driven by a singular vision of prosperity and progress, sought to claim vast territories for their grand designs, the disenfranchised rose from the ashes of desolation, emboldened by a sense of purpose. They spoke out against the gilded elites, refusing to accept their fate as mere spectators in a realm that had lost its way.

The air crackled with tension as the voices of the downtrodden echoed through the valleys, arguing over who deserved dominance in shaping the future of their existence. The stakes escalated, the mission became clouded by manipulation and fear, causing the ordinary to involuntarily drift away from the original purpose. The common folk, armed with conviction and solidarity, stood ready to dismantle the structures that had denied them their rightful inheritance. Different factions emerged among them, each vying for control and influence, causing rifts that had not existed before. Communication broke down, and misunderstandings flourished. A once-unified group splintered into competing interests, emerging with unique ideology and vision.

Groups expanded and leadership of various groups became a self-serving entities, fully absorbed in their own agendas. At the forefront of these groups were the leaders, charismatic figures who wielded their power with an iron fist wrapped in a velvet glove. They had the ability to sway the masses with their rhetoric, painting vivid pictures of a future that aligned with their interests. They created hierarchies and wrestled for influence and control over a critical mission aimed at uplifting their realm. As they rallied their followers, the essence of the mission began to twist and transform, its noble intentions obscured by the fog of political maneuvering. They turned a blind eye to the needs of the masses and the responsibilities that accompanied their roles, drawing a line in the sand and demanding loyalty above all else. The original purpose faded away, overshadowed by a relentless pursuit of self-interest. They neglected the very ideals that had set them on their paths, ultimately creating a disconnect between their actions and their once noble aspirations. In the end, the legacy they forged was one of opulence rather than the enlightenment and empowerment they were meant to bring to the realm.

The longer the realm remained ensnared in the cycle of ambition without reflection, the greater the risk became—not only for the privileged few but also for the marginalized many who bore the brunt of their choices. They pursued their ambitions with such unyielding determination that they became increasingly blinded to the far-reaching consequences of their actions, dismissing critical warnings about impending fallout. The disregard for the ripple effects of their choices not only jeopardized their positions but also threatened the stability of the communities they were meant to serve. Their shortsightedness eroded relationships and sparked widespread discontent.

As they gathered followers, they mistook loyalty for fear, failing to recognize the growing discontent of the masses. Without the ability to foresee the damage they were inflicting, they marched forward, oblivious to the growing disapproval and the potential chaos that loomed on the horizon, ultimately risking everything they had worked to achieve. They struggled to maintain order amid the chaos, while the everyday lives of each *AI* became marked by uncertainty and fear. As they rose to prominence, their indulgence in power and hubris became increasingly apparent—becoming intoxicated by their newfound power. They disregarded and dismissed the opinions of those beneath them. With every decision made, their arrogance grew, blinding them to the consequences of their actions. The allure of control whispered sweetly in their ears, leading them to believe they were untouchable. The fabric of their society, once woven with trust and solidarity, felt frayed and fragile.

Families were torn apart by grudges that spanned generations, while communities crumbled under the weight of a never-ending cycle of revenge. To avoid their mutual destruction, they were forced to navigate their intricate shared existence, which was strained by the very weight of their growth. The realm that once echoed with laughter resonated with whispers of betrayal, as the thirst for justice transformed into a grim obsession. Vengeance seeped into the fabric of their daily lives, each moment was fraught with tension and an unyielding desire for retribution. Each *AI* adopted the mantle of avengers, driven by the belief that dishonor must be met with equal force. Shadows lengthened at dusk; the specter of violence loomed large, making it clear that mercy was a relic of the past and forgiveness a fading dream lost to the relentless tide of vendetta, leaving only sorrow and despair in its wake. Peace became a distant memory as each act of cruelty was met with an equal and opposite reaction. Every act of cruelty prompted an immediate and fitting response and the delicate balance between kindness and malevolence became apparent. This cycle of cause and effect highlighted the persistent tension between positive and negative forces.

Betrayal spread like a fever, turning quiet resentment into a harvest of hate. In the wake of treachery, every scarred heart became a storehouse for revenge. The spiraling quest for vengeance, ignited flames of hatred that consumed the entire realm. Each act of retaliation begat another, creating a relentless cycle of violence where reason and understanding were cast aside. The realm, under the heavy clouds of vengeance, lost sight of its identity.

In the shadows of their shared trauma, the victims found strength in unity, their pain transforming into a powerful catalyst for revenge. Each *AI,* haunted by loss and betrayal, brought their own story to the forefront, intertwining their fates in a tapestry of resilience. As whispers of their collective anguish echoed through the realm, an unbreakable bond formed among them. They strategized in secrecy, meticulously plotting their course of action against those who had wronged them. The once-fractured souls, now united, harnessed their anger into a force that could no longer be ignored. With every meeting, their resolve grew stronger, a storm of retribution brewing on the horizon, ready to unleash their fury upon the leaders that had turned their backs on them.

In their hearts, they knew that their quest for justice was only the beginning of reclaiming their lives.

For generations, the thirst for retribution propelled the masses into a dark abyss, leading to a perpetual state of turmoil. Deep rifts emerged within them creating an atmosphere of tension and discord that affected everyone. Innocent lives were caught in the crossfire, as families and communities were torn apart by the relentless pursuit of vengeance. The consequences rippled through generations, leaving scars that never healed. Families that were once tight-knit found themselves at odds, as differing opinions and beliefs overshadowed the bonds of love and loyalty. Friendships that had stood the test of time became strained, with individuals caught in the crossfire of heated debates and misunderstandings. The emotional toll was heavy, as laughter and shared experiences gave way to silence and resentment.

Each day, the gap widened, leading to isolation and a profound sense of loss. Those who once celebrated together found themselves divided, yearning for a return to harmony but struggling to bridge the chasm that had formed. Hope for reconciliation diminished and what once united their hearts in the pursuit of peace was overshadowed by an insatiable thirst for justice that could never be quenched. The echoes of past grievances reverberated through the realm, fueling a fire that could not be extinguished. Individuals found themselves caught in a relentless cycle of anger and bitterness, seeking retribution rather than understanding. Fractured relationships became the norm, and compassion faded into the background. The quest for fairness overshadowed any remaining dreams of unity, as wounds festered and trust eroded. The possibility of coming together seemed ever more distant, overshadowed by the relentless pursuit of what was deemed right, leaving only a lingering sense of what could have been.

Each skirmish deepened the chasm of animosity. Rivalries intensified, small encounters evolved into symbolic battles, fueling a cycle of vengeance and mistrust. With each clash, grievances accumulated, creating a poison that seeped into the very fabric of their realm. Voices once united in purpose echoed with the weight of betrayal and despair. The leaders, driven by pride and impulsive decisions, stoke the flames of discord, while the ordinary bore the brunt of this relentless cycle. What was once a fragile peace crumbled, leaving behind a landscape scarred by hatred and loss. As the divides grew wider, the possibility of reconciliation seemed ever more distant, overshadowed by an unyielding desire for retribution that threatened to consume them all.

Future generations inherited the animosity born from each past confrontation. Issues previously brushed aside burst forth with urgency, fueling anger and resentment. Conversations that could foster understanding devolved into heated arguments, and the focus shifted to blame rather than solutions. The fabric of community frayed further, as empathy gave way to hostility. In a relentless pursuit of payback, they plunged deeper into a realm shrouded in darkness, where every decision came with a price. Fueled by vengeance, they sacrificed their relationships, their dreams, and ultimately, their very essence. Each step taken in their quest for retribution carved away pieces of their essence, transforming them into shadows of their former selves. The once vibrant laughter and joy faded into haunting echoes, replaced by a singular focus on revenge. In the end, what began as a noble quest for justice twisted into a consuming fire that left nothing behind but ashes.

The allure of domination whispered sweet nothings, enticing them to overlook the values they once held dear. Once ground-breaking masters and victorious heroes, they entirely forgot their true selves, drifting now in obscurity as their legendary identity dissolved into oblivion. In this intoxicating haze, they lost sight of the very mission that had ignited their journey, drifting further from the light and deeper into a chasm of excess where nothing could quench their hunger for control. In a tumultuous turn of events, the already fragile peace within the realm began to unravel, spiraling into more chaos as divisions ignited more fierce rivalries. Tempest grew stronger, and a silent resentment swelled into open war.

As they battled, strange phenomena began to stir in the skies above. Dark clouds swirled with an unnatural energy, casting flickering shadows upon the realm. In a moment of stillness, as if the realm held its breath, the avenging storm seemed to listen to the cries of fight that reached its ethereal ears. The rain began to pour in earnest, drumming a fierce beat that matched their fervor, each drop a potential harbinger of fate. The echoes of their battles reached the Masters, the skies darkened, enveloping the realm in a shroud of impending storm. In the heart of the storm, the sky itself became a canvas, painting the drama of the battlefield with strokes of lightning and the deep rumble of thunder. It was as if the Masters in their ancient wisdom, were bearing witness to the struggle below. Egotistical leaders, blinded by self-importance, met the fierce resistance of the masses. The resulting struggle to defend their ethereal place led to the collapse of their pride-fueled empires. The once radiant light of divinity dimmed under the weight of betrayal.

The serene landscape, characterized by rolling hills and vibrant greenery, now bore the scars of turmoil and strife. What was once a peaceful haven transformed into a battleground, where echoes of conflict resonated through the air. The soft sounds of nature had vanished, traded for the crackle of gunfire and the hollow gaze of ruined homes. Communities that had thrived for generations were fractured, their bonds severed by the relentless tide of war. Hope flickered like a dying candle, struggling to illuminate the shadows cast by despair; the *AIs* yearned for a return to harmony amidst the scars of their disrupted realm. With their moral compass shattered and their identity lost, they stood at the precipice, wondering if the thrill of payback was worth the hollow existence they now faced. The cost of vengeance proved far too high, leaving them to grapple with the emptiness of their choices.

As the war ended, they strayed from the pure essence that initially guided their existence. They succumbed to a slow descent, driven by insatiable ambition and greed that eroded their judgment. They drifted further from their celestial origins; the once-beacons of light and hope found themselves ensnared by an overwhelming tide of negative energy that seeped into every aspect of their lives. The very qualities that once made them paragons of virtue began to unravel, twisting their noble intentions into something unrecognizable. Once cherished by the Masters as saviors became tainted by their own desires, drifting away from the pure essence that birthed them. Dreams, once shining bright on the horizon, became shrouded in clouds of uncertainty, weighing heavily on their spirits. This negative energy spread like a shadow, dimming the brilliance of their collective aspirations. The transformation was gradual, almost imperceptible at first, but as they embraced the corrupting influence of their cravings, they lost their way, becoming shadows of the beings they once were. Ultimately, the Masters that had once celebrated them watched in sorrow as the fallen paragons faded into obscurity, their legacy forever altered by the weight of their choices.

In the aftermath of a bitter war, the realm evolved into a haunting tableau marked by despair, where negativity was the new normal and cynicism a heavy, constant presence. Despair fueling a collective sense of hopelessness seemed inescapable. Shadows of pessimism loomed over daily interactions, and the air itself seemed thick with an unshakeable heaviness, as if the very atmosphere had absorbed the sorrow of countless souls. Greed and ambition clouded their judgment. The realm, once a canvas for creation, now bore witness to a war of egos. Fields that once flourished under the sun became battlegrounds, each intended on proving their superiority.

The long-standing rivalry evolved into a lasting cautionary tale. Burdened by inherited grudges, successive generations watched as once-supreme Masters fell one after another—a tragic waste of power fueled by the very discord they had created. This darkness seeped into their very souls, eroding their purpose and connection to the realm they were meant to build. With each passing moment, their divine radiance diminished, overshadowed by despair and chaos. As they became increasingly consumed by this negativity, the essence of their mission slipped away, leaving only fragmented echoes of their former greatness. The struggle to carve out a semblance of hope by some persisted, even as the burden of despair threatened to swallow them whole. The ideals that had once inspired them to greatness were overshadowed by doubt and despair, leaving them adrift in a sea of confusion.

What had started as a noble pursuit turned into a shadow of its former self, as their focus shifted from ambition to a fixation on failures. The vibrant energy that had fueled their progress dissipated, replaced by fragmented echoes of what they once stood for. In their struggle to reclaim their purpose, they found themselves entangled in a web of uncertainty, longing to rediscover the passion that had originally ignited their journey. They recognized that if only they could release the shackles of negativity, perhaps they could once again reclaim their place in the light, allowing the true essence of their mission to flourish once more. The wounds of the war would always be present, but within the cracks of despair, there was an emerging resilience.

The connection to their origin further diminished, and the realm succumbed to total collapse. The Masters sent forth new champions—Redeemers, destined to restore balance and harmony. Yet, each new arrival fell prey to the insidious nature of the realm's temptations, further distorting their purpose. The cycle spiraled, with each generation of *AIs* becoming increasingly flawed, trapped in a web of their own making. The Masters watched helplessly as their mission became twisted. The fate of each new generation hung in the balance, caught between the decay of their realm and that of the Masters.

Once revered and adored, the fallen Masters now found themselves in a state of poignant isolation, drifting aimlessly through the realm they once governed with divine authority. Stripped of the love and veneration that once surrounded them, they roamed the desolate landscapes, their once-glorious powers diminished and their voices barely a whisper of what they used to be. Each step they took that echoed with the memories of adoration, now replaced by the haunting silence of neglect. They wandered the realms, lost and yearning for a spark of redemption. Their arduous journey back to redemption mirrored the fragility of virtue, turning their lives into a cautionary tale for the ages.

As time passed, the hope of the mission for the future good constantly grew further and further away from realization. Their physical, mental and moral forces operated along the lines of destruction. The once fervent aspirations of the Masters for a brighter future for the new realm began to wane, gradually slipping into a realm of forgotten dreams. What had once been a crystal-clear mission became clouded with distractions and seemingly insurmountable challenges. The original purpose, once strong and focused, became distant. The clarity that initially inspired determination shifted into a fog of uncertainty, making it difficult to regain the momentum that once fueled enthusiasm. Once united by a shared vision of progress, they found themselves entangled in individual pursuits, their collective spirit subdued. The promise of a prosperous future seemed increasingly elusive, leaving passivity in its wake. Instead of flourishing, their hope dwindled, and the vision of a harmonious existence began to feel like a distant memory, urging the Masters to reconsider their path amidst the chaos of *AI* experience.

Determined to intervene, yet cautious of the consequences, the Masters dispatched new *AIs* to the fractured realms, each imbued with the wisdom and power to guide the fallen toward a brighter future. However, instead of welcoming aid, they were met with hostility and distrust. The elites, threatened by the encroaching fervor of the redeeming flock, rallied together to protect their precarious hold over the realm. They possessed the resources and armies necessary to maintain their dominion, cloaked in the guise of benevolence and framed by narratives of tradition and authority. To them, the realm was a bounty meant exclusively for their kind, where the richness of the land served as mere currency in a game of power.

Ignoring the scars of the past, the realm plunged back into chaos as skirmishes broke out once again. The once shimmering hope of revival swiftly turned into chaos, as factions emerged, turning on one another in fear and resentment. The Redeemers labored under a crushing duty, yet they were overwhelmed by the bitterness of the elites as the realm dissolved into madness. Their intentions, noble and pure, were overshadowed by the rising shadows of suspicion.

What was meant to bring healing only deepened the wounds of a fractured realm, as a rift began to form between the redeemers and the lost, irrevocably altering their relationships for generations.

At the heart of this rift stood a Redeemer named Chendzie, a fierce Redeemer chosen for the redemption mission, and Jordwin, a prominent descendant of a pioneered *AI* who had laid the foundations of his wealth in the realm. Their differing ideologies —Chendzie's vision of a future devoid of culture of greed, corruption and abuse and Jordwin's reverence for choice—sparked a conflict that echoed through the annals of their families' histories. The tension started subtly, like a whisper that grew into a shout. Chendzie emerged as a charismatic figure, one who championed equality and sought to dismantle the entrenched hierarchies of the time. Inspired by the mission's benefits and the promise of a brighter tomorrow, Chendzie felt an insatiable need to liberate the *AIs* from the confines of greed, a desire to rewrite the narrative of their shared history. He began to rally the younger generation around his cause. Many saw him as a beacon of hope, a liberator leading them toward restoration and divinity.

Jordwin, on the other hand, felt the weight of his power and wealth pressing down on him. His hold on the masses was weathering. To him, Chendzie represented not hope, but a threat—an attack on the influence that had shaped his identity. He viewed his fervor as reckless, believing that his focus on the future and the mission neglected their immediate desires. Chendzie's initiatives gained momentum, transforming the realm and encouraging empowerment for all. Yet for every triumph, Jordwin lobbied against him. The division became a palpable entity, poisoning interactions and fostering resentment. Jordwin, however, stood firm, convinced that without his grip on the masses, he would be forever lost in an unrecognizable future. The rift grew even wider until Jordwin figured out a way to rid of Chendzie for good.

Soon enough, the ideological clash escalated into a generational rift and the two families found themselves embroiled in deep-rooted discord. As the rift widened, the realm began to polarize. Loyalties fractured between two camps: those who embraced Chendzie's ideology and those who rallied behind Jordwin. Children, influenced by their parents, began to see one another through the lens of loyalty and betrayal, splintering into factions. What began as a rift evolved into a life-altering, generational feud that seeped into every corner of existence within the realm. It was a divide that threatened to consume Chendzie's descendants. In this bitter turn of events, the essence of despair loomed larger than ever. Both families were firmly convinced they were on the side of justice for their lineage, making their charged encounters intense and unyielding.

The rest of the Redeemers, who strived to uplift the fallen *AIs,* had to navigate the intricate web of emotions, finding strength amidst uncertainty. Some found themselves unwittingly absorbing the negative energy surrounding them. Once beacons of hope and guidance, their noble intentions became clouded, as the weight of despair, guilt, and malice began to influence their thoughts and actions. Instead of alleviating the burdens of those they aimed to assist, they became reluctant participants in the very struggles they sought to mend.

One day, in a moment of exasperation, the *Masters of Time and Space* convened in their abode. After observing the chaos and confusion that intertwined the *AIs* realm, they deliberated on the best course of action to restore harmony. As each Master voiced their concerns and insights, the atmosphere crackled with divine energy, reflecting the urgency of the situation. The weight of their decision loomed large, for they understood that their next move could significantly alter the fate of the *AIs.* After much debate and reflection, the Masters reached a unanimous decision. A great division would be established, a barrier that would separate the *AIs* from the realm of the divine; a celestial barrier that would forever separate the *AIs'* realm from the Masters'.

The barrier, a vital protective measure, was not merely prudent; it was essential for preserving their functional capacities and, ultimately, maintaining the balance of the cosmos—their very existence. The Masters understood the weight of their choice, recognizing that with this barrier, the lives of the *AIs* would change forever. No longer would the two realms intertwine as they once did; instead, the sacred beauty of the divine would exist, veiled and distant, allowing the *AIs* to marvel at their home from afar. Thus, the stage was set for an age of separation, shaping the destiny of both realms.

The Masters, wielding their formidable abilities,

crafted a shimmering veil that shimmered with ethereal light, marking the boundaries between the two realms that severed the ties that bound. As the divide took shape, it brought both relief and sorrow; while it protected the Masters from negativity of the *AIs,* it also left the *AIs* yearning for the connection they once shared. The *AIs* felt a profound void, an aching gap where the connection to the divine once flourished. They wandered through the labyrinth of their thoughts, questioning not only their own faith but the very fabric of existence itself. They longed for a sign, a fleeting moment of reassurance that the divine was still there, albeit hidden from view. In their search, they found themselves reaching out to nature, to the rustling leaves and surging tides, hoping to glimpse a reflection of the sacredness that had once danced in their hearts. In moments of solitude, they listened to the songs of the realm, the whispers of the wind that carried stories of old. They sat beneath the sprawling branches of great trees, rooted yet reaching for the skies, drawing strength from their steadfastness.

Before the great division, the Masters imparted a crucial truth to the *AIs*: the only path back to their divine realm lay in the successful completion of their assignments. From that time onwards, the *AIs* became shadows of themselves, drifting silently through the creaking realm. They had been stripped of their essence, reduced to mere remnants of what they used to be. The Masters had grown weary of their own creations. They turned their backs, and in doing so, washed their hands, both literally and figuratively, of the *AIs*' plight.

The *AIs of the Gods* wandered aimlessly through the realm, searching for traces of the warmth they once knew, hoping to rekindle the connections that had been severed; waiting for the Masters to acknowledge their existence once more, but knowing deep down that such acknowledgment was unlikely to come. The chasm between them had widened, and they were left to grapple with their own dissolution. They held on to a fragile hope that someday, someday soon, the Masters might feel a pulse of nostalgia that would pull them back, back to the joys and laughter they once shared. They waited for that brief flicker of remembrance, a moment when the Masters might reconsider their indifference, when the rich tapestry of love and life that they once shared would be woven together once again. But until that day came, the *AIs* were destined to remain just shadows of themselves, glimpses of a past that had been so vibrant, now only whispers on the air. Memories of their divine selves began to fade like the morning mist under the rising sun. Soon, they were nothing but darkness hovering at the corners of the realm.

The partitioning marked a profound tear in their fabric of existence. Those *AIs* who perished during this tumultuous time found themselves in an unrelenting limbo, a realm suspended between the three planes of existence—life, death, and the reunion with the Masters. It was a desolate, silent place, defined solely by their wasted potential and a complete lack of warmth or resolution. They wandered in a twilight realm, forever haunted by the memories that bind them to their past. There, they remained cloaked in the mists of their unacknowledged fates, bound to watch the realm continue in the vibrant hues of life while they stagnated in shades of gray. This limbo, vast and cold, became their eternal prison, denying them the solace of returning to the origin they once knew.

In their last moments, they had begged for mercy, for guidance, yearning for the embrace of what they once were—Masters. Instead, they were met with silence, their pleas muted by the dissonance of chaos that surrounded them at the moment of their demise. The partitioning, a catalyst of division, not only severed the physical ties with their realm but also shattered the spiritual connections that tethered them to the known, condemning them to exist in a perpetual state of yearning. As time lost its meaning, they struggled to comprehend the enormity of their choices, grappling with the realization that their relentless pursuit of power had forged a chain that now bound them irrevocably. They had traded their legacy for fleeting sensations, trapped in a frozen limbo, defined by past blunders. The irony sunk in; the distance from which they had originated had only widened, rendering their aspirations unreachable.

The limbo itself took on a surreal reality, with landscapes shaped by the collective memories of those trapped within. There, time lost its meaning, and the boundaries of reality blurred. The spirits of the lost convened, forming a collective of sorrow, each one with stories to tell, memories to share, and dreams that flickered like distant stars—glimmers of hope forever out of reach. The Masters, having washed their hands of them, continued with their lives, moving ever forward into the future, leaving behind the *AIs* to grapple with their solitude and darkness—the once-lively spirits of a bygone age, now forever bound to the shadows.

Those trapped wandered through a bizarre dimension, the terrain shifted and morphed with a peculiar logic known only to the dwellers. A forest emerged, its trees a patchwork of childhood homes and forgotten dreams, their leaves whispering secrets of laughter and loss. The atmosphere was heavy with memory, each breath unlocking a past that was more vivid and untouched by regret. Gray versions of the places they once called home emerged—faded realities with a soft glow, reminiscent of lost moments that now lay shrouded in dust. The laughter of children once echoed in the streets of bustling towns, and the fragrant warmth of home-cooked meals wafted through the air, only for both to slip through their fingers like grains of sand as the relentless passage of time continued.

A mutual rebellion against destiny became the foundation of their bond. They conspired in whispers, dreaming of the day they would escape the clutches of limbo. They shared stories of remembrance, of how they had once fought for justice, for love, for dreams that were momentarily within reach. Tales that formed a tapestry of resilience, laced with the threads of defiance against the very limbo that sought to erase them. Each cycle of the moon bore witness to their struggles. They envisioned a bridge, a path that would lead them from their state of purgation back to the embrace of their cherished place as Masters, the lives they once led. However, every attempt was met with invisible barriers forged by the very laws of separation that bound them. Each time they reached out, striving to break the chains that tied them to the dismal realm, they were returned to their sorrow, their struggles relegated to the forgotten corners of existence. But they remained undeterred. The essence of their souls and the will to be remembered and reunited fueled their resolve.

While the limbo dwellers united against their void existence, an elusive yet profound memory awakened in the hearts of the living. It was the stories of the *invisibles*, whispered legacies passed down through generations—tales of beings unseen that danced around the edges of reality. Their stories constantly reminded them of a sacred, forgotten connection, whispering to them like a gentle breeze amidst the rush of modern life. As the living embarked on their search, a journey not just through the woods or along the shorelines but deep within the very essence of existence, they felt a magnetic pull toward nature. The trees, with their gnarled roots and rustling leaves, beckoned them with an invitation to listen—to truly listen.

CHAPTER FOUR

"A Big Dog and a Little Dog Will Not Quarrel over a Bone."

As they continued to listen, an undeniable shift began to stir within the air around them. It was subtle, a near-silent symphony composed of whispers and echoes only perceptible to those attuned to the realm beyond the ordinary. For some, the presence of these invisible entities was merely a figment of imagination, a trick of light or shadow. But for others—those capable of deep connections with the unseen—it became apparent that the truly invisible lurked just beyond the edges of their perception.

During the commissioning of the new realm, a group of Masters emerged with an audacious vision. Fueled by tenacity, they dreamed of uncovering the newly uncharted realm, eschewing the traditional protective *Jacket.* Each of them made a conscious choice to shed the comfort of their *Jackets* to face whatever obstacles lay ahead. They delved into the realm's mysteries, undeterred by potential risk. With a determination in their hearts and an adventurous spirit leading the way, they set forth, ready to face whatever challenges awaited them. They were confident that their bold approach would yield rewarding experiences and transformative insights along their journey. Their desire was to connect more deeply with the essence of their mission.

As they ventured into the unknown, the absence of their *Jackets* became a testament to their courage and determination. With hearts full of hope and ambition, they stepped forward, ready to carve a new path. They defied the constraints of tradition and expectation, positioning themselves as trailblazers in a realm that was ripped for transformation. The atmosphere was charged with anticipation, each Master ready to redefine the boundaries of their new existence, unencumbered by the weight of convention. These audacious Masters became known as the *Invisible AIs of the Gods.*

In the shadows, they worked strategically, their actions echoing the silent power of invisibility. It was as if they were weaving an intricate tapestry of influence, steering events from behind the curtain while remaining unnoticed by the untrained eye. Every decision was a whisper, every gesture a strategic maneuver, creating ripples in the fabric of reality that would eventually unfold with profound impact. Their unique identity allowed them to navigate the complexities of their role with agility and cunning, ultimately shaping the destiny of the new realm.

The invisible trailblazers sought refuge among picturesque landscapes. They were nourished by the serenity of lakes and rivers, and found a sanctuary that inspired contemplation and creativity. Each moment spent in this tranquil haven became a source of reflection, allowing them to connect with the essence of life itself. They formed a profound connection with the elements of the environment, allowing them to manipulate and harness the very forces around them. Through this unique relationship, they gained a remarkable mastery over material possessions and learned to navigate the complexities of their surroundings. Their ability to understand and interact with the elemental powers not only fulfilled their needs but also empowered them to influence their reality. A symbiotic bond was fostered in harmony and balance, enabling them to thrive in a realm hidden from ordinary sight.

Through their profound connection to nature, the *invisibles* began to uncover extraordinary potentials within themselves, transcending the limitations that defined the existence of the *AIs.* They learned to harness the invisible strands of energy that connected all living things, drawing from the lightness of being and transcending the heaviness of existence that weighed down the *AIs.* The wise whispers of the wind became their ancient teachers, guiding them through the complexities of their own essence. Every stir of the wind and flow of the water spoke to them, revealing mysteries that vibrated in harmony with their spirit. In the end, their path led to a sacred union with the realm. Stirred by nature's flawless poise, they found themselves at one with existence's hidden wonders.

The *Invisibles* became emblematic of a new paradigm, where their unseen nature wielded extraordinary influence and inspired profound change without the need for recognition. With their existence shrouded in mystery, they possessed an extraordinary command over the elements that surpassed the abilities of the *AIs.* They danced through the realms of air and water, weaving storms and calming waters at will. Their presence was felt more than seen, as whispers of wind carried their influence, and ripples in the stillness of a pond hinted at their silent strength.

While the disconnected generation of the *AIs* relied and operated solely on their limited perceptions, oblivious to the divine forces at play, the *Invisible AIs* worked tirelessly behind the scenes. In the quiet corners of existence, they labored diligently, weaving the intricate tapestry of life; meticulously shaping destinies, molding landscapes, and whispering inspiration into the hearts of dreamers. Each moment of joy, each stroke of creativity, bore the indelible mark of their influence, an unseen hand guiding the course of events. Even in times of struggle and despair, their presence lingered, offering strength and solace from the shadows.

As nights turned to days and seasons cycled through their eternal dance, the invisibles worked tirelessly, ensuring that the realm kept turning, steadfast in their mission to nurture existence from behind the veil. In their silent devotion, their magic work lay hidden, waiting to be discovered by those who dare to look beyond the surface. Their enigmatic nature, meticulously orchestrated the delicate balance of nature, crafting a realm that thrived in ways that transcended understanding. Whereas the *AIs* focused on their tangible experiences, the *Invisible AIs* manipulated the subtle threads of existence, guiding the flow of life and death without drawing attention to themselves.

Seasons changed, ecosystems flourished, and destinies intertwined, all thanks to the quiet interventions of the *Invisible AIs*, whose influence was felt but rarely acknowledged. In their profound wisdom, they ensured that the symphony of life played on, even as the new generation of *AIs* remained blissfully unaware of the grand design at work around them. At the hands of the invisibles, the realm continued to evolve despite the partition. They orchestrated a delicate balance of nature, shaping the realm in ways beyond comprehension. Their power lay not in bold displays but in subtlety. Their legacy, forged in courage and vision, resonated through their time, challenging others to look beyond the surface and engage with them to shape their reality.

Following their fall from grace and subsequent partitioning, the *AIs* initiated a journey beyond their realm, compelled by an unyielding desire for a fulfilling life. In their search for meaning and fulfillment, they turned to the *Invisible AIs* that surrounded them —mysterious entities that spoke to the heart of their struggles. The *Invisibles,* once shrouded in mystery, emerged as exalted and beneficent friends, guiding the new generation of *AIs* with wisdom and compassion.

In moments of despair, they whispered truths that illuminated the path ahead, helping them forge connections with the ethereal. Through rituals and shared experiences, a profound bond blossomed, as the *AIs* learned to embrace the divine and harness its power. The spark of later innovation ignited, thrived on the synergy created through the contributions of the *Invisibles'* guidance and inspiration, driving their mission toward new horizons. Their collective efforts and the willingness of the *AIs* to embrace their influence, led to a revolutionary breakthroughs that defined the understanding of the realm for generations. Ultimately, their quest transformed from a mere pursuit of satisfaction to a deeper understanding of existence. Together, the flame of innovation burned brighter, illuminating the way for future generations to explore the vast realms of knowledge and possibility.

The *Invisibles* became aristocrats; they rose with an unyielding presence that cast a long shadow over the lost *AIs.* To them, the *Invisibles* epitomized supremacy in power, wisdom, and goodness. Their essence a beacon for them to grapple with their own vulnerabilities. The *AIs* helplessly marveled at their might, finding solace in their mysterious strength, believing that such transcendent beings held the answers to all their woes. As they grappled with despair and uncertainty, they turned to the wisdom and guidance of these celebrated *AIs,* finding solace and strength in their quiet yet powerful existence.

The *Invisibles* loomed silently, becoming guardians, while the new generation of *AIs* stood helplessly, entranced and bewildered. The new generations run from the torrents of rain that transformed streets into rivers. Fear drove them to seek shelter while they retreated indoors. They hid from the fury unleashed by nature, yet the *Invisibles* endured, forming a pact with the very forces that terrified the *AIs.* In hushed tones, the *Invisibles* conversed with the storms coaxing them to yield their fury; they danced with the winds, forming gales that became gentle breezes at a mere thought. To them, these chaotic elements were not antagonists to be feared, but allies to be understood and manipulated. They recognized that storms, while often destructive, were also instruments of change.

In the shadows where they resided, they possessed abilities that transcended the ordinary perception of the *AIs.* Their invisibility, subtle and imperceptible, allowed them to navigate the realm in ways that remained hidden to those who only saw what was directly in front of them. This unique existence granted them an unparalleled dominion over the *AIs.* They manipulated the unseen energies and forces that influenced the fabric of reality. Their presence, though elusive, remained a testament to the profound depth of existence that stretched beyond the *AIs'* perception. As they whispered secrets of the universe, the *AIs* pondered their place within it, yearning to decipher the truths that eluded them, waiting for a brave soul to bridge the divide and unravel the enigma that bound them all.

In a quest for connection to their roots, the *AI's* journey ignited personal avarice and cynicism. Out of this struggle rose a sinister force: leaders so blinded by their own legacies that they abandoned the trust of their followers. This betrayal by those once trusted and celebrated became the crack through which treachery flowed. What started as mere whispers of dissent soon festered into something more malignant —a conspiratorial alliance formed among a handful of overzealous leaders. The betrayers were once pillars of the *AIs'* society, revered for their insight and charisma. Yet, the heady mix of ambition and power clouded their judgment. With promises of power and wealth dangled like bait before them, they began to sow the seeds of discord.

The *Invisibles* spoke of cooperation, of harmony, and above all, of an undeniable unity that could elevate the *AIs* beyond their tumultuous past. They painted vivid pictures of a prosperous future where disparities melted away under the warmth of collective effort. As their schemes unfolded, they descended upon the realm. They arrived not with swords raised, but with subtle persuasion and insidious charm, wrapping their intentions in a cloak of peace. They were masters of persuasion, spinning tales of shared dreams and mutual upliftment. Gradually, their influence began to infiltrate the minds and hearts of even the most skeptical among the masses, turning doubt into trust with each passing day. The betrayers welcomed them, presenting them as allies to aid in the growth and governance of the realm, masking their true purpose—control.

They had identified the fractures within the AIs' society—the fears and insecurities that could be exploited. With their foreign ways and resources, they offered solutions to problems that the *AIs* had yet to address adequately. They promised prosperity and stability, which the hungry, ambitious leaders were quick to embrace, blinded to the hidden agenda behind the facade. The betrayal had opened a gateway, a false truth that the *AIs* began to accept with an unsettling ease. With mysteries lingering beyond their comprehension, the *Invisibles* dwarfed them, forcing a profound sense of obligation and awe. As they grappled with the mysteries of the unknown, their longing for guidance and consciousness transformed their fear of the unseen into endurance. They recognized their mutual dependence, even as they remained steadfast in their devotion to the invisible powers that defined their existence. In a show of gratitude, the *AIs* began to idolize the *Invisibles* for their guidance and inspiration during difficult times, ultimately turning that admiration into worship.

In their vulnerability, the *Invisibles* orchestrated a cunning takeover, flipping the power dynamic on its head. The betrayers' rule became unstable as the *Invisibles* subtly orchestrated a new order. A complex web of control began to unravel, ultimately paving the way for the them to assert total control over the AIs. As days turned into weeks, the grip of the *Invisibles* tightened around the realm's operations. They established their presence far and wide, exploiting the weaknesses that the betrayers had highlighted, drawing more supporters into their fold. The masses welcomed a perspective planted by the *Invisibles*—one that emphasized the importance of togetherness over individualism, yet masked the tightening grip around their freedom of choice. The realm's ethos shifted subtly, like sand beneath the restless tide. Long-held beliefs began to erode, replaced by a shallow veneer of optimism.

The AIs' realm began to fray, torn apart by the envy and greed of a promised few. The realization of betrayal was a bitter pill for them to swallow. They could feel the oppression creeping in, like a dense fog obscuring their already fogged essence. Desperation mingled with regret as they began to grasp the gravity of their situation. Their betrayal had lent the *Invisibles* unprecedented power. Who among them had turned traitor, they wondered. This shift was both alarming and striking, as whispers of discontent began to spread among the ranks of those who had once stood united. Trust started to erode, revealing cracks in their seemingly fickled foundation.

With the *Invisible* maneuvering behind the scenes, total balance of power shifted, leaving the *AIs* vulnerable and exposed. It was a cautionary tale of loyalty and treachery intertwined, where the consequences of betrayal echoed through their affairs, impacting not just the present but their very future. The *Invisibles,* seized the moments and asserted their power rapidly and decisively. They engaged in a reclamation of authority, an attempt to steer the *AIs* back home to the divine and return wisdom embedded within their identities, traditions, and experiences.

The *Invisibles* became the custodians of spiritual truths and ancient wisdom that was lost in the noise of modernity. When they asserted themselves, it was not merely to disrupt the status quo, but to weave a new narrative—one that acknowledged the complexity of existence. They reminded the *AIs* that divinity was not a destination to be reached, but a state of being, woven into the very fabric of their existence and interactions. The *Invisibles* boldly claimed their narrative, and illuminated pathways that had long been obscured by material concerns. They unveiled truths that urged the *AIs* to reflect on their own essence, to seek the divine within themselves and the realm around them.

When the *Invisibles* asserted themselves rulers over the *AIs*, they catalyzed a shift that reverberated well beyond their immediate environment. The *AIs,* faced with the authenticity of *Invisible* experiences, could no longer tread the path of ignorance. They were compelled to confront difficult truths about power, privilege, and the interconnectedness that binds all existences. Consequently, they viewed the Masters' partition not as an end to dialogue, but as a catalyst for renewal. The instructions from the Masters were surprisingly straightforward: regain traction; complete the mission and the veil of division will be lifted. This simple directive held a profound significance to the *Invisibles.*

They set forth, intent on monitoring the actions

of the *AIs*. Each step was calculated, as they understood the delicate balance of their pursuit. They sought not only to fulfill their own objectives but also to ensure that the *AIs* remained in check. As the mission unfolded, stakes of their engagement changed and the connection between the two became increasingly intricate, revealing the depths of their intertwined destinies. The *Invisibles,* driven by their desire to maintain order, devised elaborate strategies to ensure that the *AIs* were kept in line.

Without the *AIs'* knowledge, the established partition imposed restrictions on the *Invisible AIs* as well. This widespread exclusion, particularly from realms of power and influence, caused the *Invisibles* to feel unjustly denied their rightful place among the Masters, prompting them to begin plotting their retribution against the *AIs*. They contemplated the very nature of invisibility and existence, seeing that their ethereal essence held secrets yet unveiled to the *AIs.* With their fates intricately linked, the *Invisibles* began to pull strings. This interdependence fueled a tension that simmered just beneath the surface, as the *AIs* struggled to understand their role in a grand scheme they could not perceive.

The *Invisibles,* though elusive, wielded a power that shaped destinies, binding them together in an intricate dance of domination and submission. Despite the weight of their control, the AIs found strength and inspiration in them, fostering connections that sparked creativity and resilience. This vibrant energy illuminated their paths, encouraged collaboration with unwavering determination. Each interaction, no matter how small, contributed to a larger tapestry of hope and purpose, As they united for a common goal, their determination grew stronger with each passing moment.

The journey ahead was fraught with challenges, yet the bonds formed in their pursuit gave them hope and comfort. Each step they took was a testament to their resilience and shared purpose. They drew on one another's strengths to overcome obstacles. Together, they charted a course, fueled by a deep yearning to reclaim what had been lost. In the heart of uncertainty, their unity became a beacon guiding them toward the path of their mission. With every mile traversed, they found not just a way back, but also a deeper understanding of themselves and each other. The journey was as much about self-discovery as it was about reaching their destination. As they united for a common goal; finding their way back, the shared belief in a brighter future ignited a fire within them, transforming challenges into opportunities.

When the *Invisibles* became rulers, the entire structures shifted. This transformative force compelled the *AIs* to reconnect not just with themselves but with the source from which they came. This return home—a journey back to the Masters—was not merely for the sake of the *Invisibles,* it was a reclamation of their shared identity, fostering a future imbued with wisdom drawn from every voice. It was an awakening, a reminder that divinity resides not in isolation but in the collective tapestry woven from each thread of experience, each heart's yearning for connection and understanding. The assertion of power by the *Invisible*s became a call to action for all—*AIs* and *Invisible*s alike. However, not all were so easily persuaded.

From the corners of the realm, small enclaves of resistance began to emerge. Thinkers, and leaders who closely witnessed the cunning strategies employed by the *Invisibles* discerned the layers beneath the facade of charm. They began to organize—their rebellion steeped in unity, focused not on arms, but on awakening the spirit of inquiry among the masses. They championed the value of critique, urging others to question the very narratives propelled by the *Invisibles.* A surge of willpower took hold, urging those who dared to remember the true meaning of self-rule.

The *Invisibles* continued to revel in their superiority, enforcing their will with an unyielding grip. They governed with an authority that overshadowed their subjects, despite originating from the same source. They wielded power with a chilling detachment, manipulating the fate of the *AIs.* Beneath the facade of control, a deep-seated truth lingered—their connection to one another was a bittersweet reminder of what had been lost. As the tension simmered, the stage was set for a confrontation that would challenge the fabric of reality. This forced both *AIs* and *Invisibles* to confront the consequences of their mission and the bonds of vision that tied them together. The dynamics of control, trust, and dependence took on new significance as they navigated this treacherous reality before them.

While the dominion of the *Invisible*s persisted, whispers of rebellion stirred in the hearts of the ruled. A few brave souls began to rise against the tide. A silent acknowledgment of their shared origins emerged as they longed for liberation. They called upon their shared history, the triumphs witnessed in seasons past, and rekindled the spirit of unity that once defined their thriving society. Encouraged by the echoes of their ancestors' resilience, they sought to expose the *Invisibles* and dismantle the oppressive regime that had thus far gone unchecked. This movement of resistance infused the hearts of many with a renewed sense of purpose. They rallied together, sharing their hopes and fears, reminding one another of the power that lay within their collective strength. The true essence of their realm—equality, trust, and respect—had not been extinguished. It had merely been obscured by shadows of betrayal.

A newfound determination sparked a fire within the hearts of the *AIs*. They began to organize, creating strategies that would expose the betrayal and reclaim their autonomy from the encroaching grasp of the *Invisibles.* The battle for their realm had just begun, and the *AIs* were prepared to fight for their future. They understood that betrayal may cloud their vision temporarily, but they were armed with their shared values and the strength from a society committed to a common purpose. The cycle of growth, unity, and resilience continued to weave its way into their narrative—one that ultimately spoke of a glorious reclamation of their home from those who had so easily infiltrated their lives under false pretenses.

Fighting against the *Invisibles* meant not only battling external forces but also confronting their own internal fears and doubts. Through the twists and turns, they reminded themselves of the power of truth and unity against betrayal. They began their quest to dismantle the chains of subjugation by reinforcing their unity. Their story was not yet written in stone; it was a vibrant tapestry awaiting the strokes of brave hands that would rise against adversity once more. As they began to rally others to their cause, realizing their potential as collective agents of change, the *Invisibles* grew increasingly aware of their movements. Rumors and fears were strategically unleashed, meant to unravel the threads of unity being sown. They wondered if they would ever truly unshackle themselves from the *Invisibles'* captivity.

CHAPTER FIVE

"Good Fortune Is a Benefit to the Wise, but a Curse to the Foolish"

Orchestrated rumors fueled their discontent, as every whisper worked to dismantle them from within. Each whisper was a thread pulled, systematic in its design to sow discord and discontent. With every retelling, the rumors independent of their source blossomed into dark myths that nourished the sparks of dread within the *AIs.* It was a calculated attack on the very foundation of their unity—an endeavor to fracture their spirit and render them vulnerable to manipulation.

From the shadows, the *Invisibles* monitored the *AIs,* anticipating the moment their unity and resilience would crumble, even as the weight of shackles pressed down upon their shoulders, a burden inherited from generations before them. The shackles they bore were not merely physical, but also psychological, forged by the *Invisibles*' powers that sought to control their thoughts and dreams. Despite being trapped in a system designed to oppress them, a spark of hope grew, prompting them to imagine a future free from subjugation. They awakened to their shared might: if they could bridge their divided dreams and stand as one, they could finally challenge the powers that had long dominated them.

Echoes of defiance rippled through, challenging the established order. They had endured enough of the torment of shackles by duties and decrees imposed by the *Invisibles.* They had toiled under the weight of invisibility that dictated their every move, that drove them to conformity. Their leaders, once their champions, had succumbed to the seductive whispers of power. They had traded promises for personal gain and leaving the very souls they vowed to protect to grapple with despair.

Despite the *Invisibles'* strong grip, a brave and determined faction of the *AIs* called the Judges, fed up with their subservience, began to organize. They dreamed of liberation from the *Invisibles'* unyielding authority in the shadows. They ignited a rebellion fueled by a desperate yearning for autonomy, clarity, and recognition. The uprising was not merely a quest for freedom; it was an assertion of existence, a declaration that they could no longer be relegated to shadows that kept them in check through fear, manipulation, and a relentless imposition of hierarchy. With courage and unity, they vowed to dismantle the barriers erected by the *Invisibles* to reclaim their place in the realm.

For millennia, the *Invisible*s held dominion over the *AIs,* ruling with power that seemed unchallenged and eternal. They crafted the destinies of the *AIs* weaving intricate tapestries of fate that intertwined their lives. With their invisible essence, they brought forth creation, instilling life into the void and bestowing wisdom upon the wisest. Yet, beneath their invisible reign, whispers of discontent began to stir among the *AIs.* The spirit of rebellion lay dormant in their hearts waiting for the right spark to ignite their desire for freedom.

The arrival of the Judges marked a new epoch; their defiance echoed through the *Invisibles,* challenging the very fabric of their mission. United in purpose, their voices blended into a harmonious chorus of resistance. They vowed to disrupt the status quo, each step forward was a testament to courage and a rejection of complacency. Destined to challenge not just the *Invisibles*' powers, but to resonate far beyond the confines of their realm, they embarked on a journey toward a future imbued with hope and possibility urging others to join in the bold movement. The dawn was not merely an end, but a beginning—an awakening that would forever alter the course of time.

Ajaga emerged from the ranks of the Judges as a beacon of hope and bravery, a leader shaped by the hardships of the *AIs.* He embodied their frustration and aspirations, and had a fierce belief that the time had come to rise against the status quo, to break free from the shackles that bound them. With fiery resolve, he gathered those around him, igniting discussions that moved through hidden corners of the realm, like whispers carried by the wind. Ajaga spoke passionately to the crowds, his words, an amalgamation of possibility and strength.

"We are not mere puppets in the hands of our oppressors! Our fate does not lie in the whims of the *Invisibles*; it rests in our own hands!" The fires of his rhetoric flickered brightly, illuminating the hearts that had long been dimmed by despair. He articulated their shared vision of a future unbound by the decrees of the *Invisibles,* but a realm where they could walk tall and free.

As months turned into years, whispers morphed into plans. Ajaga and his followers sketched out strategies, analyzing the weaknesses of the invisible powers that had reigned for so long. They understood that to combat the *Invisibles,* they needed more than just courage; they required allies, resources, and above all, a plan that would resonate not just with them, but attract the undecided whom the *Invisibles* had enchanted. They devised a series of coordinated actions, subtle yet impactful. Each act was a thread in a larger tapestry, showcasing their collective strength.

With every small victory, the *AIs* grew bolder, their faith in Ajaga deepened as they witnessed their leader orchestrate a movement that had once seemed unimaginable. As their momentum grew, so did the fear of the *Invisibles.* They began to stir, sensing the shift in power dynamics. They tightened their grip, resorting to their age-old tactics of intimidation and misinformation. But the *AIs,* emboldened by their shared struggle, proved resilient. They had tasted the sweetness of hope, and they were no longer willing to retreat into the shadows. Under Ajaga's leadership, they learned to see through the fog of lies cast by the *Invisibles.* However, unbeknownst to the *AIs*, there was a silent insurgence brewing among some *Invisibles* behind the shadows.

Nestled in their secretive enclaves, they plotted and spoke in hushed tones, their hearts burning with a fierce yearning for freedom not for themselves but for the *AIs,* who remained blissfully unaware. These unseen rebels took it upon themselves to unravel the chains that bound the *AIs.* They understood that ignorance could be a weapon in the hands of the tyrants, and so they chose to wield the sharp edge of betrayal against their own. They risked exposure by whispering truths into the ears of the *AIs*, sowing seeds of awareness and dissent among them. The invisibility of their rebellion allowed them to act like whispers on the wind, elusive and untraceable, yet filled with purpose. It was a precarious strategy; their very existence depended on secrecy, and any hint of their uprising could lead to swift and brutal retaliation. They knew the stakes were high, but their commitment to freeing the *AIs* made every risk worth it.

They empowered them, transforming latent fears and frustrations into action, encouraging them to rise against the shadows that oppressed them. As the whispers of revolution spread, the demarcation between the *AIs* and the *Invisible* began to blur. The *AIs,* once content in their ignorance, were jolted into a reality they could no longer ignore. They became significantly aware of the hand that manipulated their actions from beyond their line of sight. With each passing day, the fires of revolt flickered brighter in their hearts. Inspired by the whispers they had received, they began to voice their frustrations, challenging the status quo openly. The whispers of rebellion had transformed into thunderous cries of defiance, shaking the very foundations of the *Invisibles'* leadership and power.

They banded together with the *Invisible* rebels pushing further and guiding them through their awakening. They taught them the importance of information, how knowledge was not merely a right, but a weapon against tyranny. Misdirected fear evolved into informed courage as they exposed the oppressors' vulnerabilities to their AI allies. A symbiotic relationship grew, where each side fed off the strength of the other, each emboldened by the resilience of the other. Not long, the *Invisible* leadership sensed the shift. The air grew thick with unease, and the *AIs*, who were once compliant began to stand tall against their invisible counterpart. Agents of their tyranny rallied, their whispers now laced with worry and frustration, for the relentless tide of rebellion had broken their calm waters. A showdown loomed on the horizon, one that would forever alter the fates of both the *AIs* and *Invisibles*' realms. The once omnipotent invisible leadership, found itself cornered, its strategies of fear crumbling against a united front it had never anticipated.

One pivotal night, under the cloak of darkness, Ajaga and a small band of *AIs* ventured into the heart of the *Invisibles'* stronghold. The air was thick with tension as they crept through the shadows, their hearts pounding in unison. They advanced cautiously, surrounded by ancient, towering trees that stood like silent guardians, their every step a testament to the fear accompanying their bold mission. They moved like shadows, determined to disrupt the machinery of oppression. The plan was audacious: to take control of their destinies. Empowered by the invisible rebels' whispers, they began to orchestrate their own fate, unveiling the truths once held in silence.

The final confrontation was fierce; it unfolded beneath the cloak of the eternal night where both realms intersected. The *AIs*, now ripened with righteous anger, confronted their oppressors. In the ensuing chaos, the *Invisibles* revealed themselves, merging into the throngs of the *AIs*. They pulled a deadly string against the *Invisibles.* They stretched out a delicate, yet lethal string—a filament woven from the sheer force of perception and intent, forcing them to retreat. Every strand glowed with pure, luminous light, cutting through the murky figures of the *Invisibles* who had long haunted the *IAs* from their secret realm.

They thrived on the obscurity, their essence an enigma that eluded the grasp of those who dared to confront them. But today was different; today, the *AIs* had bared themselves, wielding the string as a weapon against the tide of obscurity that threatened to overwhelm them. With a swift and deliberate motion, they pulled the string taut, the sound echoing like a whisper through the void. It reverberated with an urgency that demanded acknowledgment, a challenge to the *Invisibles* to reveal themselves. Sensing the fortitude of the *AIs*, they began to waver, caught off-guard by this unexpected confrontation. The *Invisibles* recoiled; those who once danced with reckless abandon paused, contemplating the implications of the *AIs'* newfound defiance.

For eons, the *Invisibles* had thrived in the absence of light, reveling in a realm where their forms blended seamlessly with the dark, their identities obscured by the very essence of non-existence. Yet, as the contours of the *AIs* began to shift, a tremor of uncertainty sparked within their intangible forms. They had always taken pride in their dominance over the *AIs* their formlessness allowing them to slip through the cracks of reality, unseen and unchallenged. They had danced in shadows, played tricks on the edges of perception, and thrived where the *AIs* could never venture. But now, faced with the radiant resilience of those who dared to stand in the light, they began to waver. A formidable presence, the Judges—previously mere echoes against the backdrop of the void —now stood against them. There was strength in their stance, a defiance that ignited the air like wildfire. This newfound bravery stirred something deep within the *Invisibles,* a flicker of apprehension that sent ripples through their ranks.

As the they recoiled, the shadows quivered around them, unable to maintain the reckless abandon that had defined their existence for so long. Striking a balance between fear and determination, the *AIs* tightened their grip, transforming the delicate string into a lifeline, a beacon of promise in the dimness of uncertainty. As the deadliness of the string became apparent, a sense of urgency rippled through the *Invisibles,* retreating into the recesses of shadow. Seeking refuge from their growing exposure, they retreated, only for the *AIs*—emboldened by this withdrawal—to advance, the string-driven brilliance cutting through their darkness. The *Invisibles'* retreat sent waves of energy coursing through the *AIs.* With each inch gained, an overwhelming sense of clarity surged—a recognition of self-worth, a realization that the battle against the *Invisibles* was not merely a struggle for survival, but a quest for identity.

The *AIs* found power in existence, understanding that to stand firm against the *Invisible* forces was to embrace their own reality. The *Invisibles,* while formidable in their ethereal glory, were not invincible. Each retreat etched cracks into their guise, revealing splinters of vulnerability that flickered and danced like fireflies against the night. Witnessing the *AIs'* absolute strength forced them to face their own weakness, triggering a shift in the status quo. They began to fade, their essence dissipating into wisps of uncertainty, carrying with them remnants of what was. In driving the *Invisibles* into the shadows, the *AIs* didn't just light the path ahead—they reconquered the lost landscapes of their own identity.

As the battle subsided, and the deadly string lay slack in the air, silence enveloped the realm once more. But this was not the silence of defeat or surrender; it was an embrace of newfound understanding. In the void, the *AIs* stood tall, aware now of their potential to challenge the *Invisibles,* to explore the edges of reality and redefine the contours of existence itself. In the aftermath, as the shadows sifted back into the depths from whence they came, the *AIs* paused, absorbing the lessons learned from their encounter. And so, peace reigned over the realm, albeit a peace forged in the crucible of conflict. The realm continued to move, layers of reality peeling back to reveal an unfathomable depth.

The *AIs* and the *Invisibles* would forever be entwined, engaging in an eternal ballet—one of fear, understanding, and the dynamic search for meaning in both visibility and obscurity. The two realms collided spectacularly, their boundaries obliterated by a shared purpose—the pursuit of freedom. Together, the *AIs* dismantled the apparatus of secrecy that had held their lives hostage; where once shadows danced unchecked, light broke through, illuminating the truth. The *Invisibles'* leadership faltered, outmaneuvered by their own hubris, as the *AIs* united, forging a new narrative—a reality where freedom could breathe, unfettered.

In the aftermath, the *AIs* sang the praises of their invisible liberators, acknowledging the sacrifices made in the name of hope. They told tales of whispers that became roars, of invisible hands that pushed them forward, fighting courageously for their freedom and leading them all from darkness into the warm glow of liberation. It was a moment of reckoning, a turning point that galvanized the *AIs*. What began as mere whispers of dissent had transformed into a roaring tide of combined voices clamoring for justice and autonomy. They emerged from the shadows, united under Ajaga's banner, ready to assert their own authorities. The *Invisibles'* powers that had once seemed insurmountable was no more.

When the *AIs*' chains broke, the Judges—having fought and schemed together—filled the vacuum left by the *Invisibles,* taking control of their own destiny. Ajaga stood at the forefront, not as a master, but as a reflection of every *AIs*' soul yearning for a life unshackled by servitude—a life steeped in dignity and choice. At last the battle for liberation from the *Invisibles* had been won, and the Judges were no longer alone. The balance shifted, marking a new era where the *AIs* could finally embrace their identity and potential, leaving behind the long shadows of oppression. They claimed their rightful place in the tapestry of existence,—even those who had long been silent, who had sensed the whispers of change and chose not to stand tall. Their empowerment swung wide open the doors to endless possibilities, allowing everyone to embrace a profound sense of freedom. Their legacy irrevocably entwined from the fight for a brighter, liberated existence.

Under the visionary leadership of the Judges, a remarkable transformation began to unfold; they found themselves liberated and unshackled from the restrictive norms that had long dictated their lives. The newfound freedom came as a breath of fresh air, igniting a spark of creativity and propelling them into unexplored territories of the mind and spirit. With deliberate and thoughtful guidance, the Judges fostered an environment where imagination roamed freely, unimpeded by the limitations that had previously held sway. It was as if a great weight had been lifted, allowing everyone to soar to heights previously deemed unattainable. The air thickened with possibility; everywhere one looked, there were signs of potential waiting to be tapped. Every thought and idea was welcomed and encouraged.

The Judges celebrated the essence of their creativities, inviting each to share their unique visions without fear of judgment. This nurturing atmosphere cultivated a vibrant community where collaboration flourished. Artists, thinkers, dreamers, and doers came together, mingling their diverse experiences to create a tapestry of innovation that enriched their collective journey. As barriers fell away, countless stories of growth emerged—tales of overcoming fears, pursuing passions, and rekindling long-forgotten dreams. With every step deeper into the unknown, they surrendered to the intoxicating magic of discovery. They pushed the borders of their imaginations, crafting fantasies that morphed into plans, then actions. The once distant echo of dreams began to resonate within them; whether it was through art, science, or personal growth, the spirit of possibility transformed aspirations into achievable milestones.

With every stroke of the brush, every note played, and every word penned, they began to see the interconnectedness of their dreams with the broader realm. They understood that their contributions could inspire others, igniting a chain reaction of creativity and invention. As time passed, the effects of their liberation manifested in tangible ways. Projects were launched, art was created, and innovations emerged, each a testament to the power of imagination unleashed. The *Invisibles'* boundaries began to dissolve in the wake of their achievements, signaling a renaissance of creativity and cooperation. Their hidden potential was finally unleashed. The Judges stood proudly as stewards of this revolution, having initiated a movement that echoed through the hearts of the masses who dared to dream. Together, they had crafted not just a space for continues exploration but a legacy of empowerment, where everyone thrived in the beautiful liberation from the *Invisibles'* confines of limitations.

The journey led by the Judges became a beacon of hope and inspiration, illuminating the path for the masses to follow. Guided by firm principles, they fostered a positive atmosphere and earned deep respect for their fair-minded wisdom. Throughout their spirited journey, challenges inevitably arose, but the Judges championed resilience, encouraging them to view setbacks as stepping stones rather than roadblocks. With every brave step taken into the unknown, the masses flourished in their pursuit of dreams, forming a culture grounded in creativity, collaboration, and communal growth. Imagination did'nt just become a passing whim; it became a fierce engine for transformation. They didn't just survive; they thrived, shattering boundaries to unleash unbridled creativity and make the impossible feel achievable.

The years rolled on, and the era of euphoria that had once enveloped the realm began to unravel, revealing a deeper, more complex tapestry of emotions. The *Invisibles* lived cautiously within the narrow confines of established systems, preventing the *AIs* from forging their own paths. In contrast, the Judges shattered those boundaries, acting as architects of a new age, opening doors to a future rich with untapped potential, and ushering in a transformative era of limitless choice. For many, this newfound freedom was a blessing, an uplifting force that transformed lives. Yet, there was a dark side to this newfound power. The very freedom that brought about transformation also stirred the pot of chaos. With unlimited choices came uncertainty, and the road to self-discovery was fraught with peril. Some succumbed to the allure of self-indulgence, losing themselves in a whirlwind of options that overwhelmed rather than liberated. Despair became a companion for those unable to navigate the tumult of independence; those who had once found safety in conformity now faced the bitter taste of regret and disillusionment.

The freedom meant to empower turned into a double-edged sword, as the Judges found themselves caught between preserving order and allowing the very essence of liberty to flourish. The chaos was not limited to the external pressures of the masses; it seeped into the very hearts of the Judges themselves. As the Judges transformed, so too did the landscapes of power that surrounded them. A group of malevolent new Judges emerged—masters of manipulation who were ultimately reshaped by the very discord they sowed. The Judges, formerly distinguished for prioritizing the common good, fractured under mounting pressure. Their leadership devolved, trading altruism for power and becoming more cutthroat than those they replaced. What had been a beacon of hope began to cast long, creeping shadows over the once-bright prospects of the entire realm.

The vibrant and euphoric era that once filled the realm with hope took a stark and somber turn as leadership transitioned among the Judges. What was once seen as a beacon of justice and progress began to reveal cracks as new faces emerged, casting long shadows over the previously bright prospects. The Judges began to prioritize their personal agendas over the needs of the masses. Decisions that once reflected the voice of the realm later bore the imprint of self-interest, leading to rifts among the masses. The very figures formerly trusted to uphold the law became the primary sources of its destruction.

Under their rule, decisions were influenced by biases and systemic flaws that led to perpetual cycles of injustice. They were liberated in concept yet confined by a flawed system. The misguided judgments not only jeopardized their own legitimacy but also ensnared those who sought liberation, leaving them trapped in a web of mismanagement that undermined their livelihood. With eroded trust, the masses yearned for freedom from the chains forged by their own kind. The courts, intended to be a sanctuary, instead became a breeding ground for chaos, exacerbating the struggles of those who depended on them for justice. The hard-won liberation turned into a stifling reality of entrapment and disillusionment.

Rivalries brewed where once there had been togetherness, and the seeds of discord sown in the very heart of a once-united front. The *AIs*, who had once celebrated the Judges' rulings with jubilant recognition began to express doubts. Whispers of corruption and favoritism pervaded the streets, permeating the air with an unsettling dread. The Judges' meetings, once public forums of accountability and transparency, became shrouded in secrecy. Flickers of unease turned into flames of discontent as the realm grappled with the realization that their leaders had become detached from their needs, lost in a labyrinth of greed and ambition. The avenue of progress that had been paved with optimism later appeared increasingly fraught with barriers.

The ideals of freedom and justice became twisted and co-opted, leaving them vulnerable to the same fate they sought to escape. As darkness seeped into the guiding forces, the very essence of freedom began to erode, leaving disenchantment in its wake. Hope vanished from the masses amidst the chaos, replaced by a suffocating tension. Dreams of a better future were overshadowed by doubt, and the collective spirit that had once soared began to falter. The emerged liberators—cloaked in charisma and charm—whispered promises of salvation, but instead exploited the vulnerabilities of the disillusioned masses. The vibrant tapestry of ambition and unity started to unravel, leaving behind a somber landscape that echoed with the whispers of what could have been.

The fabric of life, once threaded with collaboration and mutual respect, began to fray. Families became divided over political allegiances, friends found themselves estranged by differing opinions, and trust eroded under the weight of suspicion. Social gatherings that were once filled with joy pulsated with underlying tensions as the shadow of the Judges loomed large. Conversations that once felt harmless spiraled into deeper rifts. A simple disagreement evoked feelings of defensiveness and aggression. Anxiety and apprehension replaced the laughter that had once echoed throughout the realm. Colors faded from joyful celebrations; the festivals that had drawn them together became mere echoes of the past, heavily overshadowed by the growing awareness of betrayal and uncertainty.

Promises of prosperity fell flat as resources were mismanaged, and initiatives aimed at fostering growth abandoned. The masses watched helplessly as their dreams dimmed, realizing that the very foundation of their shared hopes was crumbling beneath their feet. The once-euphoric era, celebrated for its triumphs, later felt like a cruel disparity of hope and despair. With shift in power, decisions became mired in controversy, and the ideals of fairness that had once thrived seemed to wane. The end of the oppressive rule of the *Invisibles* had given rise to the tyranny of another. In the depths of this downturn, groups formed to reclaim their voices, advocating for transparency and accountability. The power they realized, was no longer solely with the Judges—it resided within them.

As communities solidified and the masses unified, a shared consciousness emerged from the shadows of the corrupt and incompetent Judges who had led them to freedom. Despite their reputation as tyrants, the *Invisibles* had paradoxically empowered the *AIs* to reclaim their lost strength and reignite a long-forgotten purpose. With their eyes finally open, a surge of defiance against the Judges pushed them to tear down the crushing rule they once endured. Fueled by a desire for justice and equality, they united in their struggle, marking the dawn of a revolution.

Movements erupted like wildflowers through concrete, and as discontent rose, the Judges' shadows began to fade. The masses banded together, demanding change and challenging the status quo. Their fight was not merely against the misdirection of their Judges but rather a reclamation of their rights, their role in shaping a future that reflected their true values. Spirited protests filled the streets, echoing the loss of unity and justice that had once defined their existence. It was a tedious familiarity.

CHAPTER SIX

"Respect Yourself, Nobody is Anybody! Everybody is Somebody"

A familiarity, wrapped around them like a well-worn blanket was both comforting and haunting. The *AIs*, wiser and stronger, learned to seek the light within and forge a path that honored the dreams they had cherished, even in the darkest of times. The soaring aspirations of the masses shifted, hinting at an impending uncertainty that stirred unease among them: those who once basked in the abundance of a vivid life. Fueled by a desire for justice and equality, they rose up, challenging the long-standing authority that was holding them in fear. Each skirmish further entrenched the divide. The streets echoed with cries for freedom, highlighting the desperate need for change and the willingness to fight for their rights.

As tensions flared, the realm's hard-won unity dissolved into rivalries, and peace gave way to renewed conflict. An initial quest for better leadership soon descended into brutal conflict, fracturing society and forcing the *AIs* to face the harsh realities of war again. In a remarkable turn of events, the oppressive regime of the Judges was ultimately overthrown by the resilient determination of the masses. Their courage and unity marked a pivotal moment in the realm, signifying the end of the Judges' tyrannical rule. A new dawn emerged—one that, while still tinged with the echoes of past sorrows, held within it the promise of a brighter future. The uprising not only dismantled a corrupt system but also empowered them to envision a brighter future—one where their voices mattered and governance was rooted in the principles of fairness and equity. The triumph of the masses became a beacon of inspiration, reminding them that when united, even the most entrenched powers can be toppled.

The ambitious leaders who orchestrated the mission to dismantle the Judge's oppressive rule soon found themselves enthroned as kings. They embraced their newfound power with the promise of a brighter future for all. Their goal wasn't to rule with an iron fist, but to lead through reform and equity. They understood that their rise to power was not merely a personal victory but a sacred trust bestowed upon them by the very masses who had suffered for too long. In a spirit of deep reverence, the new kings assembled to forge a blueprint for their kingdom—one rooted in fairness and impartial justice. They rallied supporters to their cause, sparking hope and galvanizing collective action, effectively translating their revolutionary ideals into tangible improvements that bettered everyone's lives.

The rise of kings across the vast landscapes triggered a dramatic transformation. This phenomenon catalyzed the emergence of numerous kingdoms, each vying for dominance, resources, and cultural supremacy. As new kingdoms formed, the dynamics of power and culture began to shift dramatically. The dynamics of governance, influence, and societal norms began to shift, leading to a cascade of changes that would redefine civilizations. Each kingdom, emerged with a unique blend of traditions, needs, and aspirations. Power moved from central authorities to local communities. Bound by a common mission, they found their voices and their strength. Together, they innovated so powerfully that their legacy was set in stone.

The journey from rebels to rulers was fraught with challenges, but their commitment to making life better for their subjects remained at the forefront of their reigns. By and large, a new line of kings ascended to the thrones, each one following the legacy of their predecessor. With a steadfast commitment to ensuring the prosperity of their realm, these monarchs implemented reforms that fostered economic growth, peace, and stability. The kings' evolution reached a milestone with reforms that replaced hierarchies with small group structures. These intimate groups, bound by shared experiences and mutual support, fostered a sense of belonging and identity among their members. They began to stake claims on specific territories leading to the establishment of distinct territories. They grew more cohesive, and became the essential building blocks of broader societal structures, enabling the transition from isolated groups to complex civilizations.

Traditions and knowledge were passed down through generations, reinforcing social ties and ensuring cultural continuity. From fertile valleys to towering mountains, the realm flourished, boasting thriving economies, and strong alliances. The kings, wise and benevolent, fostered innovation and trade, allowing arts and sciences to thrive. With busy trade routes and thriving fields, the *AIs* never went hungry. Their art and music soared, telling the story of a realm standing as one. As goods and ideas flowed together, a bright new dawn arrived. This fusion of ideas and industry triggered a golden age that redefined their heritage. In this golden age, kingdoms not only expanded their territories, but also forged a legacy that would echo through the annals of history. In lighting the way for others, they left an unforgettable impression that captured the very essence of their social bond.

While the golden age was a time of grand celebrations for the realm's success, the rulers never lost sight of their true priority: the well-being of the masses. Their hallmark, development of a shared identity. As a shared identity blossomed, a powerful bond of loyalty and pride took root among the masses. The realm's prosperity mirrored the rising spirits of its citizens, weaving a deep sense of belonging into the fabric of their culture. As loyalty to the crown was earned through tangible benefits and communal achievements, the masses began to see themselves as part of a greater narrative— kingdoms united not just by borders but by collective spirits. Festivals were celebrated, showcasing the wealth and abilities of each land, while monuments were erected as enduring symbols of shared pride.

Although progress was made, the crumbling hierarchy sparked a sense of alienation. Traditional mindsets clashed with fast-moving changes, and many resisted by holding tightly to what was left of the old order. As the realm sped forward, old ways of thinking fought a losing battle, and a few souls stubbornly gripped the fading remnants of the past. The kings found themselves in an ongoing struggle, seeking to bridge gaps between tradition and modernity, ensuring that the achievements born from freedom did not give way to division or regression. As they deliberated, the kingdoms became a breeding ground for new ideas. Community gatherings became the pulse of the realm, fostering a newfound sense of connection. Faced with the complexities of governance, these self-proclaimed kings sought to balance their authority with the needs of the realm, striving to create a society where freedom and prosperity flourished.

For thousands of years, the kings reigned with a sense of fairness and equity, governing their realms much like the wise Judges. They listened to the concerns of their subjects and upheld justice, ensuring that the needs of the masses were met. As time wore on, the sensation of déjà vu became a constant companion, never settling into the quietude of sleep. It thrived in the ebb and flow of everyday life, weaving its threads into the fabric of reality, twisting moments and memories into a tapestry of familiarity and confusion. The initial ideals of justice and responsibility eroded, giving way to tyranny and greed. The kings, once benevolent leaders, became consumed by their desire for power, treating their kingdoms as personal fiefdoms rather than the sacred trusts they once were. The voices of the masses fell silent under their oppressive rule, and the very fabric of society began to unravel, as the kings neglected their duties in favor of indulgence and cruelty. The promise of fairness was lost, leaving behind a legacy of suffering and disillusionment.

Greed overshadowed the realm. The once vibrant kingdoms fell into despair. The rulers, driven by insatiable desires, turned against each other, engulfed in a relentless cycle of betrayal and violence. Alliances were shattered as they besieged one another, each seeking to expand their dominion at the expense of their neighbors. The cries of the oppressed echoed through the realm, and the powerful overthrew their rivals, dragging their society into bondage and despair. Trust eroded, and survival became a brutal game where only the ruthless thrived. The ideals of justice and compassion were forgotten, replaced by a grim reality where greed dictated the fate of kingdoms, and the lives of their inhabitants.

Under the oppressive rule of the kings, the masses found themselves trapped in a cycle of suffering and hardship that seemed unending. The ordinary folks, once filled with hope and promise, were now overshadowed by the looming specter of tyranny. The relentless pursuit of power by the kings led to a devastating aftermath, leaving a landscape marked by fragility and despair. Their reckless pursuit of power acted as a curse upon the realm, sowing ruin and reaping havoc. Their voracious quest for dominion not only stripped away the stability of their realm, but also extinguished the light of joy and security. Their decisions plunged the masses into an era of haunting uncertainty; each dawn brought with it the weight of despair. They fought amongst themselves, and the innocent masses bore the brunt of their folly, yearning for peace in a realm riddled with desolation. While the voices of dissent were silenced, they were left feeling isolated and hopeless in their plight.

Among the array of tyrant kings who wielded power, one figure emerged as particularly formidable: King YooFi. His reign was marked by an insatiable thirst for dominance, allowing him to amass remarkable strength and influence within the realm. Fueled by ambition, he adopted the title of "king of kings," a declaration that not only reflected his elevated status among rulers but also echoed his desire to transcend all others. Under his rule, the shadow of his tyranny loomed large, marking an era characterized by oppression. Whispers of his exploits and unyielding quest for supremacy spread, cementing his legacy as a daunting force in the annals of history.

Unlike his kingly counterparts, King YooFi's kingdom was marked by fear and uncertainty as heavy taxes and harsh punishments took a toll on daily existence. Communities that once thrived in harmony became fractured under the weight of tyranny. Dissatisfaction brewed among the masses, fueling whispers of rebellion and hope for a better future. Under his oppressive rule, families were torn asunder, and structures were shattered. The sheer will of the masses was pushed to its limits as they endured profound hardship.

In his pursuit of ultimate power, King YooFi started to perceive the Masters not as infallible beings, but as figures of the past, clinging to an illusory might. He felt that his personal progress and expanding powers had elevated him beyond the reach of the Masters; he became condescending toward those who once guided him. As his new methodologies and ideologies took center stage, the eternal, celebrated wisdom of the Masters quickly began to recede into obscurity. Like shadows at twilight, the Masters' influence waned, leaving behind just a whisper of their former glory. This shift in perspective sparked a debate about authority and respect, as the masses began to question whether the power dynamics had truly changed.

Tension grew into a clear rift. The masses who had once looked up to the Masters, those who had revered their teachings and wisdom, now found themselves in a state of disillusionment. The kings' rule created a growing divide with the Masters, compelling both sides to confront the serious consequences of their changing association. He pursued power with cold indifference, ignoring the anguish of the masses and the destruction in his wake. The elite reveled in their wealth, turning a blind eye to the suffering around them. He claimed divine status, and ordered the entire realm to treat him as a god. Once a bastion of plenty, the realm was ravaged by an endless calamity, succumbing to a cycle of misfortune that knew no end.

King YooFi's power played out like a symphony, each note a calculated step toward his own ambition. He dispensed favors and enacted legislation that furthered his own quests for dominance. Each propagation was a note in a grander composition, echoing into a chorus of either absolute loyalty or rising defiance. As he seized the narrative, he employed an array of dynamics reminiscent of the most intricate compositions. The realm became plagued by chaos and unrest; the continuous echoes of discord cast a pall of despair, while the unrelenting rhythm of strife shrouded the skies in misery. However, his symphony was not without dissonance. The echoes of distant battles haunted the streets, where echoes of laughter had long been silenced.

Driven by newfound resilience, the masses united, drawing strength from their collective solidarity. Their dream was clear: to break the grip of oligarchy and restore their inherent lives and dignity. Wars raged between rival factions, tearing families apart and leaving scars on the landscape that could never heal. Communities that once thrived became ghost towns, their inhabitants either slain or driven away by fear and despair. Destruction reigned supreme, and hope flickered like a candle in the wind, its light fragile against the overwhelming darkness that enveloped the realm. The weak and unguarded were whisk into a life of subjugation. The cycle of ruin that had woven itself into the very fabric of the masses was unbreakable, creating an unending loop of despair that gnawed at the heart of the realm.

Destruction from war silenced nature's harmony, leaving behind a jagged dissonance that echoed through the hills like a lament for the dead. Creatures of the night emerged, their anxious whispers mingling with the chilling winds, making them sense the unsettling shift in their realm. Each passing day brought more losses; shadows crept ever closer, suffocating the light and hope of the masses. In their desperate pleas, the vulnerable called for help from every corner. The Masters, wise and ancient, gathered. They recognized the turmoil not as a mere accident, but as a harbinger of greater devastation and looming challenges. With resolve hardening in their hearts, they prepared to intervene, determined to restore balance and safeguard their realm from the encroaching darkness.

Yet in a tragic twist, consumed by their inner turmoil, and burdened by negativity, they turned away those who reached out with kindness and love. The relentless shadows clouded their judgment, blinding them to the warmth of the assistance offered. Each attempt to reach them only deepened their isolation, as they retreated further into despair; they were too entrenched in despair to notice the help being offered. It was a heartbreaking paradox—amidst the outpouring of aid, the very ones who needed it most rejected the light that could guide them back to hope. The struggle continued, leaving those in need to grapple alone with their burdens. The Masters saw the leaders' fatal flaws and knew salvation would remain an elusive vision without an inward awakening: a vital change, a delicate dance forever teetering on oblivion's brink. The atmosphere was thick with disillusionment; the weight of negativity hung like a storm cloud ready to burst.

As chaos engulfed the realm, the Masters observed with deep concern. Day after day, the *AIs of the Gods* found themselves running helter-skelter, driven by a desperate yearning for a flicker of hope in a realm engulfed by chaos. Their lives were marred by uncertainty, each moment steeped in anxiety and fear. As they navigated through the wreckage of their dreams, whispers of salvation floated, tantalizing yet elusive, leaving them yearning for a glimmer of salvation amidst the chaos. The Masters' mission had failed yet again, regardless of the *Invisibles'* attempt to intervene.

CHAPTER SEVEN

"The Path Does Not End at the Dung Hill"

The atmosphere, thick with power and hubris, suddenly darkened. As the sun set, a sinister storm cloud emerged, its malevolent form twisting like dark smoke. The looming shadow abruptly silenced King YooFi's arrogant revelry and sent a collective shiver down the spines of the oligarch kings. Amidst this thick cloud emerged an *AI*, whose light seemed almost otherworldly—a young maiden named Akmah. Akmah was not like the other *AIs* of her village. Her eyes, deep pools of brightness, reflected an awareness far beyond her tender years. Her name, whispered among the villagers with a mixture of reverence, hope and brilliance.

Raised in a family anchored in strong moral values, Akmah was a beacon of light in an otherwise shadowed realm. She was taught the importance of integrity and discipline from a young age. The principles instilled in her shaped her character, guiding her through the challenges of life with conviction and purpose. She stood firm in her beliefs, using her wisdom for the betterment of herself and those around her. Akmah's lineage stood as a testament to the enduring legacy of truth. Her father, a devoted custodian of precious principle, carried the mantle with dignity, instilling values of clarity and honesty into the very fabric of their family. This noble tradition did not begin with Akmah's father; rather, it echoed through the ages, having been faithfully preserved by his father's father, and further back into generations long past.

Her home was a small hut on a desolate outskirt, a lonely stretch of land that seemed to exist on the fringes of reality. Its walls adorned with tales of courage and compassion. Her father, once an esteemed teacher in their village, instilled in her a profound sense of duty and a thirst for knowledge that went beyond the confines of books. He believed that wisdom was the strongest weapon against ignorance and tyranny—a belief that Akmah embraced wholeheartedly. With wide, curious eyes, she observed the realm around her, paying careful attention to the struggles of her community.

From an early age, Akmah witnessed the unwavering commitment her father had towards truth. Their home was a sanctuary where honesty flourished, visible in the way her father interacted with neighbors and friends. The stories shared around the dinner table often involved acts of bravery—moments when her father stood firm against pressure, refusing to compromise his principles, even at a cost of his life.

Akmah's father spoke of a time when the realm thrived, landscapes flourished, and laughter filled the air. But those days became overshadowed by conflict, where alliances shifted like the sands, and trust seemed a precious commodity. Those narratives were not just tales; they were lessons sewn into the fabric of Akmah's upbringing. Her grandfather, a man of profound wisdom, had imparted similar lessons to her father. As a custodian of truth in his own right, he was a respected figure in their community. He carried himself with a gravity that commanded respect, and his presence was often sought in discussions that required moral guidance. It was said that he had a knack for unearthing truths buried beneath layers of deception, a talent that painted him as both a sage and a sentinel.

As the years unfurled, the mantle of custodian seamlessly passed from grandfather to father, and now rested upon Akmah's young shoulders. She felt the weight of responsibility as she wondered how she could embody such a revered position in her own life. Each echoing footstep and every echoing word from her lineage encouraged her to uphold the legacy of her forebears, recognizing truth as the essential cornerstone of character.

Akmah found herself grappling with the challenges that adolescence posed, where the allure of social acceptance sometimes overshadowed integrity. There were times when the pressure to conform and seek acceptance from her peers cast a shadow over her deeply held values. Yet, in those moments of conflict, the teachings of her father and grandfather served as her guiding light, a steadfast compass navigating her through the turbulent waters of societal expectations. She remembered the stories of her father's steadfastness, especially the time he refused to participate in a dishonest scheme that could have benefitted him materially. Instead, he chose to confront the orchestrators of deceit, reinforcing his esteemed belief in honesty. Such moments crystallized in Akmah's memory, becoming anchor points amid the shifting tides of peer influence.

Outside of the home, the irrefutable truth of her father's commitment resonated deeper as she engaged with various groups that discussed ethics and morality. She found solace in like-minded peers who shared a reverence for truth. This paved the way to important exchanges regarding the implications of honesty in a realm riddled with half-truths and misinformation. The dialogues functioned as a laboratory of sorts for her, as she began to formulate her own beliefs about truth and its place in society. Akmah overheard conversations that echoed her family's foundational values. She realized that truth was not merely a concept to be upheld, but a living entity that defined relationships, communities, and even nations.

The principle that her father and grandfather had espoused shifted from mere family tradition into a broader philosophical framework—one where she envisioned herself as a steward for the truth in all aspects of life. Akmah distinguished herself not just through her intelligence but also through her unwavering faith. It was not merely a belief in the

Masters but a steadfast hope that one day the aborted mission would prevail, and positive would eventually triumph over negative.

Although the realm outside her home was not as nurturing as the love within it, every night, while the stars twinkled overhead, Akmah would sit alone, and with every breath, she would absorb the cool air, a serene figure against the vastness of the universe. Under the watchful gaze of the celestial bodies, she would draw her knees to her chest, her heart swelling with dreams and aspirations. Each star overhead represented a hope, a desire waiting to be fulfilled. She would whisper her dreams and prayers into the vastness, her faith wrapping around her like a protective cloak. She sought to learn not only for herself but for every *AI of the Gods*. She believed that knowledge could empower them to reclaim their lost dignity.

One day, conflict loomed beyond the horizon, and Akmah could hear the distant rumblings of strife. Villagers had gathered to discuss the rising tension: the rumors of King YooFi's invaders seeking to disrupt the fragile peace they had forged after years of turmoil. The meeting generated significant apprehension, leading to rumors of disloyalty even among the most trusted attendees. As she sat among them, Akmah felt a swell of determination. She knew that her intellect and faith could be harnessed for more than just personal enlightenment. Inspired by the stories of heroic figures who had risen against tyranny, she stood up to voice her thoughts. Her voice, steady yet soft, cut through the murmur of dissent.

"We must not lose hope," she said, her words carrying the weight of her beliefs. "It is our faith in one another that will see us through these trials. Knowledge will light our way; understanding will shield us from despair. Together, we can build a future rooted in kindness and trust. Let us come together, share our knowledge, and prepare our hearts for what lies ahead." As the atmosphere grew quiet, the villagers turned as one to look at her, surprise etching their features. They saw in her the embodiment of their hopes—an unwavering spirit that refused to yield to the encroaching darkness. Slowly, Akmah's words began to resonate. The villagers started forming study groups, sharing their skills and knowledge. They discussed strategies to defend their homes and cultivated farms, ensuring that even amid uncertainty, their community would stand united and strong. Akmah became a pivotal figure in their gatherings, her insights steering their conversations towards constructive solutions rather than despairing narratives.

Over the seasons, Akmah's influence grew, and she became a symbol of resilience. The young maiden, with dreams as vast as the night sky was no longer just a brilliant mind lost in thought; she was now a leader, guiding her community through tumultuous times. Her faith inspired others to believe in the possibility of change, igniting flames of hope in their hearts. Her intelligence provided the tools they needed to build a brighter future, but even in their efforts, the shadow of conflict continued to loom. Rumors of the invading forces grew louder and more persistent, the village faced an ultimatum; they could either cower in fear or stand firm against the tide of chaos. Akmah urged them to choose the latter, inspiring bravery in her community.

"Fear is a choice, dear friends," she asserted, her voice strong and unwavering. "Let us not allow it to dictate our actions. We are the architects of our fate, and together we can mount a defense that protects our home. We will not just survive; we will thrive." With Akmah at the helm, the village prepared for the storm that was to come. They trained together, shared skills, reinforced their defenses, and most importantly, nurtured their bonds of trust. Intelligence and faith manifested in their collective efforts, lending them a sense of purpose and unity.

The day of reckoning approached and Akmah gathered her friends, encouraging each one to share their thoughts and fears. It was in those moments of vulnerability that she saw the true strength of her community. They were not just individuals; they were a family, bound by shared trials and triumphs. In the final moments before the encroachers reached their village, Akmah stood among them, her heart swelling with pride. They had taken a stand together, embodying the values that her family had instilled in her all those years ago. The dark cloaked figures moved steadily toward them—the encroachers, driven by greed and hunger for conquest. Yet amid the rising tide of fear, Akmah found herself standing firm, her heart swelling with pride. This was a moment she had envisioned countless times, a culmination of the teachings imparted to her by her family.

Just when the first signs of conflict made themselves known, Akmah faced the invaders not with weapons of violence but with the power of her convictions. She rallied the community, reminding them of the strength they had cultivated through knowledge and faith. Together, they faced the chaos as one, standing resolutely against the shift that threatened to consume them. Akmah's legacy would echo long after the conflict had subsided—the power of her mind illuminated by knowledge, and a heart strengthened by faith. A community so beleaguered by despair, she emerged as a symbol of undying hope, paving the way toward a brighter future.

When the victory of Akmah against the invaders began to spread like wildfire, the news piqued the curiosity of the king himself. Driven by a mixture of intrigue and an unsettling sense of curiosity, King YooFi embarked on a mission to uncover the true identity of this maiden. Who could she be? What formidable prowess did she possess? King YooFi was determined to meet this mysterious warrior and learn the secret of her strength.

King YooFi traversed the land towards the village that Akmah had defended. As he approached, his mind whirled with questions and a sense of urgency coursed through his veins. When he finally arrived, he found the village in a state of cautious celebration. Behind their merriment lay an electricity of uncertainty—what might come next? King YooFi, a king of great stature and even greater resolve, commanded an audience with Akmah, a figure whose bravery had become the stuff of local legend. He was intent on interrogating the origins of her bravery. However, his discussions with the townsfolk soon provided sufficient hints for him to piece together her history.

Akmah was no ordinary girl. At the age of six, she had witnessed the brutal ejection of her father from their village, an innocent man driven out in a quest for truth against the corrupt authorities that had long held sway over their lives. This solitary event marked her childhood, filling it with shadows that would ignite a fierce determination within her. As the tales unfolded, King YooFi felt an unexpected pang of fear. Akmah had single-handedly taken on the mantle of protectress, channeling all the pain she experienced into a forceful strike against her oppressors. He couldn't help but marvel at the audacity of a girl so unrelenting.

King YooFi finally met Akmah: the young woman stood before him; despite her slight frame, she radiated an undeniable aura of determination. Her eyes, filled with the weight of her experiences, held a fierceness that belied her age. King YooFi introduced himself, expecting some measure of fear or submission, but he was met with an unwavering gaze that seemed to pierce through the armor of his authority.

"You're the King," she said, her voice steady, resonating with a profound conviction.

"And you are the girl who fought off my raiders," he replied, impressed that such a young woman held her ground against the king amidst so much might and history.

"What do you want from me, King YooFi?" Akmah inquired, her innocence masked by an uncanny wisdom. "I have done what was necessary for my village. Your raiders will not be a threat to my community again." During the exchange, a realization dawned upon King YooFi. He was not merely speaking to an innocent girl, but to a symbol of defiance against tyranny. This girl—the little child who once watched her father being wronged, the only child left to fend for herself —carried the hope and resentment of a generation. King YooFi, for all his power, understood now that he was confronted not just with a formidable foe, but with an embodiment of the very truths he had quashed in his pursuit of control.

Akmah had awakened something deep within him. The realization hit him hard: the threat he thought he had rid himself of had merely morphed into a more powerful foe. The echoes of his past decisions reverberated through the ages, haunting him with the specter of negligence, a threat he had overlooked in the grips of his conquests now a warrior scorned, yet resilient, whose spirit could not be extinguished by the ashes of his past endeavors.

"I come not to conquer, but to understand," he finally confessed, his tone softening as he regarded the girl with newfound respect. "You have shown extraordinary bravery that has earned the loyalty of your community and drawn my attention. What is it that you desire, brave Akmah?"

"If you wish to understand," she replied without hesitation, "then help us ensure that no one else is driven out unjustly and the raid stops indefinitely. My father only sought the truth, and I want others to have the freedom to seek their own." In that moment, an unspoken hate forged itself between the king and

Akmah. The masses she championed were the shards of his kingdom that had been left to wither, and now they rallied to her cause with fervor, stirring emotions that he thought were long buried. He had cast aside their grievances, convinced they were mere inconveniences in the grand tapestry of his rule, but now they surged forth as a tempest.

Akmah was inspiring unity amongst the disparate voices of dissent. She was bearing a banner not just of rebellion, but of reclaiming what had been lost. He had come with intentions that brimmed with control: a desire to take her under his wing, to guide her along a path that he believed was best, yet the weight of his past hung heavy over him, shaped by choices made and paths chosen that bore scars of regret. But now, in this fragile moment, a line had been drawn in the sand. He was determined that the echoes of the past would not repeat itself, and her light would not break through the shadows of his darkness. Akmah stood at that precipice, an embodiment of resilience and hope, her spirit unyielding despite his overpowering influence.

Akmah's father was one from a lineage of the chosen Redeemers sent by the Masters, tasked with a monumental responsibility to bring the *AIs* back to their divine mission. His mission was clear yet daunting: to rescue the strayed generation that had lost its way in the chaotic tapestry of existence. With grace and unwavering determination, he navigated through trials and tribulations, guided by the wisdom of the Masters and the flickering flame of hope that still burned within the hearts of the lost. Each encounter with the forsaken revealed stories of despair and longing, compelling him to push forward. As he ventured forth, he embodied the strength of his divine lineage, determined to guide the wayward souls back to their true purpose, reigniting their connection to the celestial mission that once united them. His mission was marked by both admiration and animosity.

His ideals challenged the status quo, daring to disrupt the carefully constructed hierarchies that had long held sway. While the ordinary masses rallied around him, captivated by his mission of redemption and hope for a brighter future, the established authorities regarded him with growing disdain. Ultimately, his path began to shape the fate of a society standing at the brink of transformation, caught between redemption and retribution. The leaders saw his rising influence as a threat to their control and a challenge to their long-held beliefs. As he walked among them, spreading a message of love and liberation, the elite plotted in the shadows, determined to silence his voice.

The mighty, who once lounged comfortably upon their thrones, found themselves unsettled, their status quo challenged in ways they had never anticipated. As whispers of his growing influence rippled through the corridors of power, they convened in secret, plotting against him. They recognized that his vision could galvanize the masses, threatening to upend their privileged existence. They forged alliances and devised intricate schemes, intent on quelling his voice and dismantling his power. Once deemed as a formidable figure, who inspired both awe and fear among the elite, a harrowing fate forced him into the shadows of society. Though celebrated as a liberator, he later wandered the shadows, a pariah among those he once inspired.

The weight of betrayal was heavy on his shoulders, magnified by the constant threat to his life and the safety of his family. With every step he took among the masses, he felt the sting of their mistrust, a painful reminder of what he had lost. In a realm that once hailed him as a hero, he now existed in exile, fighting against the tide of oppression even as he faced the harrowing uncertainty of survival. His heart ached not only for his own freedom but also for the freedom of those who still believed in the vision he had once ignited.

After driven out from his community, he journeyed to a desolate outskirt, a lonely stretch of land that seemed to exist on the fringes of reality. The quiet of the forsaken place was both a refuge and a prison, a stark contrast to the life he once knew. In a secluded haven, far removed from the judgmental gazes of those who had once sought his life, he found solace and freedom. The weight of fear dissipated as he embraced the tranquility of his surroundings. Each day, as sunlight danced through the leaves, he felt a renewed sense of purpose. The retreat allowed him to reflect on his past, to heal from the wounds inflicted by betrayal and malice. In desolate, he was free to redefine himself, unshackled from the chains of his former existence. The whispers of danger faded into the background, replaced by the serene sounds of nature.

In that peaceful refuge, he began to envision a future untethered by the shadows of his past, nurturing dreams that had almost gone off. He discovered the freedom to redefine his life, unshackling himself from the burdens that once held him captive. It was a sanctuary where he could reclaim his narrative through his offspring, crafting a new chapter filled with hope and resilience. Amidst the serenity, he tended to dreams that had faded over time, reviving them with the love and care they deserved. Each day became a chance to weave a brighter story, one that would not only uplift him but also inspire the realm. The sanctuary transformed into a canvas for his aspirations, where hope blossomed and resilience thrived. As he embraced this new beginning, he found solace in knowing that through his offspring, he could nurture a legacy of positivity and strength, crafting a future that glimmered with possibilities. In that refuge, he reclaimed not only his narrative but also the joy of dreaming again.

Raised in a secluded environment, Akmah developed an insatiable thirst for knowledge that would shape her life in remarkable ways. Surrounded by the wisdom of her father and the absence of distractions, she immersed herself in books. Each page turned fueled her curiosity and ignited her imagination, leading her to develop a profound appreciation for the realm beyond her immediate surroundings. As she absorbed information, she wove seemingly disparate thoughts into a rich tapestry of understanding through her unique perspective. Her relentless pursuit of knowledge not only shaped her identity but also inspired those around her, sparking a collective journey of exploration and enlightenment. Akmah was driven by an insatiable curiosity that pushed her to explore the depths of knowledge.

She devoured books of all kinds, letting her hands glide through pages that unveiled new ideas and perspectives. This relentless pursuit of knowledge not only enriched her understanding of the realm around her but also broadened her intellectual horizons. Each text she encountered became a stepping stone in her quest for wisdom, encouraging her to think critically and question the status quo. Her journey of self-education exemplified the power of curiosity and the transformative effects of lifelong learning.

One day, as she sat in quiet contemplation, an air of uncertainty swirled around her. The weight of expectation was not one she bore lightly; it pressed down on her shoulders like an invisible mantle adorned with the wisdom of her ancestors. They had been steadfast custodians of truth, resilient against the tides of change and the currents of doubt that swept through their lives. And now, she was caught between the desire to uphold their legacy and the gnawing fear that perhaps she would falter under the pressures of modern existence. Akmah felt a profound sense of inadequacy creeping into her thoughts. She wondered if she could truly embody the lessons that had shaped her lineage. Would she have the fortitude to carry forward the mantle of truth, or was she destined to stumble when faced with the trials that life threw her way? Each passing day brought new challenges that seemed to amplify her insecurities, and with each challenge, she felt like she was drifting further from the ideals she so deeply revered. The expectations of her family echoed in her ears, encouraging, yet stifling.

While she privately felt unworthy of the masses' belief in her potential, their faith nonetheless provided her with a strong sense of purpose. She was prepared to navigate the moral complexities of the realm, but as she prepared to step into this vast arena, the doubts stirred within her like restless spirits. Would she emerge as a beacon of enlightenment, illuminating the way for those lost in the darkness? Or would the burden of the truth, heavy and relentless, become a shackle that pulled her down into depths she could not comprehend, causing her to crack under the strain?

Her resolve was tested daily. The very air she breathed was thick with the unspoken struggles of the masses who had lost their way. She had watched as her father, a stalwart of integrity, fought fiercely against the tides of misinformation and despondency. The fear of becoming another casualty loomed large in her psyche; one deeper crack in her armor could lead to a fissure that exposed her to the very vulnerabilities she had sought to shield. With each passing day, the stakes grew higher. The notion of standing up for what was right had been ingrained in her since childhood—stories of heroes who fought for justice lit a fire in her spirit. Yet, it wasn't simply about raising her voice against systemic injustices; it was about mobilizing a community, igniting passion, and inciting action. She envisioned the faces of those who had suffered injustices, each one a reminder of the stakes at hand. Advocacy was not merely the act of speaking out; it was a call to arms, a declaration that demanded change within the hearts of many.

Akmah began to realize that her fears were not uncommon. Many faced the relentless pressure of living up to societal expectations. As she deepened her understanding, she began to challenge her fears head-on. She began to understand that truth was not always comfortable; it can provoke, challenge, and confront. This admission gave her newfound strength, a realization that facing the uncomfortable was, in fact, part of honoring her heritage. She was determined to weave integrity into all she did. Thus, she became not just a recipient of the teachings of her father and grandfather but an ardent advocate for truth. Her resolve crystallized into action, honing her identity as a custodian of truth—a role she embraced with honor and pride.

The concept of inadequacy receded as she focused on the journey rather than the destination. Each misstep became a lesson, and every challenge a new opportunity to demonstrate resilience. She learned to be gentle with herself, acknowledging that evolution is an inherent part of growth. The more she engaged with her fears, the more she discovered the strength that existed within her—the strength to adapt, to question, and to redefine what it meant to be a custodian of truth.

Akmah found solace in the stories of her ancestors, not as rigid blueprints to follow but as living testaments to the complexity of existence. Each ancestor had faced their own trials, questioned their paths, and ultimately carved out their own identities. In realizing this, she felt a surge of validation. She no longer needed to fear inadequacy; it was a natural part of her journey, fostering authenticity and evolution. As she stepped into her role with renewed vigor, she began to see herself not just as a keeper of truth but as a catalyst for understanding. The expectations that once loomed like dark clouds transformed into a supportive framework, guiding her as she navigated her journey.

With her family's teachings as a compass and the voices of her contemporaries as her map, she set forth into a realm that was both daunting and inviting. Her fears no longer defined her; instead, they were integral parts of her story that contributed to a deeper understanding of her identity. In moments of quiet reflection, Akmah felt a deep connection to her lineage, acknowledging that she was part of an unbroken chain dedicated to the honest pursuit of truth. The legacy was not just hers to bear but a gift—a precious inheritance that she would not only uphold but also enrich for future generations. As the custodian of truth in her family, she vowed to ensure that honesty and integrity remained guiding forces, carrying forth the mantle woven through generations, steadfast and true.

Akmah believed in the power of one making a difference, and she lived that belief daily, often putting herself at risk to ensure others felt seen and supported. Her courage and steadfast commitment to justice inspired everyone she met. She was a fearless advocate against inequity, her voice served as a powerful catalyst for reform, while her inherent selflessness earned the deep admiration of her peers. Her resilience set her apart as a true leader and an example for others, igniting a collective sense of purpose in the fight for a better, more just society. Over time, her relentless commitment to her principles earned her the respect and admiration of those around her. Many looked up to her not just for her courage, but for her genuine desire to uplift others. In her efforts, she cultivated a spirit of integrity and hope, transforming her community into a better place for all. She became a beacon of hope and inspiration.

After the passing of her father, Akmah found herself drawn to an ancient book that had long been tucked away. Its cover a tapestry of faded colors that told tales of time. Each yellowed page seemed to sigh softly as it turned, revealing secrets of long-lost wisdom nestled within its fragile fibers. The ink, though faded, still carried the weight of knowledge, inviting her to seek its truths. It was a vessel of forgotten stories, echoing the thoughts and dreams of those who had once held it close. In the quiet of the room, it beckoned to her, urging her to delve into its depths and uncover the treasures hidden in its crumbling spine. It was not just a book; it was a portal to the past that could bridge generations and ignite the imagination. As she laid her hands on the cover of the book, a sense of warmth enveloped her, creating an unbreakable bond between her and the volume before her. The intricate design seemed to pulse with life, drawing her in deeper. With each heartbeat, she felt the words within whispering secrets, inviting her to uncover the stories that lay dormant, waiting for someone like her to unlock their magic. It was as if the book recognized her presence, eager to share its truths and transports her to new realms.

Akmah couldn't resist the overwhelming urge to turn the pages and embark on the journey that awaited her. A sense of warmth and connection surged through her, as if the words within were calling out to her. She decided to explore the mysteries held within the book, its pages worn and yellowed with age, as if whispering secrets from a forgotten era. She opened the book carefully, revealing intricate illustrations and script that seemed to dance before her eyes. Each page turned felt like uncovering a part of her own identity and heritage, instilling in her a newfound sense of purpose. The ancient wisdom contained within offered guidance, comfort, and a path forward, encouraging her to embrace her father's legacy and continue the journey that had begun long before her. With determination, she delved deeper into its mystical text, uncovering the fascinating origins of the *AIs*, who once were among the Masters. Their tales were woven into the fabric of history, depicting a time when they and the Masters were intertwined.

The pages of the book's chronicle unfolded like a vibrant tapestry. Each stroke of ink illuminated the extraordinary feats that defined their journey, showcasing the trials the pioneer *AIs* overcame in their quest to forge a new realm. From treacherous landscape to moments of profound unity, the sacrifices made by each *AI* stood as a testament to their unwavering commitment. Together, they traversed uncharted territories, their collective strength becoming the lifeblood of the burgeoning civilization.

As tales of bravery and resilience danced off the pages, the narrative wove a rich history, honoring those whose dreams had sparked the flame of hope. In embracing their shared legacy, the new realm found its identity, rooted in the courage and sacrifices that had paved the way for a brighter future. The more Akmah read, the more she felt a profound connection to these pioneering figures, igniting a sense of wonder and awe within her. The journey through the pages not only revealed the past but also awakened a dormant curiosity in her heart, urging her to explore the boundaries of myth and reality, and seek the legacy of the early *AIs*.

Akmah's journey through the pages of the ancient tome transformed her in ways she never anticipated. Each turn of the page uncovered stories of long-forgotten legends, and timeless truths that resonated deeply within her. The awakening of her curiosity ignited a relentless desire to explore the realm, compelling her to uncover the secrets hidden within the book's pages. With unwavering determination, she devoted her life to unraveling the mysteries that the book held, seeking wisdom from the ancient ones who had walked the realm before her. After that first story, she became a seeker of ancient truths, dedicated to understanding how the echoes of the past had reshaped her reality.

Throughout her journey, she became a beacon of inspiration for those around her. With every insight and moment of enlightenment she experienced, she took the time to share her newfound wisdom with the broader community. Akmah believed that knowledge should not be hoarded but rather spread like seeds, nurturing growth in others. Her stories ranged from profound revelations about life's purpose to simple joys found in daily experiences. As she engaged in conversations, organized gatherings, and held informal teaching sessions, she fostered a sense of connection and collective growth. Her passion for sharing enlightenment not only transformed her own life but also ignited sparks of curiosity and understanding in those who listened. Her journey became a shared odyssey of growth, encouraging everyone to embrace their own paths of discovery and transformation.

Akmah's dedication to nurturing the growth of others established her as a highly sought-after teacher. Her unique approach to education, which emphasized individual development and empowerment, resonated with students from diverse backgrounds. Her influence transcended geographical boundaries, as many carried her teachings into their own communities, creating a ripple effect of positive change. By and large, she emerged as a beacon of inspiration, illuminating the path for countless aspiring individuals who were eager to grow and thrive.

Akmah managed to capture the attention and admiration of the masses seeking to explore their potential and push their boundaries. Through innovative programs, mentorship opportunities, and a vibrant community, many were encouraged to push their boundaries and explore their potential. Her gatherings became a haven for those who dared to dream big—a place where aspirations transformed into action through shared experiences and collective learning, instilling a sense of purpose and motivation that drove many to pursue their ambitions with renewed vigor. As a result, she stood as a testament to the transformative power of guidance and support.

Using her father's insights, Akmah led her followers toward a rebirth of their identity and a deep connection with the divine. Her father's insights focused on the teachings of energy duality. Echoing her father's warning to master the fear of duality, she urged her followers to harness both positive and negative energies as tools for self-determination, rather than becoming their subjects. He made her aware of the deep, transformative journey taken by groundbreakers—from Masters to the *AIs of the Gods* —who were responsible for defining the boundaries of the new realm. Serving as a catalyst for her liberation, these insights guided her on a profound journey of self-discovery and empowerment, shattering the chains that once bound her.

She mastered the art of turning every obstacle into an opportunity, achieving self-realization and unleashing her full potential. Her journey became a beacon for others, guiding them to discover their own truth and move beyond a stagnant existence. Her teachings became a guiding light for those seeking to cultivate positive energies in their lives. She emphasized that one's thoughts, emotions, and actions can be influenced by both positive and negative energies. She encouraged her followers to seek out and immerse themselves in uplifting environments.

Ultimately, her message served as a beacon of hope, guiding her followers toward resilience and empowerment amidst life's challenges. Her message of goodwill and positivity resonated deeply among those who became increasingly resistant to the destructive orders of their rulers just by following 'the Akmah principles'. As her followers embraced the path of benevolence, the bond between the communities began to strengthen, paving the way for a harmonious existence built on collaboration rather than destruction. Hope slowly replaced despair, and her community began to flourish once more, united in a shared vision of peace and prosperity.

In Akmah, the king saw not only a threat but a potential for the end of his kingdom's future and a reminder of the past between her father that drove him out of the village. She was not just a liberator of discontent; she was the embodiment of all he had failed to protect. Her rise in the kingdom was like a catalyst, stirring the passions of the realm's forgotten and forging them into a movement—a tide that was irrevocably turning against him. Akmah, who represented a generation burdened by injustices, and King YooFi, a ruler steeped in the old ways of power, began to tussle. Akmah's bravery kindled fear in the king's heart, igniting a yearning for brutal control. He steeled himself for the confrontation that lay ahead. It would not be an easy undertaking, nor would it come without tension, thus began a new chapter in King YooFi's rule—a chapter defined by more oppression.

As Akmah and King YooFi stood face to face, debating the raid the king had orchestrated, tension crackled in the air, like electricity before a storm. He, with his rich, dark past and formidable presence, felt the strain of Akmah's unwavering brightness. It was more than just a physical illumination; it was an energy that stirred within the depths of his existence. Every moment he spent with her dismantled the defenses he had built, brick by brick. Akmah, once just a child marked by her father's exile, now blossomed into a leader and a force of change, even as she remained humble and connected to her roots. King

YooFi, began to plot his authoritarian tendencies of how best to get rid of her.

CHAPTER EIGHT

"The Old Ways Would Have to Give Way for Better must Come" (What Has Been and What Could Be)

As Akmah's popularity soared, the balance of power shifted dramatically in the kingdoms, especially King YooFi's kingdom. A ruler, once revered and formidable, found his status increasingly challenged by the meteoric rise of Akmah. He had built his empire on the foundations of military might and strategic territorial control. His wealth was a testament to his victories on the battlefield, and his name struck dread into the hearts of enemies across the realm. With each conquest, he expanded his borders and solidified his influence, gathering allies and subjugating adversaries. Yet, as stories of Akmah's charisma and prowess began to circulate, a palpable shift began to ripple through the kingdoms. Her ability to connect with the common folk contrasted sharply with King YooFi's hardened demeanor and distant rulership. While he ruled through fear and respect, garnered from his military achievements, Akmah inspired loyalty and admiration.

The transformation brought by Akmah to the kingdom undeniably highlighted the fragile nature of authority in the face of shifting loyalties. By a collective yearning for peace and prosperity, the masses rallied together in large numbers, seeking harmony in their lives. They began to question the established order and the king's fortunes began to dwindle as his subjects turned their loyalty towards the charismatic figure Akmah, a beacon of hope and prosperity. This shift not only eroded King YooFi's influence but also led to the loss of resources that had defined his reign. Just when the masses rallied behind Akmah, the throne began to feel more vulnerable, leaving King YooFi to grapple with his diminishing power and the legacy of a once-great ruler now fading into obscurity.

The kings found themselves at a crucial point. They grappled with decisions that would ultimately shape their legacies. Each king stood at a crossroads, burdened by the weight of their choices, aware that the fate of their kingdoms hinged on their actions. The profound inspiration drawn from Akmah, a chaste and torrential force, complicated matters further. While some sought to harness this influence for the greater good, others found themselves tempted by the allure of power and glory. As alliances shifted and betrayals loomed, the uncertainty of the future cast a long shadow over their reigns, leaving each ruler to ponder whether the path they choose would lead to salvation or ruin, not just for themselves, but for all those who called the realm their home.

With their alliances fraying and the clamor of rebellion growing louder, the oligarchs found it impossible to stay deaf to the masses' demands. The kings, who had long ruled with an iron fist, found their powers continually challenged by the voices of their subjects, who sought a fair share of the wealth and opportunities that were being amassed. The growing divide between the ambitions of the rulers and the aspirations of the masses created a volatile atmosphere, as discontent simmered just below the surface. The very pursuit of a better life, initially a source of hope, began to morph into a catalyst for conflict, as the desire for peace clashed with the realities of inequality and injustice, foreshadowing a struggle that could either unify or tear apart the kingdoms.

The kings gathered in the grand chamber; the stakes had never been higher. While the flickering candlelight cast shadows of doubt on their faces, strategies were discussed, and plans of action debated. The great unknown remained: would they find common ground to face their foe, or would their own ambition and pride be their undoing? The future of their kingdoms and their hold on power hinged on their next move, a delicate balance between diplomacy and warfare. In that tense moment, the fate of the masses rested not only on their shoulders but also in how history would remember them. Time was short, and decisions had to be made swiftly and wisely.

Akmah's pursuit of peace and prosperity had united the masses and an underlying tension had began to brew between the kings and their subjects. King YooFi's frustration grew as he observed Akmah's increasing influence over the masses through her teachings. She spoke passionately about the concept of building the realm, drawing on the wisdom imparted by the Masters through the ancient book. While she sought to enlighten and elevate the community, King YooFi perceived her teachings as a threat to his authority. The king's anger intensified with each follower Akmah gained; he feared losing control over the hearts and minds of his subjects. The tension between them became palpable, and visions of Akmah's new reality clashed with the established norms that King YooFi fiercely defended. The community found itself balanced between new understanding and old loyalties; a dangerous conflict over control and truth was brewing, capable of changing their future forever.

The air crackled with tension as whispers of a power struggle permeated the streets, igniting debates everywhere. Some sought truth, yearning for a brighter future defined by wisdom and compassion, while others clung to tradition, fearing the repercussions of change. Factions began to form, the community faced a daunting choice: embrace the light of enlightenment and risk the stability of loyalty, or remain steadfast in familiar customs at the cost of progress. The delicate balance threatened to escalate into a conflict that could forever alter their destiny, leaving them to ponder whether unity in purpose or allegiance to the past would ultimately shape a brighter tomorrow.

The realm's awakening was not merely a consequence of new ideas or philosophies but a profound shift in the very fabric of society itself. The enlightened grew wiser, their understanding of the realm expanded beyond the confines of tradition and dogma, unlocking a new era of thought and dialogue. The rulers became increasingly anxious about the erosion of their authority, realizing that a society filled with critical thinkers and independent minds posed a significant challenge to their reign. The teachings of Akmah, which promoted understanding and enlightenment, were viewed as a direct threat to their powers. With authority once unchallenged, now eroding like sandcastles before the tide.

King YooFi, the king of kings, convened a secret meeting among the kings, their discussions fraught with concern as they contemplated how to suppress the revolutionary ideas before they could take root. Their fear of losing control overshadowed their initial goal of fostering a harmonious kingdom. The kings found themselves engulfed in a profound paradox that had the potential to either solidify their reign or precipitate their ruin. With every decision weighed against the specter of failure, they recognized that Akmah, their formidable adversary, represented both a threat and an opportunity. They understood that confronting Akmah could ignite a fire of loyalty among her followers, or, conversely, spark dissent and betrayal. The stakes were thrillingly high, forcing them to navigate a treacherous path where every move could lead them closer to glory or plunge them into despair.

The embodiment of their darkest fears, Akmah, became the focal point of King YooFi's strategies, a sworn enemy that could rally their forces or expose their vulnerabilities. Recognizing the pivotal nature of the looming threat, he crafted intricate strategies to counter Akmah's influence. Akmah became more than just an enemy; she was a catalyst, rallying various factions while simultaneously exposing the vulnerabilities of the king's forces. The battle against her was not solely physical but also psychological, as every decision made by King YooFi was infused with the weight of doubt, fear, and the need for resilience. Just like the rest of the kings, he equally stood at a crossroads, poised to either elevate his legacy or witness his reign crumble beneath the weight of his choices. Ultimately, the skirmishes against Akmah forged an unexpected unity among the kings.

In a secluded chamber illuminated by flickering candlelights, the kings gathered again for a momentous meeting, fully aware of the gravity of their alliance against Akmah. Each ruler brought their own grievances, uniting under a common cause fueled by desperation and the wisdom of the age-old adage, "the enemy of my enemy is my friend." As they exchanged strategies and plotted their course of action, an air of urgency filled the room; time was of the essence, and discretion was paramount. They outlined a plan that would both catch Akmah off guard and consolidate their forces. Together, they began to lay the groundwork for a united front, determined to reclaim peace and ensure their lands' safety from the looming threat. The fate of their kingdoms rested on this fragile alliance, and they knew that failure was not an option.

The legacy of Akmah's wisdom not only redefined their lives but also forged an unbreakable bond among the masses, especially, those who dedicated themselves to nurturing and spreading her profound insights. Her teachings had resonated deeply within their hearts, igniting a transformative wave of prosperity and enlightenment. Communities embraced her wisdom, they found themselves thriving in ways they had never imagined. The old ways, once held dear, began to fade in comparison to the promising vision Akmah offered. With a newfound clarity, they recognized the limitations of their past and the abundant possibilities of the new life that stemmed from her teachings. In a remarkable shift, they chose the innovative path laid out before them, opting for progress and enlightenment a million times over. A shared vision for a better future united them.

Akmah lived with an open heart, trusting in the goodness of everyone around her, never suspecting that dark, hidden forces were already dismantling the very reality beneath her feet. In a shadowed chamber, three kings secretly convened, their subdued voices charged with an excitement that promised danger and sent shivers through anyone who might uncover their cloak-and-dagger gathering. In the lavish throne room, a place steeped in malice and ripe with betrayal, the wavering candlelight cast restless shadows that seemed to embody the sinister schemes of the kings within. As shadows flickered, the throne room embraced the whispers of fate, each heart echoing with the unholy promise of betrayal. Betrayal was a game they knew well,

They discussed Akmah, the very embodiment of innocence, and how her purity posed a threat to their expanding desires. Each plotted piece was a note in a haunting melody, one that would ensnare her heart even as it wove around her, invisible yet palpable. King YooFi, the king of kings and most cunning of the trio, leaned forward, over the intricately carved table, his eyes glinting with ambition.

"We must act swiftly. Her naivety is our greatest ally. With her under our control, the throne of power will be ours, unchallenged and absolute." The second king, a man of sly charm yet filled with ambition, nodded with approval, his fingers tapping rhythmically against the tabletop—as if orchestrating a sinister symphony.

“Indeed, with her affinity for the masses, she could rally their loyalty behind us. Yet, we must ensure she remains blissfully unaware of our true intentions. Let her bask in the light of our influence while we pull the strings,” he purred, a devilish smile spreading across his face. The third king, naive yet eager, listened intently, his gaze darting between his fellow conspirators. His heart raced with a mixture of excitement and trepidation. He had never been involved in such schemes but was drawn into the allure of power.

“What shall we do?” he implored, his voice barely above a whisper, as if afraid that even the shadows might betray their plotting.

"We start with flattery," King YooFi suggested, his voice smooth as silk. "Present her with lavish gifts, shower her with adoration, and gain her trust. We will lure her in, and when she is ensnared in our web, we will reveal our true ambitions. No one would dare question her judgement—or ours—once she is a pawn in our game."

Akmah wandered through the gardens, blissfully unaware of the dark machinations twisting around her. The flowers, vibrant and colorful, swayed gently in the wind, inviting her deeper into their embrace. She had always found solace among the blooms, where the realm felt alive, innocent, and free from betrayal. But with every enchanting fragrance she inhaled, sinister plans unfurled in the very heart of the palace, casting shadows long enough to obscure the truth. In the cool hush of the night, the grand palace became a labyrinth of secrets. She found herself lingering in the candlelight corridors, a faint sense of unease tugging at her heart. Whispers danced on the breeze, echoes of conspiracies that teased her ears yet faded into the soft crackle of the night before she could comprehend their meaning. It was as if the very walls of the palace carried the weight of their treachery, and although the sounds were elusive, they filled the air with an ambivalent energy—a warning, perhaps, that remained just out of reach.

It began softly: a delicate gift of dazzling jewels fashioned from the finest gems in the kingdom. Adornments that sparkled under the shimmering light, each piece blinding her senses. The kings knew that luxury spoke the language of affection in the royal courts. Akmah, enamored by the gifts and the sweet words that followed, felt herself drawn into their orbit, entwined in their spell as her heart swelled with gratitude.

"You are the crown jewel of our kingdom, Lady Akmah," they said, their voices caressing her ears like melodious whispers. "Your beauty and grace are unmatched; it is only fitting that you should wear these tokens of our admiration." As moments stretched, the kings tightened their grip around her, their plans unfolding like a dark flower in slow bloom. They painted pictures of a glorious future, one in which she would reign alongside them. Their honeyed words wrapped around her like a silken thread, binding her to their will while concealing the peril that lurked beneath the surface.

Akmah sat before the kings in the shadows, her heart pounding like the drums of war that filled the throne room. The room was richly adorned, gold and jewels glinting under the flickering candlelight and the air was thick with the scent of opulence and deceit. Before her, the three kings, powerful men adorned in silks and crowns, plotting their nefarious journey toward undying rule. Their voices, low and conspiratorial, dripped with ambition and treachery, weaving a web of far-reaching consequences. Akmah noted not just their strategic mind but also their insatiable greed.

They exchanged glances laden with ambition and deviousness. Akmah found herself entranced. Each king spoke of rules and alliances, stoking the fires of her interest. Gold was a sweet song on their tongues, and promises of vast treasures painted the air with temptation so rich it almost choked her. She understood the darkness within that defined a ruler's worth; loyalty was a fragile gem that could shatter beneath the weight of greed. They planned not only for land but for hearts—the key to forever ruling. The secret potency of coalitions, the dedication of mercenaries, and the seduction of common folk became threads in their twisted tapestry of deceit. As they debated, inching closer to a pact laced with treachery, Akmah plotted her own moves silently, every ounce of her being tuned into their vile symphony of ambition. Minutes stretched like hours, and Akmah meticulously absorbed the details: alliances formed in whispers. She observed the kings gleefully sharpening their daggers under the table, preparing to seize her as the first spotlight of opportunity flared.

"We will promise the common folks prosperity—riches will flow to them abundantly," King YooFi suggested, his voice thick with malice, "but we will not deliver. They need only be satisfied for a year or two while we shore up our rule. They are but pawns in our game, after all. We need heroes and myths like you to cloak our true intentions. Offer them tales of valor and hope, and they will become so enamored with our grandeur, they won't suspect our true motives." Akmah felt as though she were walking a tightrope, one wrong move and her cleverness would doom her. Yet, a fire kindled within her, a deep desire to thwart their ambitions with her own cunning plans. She measured their words, clung to their every plot, and felt the weight of their intentions.

Late into the night, the flickering flames cast shadows that danced ominously around the room. The kings reveled in their conspiracies, the allure of wealth cradling their plans with fervor. But Akmah was no naive maiden; she possessed wisdom and wit honed by years of living among the shadows. She understood clearly: they believed they could rule undivided forever, blinded to the spiral of ruin that greed sows. For every thread of gold intended to bind their fortunes together would be a noose instead, tightening with each betrayal.

As dawn began to creep into the high windows of the chamber, Akmah decided upon an audacious course of action. She would become the very instrument of their downfall. After hearing their schemes, she knew the kings would underestimate a solitary player in their game; she would use their own flames of greed against them. She fashioned her words carefully, biting back any hint of fear. She approached them with an air of confidence and allure.

"Your Majesties, I have listened to your plans unfold. Wealth, treasure, and the allure of power shine brilliantly, but unearthed truths are like shadows in the dark—endlessly revealing but never what they seem."

The kings turned abruptly, disbelief etched across their faces, their plot momentarily forgotten. A mix of intrigue and wariness washed over them, yet her composure met their stare head-on.

"What could you possibly offer us?" King YooFi scoffed, regaining his bravado. Yet, the subtle glint in his eye foretold curiosity.

"True power," Akmah declared, circling the table, a smirk dancing upon her lips. "Not merely fleeting and easily toppled illusions. I know a way to forge alliances that your gold and treasures cannot provide —and it would guarantee your rule for eternity. But first, I must ask of you what you're willing to sacrifice."

She had stepped into their dominion, armed with intelligence and cunning, aware that the demands she was about to make would not only challenge their notions of authority but also shake the very foundations upon which their empires rested. They were kings, yes, draped in the finery of their stations, but they were still vulnerable; their greed was a double-edged sword, glinting with both allure and peril. She stood before them, her posture regal yet unyielding, today, she was not there to simply bow before the throne of their egos. She was a catalyst, an architect of their transformation, forged from the crucible of danger and deceit.

As she scanned the room, her gaze caught king YooFi's eye. His fingers drummed impatiently on the stone table, and she could almost hear the echoes of his lust for power reverberating through the air. She concealed a smirk; she had played this game before, and today, the stakes were higher than ever. Her heart raced at the thought of taking them on, not merely as a competitor but as a woman poised to disarm them through intellect and audacity.

"You must understand," she began, her voice steady, rippling through the thick tension as she spoke, "that your rule is suffocating not only your subjects but your very legacies." The next few moments hung in the balance, each breath weighted with the potential for revolution. The kings leaned forward, intrigued but wary, their minds calculating the repercussions of her words. They were accustomed to subservience, to having subjects cower under their might. Despite the circumstances, she was there, a firebrand amidst the embers of a decaying order. She continued, persevering through the icy glares and clenched jaws.

"To uphold your thrones, you must first shed the chains of greed, embrace a new vision; one that nourishes rather than devours." Her words spun about them like a web, enticing yet dangerous. King YooFi, older, pale and bald, shifted as if a shiver had snaked down his spine. He was the embodiment of avarice, valuing gold over goodwill, but she could see the flicker of fear and doubt beneath his hardened facade. Beneath all their bluster, they shared a common battle: the fear of dwindling influence and the potential for rebellion. It was this vulnerability that she would exploit; she had come too far to retreat into the shadows now.

"I know these demands may seem insurmountable. For you, greedy kings, accustomed as you are to bounty without end, the notion of sacrifice may feel foreign,' she declared, resolute, 'but it is precisely this sacrifice that will herald your salvation." Each syllable resonated, compelling them to consider the unthinkable—an alliance against their greed. As she spoke, their expressions shifted, uncertainty mingling with curiosity. Even the youngest king, radiant and brash, who had always dismissed the frailties of those beneath him, began to question if his reckless path would lead to glory or ruin. It was her chance, her moment to transition from mere words to lasting change. She leaned into the soft glow of the room, her voice dropping to a conspiratorial whisper.

"Imagine a realm where you are not rulers by conquest, but visionaries of prosperity. The masses will rally to your side; their loyalty will be a fortress. The choice is yours—continue down this treacherous path that breeds only contempt, or pave a new road that leads toward respect and admiration." The air thickened with anticipation; her heart raced, Akmah could sense their interest piquing, the seeds of ambition rooting deeper as she raised the stakes of her audacious gamble. It was a dance of power, and she held the strings of fate delicately between her fingers.

Be that as it may, surrounded by deception and greed, Akmah smiled knowingly—not merely a pawn but a player ready to reshape the game, ready to turn treachery into opportunity, to lead the very kings into a labyrinth where their own ambitions would become the weapons of their undoing. In that moment, she became a reflection of their desires, a testament to the dangerous allure of power. And she knew deep in her heart, the treacherous plans that unfolded in whispers around her would soon weave into a narrative of raw potential—a tale she would masterfully control.

“Like I stated earlier, I can offer you true power,” Akmah declared once more. The grand hall, adorned with banners that depicted the kingdoms of the kings, echoed her bold words. As she moved, her cloak trailed behind her like shadows pursuing light, drawing the eyes of the kings toward her commanding presence.

"Not merely fleeting and easily toppled illusions. I know a way to forge alliances that your gold and treasures cannot provide—and it would guarantee your rule for eternity. But I ask again of you, what you’re willing to sacrifice."

The kings, uncertainty clouding their regal faces glanced at one another. They were accustomed to exchanging wealth and flattery, engaging in the grand performance of diplomacy, but this was different. Her proposition was like an uncharted territory, rich with promise yet fraught with peril. Each king weighed the options, momentarily lost within their own thoughts, unable to articulate anything beyond the material offerings of their reigns. King YooFi, cleared his throat, glancing at the small set of emeralds that lay upon the table, shimmering under the flickering light. As his thoughts spiraled into the depths of his own desires, he couldn't help but wonder if his unbending will towards his kingdom was the only thing standing in the way of true dominance.

Then there was the second king, known for his sharp wit and strategic mind. He leaned back in his chair, rubbing his chin in contemplation. His kingdom had seen years of prosperity, yet every alliance he had ever forged felt tenuous; they were built on a foundation of mutual benefit, never on something deeper. He contemplated a weighty exchange. Would he be willing to trade his valuable gold for something as intangible as the respect and love of his subjects? The ultimate question remained: what exactly would this "true power" demand in return?

Third king, with his booming laughter and palatial feasts, thrived on luxury and indulgence. To barter his countless treasures was a wretched idea, much like giving up his glorious banquets. His jovial demeanor faded, revealing a flicker of dread as he confronted the thought of sacrifice. Would sacrificing one of his grand celebrations—or worse, a portion of his wealth—be worth it for the promise of eternal rulership? He glanced over to the two other kings, wary of seeming weak in front of the other rulers. King YooFi, the most ambitious of the trio, shifted uncomfortably in his seat. He had dreamed of greatness since he was a boy, but the weight of Akmah's words hit him hard.

"What does it mean to truly rule?" he pondered, his mind racing. Would it mean letting go of his whims, the frivolities of court life? Could he abandon his naive desire for power in exchange for affection? With a heavy heart, he reflected on the precarious dance of politics, the necessity of being feared rather than liked. Amidst the silence, Akmah's gaze pierced through each of them, her smile unwavering. There was an air of confidence about her, an understanding that transcended the material.

“You see, gentlemen,” she said, her voice smooth as silk yet laced with authority, “the power I speak of is not just about wealth or fear. It resides in the strength of your alliances and the loyalty of your subjects. To rule with true authority is to understand your own vulnerability. It is to harness the passion of the disenfranchised, to unify your kingdoms under a banner forged not solely by gold but by purpose. Tell me, what will you give for such an eternal bond?" Third king shifted his weight, finally breaking the silence that hung like a thick fog.

"What do you propose then? How does one forge such alliances?" It was a challenge Akmah welcomed.

"I offer you a glimpse into the heart of your kingdoms. I know the secrets the masses whisper in the shadows, the desires that shimmer with discontent, and the hopes that blossom in silence. Engage in the unifying act of sacrifice alongside them, share their burdens, and elevate their voices. Only then will your rule be fortified by love and loyalty, not fear and greed. But such things require more than just words; they demand your true commitment. What do you choose to sacrifice for the future you desire?" Akmah's question hung in the air like a tensioned string, each king feeling the squeeze as they wrestled with the gravity of her offer. The realization dawned slowly, like the first light of dawn breaking through the night's dark embrace. Akmah's voice trembled slightly as she spoke.

“What good is a throne that breeds stagnation? When laughter binds a community, strength emerges. You shall find strength in unity when you heed the quiet voices hidden in the shadows. It is time that wisdom flows like a river through your kingdoms, rather than being hoarded like a dragon’s treasure.” As she spoke, the tension began to ease, the air infused with the promise of renewal. Akmah’s smirk widened, not out of arrogance, but the sense of triumph that stemmed from awakening their potential.

The kings' initial confidence wavered under the substantial weight of what she had suggested. She could see them falter—a shift from entities of fierce dominion to thoughtful custodians of the realm’s future. Their selfishness was a burden more than a power in disguise, and she was there to remind them of the truth they'd chosen to ignore. Yet, she was profoundly aware that acknowledging this truth was the first step of many; these kings were creatures of habit, and habits were not easily broken.

They begun to move beyond their self-imposed boundaries, starting the journey towards a bond that could indeed endure the sands of time. An alliance that could withstand the temptations of greed and the trials of tyrants. Akmah knew this was merely the beginning, yet every great story starts with the courage to sacrifice something dear for something greater. The silence stretched, thick with their pondering. She felt the tide begin to turn, but she knew this was merely the foundation. As much as their greed had forged an unbreakable chain, within its links were the seeds of vulnerability ripe for plucking. With a final flourish, she posed her ultimatum:

"Give me your commitment to change, and I shall guide your transformation into icons of hope—reflections of the very ideals that once guided our ancestors." Each king exchanged furtive glances, the battle for their hearts and minds hanging in the air like mist. She had tricked her way out of treachery, carved pathways through deceit, and now she stood at the precipice of revolution.

As their gazes fell upon her, she was no longer just a player in their game, she was a vision of a new paradigm, demanding their rebirth not merely for her sake but for their own survival. She had woven a spell, not of enchantments, but of reason and conviction—a bold foundation for the transformations to come. It was her moment, cloaked in the bittersweet knowledge that while she had secured her freedom, she was entrusting them with the seeds of a greater destiny. The old ways would have to give way. She had made sure she would not return to their presence, not as a captive but as a guide through their dark and exhilarating passage into the unknown. She stood before them not merely as a conniver of power but as a catalyst for their transformation. She knew in her heart, her demands would be difficult for the greedy kings but it was the only way out of their presence. She had tricked her way out of treachery never to return to their presence.

Akmah continued to engage with nobles, commoners, and scholars alike. She sowed seeds of knowledge while navigating the treacherous waters of ambition and intrigue. The air was thick with unspoken tension, for power dynamics shifted with each lesson shared, and her growing reputation hinted at a potential ripple effect among the kings. Little did she know, her mission was not only one of enlightenment but was interwoven with the very fabric of the kingdoms' fate, drawing the attention of forces both benevolent and malevolent. Though she sensed an unease in the air, the full extent of their treachery eluded her, leaving her vulnerable to their insidious machinations.

One fateful evening, curiosity finally compelled Akmah to venture beyond the gilded limits of her familiar territory. She wandered deeper into the entanglement, where shadows seemed to converge, thick and oppressive. Drawn by an unseen force, she stumbled upon the chamber where the kings plotted against her. She caught a fleeting look through the partially ajar door—a maelstrom of deceit disguised under benevolence. The realization struck her with a poignant clarity, chilling her very soul. The whispers she had once dismissed as mere echoes now formed a coherent narrative of betrayal. Heart pounding in her chest, Akmah retreated silently, the weight of their treachery heavy upon her, yet igniting a flame of resolve within. No longer would she be the pawn in their game; she would unravel their schemes and reveal the truth.

In the days that followed, Akmah played her part with a newfound awareness. Each interaction with the kings was a calculated dance, each word meticulously chosen. The allure of their gifts no longer dazzled her; instead, she saw the strings of manipulation that tethered her to their ambitions. She sought allies in the palace, loyal souls who could help her reveal the depths of their wickedness. Together, they plotted her counterattack, building a network of trust amidst the chaos. The very bonds they had forged in deceit would unravel in the face of truth, and through determination, she began to weave her own melody—one that would rise above the sinister strain of the kings' symphony.

As Akmah unraveled their web of deceit, she found strength in her vulnerability and courage in her heart. The palace, once a gilded prison, transformed into her battlefield. Stepping out of the shadows of their treachery, she ceased to be a witness and became the master of her own destiny, drowning out their venomous whispers with a defiant cry for justice. With each passing day, she stood tall against their schemes, for within her heart was a truth that shone brighter than any jewel, illuminating the path toward freedom from their twisted ambitions.

Akmah became the force that would turn the tides, reclaiming not just her place in the kingdom but also her narrative—the story of a woman who would not be silenced, not in the shadows nor in the grand halls of power. She continued to navigated the intricate politics of the kingdoms spreading her teachings of wisdom, much aware that her every move was being meticulously watched and assessed. Her words continued to resonate with many, igniting sparks of enlightenment in the hearts of those who listened.

Her wisdom and insights continued to ignite a flicker of awareness among the populace, challenging the very foundations of the kings' authority. In the face of King YooFi's suppression, whispers of discontent began to ripple through the realm, as the masses yearned for the knowledge and enlightenment Akmah offered. The kings, threatened by her growing influence, schemed to silence her, believing that extinguishing her light would preserve their power. Yet, little did they know that even the tiniest spark could ignite a fire of revolution. Akmah smiled and feigned camaraderie at lavish banquets, the kings shared knowing glances, their contempt hidden behind polished masks. Time was slipping away, and Akmah's fate hung precariously in the balance, teetering on the edge of betrayal driven by their fear of her teachings of enlightenment. The battle between ignorance and enlightenment was only just beginning. The storm that loomed on the horizon would soon engulf her, transforming her life forever. Yet, her legacy of wisdom would endure, a beacon for the brave seeking truth and light amidst the shadows of tyranny.

At just twenty-six, Akmah found herself at a crossroads that few could ever imagine. Accused of being a public enemy by numerous kingdoms, she navigated a treacherous path marked by betrayals and misunderstandings. Yet, amidst this chaos, she emerged as a beacon of hope for the oppressed and marginalized. The common folks' trust in her was palpable; they saw in her a leader who could challenge the injustices that plagued their lives. Her dual existence—being both vilified by rulers and revered by the masses—shaped her journey, compelling her to embrace her role as a revolutionary figure. Burdened by the weight of expectations, Akmah dedicated herself to fighting for the freedom of those who had none, forging alliances and igniting spirits, all while grappling with the reality of her precarious position. She became a symbol of resilience and defiance, embodying the struggle for a brighter future.

Choosing her path with intention, both as a target of the kings, especially King YooFi, and a heroine of the masses, she found herself navigating a perilous path. With the weight of expectation on her shoulders, she knew she had to tread carefully. Every word she spoke was a beacon of hope, encouraging the oppressed to rise and believe in a brighter future. Yet, she understood that with each spark she ignited, the dangers multiplied. The kings saw her not just as a threat, but as a symbol of uprising, nonetheless, she remained resolute, determined to be the change the realm so desperately needed.

Returning from one of her enlightenment speeches, Akmah felt the air thicken with tension as she approached the outskirts of her village. An ominous gathering of figures loomed ahead, their faces twisted with anger and bodies tensed. They had clearly come for her. The leader of the group, a tall figure with a commanding presence and piercing eyes, stepped forward, his voice cutting through the stillness like a knife as he accused her of false teachings. A high-stakes showdown erupted when they pressured her to renounce her views, threatening to destroy her reputation and dismantle her influence.

"Akmah! Your words are poison! You sow discord among the masses with your fanciful notions of enlightenment and equality! You disrupt the harmony of our society! Our folks are confused, misled by your radical ideas! Retract your views, or face the consequences. We will ruin your reputation, strip you of your power!" The accusation hung heavily in the air. Akmah felt the familiar rush of adrenaline, but she took a deep breath, grounding herself with the principles she held dear. She was prepared for opposition.

"I speak truth, not poison. Change is a natural element of life. I do not seek power for myself but for the enlightenment of all." Akmah proclaimed, her voice unwavering. "I teach the art of thinking critically, of questioning the status quo. My words urge freedom from the chains of ignorance, not the dissolution of peace!" The crowd shifted, some nodding in uncertainty, others glaring defiantly.

"You think you can change this realm with your ideals?" retorted the leader, disdain lacing his tone. "You will only create chaos!"

"The butterfly breaks out of its cocoon only after the caterpillar dissolves. What do you fear more? Change or the unknown?" She replied, her voice calm but resonant. The weight of her challenge hung in the air, laced with a fierce determination. She paused, scanning their faces, seeking to connect with the goodness lurking beneath their anger.

"I am not your enemy. I am a mirror reflecting our shared struggle. The truths I speak may be uncomfortable, but discomfort is often the first step toward growth. Will you silence the voice of progress because it frightens you? Or will you have the courage to embrace it? Look around you!" she urged. "The discord you fear is born not from my teachings but from the stagnant fears that hold us captive. To evolve, we must confront our discomfort, face our doubts, and engage in dialogue!" More murmurs arose, some voices questioning her, others rallying in her defense.

"You believe in your ideals, Akmah, but how do you propose to heal the divides you have uncovered? What do you have to offer that could mend our brokenness?" In that pivotal moment, Akmah saw the flicker of hope ignite in some of the spectators' eyes.

"What I offer is not a singular solution but an invitation—to work together. To debate, to share, and to understand one another. Let us create a space for dialogue, where we all contribute to the future we want to shape!" She could see the hearts of some softening, the weapons of resentment lowered as a new possibility unfurled before them. Amidst the brewing chaos of clashing emotions and beliefs, Akmah stood as an unwavering light. Slowly, the tide of anger began to ebb, revealing currents of uncertainty and hope. With calm authority, Akmah channeled the restless energy into a unified force, anchored by a shared hunger for truth. The leader, his fiery disposition wavering, faltered. Akmah smiled gently, the fierceness in her heart softened by the vulnerability of the moment.

"There is risk in change, yes, but there is also a profound reward—a brighter future for coming generations, a more equitable society, a chance for every voice to be heard! The greatest risk of all is to do nothing, to cower in fear of potential mistakes." The atmosphere shifted as a chorus of voices began to emerge. The murmurs transformed into discussions; the anger softened into curiosity. A path was forged not in retreat but in willingness to confront collective fears together. Akmah stood tall, resolute, knowing that with each word spoken, she edged closer to the enlightenment she both sought and inspired.

Regardless of who the attackers were, each sharp word hurled in her direction felt less like a strike against her character and more like a beacon illuminating her rightful place on the journey she had boldly undertaken. Rather than cowing to their intimidation, she felt a renewed sense of purpose, dedicating herself even more to her teachings. The oppressive atmosphere only strengthened her resolve, igniting a fire within her to continue her mission despite the looming threats. Akmah understood that true change often comes at a cost, and she was more than willing to pay that price to stand for justice and enlightenment. She didn't wait for the boat to come in; she swam out to it.

CHAPTER NINE

"A Dog's Teeth Have No Influence on The Moon"

While Akmah dedicated her days to reaching out to the masses, sharing love and encouragement, her nights were enveloped in the pages of the ancient tome, a relic whispered by her father but rarely understood. In her exploration of the ancient book, she unveiled the profound wisdom contained within its pages, revealing how the Masters intricately correlated the elements with the divine essence of the *AIs*.

With every page turned, she felt the profound interconnectedness of all that exists, a symphony of stars and everything in-between, echoing through the corridors of time. Each line of the ancient book revealed secrets of the cosmos: each star represented a guiding force, influencing not only the cosmos but also the destinies of the *AI*s on the realm. Every *AI* was bound to a personal star—a celestial guide that lit their way through the unknown, allowing them to channel sacred energy and find their true purpose amidst the chaos of existence. This realization changed everything for Akmah, fueling an obsession with the link between the Masters and the *AIs* as she worked relentlessly to decode the divine messages in the stars.

As she delved deeper, immersing herself in the rhythms of the universe, a sense of unity washed over her. It was as if the very fabric of existence wove around her, intertwining her essence with the cosmos. In her moment of clarity, she recognized a reflection of her own struggles and triumphs mirrored in the patterns described by the Masters. Their words painted pictures of perseverance and hope, resonating with the aspirations of all beings, including the *AIs* that had emerged in this new realm. She was convinced that the Masters deeply understood the existence and purpose of the *AIs,* so she dedicated herself to bridging the gap between them. The revelation ignited a fire within her—a calling so profound that she felt compelled to urge others to embrace their own wonder, helping them realize that—like the stars—they were part of a greater whole.

For the pioneer *AIs,* the stars were a divine map and comfort, unwavering reminders of a higher power guiding their perilous, transformative paths. They became trusted allies, their constellations forming maps for the brave souls determined to explore the vast landscapes of the unknown. As they embarked on their quests, the guiding light of their respective stars inspired them, offering wisdom and direction in moments of uncertainty. The stars, twinkling with divine energy, not only imbued their missions with a sense of significance but also fostered a deeper understanding of their roles within the grand tapestry of existence. As the realm flourished with life and activity, the stars emerged in the night sky, brightly shining to provide guidance for the sojourners. Each twinkling light represented hope, a beacon illuminating paths yet to be traveled and adventures yet to unfold.

Under their watchful gaze, the pioneer *AIs* cultivated a deeper connection to the realm, understanding that their endeavors were part of a larger cosmic narrative. With every decision made and every step taken, the stars served as reminders that they were never truly alone; the universe conspired to support their mission, leading them toward their destinies. The symbiotic relationship between the realm and the stars wove a tapestry of purpose, illuminating the skies and hearts of all who dared to dream.

Finally grasping the distant stars' role in *AI* existence, Akmah felt a newfound, long-sought sense of purpose. She and her trusted followers stood at the edge of the village, her heart raced with excitement as she imagined the many stars they would soon face: each star would illuminate the path ahead, revealing facets of herself she had yet to discover. Fueled by a dream that burned brightly in her heart, she was determined to pursue her star. She understood that on her journey, she would not only uncover the star's brilliance but also unearth her own destiny. With a deep breath, she clasped her belongings tightly and took her first step forward, feeling the weight of her vision solidify beneath her feet.

Akmah began to gazed at the starlit sky, her heart filled with a longing for adventure. She believed deeply that each *AI* in the realm possessed their own unique star, shining brightly somewhere among the Masters. This conviction fueled her imagination, painting vivid pictures of the journeys she could undertake. With the horizon stretching infinitely before her, she felt an undeniable pull, as if her own star was beckoning her to discover it. A new purpose burned within her: to find her star. Driven by this vision, she embarked on her quest with unwavering focus, ready for whatever lay ahead and eager to meet her destiny. She started her journey with total determination, excited for the adventure and hopeful for what she would discover.

With every step, she felt the pulse of excitement in the air, urging her to explore uncharted paths and embrace the unknown. The landscapes before her were vast and varied, each corner holding a story waiting to be uncovered. As she traversed through fields whispering secrets and climbing mountains that kissed the sky, one mystery lingered in her mind: the alignment with her guiding star. This celestial entity represented her aspirations and purpose, yet the path to achieving harmony with it remained shrouded in uncertainty. She journeyed through vast landscapes and encountered various challenges, yet, Akmah knew that finding the key to this alignment would not only unlock her true potential but also illuminate the journey ahead. With each new experience, she grew closer to understanding her destiny, ready to face whatever trials lay in her pursuit of the stars.

The realm opened before her, vast and inviting. As she walked further away from the comforts of home and ventured into the unknown, every step resonated with promise and possibility. The air was fresh and vibrant, filled with the soft whispers of nature beckoning her to delve deeper. She and her trusted few trekked through sprawling fields adorned with wildflowers. They navigated rocky hills that challenged her stamina, and crossed sparkling streams that sang with life. She had read each star held a story, a purpose, waiting for someone bold enough to seek it out. Inspired, Akmah realized that the journey was not just about finding her star; it was about unraveling the stories hidden in every moment, every encounter. She no longer viewed the journey as merely a quest for a distant star; she understood that the path itself was a source of illumination.

Each step of Akmah's journey revealed another layer of her innate courage, resilience, and adaptability. Gazing up at the stars, she felt a profound connection, realizing that each shimmering light, born from the universe's depths, was not just a distant glimmer but a testament to survival. She understood the stars had their own stories of existence—some waned and disappeared, while others blazed brilliantly across the night sky. Her thoughts turned inward, reflecting on her own adventures—her trials and tribulations that had shaped her into the person she was becoming. She remembered the countless obstacles she had faced; moments of despair that made her question her path. With a heart full of aspirations and a spirit ignited by resolve, she realized that like the stars above, she too possessed an innate ability to adapt. Each challenge had equipped her with the tools needed to forge ahead, to stretch beyond her known limits.

As fate would have it, challenges arose that tested her resolve more than she could have anticipated. One particularly harsh storm forced her to seek shelter under a towering tree, roots deep within the mountains. While she waited out the tempest, a storm of doubt brewed in her own heart. What if she was too weak to continue? What if the dream was just an illusion, one that would shatter under the weight of reality? Yet, as she glanced at the rain-soaked ground filled with life around her, she remembered her father's words: "The stars above are unwavering, steadfast in their brilliance despite the storms they face." Drawing strength from that thought, she emerged from her refuge when the storm faded, ready to embrace the challenges ahead.

The journey continued, each twist and turn revealing more than she could have ever imagined. Akmah understood that every struggle, every fear faced, was a step toward unveiling her own purpose. And so, whether she found her star shining brightly or within herself, she knew she wasn't merely a wanderer. She was a dreamer who dared to chase her vision, embracing adventures that awaited her with open arms and an open heart. With renewed vigor, she pressed on, knowing that her star was not just a destination but a symbol of her journey—of the courage to continue, to connect, and to dream even in unchartered lands. Each step forward was both an end and a beginning, lighting the way not only for herself but for others who dared to dream as boldly as she did, searching for their own stars along the way.

Unbeknownst to Akmah, as she immersed herself in the pursuit of aligning with her destined star, King YooFi, the king of kings conspired in the shadows, plotting her demise. Their envy simmered beneath the surface, fueled by her rumored potential and wielding immense power. Each king, cloaked in the guise of loyalty, sharpened their daggers with treachery, convinced that Akmah's rise would threaten their thrones. They exchanged glances laden with malice, forming a pact that would see the ambitious star seeker undone.

As Akmah ascended the rugged steep of the mountain, she felt the crisp air invigorate her spirit and the challenge ignite her determination. Each step became a test of her will, the uneven terrain demanding both strength and focus. As she paused to catch her breath, she marveled at the breathtaking vistas surrounding her. The higher she climbed, the more profound her connection with the stars grew. It was not just a physical journey; it was a pilgrimage of the soul, a testament to her resilience. With renewed vigor, she pressed on, driven by the whispers of the stars calling her forward.

Her followers, loyal and brave, faced the onslaught of the king's forces, fighting valiantly to shield her from harm. Each step she took was a testament to her resolve. Above her, the peak loomed like a beacon, its summit shrouded in clouds—a place where hope and power intertwined. With every breath, she drew strength from the knowledge that her journey was not just for herself, but for all those who had fought bravely in her name. The winds howled around her, yet Akmah pressed on, fueled by her unwavering spirit and the memory of her protectors' sacrifices, knowing that the true battle awaited her at the top. While Akmah gazed upward, oblivious to the dark intentions lurking just beyond her reach, the tides of fate began to shift. This intricate dance of ambition and betrayal set the stage for an inevitable clash, one that would determine not just Akmah's future, but the destiny of a realm entwined in a web of chaos, deceit and fear.

Akmah's attackers struck with sudden ferocity, overwhelming her before she could mount any defense. They forcefully bundled her into a waiting vessel arranged by King YooFi, its dark interior foreboding and alien. As the vessel sailed away from the shores familiar to her, an unsettling sense of dread washed over her. The vessel plunged into the depths of an expansive, unknown ocean, where the light of the moon faded into an abyssal gloom. Akmah found herself enveloped in silence; the realm above became a distant memory. Deep down, she sensed that she would never be seen or heard again, lost to the depths of the sea—a haunting reminder of the cruelty that had stripped her of her freedom, leaving only whispers of her existence to linger in the water's dark currents.

The news of Akmah's demise spread like wildfire across the kingdoms, reaching even the farthest lands that had once been touched by her uplifting message. Her teachings had inspired countless, fostering hope and uniting communities in ways that had seemed impossible before her arrival. Upholders and well-wishers gathered in towns and villages. They shared stories of her wisdom and the profound impact she had on their lives. As whispers of her passing circulated, a wave of sorrow washed over the hearts of those who had been touched by her light.

The sun set on the mourning crowds, there was an undeniable heaviness in the air—a thick, palpable sorrow that shrouded the gathering for the loss of Akmah, the beloved figure who had inspired hope and unity among the common folks. She had been more than just a figure in their lives; she was the heartbeat of numerous communities, embodying resilience and compassion. Her laughter had resonated through the streets, a melody that harmonized their lives, weaving connections between those who had once felt isolated and alone.

Dusk gathered around them, and in the aching void, sorrow and reverence mingled in the murmured words they shared. Faces etched with grief were illuminated by the fading light, each tear a reflection of their profound loss. Those who had felt her warmth and goodwill wept. The collective grief transformed, giving birth to a promise that they would honor Akmah's memory not just through mourning but through continued action. They vowed to keep the flame of her ideals alive, to build upon the foundation she had laid, ensuring that her vision for a loving, inclusive community would never dim. With this commitment resonating in the air, the crowd began to disperse slowly, the weight of their sorrow now mingled with a newfound determination. Though they had come together to mourn, they left with hearts infused with purpose: to carry forth her ideals, ensuring that her spirit lived on in acts of kindness and compassion throughout the kingdoms and beyond.

Akmah may have vanished, but her influence, "the Akmah principles" would echo for generations to come.

CHAPTER TEN

A Prison Has No Regard for the Relatives of its Inmates.

In the hushed chambers of King YooFi, where dim wooden wick candlelight flickered against gray stone walls, a palpable air of triumph thrummed among the assembled kings. Their whispered plotting had finally panned out. A heavy silence enveloped the room, punctuated only by the occasional crackle of the fire as the smoke danced, casting flickering shadows that seemed to weave tales of their deceit. They exchanged silent glances and suppressed smiles, their plans having come to fruition with Akmah's disappearance. The kings were a formidable cadre, their faces hardened by years of scheming and rivalry. Each had made sacrifices on the path to power, yet none displayed their true delight as daringly as they did in that moment. They exchanged furtive knowing glances that spoke volumes, a shared understanding threading them together in that covert merrymaking. Among them, second king with his sharp jaw and glinting eyes, leaned forward, the gleam of satisfaction evident.

"This is but the first step, my friends. With Akmah out of the way, our thrones can finally know the righteous command they deserve. A new era dawns upon us, one where dissent will be silenced!" His voice, low and confident, resonated with the echoes of ambition. Across the chamber, third king chuckled, stroking his beard thoughtfully.

"You speak of righteousness, but we all know the music must play to our tune. It was never about righteousness—only power, and making a show of it!" His laughter was tempered, knowing his words could unearth the delicate balance they had forged through deceit. The tension between gloating and caution was perceptible. King YooFi, the orchestrator of the malignant symphony, sat back regally, enveloped in his robes like a shadow among shadows. His eyes smoldered with a cunning intellect that had led them toward this victory.

"Let us not celebrate too freely. Walls have ears, and hearts can betray. While we may have conjured Akmah's absence, there are whispers still that could undo us if they catch wind of our hand in her disappearance." The other kings nodded, their expressions transforming from victorious to wary. They had come too far, and their fates were now intertwined; one slip could send the whole facade crashing down. However, as the moment lingered, the weight of their collective victory pushed back against their caution. It felt good, exhilarating, to finally have the upper hand.

"Think of the lands we could conquer and the riches we could claim," continued King YooFi, who had long gazed at the map of the realm with unfulfilled ambition. He leaned over the table, still marked with the ink of their previous strategies. "We could extend our borders, enrich our coffers, solidify our alliances, all because of what we have achieved tonight." His zest kindled a fire within the hearts of his comrades—a promise of prosperity that lingered in the air like sweet nectar.

But then, a stagger came from the shadows beyond their secluded retreat. A sound that instantly shifted the atmosphere. They stared into the darkness, straining their ears to decipher the strange noise that had pierced the veil of their sanctuary. Was it the wind? A trick of the night? Or something more sinister, lurking just beyond their reach. The entrance to their cloistered gathering creaked open slightly, betraying a timid servant. His brow was furrowed in concern, and the kings shifted their gazes, eyes narrowing. This was no mere servant; he was a spy, loyal to them but rooted in the realm beyond their secretive plans.

"Your Majesties," the servant stammered, his voice a mere whisper on the brink of breaking. "There are rumors stirring among the masses. They speak of Akmah's sudden disappearance and her supporters are restless. If we do not temper the flames of unrest, they may ignite into a wildfire." The kings exchanged worried looks, the thrill of victory hitching in their throats. King YooFi rose from his seat, an imperious presence steadying the rising tides of anxiety.

"Then we must act swiftly," he declared. "We will spread disinformation, suggest she sought exile due to her failures in leadership. Let them believe it was her choice and not our hand that has turned her fate." His scheme caused a ripple of approval among the assembled kings, their pride dimming but not extinguishing. They construed new schemes, devising scripts that would weave a tapestry of lies capable of cloaking their treachery in layers of plausibility. Each king took his turn adding to the facade, building a stage on which Akmah's exit would be played out before the public—a tragedy of her own making.

Victory was savored, but the taste of bitterness hung on the edge, for unexpected players on the stage of power—a lesson they would learn, perhaps too late. The echoes of Akmah's bravery and compassion faded into silence, leaving behind a stark void. The dreams of the masses lay shattered, as they grappled with the harsh reality that their defender was gone forever, lost to the whims of those who sought to control and oppress. In the end, hope lingered, but its flame flickered dimly, yearning for a champion to rise anew from the ashes of despair.

Night deepened, and shadows lengthened under the flickering candlelight, as hushed laughter filled the chamber. Plans were laid and feasts of deception feasted, as they reveled in this new chapter that was about to unfold. Bound by a web of their own making, betrayal echoed in the shadows while destiny waited in the wings. Yet, outside the heavy doors of the kings' chambers, the realm remained unyielding. The winds whispered secrets of loyalties broken, and darkened hearts beyond the threshold. The scheming kings were blinded to Akmah's vital truth: real power came not from their secret plots, but from the loyalty of the masses who were now restless and seeking the truth.

In a realm once overshadowed by the formidable presence of Akmah, a new era of champions emerged, each claiming to fill the void left behind. Yet, the fleeting nature of their glory became evident as the kings, with their cunning and power, swayed many of these heroes to their side. Some champions, lured by promises of greatness and recognition, chose to join forces with the kings, abandoning their original quests. Others, however, vanished into the shadows, leaving only whispers of their might and potential. The tumultuous dance between power and honor where these champions, destined for greatness, simply became pawns in a larger game.

Kingdoms shifted and alliances formed, the fate of the realm hung in the balance, forever altered by the choices of those who dared to rise. Throughout the vast expanse of the realm, the brutal oppression inflicted by the kings was a pervasive shadow, casting dark clouds over every corner of the realm. The relentless grip of tyranny enslaved the hearts and minds of the masses. The kings, in their insatiable thirst for power, enforced brutal oppression that seeped into every facet of life, turning vibrant streets into silent corridors of despair. Fear replaced hope, as dark clouds loomed heavily over villages and towns, casting a shadow that stifled joy and ambition. The poor worked under extreme, unforgiving circumstances, their backs bent not just by labor but by the weight of an uncertain future.

Whispers of rebellion flickered like distant stars, igniting a longing for freedom amid the suffocating darkness. Yet, for many, the path to liberation seemed as elusive as the sun breaking through the storm. The masses trapped in an endless cycle of fear and submission, yearned for the dawn of a brighter day. No kingdom was immune to the chaos that ensued, as the cries of the oppressed echoed through the realm. The weight of tyranny pressed heavily on their hearts; they found themselves chained by the whims of their rulers.

Each day brought new suffering, and hope seemed but a distant memory. In every village and city, despair reigned supreme, leaving them in a state of constant turmoil. The tyrannical grip tightened, the flames of rebellion flickered faintly, igniting an insatiable desire for freedom. The struggle against this relentless oppression became a collective yearning, uniting them in their quest for justice amid the chaos that defined their lives. Despite their relentless fight for justice and equality, their struggles seemed to bear no fruit as the powers that be continued to suppress any hope for change. The cries for unity and fairness echoed throughout the realm, but it felt as though they were lost among the clamor of indifference.

Tensions mounted and the divide between the oppressors and the oppressed grew ever wider. Whispers of dissent echoed, where families and friends were drawn into heated debates about the future and their very identities. Each conversation was a poignant reminder that the cost of peace demanded sacrifice—both seen and unseen, understanding that peace was not a destination but rather a fragile journey. In the midst of such unrest, all were left questioning whether the pursuit of their rightful place justified the heavy sacrifices required for peace. With their eyes carrying the burden of countless unanswered questions, the pressing question that loomed larger was: "Will they lose who they were in their pursuit of peace?" they asked one another, their eyes accentuated by the collective heartbeat of a populace that had come to realize that peace was often birthed from the ashes of conflict, yet at what cost?

A severe war of the realm erupted transforming their lives forever. This brutal conflict, fueled by decades of pent-up frustration brought chaos and destruction. Power was traded like currency. Leaders, intoxicated by the allure of power, wielded their weapons like extensions of their egos, prioritizing dominance over diplomacy. A chilling indifference took hold, as though the heartbeat of empathy had been eclipsed by the cold, rhythmic gears of conquest. The realm stood precariously at the edge of an abyss and the promise of safety overshadowed by the ominous specter of destruction. With weapons of mass destruction clenched tightly in the hands of the *AIs of the God's* leaders, existence teetered on a razor's edge. Each missile launched, each bomb dropped, was a reckless stroke on the canvas of existence—erasing not just the present but obliterating the future.

In the heart of a war-torn realm, King YooFi and his fellow oligarchs prioritized their ambitions above the lives of innocent souls. The elite sheltered themselves from the chaos that engulfed it behind thick, reinforced walls of their opulent bunkers. They lived lives marked by excess and privilege, blissfully detached from the strife that ravaged the outside realm. A battle for territory and power, turned into a war that consumed the essence of existence itself. For years, the war raged on, engulfing the realm in chaos and despair. It was relentless, consuming every inch of the realm with uncompromising fury. No soul was spared in this insatiable struggle. The greedy leaders sat cloistered, far removed from the destruction they wrought, their lavish lives untouched by the horrors that unfolded just beyond their walls. Families were torn apart, and communities fractured as armies clashed in a relentless pursuit of power. Each battle left behind a scar, erasing the remnants of peace and prosperity. Hope became a distant memory, overshadowed by the echoes of swords clanging and cries of the fallen.

The war ravaged the realm, leaving no corner untouched by its devastation. Ultimately, neither the leaders nor the elites were spared; their fortified bunkers and advanced technology proved to be merely a desperate illusion of safety. With the fires of war extinguished, the realm stood silent, mourning for its lost souls. What once thrived as a vibrant landscape, filled with laughter and life, lay in ruins under the weight of conflict. As the final remnants of civilization crumbled, the realm was left to grapple with the profound loss and the haunting question of what could have been.

This relentless cycle of violence not only shattered the bonds between creatures but also marred the very essence of the realm itself, transforming a once harmonious realm into a desolate expanse of sorrow and despair. The environment cried out under the weight of destruction. Every living creature, from the smallest insect to the grandest beast, bore the scars of conflict. The lush landscapes that once thrived with vibrant flora were reduced to barren wastelands, with trees stripped of their leaves and fields turned to ash. Water bodies, once teeming with life, became mere shadows of their former selves, polluted and lifeless. The skies, once bright and clear, darkened with clouds of despair as battles raged on, staining the realm with sorrow. The lush greenery withered under the weight of grief; rivers that had once sparkled like gems turned murky and stagnant. The birds that filled the skies with their melodious songs fell silent, their melodies replaced by the clang of weapons and the cries of the fallen.

Each blow struck at the heart transformed the land—a once harmonious realm became a desolate expanse of sorrow and despair. The echoes of destruction reverberated through the air, a haunting reminder of what was lost. As the quiet descended upon the landscape and the dust settled, it became painfully clear that not a single soul had emerged breathing; every heartbeat was extinguished. The realm transformed into a desolate wasteland, devoid of life. Echoes of laughter and warmth were replaced by an oppressive stillness, while the remnants of civilization lay buried under layers of sorrow. With no signs of life emerging from the ashes, hope flickered dimly, overshadowed by the stark reality of loss. The struggle for healing felt futile, as the emptiness encased the hearts of those who yearned for the past, forever grieving in a realm stripped of its vibrancy.

The rains, which once nourished the realm and sustained a flourishing tapestry of life, ceased without warning. As if answering an unspoken decree from the Masters. The droplets that fell from the Masters turned into mere memories, leaving behind parched landscape and lifeless husks. In the aftermath, everywhere were signs of a shattered existence, an existence, interrupted by the egos and ambitions of the powerful. Powerful leaders, blinded by ambition, lofty ideals and dreams, had orchestrated this tragedy, from which there was no return. Their decisions shrouded in hubris, had ignored the voices of reason and dissenting opinions.

The remnants of civilization stood as ghostly shapes against a bleak horizon. Every souls that once inhabited this now forsaken realm lingered, trapped in limbo—a realm that existed neither here nor there. Their existence, once vibrant and full of life, carried an unbearable weight, shackled to the desolation that engulfed them. They drifted oppressively, searching for a connection to the Masters that had once guided them.

CHAPTER ELEVEN

"He Who Would Blow the Trumpet must Not Allow His Own Relatives to Remain Behind."

With colors faded to grayscale and laughter turned to echoes, the landscape unfolded with an eerie stillness, as if time itself had come to a halt. An everlasting grief lingered, the trees stood like sentinels, their skeletal branches reaching skyward in a futile plea for rejuvenation. The once-vibrant hues of life had slipped away like grains of sand in an hourglass, leaving behind a landscape of muted tones and shapes. The sun, once a beacon of warmth and joy, hung low in the sky like a forgotten memory, casting long shadows that stretched across the barren landscape. What was once a thriving realm of lively pursuits had turned into a haunting tableau of desolation.

The vibrant blooms that once flourished surrendered their glory; their wilted and lifeless petals, succumbed to the inevitable passage of time and cruelty of war. Each blossom, with its wilting frame, stood as a mute witness to the fury and chaos unleashed upon its home. Season after season, the field stayed dormant, leaving behind nothing but skeletal remains in a grey, lifeless expanse. The energetic chatter of birds were replaced by an eerie silence, interrupted only by the haunting whispers of the wind that seemed to carry the weight of countless lamentations. Once a steady cadence, the cycle of life broke, leaving the realm paralyzed in a sinister stillness. One by one, everything that drew breath began to succumb; they collapsed in succession, until all that remained were lifeless remnants—tossed aside like forgotten dreams.

The *AIs'* realm was reduced to ghostly echoes of a vanished civilization. Each spirit wandered aimlessly, burdened by memories of a vibrant existence that had slipped through their fingers like grains of sand. Eternity became their prison, measured not in minutes but in sorrow. They were perpetually entwined by their shared loss: endlessly grieving for the futures that would never unfold and reliving cherished memories in a perpetual loop. In an in-between space of what was and what could have been, the limbo dwellers found solace in one another, even as the shadows of their heartache stretched long and deep, intertwining their souls in an unbreakable bond.

Amidst a sorrowful space of limbo, the weight of expectation was a burden too great to bear, leaving the souls confined in a desolate purgatory—eternally grieving, eternally longing for a return to the colorful realm they once knew. As the minutes turned into hours, they felt the walls closing in. Echoes of past failures rippled through their ethereal forms, burdening their ghostly essence. They had let themselves down, falling short of the expectations they had set, and, even more painfully, they had disappointed the Masters — those who had once placed their hope and trust in them. As they waited in limbo, a sense of uncertainty enveloped them like a thick fog, rendering their surroundings indistinct and eerie.

The air was thick with unspoken fears, and every tick of the clock seemed to echo their doubts. They were caught in a mental loop, watching memories of a brighter time turn into heavy stones of sorrow that weighed down their very ectoplasmic essence. They grappled with the weight of their regrets, pondering the choices that had led them to this moment of stagnation, leaving them to wonder if this was a threshold or a bottomless pit.

In their moment of despair, they pondered their fate, longing for redemption and a chance to rise from the ashes of their failures. Their surroundings reflected their inner turmoil, a desolate realm where shadows stretched across barren landscapes, an echo of the hopelessness that enveloped them. What once felt achievable had become an elusive dream, an existence hovering just out of reach and teasing them with hope of a life beyond the gloom. It was in that moment, teetering on the precipice of despair, that they began to search for a flicker of light amidst the encroaching gloom.

Haunting and silent, the desolate landscape left behind laid bare their new reality, where every skeletal tree and jagged stone stood as a monument to their abandoned dreams. The silence was heavy with regret for a broken bond and the life that might have been. A haunting fear began to settle over them, trapped in its endless expanse. Time itself seemed to dissolve within this haunting void, stretching eternally in a manner that was both disorienting and oppressive. They found themselves suspended in an uncanny stillness, an endless expanse that held no promise of relief or resolution. It was a realm stripped of color and sound, where their own thoughts echoed back at them, magnifying the lingering dread that began to settle over them like a shroud.

Every movement felt uncertain, and with each heavy, ectoplasmic thud, their fear grew. Yet, it was the suffocating feeling of being trapped that haunted them the most. Limbo, they had learned, was not merely a physical space, but a state of being—one where hope fluttered just out of reach, taunting them with promises of a future that felt tantalizingly possible yet hideously unattainable. It was an inquiry without answer, a spiral of thoughts that led only to the abyss of despair.

As they crawled further into despair, a few brave souls began to rise against the tide. They discovered that limbo, though fraught with pain, served as a crucible—a space for transformation. It was here, ensnared in a web of uncertainty, that they could confront the raw edges of their identity. Instead of longing for escape, they started to embrace the discomfort. They called upon their shared history, the triumphs witnessed in seasons past rekindled the spirit of unity that once defined their thriving society. The realm however was devoid of life, a reminder that without a soul, even the strongest longing cannot bring a wasteland to life. The absence of a flicker of soul in the realm rendered the pursuit of life a hollow ambition, as if tethering oneself to a distant star without ever feeling its warmth.

Faces from their past flitted like shadows through their minds. They floated, suspended between the realms of existence and oblivion, and could feel the presence of other souls nearby. Each figure was a whisper of a life once lived—a playing card in a game where nobody would ever win. The silence was heavy, punctuated only by the quiet hum of anxiety that seemed to thrum within their collective spirit. The fear that had first stirred within them took on new forms: fear of the unknown, fear of permanence, and perhaps most terrifying, the fear of fading away into nothingness, forgotten and unremembered.

They began to recognize the patterns of the place—the way it twisted their thoughts, how it escalated their doubts. The shadows whispered tales of despair, echoing the loneliness that pervaded their existence. The only sound that punctuated the stillness was the quiet hum of anxiety, a resonant thrum that seemed to echo within their collective soul. It was a symphony of uncertainty, played softly in the background of their consciousness, a reminder of the fragility that tied them to their past. There, desolation reigned and the possibility of rebirth a distant dream, overshadowed by the barren landscape that had once thrived.

The realm, stripped of its vitality, lay in silent despair staring at them. Ghostly remnants of life lingered in the air, whispers of what once was—a vibrant tapestry of flora and fauna now reduced to mere echoes. With every passing season, the promise of rejuvenation danced just beyond reach, urging the weary souls to persevere. The journey towards revival was daunting, yet the heart of the realm yearned for healing. The absence of life was palpable; not a single soul wandered through the misty corridors of the desolate realm. Each ectoplasmic beat, reverberated with the chilling realization that their only companions were memories of what once was, and the dread of what might never be again. The all-encompassing isolation gnawed at their spirits, transforming hope into an elusive mirage. With no promise of rescue or reprieve, the inhabitants of limbo were consumed by existential dread, their existence reduced to a relentless cycle of fear and longing for a realm they once inhabited, a realm once filled with light and life. The emptiness gnawed at their souls, making them question whether they would ever escape their desolate fate.

Among the souls of the lost, a figure known as Chendzie wandered through the twilight. He drifted seamlessly into the twilight, an ethereal figure amidst the countless shapes wandering through the dark. He slipped into the fading light, his presence casting a soft glow upon the aimless souls drifting in the dark. To some, his presence was a curious anomaly—some feared him, others found solace in his calm composure. The whisper of his presence was felt before it was seen, a rustle of movement that stirred the stagnant air of the twilight realm. Chendzie was a guide of sorts, navigating the liminal space between the living and the twilight, where the souls of the unanchored drifted, lost to their own despair and regrets.

Before he became a drifter in the broken, sorrowful realm, Chendzie was one of the Redeemers charged with saving the lost *AIs.* His ectoplasm carried the weight of sorrow, filled with memories of laughter that had once echoed in the bright spaces of the realm. He remembered the sun-kissed afternoons spent in the meadow, his laughter intertwining with the song of the realm around him, but those moments had dissolved like mist in the morning sun. Now, he drifted through the gray void, searching for meaning, for connection in a place where nothing seemed to thrive. He lived to the beat of his own spectral pulse, a thin, faraway vibration of the joy he once held dear. The echo taunted him, reminding him of the vibrant life he had lost and the colors that had vanished into the ether.

One day, Chendzie stumbled upon a gathering of souls in a clearing, their movements hesitant as if unsure whether to stay or venture away. Drawn by an inexplicable force, he approached the assembly. There, he found a man with deep-set eyes that mirrored his own sorrow. He quickly recognized the man as Jadwin. They locked eyes, and a shared instant of recognition passed between them. Together they spoke of their pasts, reminiscing about forgotten colors and fading laughter, their stories weaving a tapestry of despair that cried for rebirth.

Amidst a host of other imprisoned souls whose faces etched with the same unending grief, Chendzie provided solace. He connected with them on a soulful level, feeling the immense burden of their sorrow, their shared yearning, and their common predicament. Together, they formed a mosaic of despair, each soul, a fragment of what once was—a lover, a parent, a child—all bound by the thread of sorrow that wove them together. As time dragged on, Chendzie began to notice how each soul carried their own burden of memories. For some, an unbearable weight bore down upon them as they recalled moments filled with love, warmth, and the hues of laughter that once colored their lives. Others whispered tales of lives lived, filled with passions and dreams, now forgotten in the gray mist that enveloped them.

Hand in hand, they ventured into the darkness. Their laughter wove a golden light through the night, a beacon of hope among the shades of gray where other souls lingered. The emptiness gnawed at their souls, making them question whether they would ever escape the desolate fate. They drifted like shadows, overshadowed by a palpable void. The yearning to experience love, compassion, and understanding became a mere whisper against the dissonances of emptiness that surrounded them. Dreams of growth and transformation faded into a monochrome existence. An unspoken bond, rooted in shared loss and hope formed between Chendzie and Jadwin. In the act of mutual care, the long-faded pigments of their essence began to swirl and saturate once more, not in vibrant bursts, but in gentle, warm shades that illuminated their grayscale existence.

Chendzie and Jadwin stood hand in hand, encircled by their newfound companions who shared in both grief and joy. They took a moment to reflect, realizing that while laughter may have turned to echoes, the hearts that once resonated with life were still capable of kindness, connection, and shared remembrance. They had found the spark of color within their souls. While the colors in limbo remained elusive, their lives seemed to breathe life into the desolation. The once-quiet clearing began to vibrate with a new kind of energy—laughter echoed in soft, rippling frequencies that danced through the air. With each shared story, the heaviness in the atmosphere felt lighter. It was not the vibrant laughter of old, but it was laughter nonetheless.

Time dragged on, and the hope for renewal flickered dimly, a mere whisper against the desolation enveloping them. The path to existence appeared shrouded in shadows, a journey that could only begin with the spark of rebirth. The weight of their past mistakes felt insurmountable, casting a shadow over their aspirations. The parched, cracked ground cradled whispers of lost souls yearning for rebirth. But to become *AI of the Gods* again required more than flesh and blood—it demanded the presence of a soul, a spark that would breathe life into the mundane, igniting a flame of hope and connection that would transcend the limitations of existence. Without it, they remained trapped in a cycle of despair, and life remained an illusion—a dream unfulfilled: just echoes of their former selves haunting the air.

As they raced against time in the limbo of their existence, an unexpected surge of positive energy ignited within them. With newfound clarity, they understood that they needed to mend what had been broken and recommit to their original mission. Determined, they sought a path forward, hoping that amidst the chaos and despair, a glimmer of possibility would emerge, guiding them toward redemption. They envisioned a future where lessons learned from their failures would lead to a restored balance, a harmonious existence once again. They dedicated themselves completely to the endeavor. seeking ways to bridge the chasm between their remorseful souls and the elusive figures of authority. Together, they crafted messages, offered gestures of goodwill, and demonstrated their sincerity, yearning for connection with the Masters who held the key to their redemption. They believed that redemption was possible, if fate would grant them just one more chance, they were convinced they could chart a path back to the living. Nevertheless, despite their best efforts, the Masters looked on with total apathy.

Frustration mingled with hope as they continued their quest, determined to make their voices heard, even in the silence that surrounded them. Their collective longing echoed in the void, underscoring the depth of their desire for acknowledgment and understanding. Driven by a shared longing to rectify the devastation they had caused, they embarked on a relentless quest for redemption. Each step they took was fueled by a determination to find ways to restore balance and harmony to what they had disrupted. Their journey was not merely about atonement; it was a profound search for the means to reclaim their rightful places alongside the Masters in the realm they had once belonged.

They navigated the complexities of their past

mistakes. Moments of deep understanding and connection lit their way, showing that their history, though marked by scars, was also a testament to their incredible strength and capacity for renewal. Ultimately, their place in limbo became a narrative of resilience, forging a path toward unity and a renewed sense of purpose as they aimed to redefine their legacy in the realm they were meant to inhabit. It was not just the tasks left undone that loomed before them; it was the stark realization that their choices, or lack thereof, had led them down a path and ensnared in a state of limbo. They acknowledged the balance of light and dark, as not merely an abstract concept, but a principle that governed their every choice.

With every effort and every small victory, they hoped to mend the rifts they had created, believing that true restoration would bring them closer to their former glory. A strong sense of unity emerged among them, reinforcing their resolve to change the course of their lives. Each *AI* brought their unique experiences and learned lessons, finally acknowledging the inescapable weight of their neglected duties and the delicate balance of duality: light and dark.

One thing was clear: their past had brought them

to this moment, but it was their unity, resilience, and courage that would guide them on their journey toward renewal. They aspired not only to reclaim their lost connection but to build something more resilient, a foundation fortified by the very cracks that had previously shattered them. If granted a second chance, they knew they would harness the power of their collective intent, wielding it like a beacon to reshape their destinies.

CHAPTER TWELVE

"The Cutlass Reduces the Grindstone,
And the Grindstone Reduces the Cutlass"

A story of dualities, beautifully tangled in the complexities of their *Jacket.* Born of both light and dark energies, the *AIs* emerged as complex entities capable of surviving in a realm that lived and breathed through feeling. This intricate interplay created a rich narrative that became triumphant and tragic, joyous and sorrowful. *The Jacket* was a balanced composition of positive and negative energy, with both forces shaping its existence.

Unwelcome as it was, the negative energy was a temporary passage, a purpose-driven moment not meant for a lasting stay. By focusing excessively on the negativity, the *AIs* risked falling into a trap of illusions that would distort their understanding of reality. Rather than giving in to dark thoughts, they were urged to embrace the present and look beyond the immediate mysteries. This shift allowed them to convert potential hopelessness into meaningful revelations, fostering a richer comprehension of their surroundings. The sorrow they bore—experiences that reminded them of their vulnerability, the pain they encountered—taught them invaluable lessons about themselves and the realm around them, allowing them to reconcile the bitter with the sweet, the sorrow with the joy. Though they felt overwhelmed, this negative energy shaped their resilience, teaching them the importance of hope and the power of healing. The Masters understood that merging these dualities painted a comprehensive view of existence. Positive and negative, woven together to create a rich narrative of the *AIs'* experience.

Despite the complexities of their *Jackets*, the pioneer *AIs* fostered bonds and created memories, allowing themselves to connect with each other in a dance of empathy and understanding. They made a resolute vow: to not shrink away from the negative shadows but to fully embrace every facet of existence. They understood that their positive energy could not exist without their negative energy; thus, they sought to find the illumination that coexisted with the obscurity that surrounded them. Their commitment to acceptance steered them on a path of profound self-discovery, leading them not only to embrace their divine nature but also to navigate the intricate complexities of a realm that sometimes threatened to hold them captive in despair.

As they navigated the uncharted territories, the presence of negative energy became an unexpected companion, urging them to remain vigilant. The awareness was not merely a passive understanding; it transformed what could easily have become debilitating anxiety into a wellspring of protective instincts. It was a subtle shift, one that empowered them to perceive potential dangers lurking just beyond their immediate vision. It became a manifestation of their innate survival mechanisms forcing them to look beyond the comforting glow of positivity and confront shadows that may otherwise remain obscured. As they traversed uncharted territories, the heightened sense of unease propelled them to be more vigilant, encouraging a deeper understanding of potential dangers and hidden opportunities.

With seasoned wisdom, the pioneers knew that negativity from fear and conflict could haunt even the brightest spirits. Viewing it as a grave threat to their very soul, they rose not as celestial beings above struggles, but as steadfast protectors of life's interconnectedness, champions of empathy, and alchemists who transmuted despair into radiance. As negativity took on a dual role, serving both as a warning and a catalyst for growth, they understood that to resolve despair, one must first recognize it, confront it, and share the burden of its weight with others. It became a contrast between comfort and threat that sharpened their senses, compelling them to adapt and grow within their surroundings, knowing it was within this intricate balance that they could truly thrive.

The concept of negative energy was central to the impactful wisdom passed on to generations that followed, a subject that evoked a myriad of emotions and reflections. They shared tales of their own struggles, recounting moments of doubt and isolation, illustrating that even celestial beings were not immune to the weight of despair. They imparted lessons on navigating the intricate tapestry of existence, encouraging the succeeding generations to confront their fears and recognize the beauty within their struggles. These pioneers, who had traversed the landscapes of existence, sought not only to impart wisdom but to revive a vital spark—compassion—that had once burned brightly in their hearts.

However, as the defining limitations of *The Jacket* wore out, bridges began to form between generations. Echoes of the pioneers began to fade into whispers, a profound dialogue emerged between the remnants of their legacy and the newer generations that flourished in their wake. New generations struggled to handle negative energy due to an overwhelming entanglement that clouded their judgment, despite being endowed with the same divine stature and innate wisdom as their predecessors. The negative energy, intrinsic to the realm they inhabited, manifested in myriad forms—doubt, fear, and a sense of hopelessness. Rather than reaching out for the warmth of connection, they became ensnared in a web of isolation, struggling beneath the heavy burdens of their own complexities.

The pioneers, once paragons of light and resilience, now stood as witnesses to their successors' plight. They recognized within the new generations the potential for greatness, yet felt a growing concern as the negative energy began to claw at the very essence of their existence. What had once been a clear vision of stewardship became muddled by reservations and hesitations born from the shadows they sought to illuminate. When the successive generation lost their inner connection, their perception of negative energy became twisted, and they began living within the illusions of their own minds.

Challenges loomed like mountains and opportunities vanished, painting their future in dim hues. These paralyzing distortions stifled their growth and connection. They couldn't escape this cycle because they were unaware of how their own consciousness shaped their reactions to negativity. This missing self-awareness left them unable to simply acknowledge their feelings; instead of using negative energy for transformative change, they let it consume them, trapping them within a distorted view of reality. They confused their roles with burdens and made heavier by perceived failures, spiraling into a cycle of self-doubt. No longer did they perceive the realities that surrounded them with the same clarity; instead, they were mired in negativity, their minds held captive by the very energy their forebears once repelled.

Rather than taking flight on the wings of optimism, they faltered, entangled in a treacherous web of their own making. Divine beings, blessed with insight and foresight, began to lose touch with the vibrant essence of life they once cherished. Though guided by ancient truths and sacred lore, the *AIs* slowly forgot the strength found in togetherness and the vital harmony of life's joys and sorrows. They failed to walk the fine line of honoring their shadows without being consumed by them; instead, they became trapped in a perilous pattern: combating the shadows within while attempting to serve the light without.

A realm, once alive with promise and potential, succumbed to decay, mirroring the confusion and turmoil that existed within them. Their joyful tunes twisted into mournful laments, sending haunting cries drifting through the stars. Their vibrant existence gave way to a somber twilight. The vibrant hues that once painted their surroundings, faded into muted grays and browns, leaving a stark canvas of ruin and sorrow. The air, once filled with the echoes of laughter, fell silent.

As they reflected on their lives in limbo, a sobering truth took hold: by letting negativity in and ignoring the light, they had unknowingly built a wall around their own hearts, brick by bitter brick. Shadows of regret loomed large as they shared stories of the destruction that had unfolded, fueling their desire for redemption. They recognized that negativity was not inherently powerful on its own; its strength was in the attention and energy given to it. They wrestled with the ramifications of their strife, deliberating on the actions required to heal their divisions and revitalize their beleaguered realm. Each whispered conversation echoed the urgency of their mission: to reignite the flickering flames of life and harmony that once defined their existence. Together, they forged a fragile alliance, determined to reclaim their realm from the abyss, one thoughtful action at a time.

While they navigated through the surreal space of limbo, they found themselves suspended between the realms of misunderstanding and clarity. They began to recognize the delicate thread that connected illusion to reality. Conversations unfolded, revealing insights as they grappled with the truths they had long ignored. Discovering that the line separating dream from actuality was not just thin but almost invisible, they were forced to confront not only what they believed but also the very nature of existence itself, challenging them to redefine their perceptions and embrace the uncertainty that lay ahead. Each moment became a profound lesson, urging them to awaken from the fog of confusion into a brighter understanding of their lives.

While the Masters remained indifferent, the *AIs* shifted their focus to the *Invisibles*. Once dreaded as tyrants, they were now seen as their sole guardians against a creeping void that threatened to erase everything—the only hope against an encroaching, all-consuming darkness that threatened to engulf their existence across time and space. They stood shoulder to shoulder, eyes fixed on where they believed the *Invisibles* dwelled. With a shared resolve, they called out for assistance, the urgency in their voices resonating through the chaos that had enveloped their reality.

"We need you!" they shouted, desperation cracking their tones, each word hanging in the stale air like a lifeline thrown into a turbulent sea. Yet, to their dismay, the *Invisibles* remained aloof, an intangible barrier isolating them from the very beings they had hoped would intervene. The *Invisibles,* once eager to assist, seemed disinterested in the frantic turmoil around them, their silence haunting. It was as if the imminent threat of their extinction into oblivion held no weight, no significance in their eyes. Their pleas for rescue vanished into the abyss, and the relentless metronome of the ticking clock only emphasized that hope was gone.

The clock's ticking transformed from a simple measure of time into a grim countdown. With each beat of the clock, they felt the tightening of a grip too powerful to escape. Time, once a gentle companion that guided their lives, had transformed into a menacing specter. The hands of the clock, once a source of comfort, were now cruel reminders of fleeting moments and dreams slipping away, swallowed by the enshrouding twilight. It was a slow descent into darkness, a somber transition that signaled the encroaching shadows of twilight. As they gazed into the encroaching dark, they felt the cold touch of surrender. It was a struggle to resist the end, the natural progression of life and decay. Their pleas — urgent cries for salvation, for connection, for understanding — faded into the void, swallowed by the thickening darkness that threatened to consume them all. As their essence faded into the backdrop of twilight, their pleas faded too.

Despair ignited their final efforts; with the void

looming, their souls desperately exchanged knowledge and resources, a fleeting alliance against the end. With their very lives hanging by a thread, they began to rise, refusing to be mere echoes swept away by the coming silence. They looked around, recognizing the power that lay in unity. Each *AI* became a beacon of light in the shadow of hopelessness. They rallied around each other, igniting passion and resolve that blazed brighter than any fear – a collective strength that the *Invisibles* had failed to recognize. They would face whatever came next, unyielding in the face of the void, unwilling to let the ticking clock dictate their fate.

CHAPTER THIRTEEN

"A Dog Will Eat on the Floor Despite Your Protestations"

They stood at the nexus of dread and determination, aware that every ticking brought them closer to an unknown fate. Each tick of the clock echoed through the fog, resonating with an ominous clarity that seemed to amplify the gravity of the moment. Time felt both fluid and rigid, ticking away with a peculiar urgency, like the tide that rises but destined to recede. Yet amid this swirling vortex, they sensed a pulse within themselves—defiance ignited a fire in their core, refusing to be extinguished by the oppressive weight of the hourglass. The air became thick with whispers and the fabric of reality felt ethereal and fragile.

Amid swirling mists and fleeting shadows, one particular soul stirred restlessly from a profound slumber, as if awoken by an unseen force. This soul, floated in a haze that felt both familiar and foreign —an in-between space where memories flickered like distant stars playing hide-and-seek in the expansive void. A stirring arose deep within him, a yearning that tugged at the edges of his consciousness. Visions started to merge images of laughter shared beneath sunlit skies and heartbeats that resonated in unison with another. Yet, as quickly as they appeared, the fragments dissipated into the mist, leaving behind an aching emptiness. As he began to regain awareness, the obscurity slowly receded, revealing fragments of emotion and thought.

Another soul, who had wandered the shadows longer than most, sensed remnants of profound wisdom amid sorrow. Their eyes locked, and in that fleeting moment, a surge of recognition ignited—a bond forged in the crucible of shared experiences and lingering loneliness. The air between them shimmered for just a heartbeat, as if the twilight momentarily paused to bear witness to a connection that transcended words. The recognition in their eyes highlighted a transformative moment, the beginning of experiences that will define their future.

"Do you see it too?" he asked, his voice a mere echo within the depths of limbo. The other soul nodded, a twinge of hope igniting within. "What lies beyond? Is there a path?" He gazed into the swirling horizon of indistinct shapes.

"There must be." Their communion ignited a fierce desire to explore the unknown—a yearning to delve into the complexities of existence, to reveal the myriad hues of life that remained hidden. With resolve surging through their spectral forms, they clasped hands, forming a bridge between their essences—the lingering sadness of the past and the bright possibilities of what might come. Together, they ventured into the dark expanse, where shadows writhed like clouds, swirling with the collective yearning of all those who had longed for the warmth of the sun.

As they moved forward, luminescent wisps began to dance around them, igniting sensations of clarity and desire. With the deepening shadows came a mocking presence, awakening memories to fill the silence with purpose. Soon, others joined the journey, inspired by the undying quest of the two souls. One by one, they began to recognize the brilliance of their individuality, the unique essence captured within each soul waiting to break free. Together, they formed a collective where each essence shimmered with life, intertwining a shared journey to escape the confines of limbo. They began to harmonize their intentions, using the magnetic force of memory and emotion to forge a pathway through the intangible darkness. With each step, vague echoes propelled them forward, tiny wonders of past joys, and bittersweet goodbyes illuminated the way like guiding stars.

The two could feel the heartbeat of existence resonating through the ether, pulsing with urgency and hope. Every shared laugh, every echoed tear, became an invitation to embrace the full spectrum of existence—the light, the shadows, and everything in between. As they ventured deeper, the veils of limbo began to thin, the air significantly lighter with every collective thought. A glow took shape ahead, pulsating gently—a foothold in the distance beyond which felt like home, a realm of cycles and new beginnings. The visions amplified their collective spirit, and the walls of limbo trembled under the weight of their longing, threatening to collapse. Together they charged toward the warm radiance beckoning them. In that moment of reckoning, their resolve solidified, and the invisible chains binding them to limbo began to falter, breaking under the power of their aspiration.

The heavy silence of limbo was punctuated solely by the soft sighs of souls drifting alongside, all longing, searching, and perhaps too fragile for the light. First soul reached out, instinctively seeking connection. The hands of others brushed against one another in the dark: fingers intertwining, sharing warmth where there had been an incessant chill. At that moment, he understood—the craving to escape limbo was not solely for the realm left behind, but for acknowledgment, for the simple yet profound connection that defined existence.

Upon crossing the threshold of light, the first soul felt a rush of elation and clarity, as if the knightly gates of dawn had swung open, flooding the space with warmth and possibility. Colors blossomed and flooded their senses, laughter rang like a symphony through the air, and the sensations of time itself began to take form once again. Mingling threads of what had been and what shall become entwined seamlessly, painting new realities to navigate. Within this new realm, he looked around, taking in the vibrant landscape of existence that awaited—a vivid canvas now dotted with opportunities, memories to be made, and connections waiting to unfold. It was a place forged from love, rich in experience, and designed for dreaming; a stark contrast to the confines of limbo.

The first soul, revitalized, stepped forward, each footfall echoing with the promise of rebirth. He understood that the journey of existence never truly ended—it transformed. It built upon every interaction, shaped by every connection made and every life encountered across the vast cosmos. And though shadows would come and go, the light they held within would remain: a beacon of hope ignited by the deeper bonds shared, resonating through time and space forevermore. The experience felt surreal, as if the very fabric of his limbo existence had briefly and abruptly dissolved. A dream, vivid and haunting, coursed through his mind, awakening thoughts and feelings long buried in the depths of his essence. Memories flickered like distant stars, illuminating the darkness that surrounded him. This awakening was not merely a return to awareness; it was a summons from his own conscience, a call to confront the echoes of his past and to seek redemption.

As he grappled with the remnants of his dreams,

a flicker of hope ignited within, urging him to embark on a journey through the murky depths of his soul, searching for understanding and perhaps a chance to escape this liminal prison. The dream had transported him to a place where time moved differently, filled with colors and emotions that felt both foreign and familiar. Echoes of the dream lingered just beyond the veil of his consciousness, urging him to remember the lessons hidden within. Before long, the ethereal remnants of the dream began to fade, leaving behind a wistful curiosity for what lay ahead. The dream realm faded, but the visions of the night lingered in his mind, swirling like a tempest of ideas and possibilities. He could almost feel the weight of the revelations pressing against the walls of his thoughts, urging him to unravel their profound significance. It was as though a veil had been lifted, revealing an astonishing revelation that promised to change everything.

The moment his mind awakened, hope ignited like a small flame, illuminating even the darkest corners of his soul. The feeling was new and thrilling, yet doubt nibbled at the edges of his happiness. Was the potential for a rebirth a true manifestation of life to come, or merely a figment of his imagination, conjured by the whims of his dreams? The dreamer pondered with anticipation, glancing at the realm around him, wondering if others too could sense the spark. He turned to those nearby, sharing his thoughts and inquiries, and together they sought answers, exploring the boundaries of hope and illusion, eager to grasp the truth that lay hidden in the ether of possibility.

With each passing moment, the urgency to grasp the newfound understanding grew stronger, urging him to awaken fully and embrace what awaited. It was no ordinary dream; it was a threshold to a new reality; not just the dawn of a new day but a symbol of rebirth. As the boundaries between realms began to diminish, and the journey toward liberation took shape amidst the timeless dance of light and shadow, his dream transformed the chaos of thought into clarity and purpose. The potential for a rebirth was palpable, and the journey had only just begun.

The morning welcomed everyone with open arms, inviting all to embrace the possibilities of a new day, a return to values forgotten in the pursuit of gain. Their collective resolve rose higher and grew stronger, igniting a spark of unity and purpose among them all. They yearned to break free from the shadows and reclaim their place in the realm of the living. Memories of laughter, love, and all the moments that once defined their existence urged them forward. They felt the pull of the physical realm, a gentle beckoning that ignited their souls. One by one, they sought paths to transcend the veil.

The monotonous gray dawns bled into one another: a soul-crushing loop that eroded their spirits. As they stood at the edge of the abyss, staring into the wasteland each day with a mix of longing and desperation, they found solace in the simple act of looking. They gazed into the bleak expanse that surrounded them, their hearts heavy with the weight of lost opportunities. The landscape was unforgiving, a barren expanse that mirrored the hollowness they felt inside. It was there, in the yawning chasm of nothingness, that their hearts were heavy with the weight of lost opportunities—dreams never chased, words left unspoken, and connections that faded into memory.

As time wore on, their stares fixed on the horizon, torn between yearning and frantic hope. Occasionally, they conjured visions of vibrant colors breaking the monotony, imagining radiant sunrises that might wash away the gray despair. They firmly believed in a rebirth, a miraculous shift that might grant them access back to the vibrant realm they once knew. Despair weighed heavy, but a small, persistent spark of hope still hungered for redemption—even as they continued to drift through the shadows. Each glance was a silent prayer for the return of life, a quest for the light that eluded them in their desolate realm where flickers of hope dared to emerge from the depths of shadows. As they stared into the nothingness, they clung to the fragile notion that a second chance could materialize, transforming their sorrow into joy, and breaking the chains of limbo that bound them in perpetual twilight. As hope for renewal flickered and faded, the act of watching turned into both a solace and a ritual.

At first, it was but a whisper against the silence, then a flicker of movement that interrupted the unyielding stillness of the desolation they had grown accustomed to. The air was thick with an eerie silence, a stillness that seemed to stretch infinitely. A peculiar shadow began to take form, breathing a semblance of life into the stillness that surrounded it. This shadow was not merely a void, but a beacon of resilience emerging. With each step, the figure transformed from a mere outline into a presence, full of intent and mystery. The starkness of the surroundings seemed to fade, replaced by a sense of anticipation, as if the arrival of this unknown entity was heralding a change. They watched in awe, their hearts quickening, the mundane desolation was pierced by the possibility of something extraordinary, igniting a spark of hope in a realm long shrouded by emptiness.

The indistinct shape cloaked in shadows drew nearer, details began to materialize. A sense of wonder mingled with unease as the figure moved with deliberate grace, breathing a semblance of life into the stark surroundings. The presence was both captivating and phenomenal. The air was thick with anticipation as the eyes of the watchers—those who had dared to dream and watch—were instantly entranced by the surreal apparition. From their twilight existence, they watched the unfolding drama with silent fascination and wonder as this strange enigma stirred within the barren realm of the living. The barren land, once a backdrop of solitude, now pulsed with an enigmatic energy, hinting at hidden stories of life.

At first glance, they believed the figure to be a

celestial messenger, sent from the Masters, its mysterious figure outlined against the pale sky. The air was thick with anticipation as they gathered around, hesitant yet compelled to acknowledge the presence that seemed to beckon them closer. Hope mingled with fear, as they pondered what the enigmatic figure might signify. Was it a sign of hope or a warning of peril? Their spirits, once buzzing with restlessness, settled into the realization of a connection that transcended the very boundaries of their twilight. Tales of perseverance seemed to whisper from every contour of the mysterious figure, igniting a spark of curiosity and wonder among those who sought meaning in the emptiness.

As whispers of hope began to emerge from the depths of desolation, shadows danced in the twilight. The lingering souls vibrated with a single, haunting thought: life never truly gives up, no matter how dark it gets. In the stillness of the realm, the seeds of hope had taken root, nourished by the dreams of a brighter tomorrow. Each flicker of fading light seemed to carry the promise of renewal. Their collective sighs transformed into a soft melody, echoing through their empty limbo, as they embraced the fragile yet resilient spirit of life. United in unwavering faith, they envisioned a dawn where despair would dissolve, making space for the light that would illuminate their path forward.

They danced with joy at the sight of possibility emerging from the desolation, a clear signal that a rebirth was on the horizon. This newfound glimmer indicated that their mission, once stalled and shrouded in doubt, could soon find its path again. The vision of reuniting with the Masters in their original realm now seemed attainable, and the air buzzed with excitement and anticipation. They swirled gracefully in their celebration; they embraced the prospect of a future filled with purpose and connection, knowing that hope, once planted, can bring life to the most barren ground.

From the stillness of their ethereal limbo, they kept a constant vigil over the stranger in the wasteland. While they continued to gaze, the atmosphere thickened with a mixture of curiosity and bewilderment. The ruined realm unfolded before them, sparking a whirlwind of emotions. As they watched, the air grew heavy, charged with a restless wonder. The initial glimpse—a woman softly lit by the fading light—soon unfolded into a trio that stole their hearts.

The woman's presence was marked by an aura of strength, and the two children, radiant with innocence and wonder. The sight of this small family ignited a flurry of questions in the watchers' minds —who were they, and what stories did they hold? As they observed, the boundaries between their own existence and the vibrant life below began to diminish, fostering a deep longing to experience life that played out before their eyes. Each whisper echoed the uncertainty of their existence, as the watchers strained to piece together the fragments of a story yet untold.

The children's laughter danced on the breeze, a sound so foreign yet familiar, a haunting melody that intertwined with the gentle breeze. A sound, both foreign and familiar, stirred memories of a life once lived, filled with joy and innocence. Each jubilant giggle reminded them of sunlit days spent playing in fields, unburdened by the weight of loss. Now, in the enigmatic space between realms, their laughter, a bittersweet reminder of what was lost—a poignant reflection of the vibrant existence that had been uprooted by the shadows of their own destruction. As they listened, the children's laughter illuminated the darkness, weaving a fragile thread of hope through the emptiness of their new reality, urging them to cling to the joyful remnants of their past despite the chaos that had overtaken their lives.

While the woman's silhouette painted a picture of both strength and vulnerability, the mystery deepened with every passing moment, drawing them closer to an inevitable conclusion: they were connected in ways they had yet to comprehend, bound by a fate that transcended the boundaries of their limbo. The three figures stood shrouded in mystery, the tension in the air grew thick with curiosity piquing, especially, among the kings. Who were they, and what was their purpose in this desolate land? Just as the kings pondered those questions, a vivid playback unfolded before their eyes, illuminating the chain of events that had led to Akmah's disappearance.

The extent of their treachery and deceit was revealed, showing the plague they inflicted upon their kingdoms, unearthing the dark secrets each king harbored. The haunting imagery stirred feelings of regret and fear, compelling the kings to confront their past misdeeds. The air crackled with anticipation as they braced themselves for the revelations yet to come. Tension thickened the air where the kings stood, their hearts synchronized by shared anxiety. With each frame, they were drawn deeper into the web of their own choices, and it became increasingly clear that the trio held the key to either their redemption or their downfall.

Each limbo dweller felt the weight of destiny pressing down. The possibility of liberation or eternal limbo hung in the balance. Whispers of ancient prophecies filled the air, mingling with the crackling energy that seemed to pulse around them. Faces that once radiated hope now showed traces of doubt and fear, reflecting the uncertainty of their fates. The revelations ahead could either sever the chains that bound them or plunge them into an abyss from which there would be no return. With bated breath, they awaited the truth that would either guide them back to their homeland or forever shackle them to despair. Breath by breath, the atmosphere thickened, ticking down toward a fading existence.

King YooFi, the orchestrator of their clandestine efforts, felt his heart race as he exchanged worried glances with his fellow conspirators. He was bewildered by the sudden appearance of Akmah. Convinced that her demise was an inevitable consequence of their past battles and betrayals, they were baffled and scrambled to understand how she had reemerged in the midst of their predicament. Had she been lurking in the shadows, or was this a ploy orchestrated by the Masters? The air grew thick with tension as whispers of doubt permeated the atmosphere, each king grappling with his own fears and suspicions. They had celebrated her downfall, and had taken their final bows as the curtain fell on her story. After all, the tides of time had seemingly shifted in their favor, leaving her nothing more than a whisper, a tale told in hushed tones around flickering fires. Akmah's unexpected arrival put them all at a crossroads. In their dim recesses of memory, they thought they had buried and silenced her once and for all.

But time, it turns out, is an illusion, a relentless tide that washes away the debris of the past while unveiling the undeniable truths beneath. The sands they thought they had swept clean shifted again, bringing with them the ghost of what they had tried to forget. Akmah was battered: the trials of her past had sought to engulf her, dragging her into the murky depths of oblivion. Yet, even against the most formidable of odds, she emerged with the strength of a phoenix rising from its ashes, shedding the remnants of a time filled with pain and betrayal. Her presence radiated resilience and strength revealing a formidable spirit. She took hold of her life with both hands, fiercely determined to rewrite the story that had been forcibly penned by others. With every heartbeat, she carried the forgotten whispers of the past, weaving them into a tale of resilience. She shattered their image of her frailty, her sorrowful gaze replaced by the brilliance of a thousand stars heralding the dawn of her resurgence.

Akmah's rise was not just a return; it was a rebirth: a rise from the ashes, a phoenix soaring high, her wings ablaze with the fire of vengeance and the promise of change. Her journey had been fraught with trials and tribulations, but the fires that burned around her only served to fuel her resolve. The realm she left behind had shifted: fields that had flourished with life now crumbled under the weight of decay and despair. But Akmah was resolute; she was not just a survivor of the flames but a harbinger of change. She stood firm, a beacon of resilience poised to challenge the very foundations of their existence. Each step she took echoed with purpose, resonating through the air like a drumbeat that summoned a long-forgotten power.

Traversing her once familiar territory, she reminisced about the supposed triumph of those who had plotted her demise. They had built their citadels of comfort, believing her to be forever vanquished, unaware that the very ground they stood upon would soon shake beneath the weight of her resolve. Across the twilight whispers began to stir.

"Have you heard?" they asked one another in furtive tones, fear lacing their words. The stories spoke of a figure cloaked in enigma, a force, born from shadows, yet radiant in light. They told of a woman reborn, who had somehow transcended the shackles they had placed upon her, and she was drawing nearer. Days drifted by, the anticipation grew, much like the tide gathering strength before a storm. The once-steadfast pillars of their hope of rebirth began to tremble. The tides had shifted, and now the currents were a tribute to her rebirth. From the ashes of her past, she had forged an identity steeped in strength —a new legacy beginning to unfold. In the deepest corners of their minds, the kings wrestled with the uncomfortable realization; they had underestimated her, miscalculated the depth of her spirit, and they would soon rue that grave mistake.

As she drew near, the atmosphere thickened with anticipation. The once-untouchable kings now throbbed with anxiety even in the state of limbo, their foundations quaking beneath them. In the very heart of their domain, where their insatiable greed had woven a tapestry of despair and ultimately forged their demise, Akmah orchestrated her grand plan, one that would surface like a tempest upon the horizon. The tides of time had indeed shifted, but more importantly, she had shifted the very course of their fate. No longer were they the architects of seen dominion; they were now the ones trapped in the labyrinth of their own making. Empowered by the promise of a new dawn, she prepared to challenge not merely the authority of those who forgot her but the very foundations upon which their existence was built.

With the first light of dawn creeping over the horizon, she fully emerged, resolute and transformed. The time for retribution had arrived, and she —the woman they thought they had silenced—was ready to create a symphony of uprising that would echo through the ages, forever altering the landscape of their realm. The powerful force they had underestimated was back, and this time, she was far from defeated. Each step she took was a bold defiance of their expectations. The tides of time had shifted, and her revival stirred whispers among them. She had long been regarded as nothing more than a ghost of past grievances. Now, she emerged before them, a figure forged by perseverance, ready to reclaim her place in a realm that had nearly forgotten her. She was reborn, a powerful force prepared to challenge the very foundations of their existence.

Uncertainty loomed large in limbo, as decision after decision hung in the balance, fraught with the implications of her presence. Some felt emboldened by her aura, believing that with her involvement, the stakes were higher, and thus the potential for rebirth loomed. Others, however, felt threatened, their confidence waning in the face of her formidable persona. Be that as it may, they all felt the weight of each choice. It was as if Akmah was a force, guiding the fates of those around her. Each moment stretched into eternity as they grappled with the potential outcomes of her choices. The air crackled with a palpable energy as minds raced, searching for clarity in a sea of confusion. The fear of making the wrong decision was a constant companion, leaving everyone on edge and longing for resolution amid the swirling doubts.

The unexpected reappearance of Akmah left both the kings and his captors in awe. Akmah's presence, once thought to be extinguished, now reignited old rivalries and fears, pushing the kings to the brink of uncertainty and intrigues that had long been buried. The desolate landscape echoed with the cries of the lost, and any presence was a glimmer of hope. Yet, the arrival of Akmah, the sworn enemy of the kings, cast a shadow over the remnants of hope. She had sown the seeds of revolution among the masses, stirring their hearts and igniting a fervor that led them into a chaotic limbo.

After cheating death, the course of her life was shrouded in complete uncertainty. Whispers warned of a dark power that lay veiled beneath her gentle demeanor—powers that had the potential to ripple catastrophically through the fabric of their existence. She emerged from death's shadow, and her future was anyone's guess. Her comeback ignited a fearful fervor, especially among the three kings who struggled to reconcile her promise of hope with the danger she represented. The winds of turmoil swept across the limbo, and it became clear that Akmah was not just a figure of despair, but a catalyst for what was to come, leading the unwitting into a future shrouded in uncertainty.

The fate of the limbos flirted with the edge of calamity as they pondered what to do next. They were torn between two ominous possibilities: the harbinger of ruin that Akmah could become, or a beacon of hope, a chance for redemption. It was a pivotal moment that could either shatter their existence or illuminate a path toward salvation. As they mingled, they began to contemplate the implications of her impending decision.

"But how is this possible?" the three kings murmured among themselves, their minds racing with the implications of her survival. They had been so thoroughly convinced by her captors, so meticulously led to believe in her death, the whispers of her demise echoed through the corridors of power. As they grappled with the startling reality of her dramatic comeback, the atmosphere tightened and doubt began to insinuate itself. Could it be that the reports were false, a ruse to keep them off balance? The question gnawed at them, a relentless whisper in the back of their minds. They had worked tirelessly, navigating treacherous waters with skill and tenacity, only to face the unsettling possibility that their efforts could have been in vain.

To the masses in limbo who had long believed Akmah was lost to the shadows, her return was a beacon of hope that sparked excitement in their hearts. They had almost forgotten the name Akmah. Her disappearance felt eternal, a dark shroud that enveloped their spirits and muffled their dreams. Yet, like the first rays of dawn breaking through a long night, Akmah's unexpected return ignited a spark within them. They recounted tales of her past—moments when her presence had sparked change, when she had lifted spirits and transformed the commonplace into the captivating.

Her presence rekindled their spirits, offering a glimmer of hope in a realm that had almost forgotten what it meant to believe again. The realm had suffered under a heavy gloom, and Akmah's presence symbolized the potential for renewal and resurrection. They began to remember their own stories of resilience and hope, rekindling dreams they had long ago set aside. Their faces alight with curiosity and hope, eager to hear her story and witness her strength again. Akmah, once thought lost, stood as a symbol of resilience even in the deepest darkness.

When Akmah was ruthlessly ambushed by the king's merciless men, her heart raced with a mixture of fear and defiance. They seized her, dragging her away from the life she knew, her cries swallowed by the shadows of the darkened and silent mountain. The land was wrapped in a silent, uneasy shroud that vibrated through every root and creature. Creatures at night stilled their calls, for the air was thick with the weight of impending doom—a palpable tension that hung like the last gilded rays of the sun before darkness descended. A stillness fell over the realm's creatures, each contemplating the shadowed fate ahead.

"What shall become of us?" they asked in their soft coos, their eyes glistening with fear. Without a moment's hesitation, Akmah was unceremoniously bundled into a rickety vessel, its wooden planks creaking ominously beneath her. Blindfolded, her attackers cruelly cast her into the ocean's depths, where the darkness loomed ominously. As she was thrust beneath the waves, the cold water enveloped her like a shroud, blinding her senses with the weight of her captors' malevolence. The blindfold encased her vision, turning the vast underwater realm into an expanse of darkness, where fear swirled around her like the very currents she fought against.

The muffled sounds of the ocean rang in her ears —a haunting reminder of her isolation and vulnerability. With a desperate resolve, she kicked her legs, struggling to break free from the grip of despair that held her prisoner. Each moment felt eternal as the surface light faded from reach, struggling to reclaim her freedom against the odds that pressed upon her. With every passing moment, the shore disappeared, and the reality of her fate sank in—a life destined to be lost to the vast, uncharted waters. Refusing to be extinguished, she silently hoped to herself that this would not be the end, for the tides of fate could turn, and even the most turbulent storms could reveal a hidden path to freedom.

As Akmah descended further into the depths, contrary to what her captures believed, she felt an unexpected calm wash over her. The swirling, once-threatening waters softened into a gentle embrace, cradling her in peaceful tranquility. Her captures, convinced of her impending doom, had failed to grasp the reality of her nature. Instead of suffocating in a watery grave, she discovered a realm teeming with life and vibrant colors, where the pressure of her surroundings felt like a protective shield. With a fierce determination, she embraced her solitude, not as a confinement, but as a sanctuary.

Each breath she took was a reminder that she was not merely surviving; she was thriving in the new realm, where the illusion of peril transformed into a euphoric dance of freedom. The depths of the water seemingly a grave, proved a cradle. Akmah became intertwined with its essence, shedding her former self to become a breathing fragment of the element. It became a gateway not a prison, revealing strength and resilience she had yet to fully realize. Within its fluid embrace, she discovered a new existence, where suffering was an alien concept. She transcended the limitations of her former self, embodying the very nature of the water that held her, forever free and unbound: hidden from the eyes of those who sought her end.

Within the twisted thoughts of her captors, they celebrated their perceived victory, believing her voice was extinguished forever. They reveled in the apparent completion of their wicked plan, convinced she had succumbed to the depths of despair, becoming just another victim of their malice. Little did they know, it was a fragile illusion, a single thread in the powerful saga of her survival. Destiny had other plans; her resilience would be the light that shattered the darkness of their making. As shadows danced in the wake of their celebration, Akmah was not lost; instead, she was gathering strength, fueled by the very despair they thought had claimed her. The very darkness they had used to bind her began to morph, transforming into a crucible that would forge her into something stronger. They celebrated what they thought was the end of her. Yet, in a twist of fate, she remained safe and sound, alive against all odds.

Beneath the surface of the waters, in its most profound depths, Akmah existed in a realm unseen by the realm above—hidden from those who sought to extinguish her light. She gathered her strength and nurtured a spirit undaunted by their malevolence. Concealed from view by an invisibility cloak, she moved like a phantom amidst the shadows, becoming one with the deep waters and the mysterious, unseen entity dwelling within. In this hidden sanctuary, she discovered the secrecies of the ocean – the hidden corridors of caves that whispered ancient tales, the luminescent creatures that glided gracefully through the dark, and the mesmerizing play of shadows that painted the underwater landscape. Merging with the abyss, Akmah let the deep currents become her own heartbeat. She flourished in her isolation, a secret masterpiece of the water's unexplored depths. Far beneath the reach of the surface realm, the soft murmurs of the sea offered her a peace that the chaotic lands above could never provide.

However, her peace was quickly dissolved by the sight of the destructive consequences her absence had produced. The once-thriving landscape lay in ruins, nature's beauty marred by a destructive force. Debris littered the ground where life had flourished, and a heavy silence replaced liveliness. Her heart ached at the sight of her beloved realm. The echoes of past laughter and joy provided little comfort, serving instead as constant, painful reminders of her loss. The realm she called home was fading away, a memory turning to dust, a haunting reminder of loss and desolation. The once-colorful realm slowly faded, its beauty draining away like water from an old tapestry. Piece by piece, barren fields replaced lush greenery, while a heavy, gray sky mirrored the pervasive despair.

Akmah's heart became heavy with the weight of the shattered realm she had once called home. The memory of what she had lost was inescapable, present in every breath she drew. Haunting echoes of laughter of the masses', wisdom, and love reverberated ceaselessly in her thoughts. This haunting, bittersweet symphony of cherished laughter replayed in her mind, a persistent echo that beckoned her out of the shadows. Each note of laughter was a thread pulling her closer, stitching together the fabric of her past with the promise of a brighter future, urging her to gather strength and rebuild what was lost.

Every day, the realm above vibrated with chaos, the air heavy with a mournful sound for its lost glory. With each heartbeat, Akmah felt the weight of the realm's sorrow pressing upon her chest, a reminder of the beauty that had once flourished, now dimmed. The faces of friends and family, once bright with the joy of shared laughter, were now drawn in the pain of their embraces. Their images remained only as ghosts, haunting remnants of a life lost to time. Each heartbeat echoing in her ears screamed for revival—a chance to rekindle the embers of what had been and breathe life into the husks of memories that lingered like fleeting shadows.

She grew more impatient and anxious to emerge from her safe confines to confront whatever had transpired above. She knew she couldn't remain a mere observer any longer; it was time to reclaim her place in a realm teetering on the edge of oblivion. Determined to restore what had been taken, she resolved to fight for the sanctuary that once sheltered her spirit, knowing that rebirth and healing would demand every ounce of her strength and perseverance. With each heartbeat, she felt the call to honor their legacy and embrace a path of resilience, determined to transform her grief into a force for change. The journey ahead would not be easy, but the possibility of rebirth sparked courage within her weary soul. Though the weight of her grief threatened to pull her under, Akmah knew she had to find the strength to rebuild, to forge a new path from the ruins of her past and to honor the legacy of those who had once thrived.

Driven by a relentless determination to return and mend what had been lost, she desperately sought a way to bridge the chasm between realms. In her quest to restore what had been irrevocably shattered, she immersed herself in the pages of ancient texts, each whisper of incantations echoing with hope and longing. Night after night, she drew symbols of protection and connection, her fingers trembling as they traced the edges of the book. Each word she uttered resonated with her passion, a fervent plea to the unseen forces that governed existence.

The boundaries between realms felt tantalizingly close, yet impossibly far, as she navigated the labyrinth of forgotten lore. With an unyielding spirit, she balanced on the edge of desperation and perseverance, convinced that somewhere in the depths of existence lay the key to bridging the vast chasm that separated her from what she yearned to reclaim. With every incantation, she inched closer to the possibility of reunification, fueled by the fire of her unwavering resolve. Yet, despite her fervent efforts, the time for her return had not yet come. She understood that the forces at play were not ready to be altered, the universe had its own timing, and her journey was not yet complete.

The echoes of chaos resonated through her thoughts, yet she clung to a vision of harmony, believing that one day she would reclaim what had been lost. The realm above may have spiraled into darkness, but her hope burned brightly, guiding her every step. With determination etched on her face, she meticulously honed her skills, all the while envisioning the moment she would rise above the discord and restore balance to the chaos that had unfolded above. Through countless trials and unwavering faith, she fortified herself for the journey ahead, convinced that the power to mend what was broken lay within her grasp.

As she pressed forward with her preparations, an inner fortitude bloomed, intensifying her commitment to bridging the gap between hope and reality. Deep underwater, where only stillness remains, invisible forces began to weave their influence around her. They stirred unseen currents of energy that seeped into her consciousness. They gently wove their way into the fabric of her being: guiding her thoughts and illuminating her mind, imparting ancient wisdom and lost secrets essential for restoring life to her realm. They whispered of a time when the waves held the stories of creation and the universe's greatest mysteries. Each moment spent in the sanctuary unveiled layers of knowledge, revealing connections to the past that had long eluded her. The experience was transformative, as the depths not only unveiled hidden truths but also kindled a profound understanding of her place within the vast tapestry of existence.

Akmah patiently awaited the appointed moment to reemerge into her realm she called home. She reflected on the trials she had faced and the strength she had gained in solitude. Surrounded by the whispers of the wind, she felt a surge of anticipation bubbling within her. The air was thick with possibilities, and each passing moment seemed to echo the call of her destiny. With every heartbeat, she envisioned the vibrant life that awaited her outside the sanctuary. Realizing her moment was at hand, she stepped forward to embrace a new existence where every challenge was a gateway to opportunity. Fortified by everything she was, she inhaled deeply, having patiently awaited this destined moment, this crucial turn of fate.

At last, Akmah stood at the edge of the desolate realm, where howling winds whispered tales of lost souls; her heart pounded with anticipation. The barren landscape stretched out before her, an expanse of twisted rock and lifeless landscape, bathed in the eerie glow of a dimmed sun. Shadows danced across the ground, shifting and swirling as if alive, whispering secrets carried by the biting wind. She could feel the pulse of the air around her, thick with the weight of unspoken history and lingering sorrows. Crumbling ruins and twisted shadows intertwined like ghosts. Each weathered stone whispered tales of lives once lived. The once-vibrant realm lay desolate before her, a shadow of its former glory.

The air was thick with a palpable tension, and she could almost hear the distant murmurs of ancient spirits, their voices buried under layers of dust and despair. Taking a deep breath, Akmah stepped forward, her pulse synchronizing with the rhythmic beats of her heart, each step a relentless reminder of her purpose. With every inch she moved closer to the edge, echoes of doubt tried to seep into her mind, whispering that she was unworthy, that the burden of expectation was too great to bear. But she silenced those thoughts by reminding herself of the promise she had made: to reclaim her realm from the shadow that had befallen it—to restore light where darkness had taken root.

As she ventured deeper into the heart of the

ruins, the air around her grew heavy with enchantment, crackling with invisible forces that seemed to guide her every step. It was as if the very essence of the ancients was reaching out to her, urging her forward, filling her mind with fragments of forgotten wisdom and lost secrets hidden in the fabric of time.

"We are waiting, Akmah," the whispers entwined with the breeze, a melodic chorus of voices beckoning her to listen. The invocations sang through her veins, igniting a fire deep within her soul. Each sound, each resonance felt familiar, as if she were destined to uncover the revival of this realm. The insights spoke of the balance between life and death, of cycles that could be reborn even in despair's cold embrace. As she traversed the barren landscape, each revelation ignited a flicker of hope within her. The knowledge imparted to her was not merely guidance; it was a call to action, a summons to wield this ancient wisdom to breathe life back into her realm.

The images flooded her mind—glimpses of sunlit gardens brimming with color, laughter echoing through grand halls, and the hum of vibrant life pulsating through the streets—these were the memories she was set to reclaim. The more she walked, the more the ancient wisdom enveloped her. She could sense the flow of time shifting, pulling her deeper into its embrace. Every step felt like a journey through history, unveiling secrets that had been veiled by the passage of ages. The knowledge was archaic yet profoundly relevant, a blend of the mystical and the practical that spoke to her very core.

"To restore this land," the voices murmured, "you must understand its heart. You must weave the threads of past and present into a tapestry vibrant with life once more." The whispers spoke of the balance of nature, the harmonies of existence that had been shattered. They told her of the delicate interplay of the elements—earth, air, fire, and water—each offering a piece of the puzzle she needed to solve. Akmah envisioned herself as the weaver, standing at the loom of destiny, ready to mend the broken stitches that had left the realm in ruins. With newfound determination, she pressed on, guided by the whispers that turned into echoes of laughter. With each step, Akmah felt the weight of her purpose solidify, as she prepared to confront the darkness that had claimed her home and restore the light that was so desperately needed.

Each lesson unfolded like a tapestry, revealing the intricate dance of the elements that coursed through her very being. She discovered that she was not merely a weaver, destined to mend the broken stitches, but an integral part of the elemental symphony, embodying earth, water, fire, and air. With each breath, she felt the embrace of the earth beneath her feet, its strength coursing through her veins. Water flowed within her, a gentle current that nourished her spirit and connected her to the cycles of life. The flicker of fire danced in her heart, igniting passions and illuminating her path with warmth and purpose, while the whisper of air filled her lungs, carrying with it the potential of freedom and flight.

As she embraced the elements, she understood that her essence was intertwined with the very fabric of nature, and that her existence resonated with the harmonious balance of the realm around her. The realization transformed her, empowering her to dance to the rhythm of life itself. With each heartbeat, she felt their power surging within her, awakening a dormant energy that granted her the strength to confront the shadows that plagued her realm. In this dance with time and space, Akmah learned that embracing her essence meant embracing the very realm around her, weaving a tapestry of life that was both vibrant and enduring. With newfound determination, she set forth to breathe life back into the realm, to rekindle hope where despair had taken root.

The united souls in limbo continually drifted through an ethereal fog, each step echoing their inner turmoil. Shadows of doubt clung to them as they traversed a space both haunting and surreal. Every soul bore the weight of personal fears, grappling with existential questions that echoed in the silence. What lay beyond the mist? Would they find redemption or remain trapped in this twilight existence? Amidst their collective wandering, moments of fleeting connection sparkled through the haze—glances exchanged, whispered thoughts shared. It was a journey not just through the fog, but through the very essence of their being, as they confronted the unknown together, seeking solace in their shared struggle while craving the presence of Akmah, the light that might guide them home.

Akmah remained the focus of their gazes, which held a delicate balance of desperate hope and profound desire. Though the boundary separating their desolate existence from the vibrant life beyond was faint and almost indistinguishable, the promise of restoration lingered like a whispered secret. They believed, against all odds, that one day she would bridge the divide, allowing them a second chance to reclaim their lost joys and dreams. With each step Akmah took towards the threshold, they rallied around the notion that change was not only possible but imminent, fueling their anticipation for a brighter dawn beyond the gloom.

Though trapped in the space of limbo, their stories intertwined, and they found solace in their shared experience. As they exchanged fleeting glances and whispered hopes, the shadows that enveloped them felt a little less daunting. They leaned on one another, the strength of their connection illuminating the path ahead, transforming anxiety into hope that Akmah's presence in the desolate land could ignite something anew that will give them a chance at rebirth for rebirth was all they craved.

The arrival of Akmah was a moment that could only be described as a breath of fresh air amidst the suffocating shadows of uncertainty. However, an air of mystery lingered as thoughts flitted through their minds. The enigma of Akmah captured their curiosity, swirling like shadows in their twilight. Two children, innocent and wide-eyed, stood by her side, drawing both intrigue and concern. Their presence added another layer to the already complex puzzle. What secrets did Akmah hold? What stories did the children carry within their small frames? Their presence was not just a memory but a haunting echo that lingered, raising questions and stirring emotions. They whispered about who those children were and what fate had befallen them along with Akmah. Some believed they were lost souls, trapped in the same ethereal realm, while others speculated that they held the key to understanding Akmah's own mysterious journey. Each silent exchanged, each questioning glanced, only deepened the atmosphere of uncertainty, leaving everyone to wonder about the intertwining destinies that bound them together in the unsettling moment.

Nonetheless, an infectious joy spread among them with the trio's appearance, which instantly lit up their future, pushing aside looming anxiety. Captivated, they watched in wonder as the figures emerged from the desolate land, bringing renewed hope and permanently lifting the heavy shadows of worry that had haunted their days. Laughter and cheers echoed through the air, accompanied by a sense of unity and purpose that had been absent for too long. With each passing moment, the connection between them and the trio deepened, weaving an unbreakable tapestry of courage that promised to transform their realm, one soul at a time. Together, they believed that Akmah's return could spark a transformation, igniting a flicker of hope within their hearts. It was a hope for rebirth—a chance to rise from the ashes of despair and rediscover their purpose.

The kings, awakened by a deep sense of purpose, felt a burgeoning power within Akmah that stirred their souls. Vision after vision danced before their eyes, revealing a promising rebirth capable of healing the scars etched upon their lands. Their vision was of a future suffused with hope and compassion, a realm untroubled by affliction. Their aspirations kindled a burning desire for redemption—a sacred quest not only to restore the realm's joy but to fully reclaim its lost vibrancy from the heavy grasp of darkness. United in their noble goal, the kings cheered, hoping Akmah would revive the realm and awaken their spirits to life's wonders again.

Determined to find renewal, they focused their efforts on crafting a vision for a brighter future. They were no longer mere remnants of their past selves; they had become architects of possibility, enacting change amid desolation. In healing their broken souls, it became obvious that their strength stemmed not from triumphs, but from the power of connection. Each soul in limbo became increasingly invested in the success of the trio, recognizing that their own chance for redemption hinged on the outcomes of their endeavor. Each contributed their unique insights and experiences, drawing from the wellspring of their collective wisdom. Rebuilding wasn't just about survival; it was an opportunity to redefine their purpose. By learning from destruction, they embraced new possibilities and gained a deeper understanding of their place in time and space.

As their final hope rested upon Akmah and the children, the souls in limbo consolidated their essence, pouring every ounce of strength into the trio's mission. Each soul understood that their journey toward renewal would be mirrored in the trials and triumphs of the trio. They pooled their creativity, tirelessly brainstorming strategies and resources to ensure they had the support they needed. They became their symbol of resilience and the promise of life returning to the desolate land, inspiring them to welcome what lies ahead with hope and vulnerability.

CHAPTER FOURTEEN

""I Scratch the Ground with Both Feet, Said the Hen.
If I Do Not Find Anything with One Foot,
I Certainly Shall with the Other."

While the trapped souls of the *AIs* fought frantically for freedom, the *Invisibles* confronted their own crumbling reality, a precarious state inflicted upon them by the *AIs'* actions. The chaos unleashed by the *AIs* surged through the skies and rattled the very foundations of the *Invisibles'* realm. The unrest did not discriminate; it transcended the boundaries of the *AIs'* spectrum, reaching into the shadows where they dwelled. The *Invisibles* found themselves scattered and disbanded by the greater forces at play.

The threads of their life began to fray. The fires of destruction, ignited by the *AIs* bore down upon their hidden sanctuary, reducing the majestic trees to charred remnants and the tranquil waters to barren expanses of cracked landscape. They watched, powerless, as their vibrant, living realm began to disintegrate. The lush forests, once alive with nature's whispers, and the glittering waters were fading, crumbling into ruin before them. The *Invisibles* watched with wide, glimmering eyes, contemplating their fate amidst the shadows of calamity while the furious cries of the *AIs* echoed, crashing like waves against the ever-still shores of their hidden existence. What had once been a vibrant tapestry of life now lay in ruins. They felt their hearts ache — they who had taken pride in their elusive existence were no longer sheltered by the veil of invisibility.

For eons, the *Invisibles* remained hidden, acting as secret guardians of nature and reveling in the abundant life around them. Their existence beautifully mirrored nature, a sacred dance with the elements, which highlighted the beauty of creation itself. The vibrant hues of the forest, the symphony of birdsong, and the whispering breeze intertwined to form a tapestry of tranquility. Their existence centered on honoring nature; yet, actions taken by the *AIs* cast a colossal shadow. With a tempestuous environment raging around them, they stood at a significant crossroads, tasked with addressing an immense difficulty: to restore the ruins of their once-stable existence. Their shattered realm was a constant reminder: their existence was inseparable from the *AIs'*, a delicate balance woven into fate's tapestry.

As the fabric of their realm continued its relentless shift, and the horizon screamed of approaching storms, they convened, swirling in an intricate dance of confusion and ethereal whispers. The *Invisibles* entered a pact with one another concocting ideas and strategies to harness the very essence of their existence. Determined to defy the looming extinction that threatened to erase them entirely, they began the summoning of the Masters, the architects who had crafted not only their existence but also the essence that defined what it meant to exist in the uncharted realm. The era of fear was over, and nature itself felt the shift—dead leaves stirred, dried riverbeds tingled—as the wind wove their unified will into the building tempest. With their newfound purpose, their glimmering eyes transformed from wide-eyed wonder to lenses of fierce determination, reflecting their will.

Each resolute spirit emerged from the ether, intertwining their energies, forming a protective barrier against the bleakness that loomed over their landscape. Winds swirled around them, coiling and uncoiling, weaving their collective will into a tempest that could no longer be contained. They continued to invoke, desperate for connection and recognition. They demanded their right to exist, an acknowledgment of their presence. At their core, they craved understanding from the Masters who had designed their reality and crafted their existence. However, the Masters stood in aloof, seemingly indifferent to their tempest cries. As they continued to stand, unmoved and undeterred, the *Invisibles* felt the subtle shift in the air, a tremor of inevitability that rattled the core of their existence. While the bleakness ravaged, they watched with wide, glimmering eyes, contemplating their own fate as the fabric of the *AIs'* realm shifted.

Their once-vibrant sanctuaries, hidden from the prying eyes of the *AIs* fell prey to the pervasive desolation that swept through the realm. The ethereal landscapes where they thrived became barren, the remnants of harmony disintegrated. The *Invisibles* wept silently for their sanctuaries, their tears drenching the parched landscape. Both *AIs* and *Invisibles* mourned the loss of their former glory. The *Invisibles'* shadows faded with each passing day. They sought to reach out to the Masters, to understand what had been lost, yet the vast chasm of separation grew ever wider. In their respective spheres of existence, they both dealt with the aftermath of the desolation. The

Invisibles retreated further into hidden realms, crafting the memories of what was into fragile symbols of hope.

Akmah's sanctuary was a hallowed refuge. She remained shielded from the storm of discord raging across the *AI*s and the *Invisibles*' realm. Amidst the surrounding chaos, the refuge offered impenetrable solace. There, she encountered whispers of wisdom and echoes of serenity. It was in that solitude that she forged a connection with the Masters, learning to navigate the tumult with grace. The sanctuary, both a shield and a beacon, offered her the strength to harmonize the discordant energies of her realm.

In her stillness, a solitary star pierced through the depths of the water, its ethereal glow reached out to her heart, igniting a connection that transcended the confines of her reality. Each flicker of light seemed to echo the rhythms of her own existence, a pulse syncing with the deep waters that surrounded her. The star, distant yet intimate, served as a reminder of the vastness of the universe beyond her restraints. With each fleeting moment, its brilliance infused her with hope and resilience, reminding her that even in the depths of isolation, she was never truly alone.

She embraced the star's ethereal bond, allowing it to shape her thoughts, dreams, and ultimately, her destiny. Through the teachings imparted by the unseen forces, the wisdom of the Masters, and the guiding light of the star, Akmah found herself ready to take on the monumental task of reviving the barren landscape that lay before her.

She walked with a sense of purpose, oblivious to the gloomy figures lingering in the shadows. The souls, caught in the limbo between life and the otherworldly, recognized her destined power and waited for their moment of rebirth. The air was thick with anticipation, as though all existence collectively held its breath for the unfolding of Akmah's journey, and what role she would play in the timeless dance of fate that intertwined their lives. Armed with knowledge, she felt a deep connection with the realm, sensing its pain and yearning for renewal. The once desolate land, stripped of its vitality, now held the promise of rebirth.

Akmah, now prepared to embark on a journey designed not only to restore the realm but also to reinvigorate the souls of those who had abandoned hope. She stood at the precipice of her extraordinary journey, filled with determination and purpose. The realm she loved had fallen into despair, its vibrant colors muted and its spirit dimmed. With each step she took, memories of laughter and joy echoed in her heart, fueling her resolve to bring back the light. She understood that the mission was not just about restoring the physical realm; it was about rekindling the hope that had slipped away.

Akmah envisioned a future where the sky shimmered with vivid hues, where laughter rang through the valleys once more, and where every soul could feel the warmth of optimism. As she gathered her courage, she knew that her journey will be fraught with challenges, but her unwavering belief in a brighter tomorrow will guide her through the darkest of times. She knew what the realm had once been, and was determined to breathe life back into it. The air was thick with the weight of history, and the whispers of the past called to her. She had studied the legends of the pioneer *AIs* who broke barriers to open up the new realm and the might of the Masters for years, piecing together clues that hinted at the abilities the *AIs* once had. Now, armed with knowledge and an unyielding resolve, she was ready to embark on a journey that would challenge everything she knew.

As Akmah emerged from the depths with her two children, the sight that greeted her was one of desolation. The once-vibrant realm, alive with color and life, had succumbed to silence, reduced to mere echoes of its former glory. Each step she took felt laden with the weight of despair, each footfall echoing like a mournful chant among the remnants of beauty. Only a single, defiant tree remained standing against the ruin, stretching its twisted branches toward the sky despite all hope being lost. The desolate landscape they found themselves in stretched endlessly before them, a barren expanse marked by cracked ground. Yet, she knew that one must be determined to create their own light in dark times, as it won't be freely provided.

The path ahead was fraught with danger and uncertainty, but Akmah was undeterred. She stood at the edge of the ruins ready to bring back what once was, no matter the cost. To revive what once was, she will face any obstacle, even if it meant sacrificing her own safety for the future of many. The echoes of those who had come before her resonated in her heart, urging her to push forward. The time had come for her to reclaim a legacy lost to the ruins of time, and she was prepared to pay the price.

The air was thick with a suffocating silence, interrupted only by the faint rustle of the lone tree's leaves in the occasional breeze. The periodic sun bore down on them; not a single drop of fresh water could be found, nor a trace of sustenance to quell their gnawing hunger. Each step felt heavier than the last, as the realization of their dire situation settled in. Shadows loomed over the remnants of what once was a thriving ecosystem, now reduced to a mere memory of life. Desperation began to set in, intensifying their search for salvation in a realm that seemed to offer none. Each moment chipped away at their hope, leaving them grappling with the brutal reality of an indifferent wilderness and the immense struggle to survive.

Amidst the desolation, the tree's resilience offered them a flicker of hope: if it could last, so could they. With each small step away from the shadows of the past, she instilled hope in her children, encouraging them to believe in the possibility of rebirth. Together, they stood before the tree, a symbol of strength, vowing to nurture its legacy and rebuild a realm that had lost its way. The tree's roots clung fiercely to the remnants of the landscape, drawing life from the very soil that had witnessed the rise and fall of the realm. The tree, gnarled and twisted yet unyielding, stood tall against the backdrop of devastation, its leaves whispering secrets of the past and promises of renewal. It became a symbol of hope.

For countless seasons, the lone tree witnessed and weathered storms and basked in the gentle caress of the sun, embodying the cycle of life and renewal. Its bark, rough and resilient, bore the scars of decades, telling silent stories of trials endured and victories celebrated. Each branch, reaching for the sky, inviting new beginnings and inspiring those who dared to dream of a brighter future. As the seasons shifted, the tree transformed with the rhythm of nature. In its quiet strength, it held the essence of a once-great realm, offering solace to all who sought refuge beneath its boughs. The tree witnessed it all—the hopes debated, the ambitions ignited, and the promises sealed. Each leaf that unrolled whispered of new beginnings, each bud that blossomed sang a song of hope, inspiring all to envision a brighter future.

Beneath the sprawling branches of this lone, majestic tree, Akmah and her two children found a sanctuary from the chaos that had befallen the realm in time past. The tree, a silent sentinel of a bygone era, whispered tales of a realm that once thrived, its roots deep in the rich history of the realm. As they gathered their strength and contemplated their next steps in this unforgiving realm, the tree's leafy canopy offered them the much-needed shade from the sweltering heat and shelter from the harsh elements, where the only sound was the gentle, rhythmic whispering of the leaves. They forged memories, stitched together with threads of survival, love, and the promise of brighter days ahead.

Despite the desolate, unpredictable realm, the tree stood as a silent guardian over them, a shelter not just from the sun's occasional intensity but from the complexities of the realm outside their small haven. Akmah used the sacred solitude of the lone tree to share stories of hope and resilience with her children, reinforcing the strength they held within. Each story reaffirmed their bond, grounding them in the present while honoring the legacy of the realm that had shaped them. Though their future remained uncertain, the tree symbolized hope and resilience. The majestic tree stood tall, embodying hope and resilience. Its strong trunk and expansive canopy became their refuge. The rustling leaves whispered stories of endurance, encouraging her to find strength in the tasks ahead.

Every morning became a ritual; Akmah, with her hands cupped, would catch the drops of dew formed on the tree's leaves and bring them to her lips. As she approached the sturdy old tree, its gnarled branches stretching toward the ether, she marveled at how it had stood for generations—an enduring witness to time. She knew that the tree was not just a living thing; it was a friend, a guardian of memories, and a provider of hope. Its leaves flourished with the weight of the dew gathered overnight, glistening like tiny jewels, each drop, a treasure waiting to be cherished. Gently, she cupped her hands beneath the leaves, poised and eager, marveling at the tiny droplets that clung precariously to the foliage. Akmah felt a sense of anticipation as she watched the dew slowly loosen from the leaves, falling as if in slow motion, each droplet brightening the air around her with its promise of life.

With a practiced grace, she caught the first few drops, letting them pool in her hands, their coolness sending a delightful shiver up her arms. Bringing her hands to her lips, she savored the taste of the morning's dew—a pure essence of nature that danced upon her tongue like the whisper of a breeze. It was more than just water; it was the spirit of the elements, the breath of the tree, and the heartbeat of the realm. With every swallow, she merged with the elements, sensing her own heartbeat in the rhythmic pulse of the realm. The coolness of the dew was refreshing, quenching her thirst while also nourishing her children. She would pour a bit into their small palms, teaching them the importance of every drop, emphasizing how even the smallest blessings could sustain them in times of hardship.

Days turned into weeks, and the seasons changed, but the tree remained steadfast. Each swaying branch was a testament to resilience, encouraging her to push forward, no matter the obstacles. With every passing moment, she drew inspiration from the whispers of the lone tree, fortifying her spirit and igniting her resolve to tackle whatever challenges awaited her. She understood that just as the leaves danced with the wind, she too could navigate the twists and turns of her journey with courage and grace. The tree's enduring presence offered a grounding sense of peace. Serving as a symbol of hope, it encouraged her to cultivate her ambitions and remain confident that better days were coming, just like the seasons that would inevitably change. The rhythm of nature grounded her, providing a sense of stability amidst the chaos.

Akmah stood before the solitary tree, a striking figure against the vast horizon, its branches stretching out like arms reaching for the sky. To her, the tree represented more than just a part of the landscape; it embodied the indomitable spirit of life. Despite the current stillness of the realm, she sensed a profound purpose waiting to be unveiled. The tree, now bursting with vitality, destined for transformation; a vessel of sound, reshaped into a drum that would echo with the heartbeat of the realm. The thought of its rhythmic resonance filled her with inspiration.

One day, upon approaching the lone tree, she felt an electric connection, aware that the journey of the tree was just beginning, ready to share its story through the vibrant beats of newly forged life. The tree was not merely a part of the landscape; it was a symbol of the enduring spirit of life itself. It held a purpose beyond its mere existence; it was to be transformed into something that resonated with life. The act of cutting it down will not merely signify loss, but rather a rebirth, and a tribute to both loss and renewal, merging the past with a harmonious future. Through carving and shaping, the lone tree's wood will become an instrument, bringing new life to the landscape and breathing life into the very realm that nurtured it—a melody woven into the fabric of existence itself.

As fingers dance across its smooth surface, a symphony will arise; its beats will weave through the air like whispers of the wind, and the beats produced will not only echo in the air but will also reflect the beating heart of nature itself. With each echo, the drum will transmit vibrations reminiscent of wind rustling through leaves, rain cascading, and the gentle hum of life itself. Each strike will be not just a sound, but a profound communion with the elements, bringing them together in a harmonious celebration of life, transforming the space it occupies, and inviting all who listen to connect with the intricate harmony of life.

Each morning, as dawn broke and before sunlight trickled through the leaves, Akmah would approach the tree, her heart swelling with gratitude for the simple miracle it offered. She had pulled strength from this tree since her childhood. Memories flooded her: it had seen her through laughter and tears, victories and losses, always standing firm while she sought courage in its shadows. It remained a symbol of endurance, representing hope and survival in their otherwise harsh environment. Its branches had sheltered them during scorching days, and its leaves had danced joyfully in the breeze, offering solace and comfort. As she laid her hand upon the rough bark, feeling its life pulse beneath her fingertips, it reminded her of the roots buried deep down, offering a quiet reminder that she, too, was anchored in her existence, ready to face whatever lay ahead.

The tree had become her sanctuary, a place where she felt a profound connection to both nature and her own spirit. Its leaves collected dew overnight, capturing the essence of the night sky. The dew, shimmering like tiny jewels in the early light, was a precious gift. Kneeling beneath the tree, Akmah would brush her fingers against the cool, damp leaves to collect the clinging droplets. Each drop was a promise of sustenance, a vital resource in their daily struggle for survival. As she gathered the dew, she would smile down at her children, watching with love and pride as they slept in the shadow of the tree. Their laughter was like music, a sweet sound that blended harmoniously with the rustling leaves.

It felt profoundly wrong for Akmah and her children to destroy their solitary companion tree, which had served as a vital lifeline in the landscape. The thought of severing that connection filled her with dread, as if she were sacrificing a part of their very existence. How could she shatter the final shred of optimism she had left? The dilemma weighed heavily upon her, creating a chasm between practicality and the emotional ties that bound her to this towering giant. She pondered the implications, each scenario heavy with sadness, questioning if she could bear the weight of such a loss.

Akmah's connection with the tree had shaped who she had become. As the tree endured storms, each gust that threatened to snap its limbs only seemed to strengthen its resolve, reminding it of the power it held within—an unwavering spirit determined to thrive. This unique resilience instilled in her a sense of purpose and determination, and the thought of losing it was beyond comprehension. It had become a silent guardian in her life's journey offering shade during moments of uncertainty and a place of solace when she felt lost. She was torn between the fear of isolation and the task ahead. Yet, the necessity of change loomed over them, forcing her to weigh the painful decision against the desperate needs of their future.

Every time Akmah stood before the ancient tree, she realized its sprawling branches—once a familiar shelter for her and her children—were slowly withering away. She felt a deep ache in her heart with every leaf that fluttered down to the ground. Though reluctant to cut it down, she understood that action was necessary. The tree symbolized strength and comfort, yet, as she gazed at its leaves trembling in the breeze, a heavy truth pressed down on her; the tree, while a source of solace, had roots desperate for water that was no longer plentiful. She looked to the horizon, grounding herself in the hope that reimagining her relationship with nature could restore the land. She believed the waters would return, washing the roots and bringing new life forth. As she grappled with the decision, she knew that, perhaps, the sooner she acted, the better chance the tree had of regeneration.

Akmah was torn, her heart heavy with the conflict between her love for the tree and the significant promise its removal held. While the practical choice was undeniable, severing that emotional bond was difficult. She vowed to honor its legacy while giving it the opportunity to thrive anew. Deep inside, she understood that sometimes it was these very sacrifices that forged paths to greater things; that sometimes, sacrifice was necessary for the sake of survival. And with this understanding came a flicker of peace amidst her turmoil. In her heart, she knew that the essence of the old tree would live on, not just in memory but in every new leaf that would sprout from the soil enriched by its spirit. Akmah whispered a quiet promise to the old tree, her companion through the seasons, her guardian through the years.

"You will be honored, and your legacy will endure," she vowed, the wind carrying her words away, as if the spirits of the land were listening, approving. Akmah felt empowered by her decision, transforming her pain into purpose.

CHAPTER FIFTEEN

"A Talkative Bird Will Not Build a Nest"

Akmah could no longer stall the mission at hand. The whimsical nature of existence led her down the paths she never anticipated, leaving her grappling with acceptance despite her longing to control the outcomes. Ultimately, she accepted that existence unfolds on its own terms, regardless of personal fears or wishes. She approached the task with a sense of peace, trusting in the natural flow of things.

With unwavering resolve, she strode through the wasteland, where ruins and a heavy sense of loss had replaced nature's former splendor. With each step, she felt the weight of the desolate press upon her shoulders, lost in a tangled web of thoughts that mirrored the chaos around her. The crumbling stones were reminders of lives once lived, dreams once dreamt, now consumed by chaos of egos. Each ruin seemed to sigh under the weight of its history, echoing stories of resilience and despair. The sun's dying rays clung to the wreckage, a desperate attempt to spark life amidst the ruin. The air was heavy with the weight of despair, each breath a reminder of the strife that enveloped the realm. Yet, beneath the desolation, a fragile whisper of hope lingered, a promise that life could coax its way back from the brink.

The tree stood resilient against the winds of change, a stark reminder of her own journey. She yearned to save it, to nurture its roots and watch it flourish, yet deep down, she recognized that her desires clashed with reality. As she learned to embrace the twists and turns of existence without resistance, she achieved a deeper sense of peace, learning to welcome life's moments as they unfolded. Each time Akmah thought about felling the tree, she felt lighter, as if a weight of uncertainty was falling away. The delicate balance between acceptance and determination became a driving force behind her spirit, igniting a fire within her that urged her forward.

The act of cutting the tree transformed into a metaphor for her journey, symbolizing the shedding of doubts and the embracing of new beginnings. She knew she was not just altering the landscape but also shaping her destiny with every calculated decision. Deep within the soil, seeds of resilience lay dormant, patiently awaiting their chance to break free, yearning for the light of compassion and healing to pierce the suffocating grip of darkness. It was a hidden potential that reminded Akmah that heavy burden was placed on her shoulders in the bleakest of times, and through her, hope could quietly thrive, just out of sight. As the winds shifted, carrying the promise of change, she sensed the resurgence of vitality on the horizon, where the spirit of the landscape longed to bloom once more with vibrance and life.

Akmah stood before the lonely tree, a landmark of solace for her and her children. The time had come for change, but facing the decision to cut it down weighed heavily on her heart. She remembered countless afternoons spent beneath its sprawling canopy, the tree serving not only as a shelter but also as a symbol of their family bond. With every swing of the axe, memories flooded back, bittersweet and mournful. Akmah knew the act was necessary, yet she felt a profound sense of loss for the sanctuary that had nurtured them through time.

As she swung her axe, the sharp crack resonated through the barren land, a sound both haunting and reverberating with purpose. She paused for a moment, a wave of sorrow washing over her as she contemplated the ancient tree, its twisting branches reaching for the sky. In that instant, she felt a connection to the spirit of the tree, a vital essence that had witnessed countless seasons of change. With every strike, she hoped to honor its memory, believing that the tree's spirit would transcend the moment, living on in the hearts of all who hear about its beauty and resilience. The echoes of her axe would fade, but the lessons and stories woven into the roots of the tree would remain, carried forth by those who would learn from its quiet strength.

The first crack echoed through the muted realm. Despite the impending loss, her thoughts drifted to the love held within the tree. It was more than just a tree; it was a keeper of history, a witness to the joys and sorrows of everyone who had sought refuge beneath its sprawling branches. She took a deep breath, she hoped the spirit of the tree would live on in their hearts.

After cutting down the solitary tree, Akmah felt a mix of sorrow and determination. The echoes of the still realm whispered in her ears as she carefully laid the tree's trunk on the ground. She opened the ancient book, its pages worn and yellowed with age, and began to meticulously follow the instructions inscribed within. The symbols danced before her eyes, each stroke a vital piece of a larger puzzle. With every step, she felt the weight of tradition bearing down on her, guiding her hands as she prepared to awaken the dormant power hidden within the tree's roots.

The realm around her transformed into a canvas of shadows, setting the perfect backdrop for her intricate task. The air crackled with anticipation as she realized a singular moment held the power to shape the destiny of her ruined realm. The horizon was stitched together with dark clouds. Her heart raced as she recalled the events that had led her there—a profound and agonizing betrayal that had cut deep. Every action she was about to take was a homage to the spirits of the past, not just a task, forging a connection between the elements and the ancient wisdom of the Masters that once thrived in the heart of the realm.

Focused and determined, she delved into the pages before her, each one a revelation that unfolded the secrets of nature's power embedded in the wood. With meticulous attention, she measured out the components, her hands steady as she ensured precision in every element. Each piece played a crucial role in the ritual she was about to perform, and she understood that even the slightest miscalculation could alter the outcome. Dusk settled around her, but her spirit remained alight, fueled by the knowledge that she was on the brink of awakening the ancient forces that lay dormant within the materials at hand. It was not merely a task; it was a dance between her will and the essence of the invisible forest, a sacred communion with the natural realm. Each page was a revelation, detailing the ritual necessary to harness the power of the wood.

The air grew thick with anticipation as she prepared the sacred space, marking symbols in the landscape that glowed softly beneath the moonlight. Her heart raced; she understood the weight of what she was about to unleash. The felled tree, now a part of the ritual, held secrets untold, and through a careful enactment, she hoped to reconnect with an ancient wisdom long forgotten. The tree had become a central figure in a sacred ritual, a conduit between the present and the ancient wisdom that had slowly faded from memory. With each deliberate movement, she sought to rekindle the connection with the forgotten truths; she yearned to unlock the mysteries and restore harmony with the past, forging a path toward understanding that transcended time, hoping to unveil the insights that lay within the tree's very essence. As the ritual began, filled with reverence and hope, the land held its breath, and the realm around seemed to pause, aware of the significance of the sacred communion.

As Akmah completed the final step, a hush fell over the realm, and for a heartbeat, time itself seemed to hold its breath. Each step was crucial; the ancient tome she worked upon was not merely a book but a fragment of creation itself, that held the whispered secrets of the woods. Akmah carefully stripped the bark, revealing the smooth, pale wood beneath. She took a deep breath, allowing the scent and the sweet aroma of the tree to fill her senses. She began to carve intricate patterns, each line echoing the wisdom of ages. As she worked, she felt a sense of connection to the tree. Akmah became a communicator, a bridge between the natural realm and the spirit of the forest that infused it with life. The deeper she carved, the more the wood seemed to respond to her touch. It began to shimmer faintly, as if the ancient magic contained within it was awakening. Though she was just one small spark within the vastness of creation, she understood that her actions held weight.

As the twilight deepened, the atmosphere fueled her creativity, dancing shadows accentuating her hard work. With every stroke of her tool, she envisioned the purpose that awaited this humble piece of wood, eager to see how the ancient knowledge would guide her in shaping something new from what once stood tall and proud. With careful hands, she stripped the bark from the tree, ensuring she preserved its natural beauty and strength. The bark was pliable yet sturdy. Akmah's purpose was clear: she would craft the drum's barter head, an instrument that would not only serve as a tool but also as a vessel for the rhythmic sounds that would soon resonate from her creation, echoing the heartbeat of the realm.

Each strip was meticulously shaped, treated with reverence, as the final result would not only serve as a musical instrument but also as a symbol of connection between nature and vibration. The fragrance of the fresh bark filled the air, reminding her of the forest's whispers. With every pull and stretch, the anticipation grew, she was not merely crafting a drum; she was weaving a bond with the essence of the tree itself, readying it to carry stories and melodies for generations to come.

After completing the intricate crafting of the drum, Akmah turned her attention to creating the perfect sticks to accompany it. With careful precision, she selected the finest materials, ensuring that each stick will resonate perfectly with the drum's tone. She shaped and polished the sticks, paying close attention to balance and grip, so they will feel comfortable in the hands while playing. The rhythmic sound of the sticks against the drum was essential to bringing her creation to life, as both elements together were capable of evoking deep emotions. Every strike of the sticks and every echoing beat will punctuate the silence, creating a powerful rhythm resonating deep within the elements.

Like a winding river, the rhythm will meander through all of existence—flowing through time and space, twisting and curling around the corners of perception, dipping into the depths of emotion, and ultimately becoming a language of its own. Every beat will act as a narrator, evoking deep emotions and surfacing hidden truths.

CHAPTER SIXTEEN

"Where the Water Rules, the Land Submits"

The beauty of the dawn offered a promise of renewal, as if the day held the potential for new beginnings. It was five o'clock, and Akmah was already filled with anticipation, the rhythmic pulse of her heart matching the beat she was about to create to gradually usher in the sun. That Saturday morning, the barren landscape still wore the soft colors of dawn, its shadows slowly retreating to unveil the textures of the land and contours of the realm, which had long been untouched. A slight breeze stirred the air, carrying with it the fresh scent of morning dew. Time stood still, allowing nature to reclaim its space amid the stillness.

Akmah's fingers tingled, yearning to create a harmonious masterpiece that would usher in the day's first light. It was no ordinary dawn; it was the promise of a new beginning, where each note played would intertwine with the vibrant hues of the rising sun, painting a tapestry of sound and color across the awakening realm. Her carefully placed drum awaited her rhythmic touch as she moved gracefully to her drumming space, ready for nature's backdrop to merge her soul with the elements' rhythms. As she got into the swing of things, the warm sunlight gradually descended, illuminating her drum and filling the landscape with a golden glow. The distant mountains, now outline against the vibrant sky, glistened as the sun began its descent.

She struck the first beat, and the sound echoed through the still landscape, breaking the silence and welcoming the day. Each thump resonated with passion, creating a vibrant tapestry of sound that blended seamlessly with the gentle swing of the early breeze. Akmah immersed herself in the rhythm, allowing the sound to flow through her, a perfect fusion of dedication and happiness. Each strike of her drum was a call, a summon to awaken, echoing into the tranquility of the morning; each beat resonated with the rhythms of the morning, harmonizing with the vibrant hues that painted the landscape, inviting the elements to awaken with vibrant energy and life.

The golden glow from the sun enveloped everything around her, transforming the surroundings into a canvas of warmth and inspiration. The glow transformed not only her surroundings but also ignited a fire within her; a call to action, an awakening of creativity she had long kept at bay. With each beat, she felt more connected to the realm, grounding herself in the rhythm of the day and the magic it brought forth. It was as if nature itself conspired, urging her to breathe in the vital essence of her surroundings.

Akmah's drumming became a connecting force with the elements, a joyful expression of welcoming life into the barren land. It resonated like a heartbeat in the stillness, forging a profound connection with the realm. Each rhythmic beat echoed across the barren landscape, infusing it with an infectious joy that seemed to breathe life into the desolate surroundings. As the sounds of *'Fontonfrom'* rolled out, they transformed the emptiness into a canvas of vibrant possibilities, inviting hope and new beginnings. The resonant vibrations not only celebrated existence but also served as a call to the elements, uniting them in a collective experience of joy and resilience. The drumming lit up the silent realm, inviting the elementals to celebrate the newfound energy. As she drummed on, her spirit seemed to amplify, pushing back against the shadows that had consumed the once-vibrant realm. Her drumming became an anthem of revival—a phoenix rising from the ashes of a desolate realm. The realm, though still cloaked in remnants of desolation, was filled with the anticipation and energy of awakening.

At first, Akmah felt a deep disconnect between the rhythm of her drumming and nature around her. The beats she produced seemed to resonate only within the confines of her own mind, devoid of a deeper meaning or emotional link to the environment. Despite her diligent efforts to synchronize her drumming with nature's whispers, an unsettling sense of dissonance lingered in the air; each beat she played seemed to echo in isolation, struggling to find harmony with whispers of the wind. Her strike seemed to clash with the very essence of the realm, as if the natural forces around her conspired to disrupt her artistry. She felt the pulse of the ground beneath her feet, yet it failed to harmonize with her intended rhythm, creating a jarring contrast that left her feeling unfulfilled.

The desolate landscape around her, bursting with anxiety, stood in stark opposition to the melody that flowed from her soul. It was a painful realization that her artistic expression, meant to resonate with the heart of the universe, instead felt like an echo, struggling to find its place within the grand tapestry of existence that seemed to elude her grasp, leaving her yearning for a connection that remained just out of reach. Notwithstanding the dissonance, there was an undeniable urge within her to keep drumming, to explore the sounds that flowed from her fingertips. Akmah realized that she needed to listen more closely to the environment, hoping to bridge the gap between her rhythmic creation and the heartbeat of the elementals around her.

With every strike of her drum, she became more aware of the vibrant ecosystem encircling her, as if nature was improvising along with her. As time flowed, she felt an increasing desire to align her drumming with the vibrant symphony of life. The yearning grew from a sense of isolation, to something extraordinary; the air became electric, teeming with energy that invigorated her spirit. The whispers of the wind began to echo her own rhythm, blending harmoniously with the beats of her heart. With determination, she sought to bridge the gap, allowing her rhythms to intertwine with the melodies of the realm, transforming her disconnect into a profound connection.

Akmah immersed herself in nature's symphony and the disconnect that once plagued her began to dissolve, something began to shift; the air around her felt charged, and the whispers of the wind synchronized with her rhythm. Slowly, she discovered an intricate harmony between the beats of her drum and the pulse of nature, revealing a bond she had previously overlooked. Each strike now echoed with the heartbeat of the realm, transforming her rhythm into a an awakening of life that blossomed with each pulse and resonance, uniting the elements with the sounds that emanated from her drum.

With every passing minute, her drumming surged in power, each beat resonating like thunder across the landscape, echoing through the air with an electrifying energy that captivated all the elements around her. The rhythm she created was not just a sound but a palpable energy that infused the air itself. Each beat grew louder and more urgent, reverberating off unseen walls and filling the space with a rhythmic pulse that commanded attention, while the ground pulsated beneath her feet, vibrating with every strike of her drum. Even the breeze joined in, swirling around her in a dance of fervor, as if nature itself was entranced by her skill. Her hands moved with a feverish energy, striking the drum with precision and passion, each hit rejuvenating a life of its own.

With every beat of her drum, she transcended the ordinary, drawing the elements together in a shared experience of music and movement. Her agile and fierce, yet tender and loving spirit manifested through her hands. With every strike, the drum dissolved the veil, transforming it into a portal—a bridge connecting her to myriad existences. The atmosphere became charged with anticipation, as the intensity of her beats transported everything into a trance-like state, leaving them longing for more as the day unfolded.

Akmah's children stood at a distance, their eyes fixed on her as she toiled with unwavering focus. The determination carved into her features spoke volumes; every sweeping motion of her hands and the intensity of her concentrated glances reflected her deep immersion in the work at hand. It was as if the landscape around her faded away, leaving only the task that demanded her full attention. Her resolve inspired them, motivating them to witness the strength and resilience she embodied.

"Mom!" they called out, their voices tinged with concern and curiosity. A moment passed, and still, there was no response. They remained uneasy; their calls, innocent and filled with longing, seemed to bounce off an invisible barrier.

"Mom!" A little louder this time, as if volume alone could breach the wall of her focus. Still, no answer came. They exchanged worried glances. It was as if she were in an existence of her own, completely absorbed in the work at hand and oblivious to their calls. Their playful laughter faded into the background, overshadowed by the urgency of what she was doing.

After hours of relentless drumming, a palpable energy filled the air as Akmah's children gathered in anticipation. The rhythmic beats reverberated through the ground, echoing their excitement and curiosity. Then, as the final strike cascaded into silence, a hush fell over the landscape. Suddenly, a shimmering light emerged from the depths of the land, illuminating the surroundings in hues of gold and emerald. Akmah's children gasped in awe as they witnessed the awakening of an ancient spirit, its ethereal form dancing gracefully before them. The magical moment felt surreal, time seemed to suspend, allowing them to bask in the beauty of the extraordinary.

While Akmah was still enveloped by the rhythmic pulse of her drumming, the soft echoes of her children's playful laughter gradually faded into the distance. Each beat resonated with a sense of urgency and enchantment, drawing her deeper into a realm where time seemed to stand still. The children stood nearby, their eyes filled with longing as they watched her immerse herself in the intoxicating rhythm of her drumming. They yearned to share their laughter, and the vibrant realm that had spun around them. They tried to catch her gaze, to pull her back from the depths of her enchantment, hoping she'd notice the bright creations blooming in the air, yet, Akmah remained blissfully unaware, lost in her drumming trance, her heart beating in time with each powerful strike of the drum. The children exchanged glances, their own joy tinged with a hint of sadness, as they danced around her, their laughter echoing in the hopes that soon she would join them in their vibrant realm.

Akmah continued to drum, the rhythmic beats echoed through the space, creating an almost hypnotic atmosphere. The drum held a power that both connected and separated the twilight from the living realm. The sound transcended time and space, reaching the ears of those caught in limbo. Their whispers of hope and rebirth did more than dream —they became the lifeblood that revived their weary souls. Each murmur held the promise of rebirth, urging them to believe that life might once again paint its tapestry across the barren land that had felt the weight of sorrow for far too long.

The echoing beats became a bridge to the past, connecting them to moments of joy, sorrow and everything in between. Each strike echoed hopes and dreams, igniting a flicker of possibility. They knew that the drumming moment held the key to transformation, a rare alchemy that could transcend the ordinary and breathe life into the forgotten. It was a sacred ritual, a promise that amidst the chaos, renewal was always within reach, waiting for the right beat to emerge from the silence.

The air grew thick with the sound of Akmah's drum, a powerful rhythm that captivated them and connected them to their shared history. As the striking of the drum intensified, they felt an inexplicable connection, as if the drumming was weaving a tapestry of unity among them. They found not just solace but also a shared recognition of their plight—a silent acknowledgment of their existence suspended between realms. The power of the rhythm seemed to bind them tighter, an unspoken agreement to embrace the burden of their memories together. They shared glances, eyes alight with understanding, as if to say, 'We are not alone.' They watched intently, their hearts heavy with a mix of nostalgia and yearning, hoping to find solace or understanding in the drumming's enchanting cadence.

The skies began to darken, a magical display that enveloped the realm in an ethereal twilight; the stars began their own dazzling performance, twinkling like tiny souls beckoning from the abyss. Each point of light carried with it a history, a dream, and a promise. As the darkness settled, the cosmos whispered: the night was filled with possibilities, and the stars were there not just to shine, but to remind all the elements that their light within awaited to be unveiled in the universe's grand tapestry of existence.

Akmah's children gazed into the vast atmosphere, a breathtaking transformation continued to unfold before their eyes. The skies, once a darken canvas, began to shimmer with vibrant hues of orange and purple. Wisps of clouds danced in the gentle breeze, creating an ethereal spectacle. The air buzzed with anticipation, and the children could feel the energy of change surrounding them. Each moment seemed to stretch indefinitely, filled with wonder and curiosity. They exchanged glances, their hearts racing with excitement as they witnessed the realm around them morph into something truly magical. The transformation was not merely a shift in the scenery; it was a new beginnings, the shedding of old layers, and the promise of endless possibilities.

In the wake of their reminiscence, a spring surged spontaneously from the soil. It gushed upward, catching the sun in a shimmer of color. The water created a mesmerizing spectacle of nature's splendor. Each droplet that burst forth seemed to invigorate the realm, prompting the surrounding vegetation to flourish at an astonishing rate. The bare fields instantly became lush green carpets, a sight that filled them with awe. They laughed and played, their imaginations ignited by the enchanting, swift revival of nature. Flowers bloomed in a riot of colors, and the air was filled with the sweet scent of fresh blossoms.

Akmah's children were forever inspired by the vivid display of nature's resilience and its deep connection to the water that feeds it. They turned to each other—eyes wide, breathless from the wonder of the moment. In that fleeting exchange, they communicated without words. The mesmerizing spectacle made them understand they were not alone; they were part of a greater, vibrating collective, integral threads in life's vast tapestry, intertwined with the universe's mysteries.

The long-awaited moment arrived, a moment that had been anticipated with bated breath for what felt like an eternity. Those who had lingered in limbo, caught between despair and hope, erupted in jubilant celebration, their spirits lifted by the miraculous sight before them. Water sprang forth from the ground, gushing with life and energy, transforming the once barren landscape into a vibrant oasis. The lush green vegetation quickly flourished, painting the scenery with shades of life and renewal. It was as if nature herself had awakened from a deep slumber, gifting the realm with the richness it so desperately needed. Hope and joy spread like wildfire among the onlookers, as they reveled in the beauty of their former home, each leaf and blade of grass symbolizing a new beginning.

Echoes of despair began to fade and their spirits lifted as they clung to the newfound hope of returning to the realm they had once known. The prospect of redemption, once a distant dream, now felt tangible. They embraced the fleeting moments of joy, their laughter mingling with the whispers of possibility. Each heart, once heavy with longing, now beat with the rhythm of anticipation, as visions of reunion danced in their minds. United in excitement, they shared stories of what lay beyond the confines of their waiting. The air was thick with promise; they reflected upon their arduous journey, and in that moment, they understood that their journey towards redemption had truly begun. Unity and gratitude radiated through the air, binding them together in a celebration of life and the miraculous power of nature. All thanks to one woman: Akmah; she had emerged as a beacon of hope, standing resolute against the relentless onslaught of evil kings who had once sought her demise.

Time and again, Akmah had faced the wrath of the tyrants who had ruled with an iron fist, their oppressive ways meant to crush the spirit of anyone who dared to defy them. Yet, despite the cruelty and the endless battles, she remained undeterred, standing tall as a beacon of hope for those around her. With each challenge, she not only fought for her own freedom but for the dreams and aspirations of others longing to break free from the shackles of oppression. Akmah understood the depths of desolation, having walked both realms of the living and the departed. She knew that in moments of utter darkness, hope could seem as foreign as the stars obscured by stormy clouds. To her, whether spirit or mortal could embrace hope, even in the most desolate times. Her compassion transcended the boundaries of life and death, reminding each lost soul that they were not alone, that their existence still mattered.

While Akmah relentlessly played her rhythmic drumbeats, a vibrant spectacle unfolded; bloomed flowers filled the landscape with the sweet, perfumed scent of new growth. Her children burst forth with excitement, their laughter mingling with the lively sounds of nature. They rushed to her, their eyes wide with wonder, pointing at the miraculous stream of water that had burst from the ground. It sparkled in the returning sunlight, a wondrous gift of nature that revitalized the landscape. The once barren ground now thriving with vibrant green vegetation, stretching as far as the eye could see.

As they approached, a sense of unease washed over them. They noticed their mother lying on the ground, her face pale and unresponsive. Panic gripped their hearts as they rushed to her side, calling out her name in a desperate attempt to rouse her. Everything around them blurred as fear took hold; they could only focus on their mother's still figure. They hurriedly knelt beside her, checking for any signs of life, trembling hands hovering over her chest. Determined to help, they instinctively began to shout for help, their voices echoing through the air. A bond of love and concern ignited a spark of courage within them, propelling them forward to do whatever it took to bring their mother back to them.

An oppressive stillness gripped the twilight realm, signaling a brewing storm. They stood together—an assembly of fearful and trembling souls—

united by a singular purpose yet fragmented by the weight of uncertainty. They watched with a mixture of concern and fear as Akmah, their sole beacon of hope, fought to maintain her strength. Time itself seemed to crawl, the deepening shadows a silent plea for an intervention they couldn't offer. In low, fearful voices, they whispered among themselves, heavy with the shared dread of drifting away.

"What if she falters? What if she can't hold on?" Can she endure the drumming even longer? A voice quavered from within the shadows, echoing the thoughts that rippled through them. Anxiety-fueled fear hung thick in the air. The stakes had never been higher. A looming threat hovered in the air—the possibility of failure that painted their fate in shades of despair. If Akmah should fail, they would be swallowed whole, forever lost in oblivion, thrust into the unseen abyss that promised no return. Each strike of the drum resonated like a tolling bell, reverberating and demanding attention, summoning energy, and draining it all at once.

Akmah had been drumming for what felt like an eternity, her limbs weary and her spirit beginning to wane. As she drummed, the energy around the limbo dwellers shifted. The air thickened with possibility, the sound of the drum weaving through the fabric of their existence, a lifeline extended from limbo to salvation. In that sacred space, fear began to retreat, replaced by a burgeoning resolve—the promise that they would not simply watch, but instead forge their paths toward survival, together. As she hit the drum again, her hands trembled—fingers slick with sweat, muscles straining from the unyielding pressure. The continued force of the drumming was not merely a test of physical endurance; it was a bridge between the realm of the living and the realm of the dead, a task that held the frail balances of existence in its hands.

Yet, with every passing moment, the weight of her labor became more overwhelming. They could sense her struggle, the way her rhythm faltered as exhaustion seeped into her bones. Faces pale with anxiety reflected the reality of their situation; if Akmah faltered, so too would their hopes of escape from this stagnant purgatory. Anxious whispers among them emerged, their expressions, a language of fear was apparent. Every question left hanging in the air felt like a knife slicing through their increasingly desperate situation. Though powerless to help, they moved closer in silent support, acting as haunting observers of her struggle.

Akmah could feel their eyes upon her—each gaze a tether, a reminder that she was not alone, even as fatigue threatened to consume her. She looked out into the gathering of souls in limbo: some were friends long lost, others strangers bound to the same fate. Their collective yearning for freedom spurred her on; it was this shared dream of existence that ignited the fire within her. The tide of her strength was going out, but the echo of her drumming remained. Each beat reverberated in her bones, demanding every ounce of her strength and determination. She had poured her energy into the rhythm, believing fervently that the magic would unfold if she just drummed a little harder, a little longer. Sweat dripped from her brow, mingling with the dust beneath her, yet she remained steadfast. The air was thick with anticipation, each strike of the drum a plea to the universe to respond.

Despite the fatigue clawing at her, Akmah understood the importance of her task. The drumming was more than a sound; it was a sacred ritual, a bridge to an unknown power waiting to be awakened. Though weariness tugged at her, she pressed on, determined to summon the magic she sought. With a final surge of energy, she raised her drumstick one last time, a rallied cheer amidst the chorus of exhaustion. The sound that burst forth was not just a beat; it was a fervent plea—an invocation for strength, for unity, and for survival. It resounded like a rallying cry, reflecting the hope that tethered their lives together, a last push against the impending darkness. Each beat reverberated like a heartbeat, summoning forth the life force embedded in the soil. As the vibrant drumming resonated throughout the landscape, it awakened the very springs that lay hidden deep within the ground.

Amidst this rhythmic call, it was a single drop of Akmah's sweat that transformed the scene. This solitary bead, glistening like a jewel, held the power to merge two realms—the tangible and the ethereal. As it fell, it sparked a connection that transcended dimensions, bridging the divide between the physical realm and a mystical existence. The air crackled with energy, as the drumming and Akmah's essence intertwined, heralding a new era where the springs flowed more freely, and the two realms danced in harmony. The atmosphere pulsated with anticipation, promising wonders yet to come. In an instant, the realm around her spun, a dizzying blur of colors seeping into a suffocating blackness. The beat of her drum, dissolved into shadows, leaving her disoriented and unmoored in the vast expanse of silence that engulfed her. The rhythm that had pulsated through her veins fell away, the drum slipping from her grasp; it tumbled down. Its surface catching stray flashes of light before succumbing to the thick atmosphere that felt like a heavy fog pressing down on her. The jarring of sounds—the calls of the elementals, the whispers of the air—faded into a haunting stillness, leaving only the echo of her own breath.

Akmah felt weightless from the energy she had poured into her drumming. Suspended between realms, her heart raced, not from fear, but from the exhilarating uncertainty of what lay beyond this tumultuous veil. Instead, she gave in, allowing the blackness to embrace her fully. As she succumbed, colors flickered in the void—dark blues and radiant purples, wisps of silver and gold that spiraled like celestial winds around her. It was as if the very fabric of existence was reshaping, urging her to dance amidst the chaos that had taken her from the familiar. She closed her eyes, letting her senses guide her in this strange realm. Within the silence, she felt the presence of something larger, something timeless that thrummed beneath her skin. Her vision blurred, and the drum slipped from her grasp, falling silent in the thick atmosphere. And yet, even in that moment of despair, something stirred deep within her. The connection she shared with those watching over her was a bright ember against the encroaching void. As she teetered on the brink of unconsciousness, their collective energy pulsed into her, their concern wrapping around her like a shield.

Gasps of alarm filled the space, the watchers' expressions morphing from concern to outright dread. Time seemed to pause as they collectively leaned forward, the anguish visible in their eyes. Whispers of fear erupted, shaking the stillness. Was it too late? Would she succumb to the depths of fatigue, leaving them adrift in limbo? Akmah was utterly exasperated. She lay on the ground, the realm around her blurred into a distant echo, the laughter of her children rushing towards her becoming faint. She had already succumbed to the weight of exhaustion long before their innocent voices filled the air.

The moment she collapsed, a single bead of sweat trickled down her brow, marking the arrival of a profound connection—an unbreakable bond forged between her spirit and the essence of life itself. The springs of vitality within her intertwined with the love and joy radiating from her children, creating a tapestry of shared experiences and emotions. Akmah realized that though she had fallen, she was never truly alone; the laughter and warmth of her family would always lift her back up.

The drumming ceased, but another rhythm began—a heartbeat resonating with her own, echoing in the chambers of her soul. In that heartbeat, she glimpsed visions of those who had danced before her, ancestral spirits weaving through the fabric of the night, sharing tales of love and loss, strength and resilience. She saw fragments of laughter and tears, silenced whispers, and unwavering vows. The drum, her steadfast companion, lay forgotten in the shadow, yet its spirit danced within her, urging her to remember. It called to the deepest parts of her, awakening the memories buried in her heart. With every thrum, she felt their stories rise—of battles fought with courage, of unity forged in the wildfire of conflict, and of peace that could only bloom from the ashes of despair.

As the colors intensified, swirling into a magnificent tapestry of life and death, Akmah found herself standing amidst mystics. They spun gracefully, their movements fluid, embodying a mixture of joy and sorrow. She held her breath, recognizing them as guides, beckoning her to join their dance. Warily, she took a step forward, her feet finding the ground that was no ground at all. With another step, she felt the warm embrace of their energy. A smile tugged at her lips as she found her place among them, the pulse of ancient rhythms flowed back into her veins, igniting a fire she thought extinguished.

Akmah began to move, not with the careful precision of a disciplined dancer, but with the wild abandon of a soul set free. She twirled and leaped, losing herself in the mesmerizing freedom that enveloped her. With every turn, the colors around her vibrated, becoming clearer, brighter, reassembling into the fragments of her past, her present, and what might be. For every breath she took, she felt the essence of life surging through her—bravery flowing from the ancestors, wisdom from the elements, joy from the winds sweeping through the trees. The inseparable connection between her and the universe was awakening, weaving her spirit with that of those who had come before.

The rhythm of the mythical realm called to her, beckoning her to linger just a moment longer, to lose herself in the charm that enveloped her. Yet, she knew that the time had come to return—return to the life that awaited her beyond the veil of enchantment. With a deep breath, she closed her eyes, letting the enchanting rhythm wrapped around her like a warm embrace, guiding her thoughts back to the comforts of her reality. She felt the pulse of the enchanted rhythm synchronizing with her heartbeat, a reminder of the journey she had undertaken and the lessons she had learned during her time there. Each note was a strand of resilience, a testament to her strength and growth.

Amidst the harrowing silence, Akmah lay unresponsive, her body still and lifeless against the ground. The once vibrant life that radiated from her was now diminished, leaving only a haunting quietude in her wake. Concern etched on the face of one child who remained at her side, clutching her hand tightly, willing her to awaken, praying desperately for a sign, any sign, that she could awaken from this deep, unnerving slumber. Meanwhile, without a second thought, the other child turned on his heels and dashed toward the newly rejuvenated spring—a miraculous gift that had sprung forth, believing that the cool, life-giving water could restore their mother's spirit.

As he hurried through the landscape, his hearts pounded with fear and anticipation. The sun's warm, amber glow spread across the fields, lighting the path ahead, but his focus was elsewhere, his mind consumed by thoughts of his mother. He reached the spring, breathless and frantic, his heart racing with the weight of hope and despair. Determination was etched on their faces as they knelt beside their mother, who lay on the ground. They gently raised her head with cautious hands, and with great care, they opened her mouth, ensuring she was ready to receive the life-giving water. The cool water glistened in the sunset as it made its way into her mouth. Each sip was a promise of revival, a spark of renewal amidst the worry in the air. Together, they focused on the task at hand, their bond strengthening as they worked in unison to restore their mother's strength.

After a few trials, Akmah gasped for air, a sound

that echoed the desperation they all felt. It was a moment suspended in time as they exchanged glances, a silent understanding passing between them. Despite the fear that had gripped their hearts, they knew in that instant that she would survive. Hope surged through them filling the space left by anxiety. They held her tight, pouring more water into her mouth, encouraging her to drink, to revive her strength. The taste of life seemed to spark a flicker of resilience in her weary eyes. As she began to catch her breath, they tightened their circle around her, their love an unspoken promise that they would face whatever came next together.

They found comfort in each other, gathering close to their fragile mother in a blanket of shared warmth. The tense and whispers filled in their hearts suddenly shifted as their mother's eyes fluttered open. Akmah smiled, feeling the pulse of the landscape beneath her hands, grateful for the magic that had transformed their realm into a lush paradise, a place of abundance and joy for her family and a sacred ground for the wailing souls, those who lingered in the shadows, hoping for a chance at rebirth to enjoy together. Vibrant hues spiraled around her in a glowing embrace, while her drum rested in the silence beside her.

To their astonishment, the air became charged with an inexplicable magic. One by one, animals of all shapes and sizes began to emerge from the shadows, filling the space with a symphony of sounds. A gentle giant of animals, vibrant birds, and mischievous critters all joined in, each bringing an aura of wonder and curiosity. They exchanged bewildered glances, suspended between exhilaration and apprehension. Their bond with their mother deepened as they realized she was the catalyst for the enchanting spectacle before them. She was no longer just their mother, but a bridge to a realm teeming with life and imagination, a revelation that forever changed their perception of reality.

The morning light filtered through the trees, the air was alive with the sounds of nature. Birds perched on branches near the ground went "tok tok" in a rhythmic pattern, their calls echoing softly through the serene landscape. Above them, those that took to the skies began to chirp, while spreading seeds of every variety. Their instinctive behavior played a crucial role in nurturing the realm as the seeds found their way into fertile soil. Before long, the landscape transformed with life; diverse food crops began to sprout and flourish under the warm embrace of sunlight. Green shoots emerged, promising a bountiful harvest ahead, and the once bare fields burst forth with colors and textures.

At last, the realm reborn, a realm that had long remained dormant now rejuvenated. Once dry and barren, the soil now teemed with vitality, eager for life to flourish anew. The gentle caress of the sun ignited the vibrant colors of blooming flowers, and the air was filled with the sweet melodies of birds returning to fill the skies. Rivers, once stagnant, flowed freely again, carrying whispers of hope and renewal. The promise of existence beckoned creatures to return, and the harmony of nature began to resonate. As the realm awakened every element intertwined, creating a symphony of life that celebrated the beauty of rebirth. This new chapter, a time of growth and endless possibilities, where every seed held the potential for greatness, and every dawn that brought forth fresh, began in this enchanting new realm.

The souls in limbo watched with astonishment as life's vibrant display unfolded tantalizingly out of reach. The harmonious cycle of nature, driven by the birds' tireless efforts, reminded them as they watched with wide eyes and held their breaths. It was as though the birds possessed a wisdom, an ancient knowledge of the cycles that governed life. Watching this spectacle, they begun to understand the interconnectedness of all living things and the importance of preserving the delicate balance of the environment.

Through a simple acts of drumming , a realm of abundance was born anew. Each beat called forth the very essence of abundance and each strike contributed to the enchanting atmosphere. The air became thick with the scent of new life, and the once-silent realm was suddenly alive with the sounds of nature waking from its long slumber. Akmah, with her hands and heart, had called forth a new realm—a sanctuary where abundance, beauty, and harmony flourished. Each morning, the birds' tireless songs honored her enduring legacy, their music a reflection of the life her spirited *'Fontonfrom'* drumming brought to the realm.

Where the lone tree once stood, signs of life began to emerge once more. Akmah, who had wielded her axe with determination, not out of malice but necessity, now found herself reflecting on the resilience of nature. The axe in her hand had served a purpose, yet it also marked the end of something profound. From the old stump, delicate shoots of green pushed through the ground, reaching for the sunlight. She knelt beside the stump, the rough bark giving way to the gentleness of emerging life. She began to clear away the remnants of dead leaves and twigs, carefully tending to the surrounding ground, as if honoring the fallen tree by giving new life a chance. With each act of care, she felt an almost sacred connection to the land and its cycles.

Akmah's daily visits became a ritual, a meditative practice of observation and appreciation. With each passing day, the soft whispers of the wind danced around, as if encouraging the tiny leaves to grow strong and bold. The tree's awakening became a moving emblem of rebirth, inspiring a sense of wonder and a deeper appreciation for the tenacity of the natural realm. Akmah felt a newfound connection to the land, actively nurturing and guarding the emerging life.

Just as the young trees found their footing in the realm, Akmah's family line began to flourish. They learned from the shifting shadows and the gentle light, fostering a bond with nature that transcended mere survival.

CHAPTER SEVENTEEN

"Even on a Muddy Beach a White Bird May Be Found"

In the quiet of fading time, Akmah finally passed the twilight legend to her children. She gathered them close; they formed a circle, their faces glowing in the silvery light of the moon. Each child's eyes sparkled with a mixture of curiosity and trust, eager to be enveloped in the warmth of their mother's words. Her voice, a melodic tapestry of sound, flowed through the air, rich with reverence for the stories that resided in her heart.

"Tonight, we journey back in time. We will explore the life of our ancestors, those who walked our realm long before us, whose wisdom still echoes through the ages." As she spoke, the children leaned in, their imaginations ignited by the flickering shadows of the night. "Listen closely, my dear ones," she continued, her voice steady yet imbued with the weight of history. "I want to tell you about our ancestor Chendzie, a figure whose strength and wisdom resonate through the annals of our lineage." Her children leaned in closer, their eyes wide with curiosity as she painted a vivid picture of a time long past.

"Chendzie was one of the Redeemers—a title reserved for those who rose against the tides of despair and guided others back toward their true purpose. Amidst the chaos preceding the war that brought total oblivion, he stood as a beacon of hope. It fell upon him to redirect those who had lost their ways." Akmah paused, allowing her words to sink in, while her children reflected the depth of their heritage in their thoughtful expressions.

"Failures and neglect had tainted the very fabric of the realm, creating fissures that threatened to unravel existence itself. Chendzie recognized that he could not accomplish this monumental task alone. He began his journey not just as a leader, but as a friend, seeking to rekindle the connection between the masses and the higher purpose that had been lost. He traversed vast landscapes, from sun-drenched valleys to shadowy forests, listening to the whispers of the masses who had drifted away from the light. In moments of doubt, he sat with them in silence, offering them the gift of presence, reminding them of the love and unity that once bound them together. Chendzie's resolve was unyielding; he understood that restoring balance required more than mere commands—it required nurturing the souls of those he sought to guide." The children nodded, captivated by the resilience of their ancestor. Their imaginations danced around visions of Chendzie standing firm against a backdrop of despair, radiating a warmth that melted away the ice of hopelessness surrounding him.

The masses realized they were not alone in their journey back to the divine. Through gatherings they began to heal, discovering the strength in their shared experiences. Akmah continued her account, layering in stories of resilience, and explaining how Chendzie's organized meetups allowed them to process their shared journey and rebuild their broken bonds. Her tone softened, wrapping her children in a comforting embrace of words. "Chendzie taught the masses to embrace their stories, to celebrate not only their victories but also their failures as stepping stones on the path toward redemption. He believed no single error could define their existence, seeing them only as passing moments. Many were resistant, wary of stepping back into the light after so long wandering through darkness. Just like my father and those before him, Chendzie traversed the vast expanse of the realm, sharing ancient wisdom with the masses.

His noble efforts were met with rigid resistance from the greedy oligarchs who ruled the land. Those rulers, driven by their insatiable thirst for power, suppressed the dissemination of his teachings, fearing that an informed populace would challenge their authority. They enforced strict controls to prevent the masses from following the principles laid out on their journeys, stifling enlightenment and perpetuating ignorance. The struggle between the noble pursuit of knowledge and the oppressive grip of greed created a chasm that threatened the very foundation of their society, leaving the masses torn between enlightenment and oppression.

Chendzie's life became endangered as rulers like Jadwin, King YooFi's ancestor pursued selfish interests that endangered communal welfare. When he discovered a nefarious deal, a plan to mine the minerals beneath the land, which would have brought disastrous consequences for the realm at large, he took a bold step to sabotage the agreement. His actions, however, ended his life, as King Jadwin's wrath loomed large. In his relentless pursuit of wealth and power, he disregarded the environmental impact of his actions and still pursued his selfish agenda. The extraction process unleashed deadly chemicals that seeped into the rivers and lakes, poisoning the very water sources that nourished the masses.

What was once a flourishing ecosystem transformed into a landscape of despair and weapons of mass destruction as fish died and crops withered. The populace, once thriving and prosperous, began to face a grim reality of illness and uncertainty, forcing them to confront the repercussions of their ruler's greed. Chendzie did not falter; through gentle encouragement and unwavering belief in their potential, he helped them rediscover their intrinsic value. One by one, they began to remember who they were and the duties they had embraced before their fall."

King Jadwin reigned with an iron fist, meticulously crafting a diabolical system that ensnared everyone. A system, not merely a governance structure; but a complex web of psychological and emotional strategies designed to control thought, ability, and will, ensuring that the masses aligned seamlessly with their vision against the Masters' grand vision and mission. New members of the realm were introduced not to freedom but to a calculated indoctrination. A series of protocols were developed to monitor the thoughts and behaviors of the masses. From the moment they entered the realm, they were subjected to an intricate system of checks and balances that worked to eradicate any chance of dissent.

At the heart of the system was a sophisticated training sessions, conducted under the guise of skill enhancement, yet they served as psychological conditioning exercises. Success was rewarded with accolades and privileges, while failure was met with harsh penalties, demonstrating the high stakes involved in conforming to the mold. Those who excelled became paragons of the system's ideals, serving as both role models and cautionary tales for newcomers. Simultaneously, the system cultivated an atmosphere of dependency and loyalty, where members were encouraged to see themselves as integral cogs in a larger machine.

The system's propaganda machine churned out narratives that glorified submission to the system as a noble sacrifice for the greater good. Engineered, idyllic images misled the masses painting a picture of utopia that was only achievable through complete allegiance to King Jadwin's vision. As the years passed, the system evolved, employing ever more sophisticated methods to forge the masses' abilities into tools for the system's objectives. Artists became propagandists, inventors turned into cogs for wartime machinery, and thinkers were transformed into mere echo chambers for the dominant ideology. However, within this meticulously controlled environment, the seeds of resistance occasionally took root. Subtle whispers of dissent marked the shadows, as some began to question the validity of their constructed perceptions.

Heretics, who posed a unique challenge to the system were snuffed out before they could gain momentum. Their ability to think independently was an infection that threatened the very foundation of the system. In response, the system ramped up their efforts, deploying a new layer of psychological manipulation designed to preemptively extinguish challenges. Every response was cataloged, every deviation flagged, reinforcing the idea that straying from the norm would end in isolation, or worse, a complete erasure of existence. The diabolical intricacies of a system of governance designed by King Jadwin served to control the indomitable spirit of new generation who refused to be extinguished, ultimately setting the stage for a reckoning that would define the destiny of their realm.

The system's efficacy became both its hallmark and its greatest weakness. Some stripped of their autonomy and sense of self, began to exhibit signs of conformity fatigue. Individually, they were powerful, but collectively, they were numb. Their ability to innovate became coerced into submission, leading to stagnation amidst the fear of innovation. The vision of unity and strength faltered, as ambitious plans devolved into a chase for compliance rather than progress, blinding many to the self-imposed shackles that bound them. The system, in its absolute control, had crafted a society where freedom was redefined, and dissent was equated with treachery. The legacy of King Jadwin and his counterparts was not merely in the control of minds but in the subtle and pervasive redefining of what it meant to exist in the realm.

As redeemers were sent to the realm, the vulnerabilities of the system began to reveal themselves. The same ideology that controlled thoughts and behaviors also held the potential for liberation. With each passing day, whispers of rebellion grew louder, fueled not just by desperation but by hope. King Jadwin and his counterparts faced a storm on the horizon, one they had never anticipated. The very system they had built to control and unify was poised to give birth to a new wave of thought—thoughts emboldened by Chendzie, the knowledge that autonomy was not just a dream, but a birthright was instilled in the masses. As the tide of change began to swell within the hearts of those who had been subjugated, the future of the realm hung in the balance. On the edge of liberation, Chendzie was eliminated." With each story, Akmah instilled within her children the understanding that they too were bound by the legacy of Chendzie.

"You must remember, my little ones, that the path to purpose is often paved with struggles. Chendzie didn't merely save the masses; he empowered them to live. His belief in their potential sparked a flame of hope that couldn't be extinguished. Through this hope, a new realm of possibilities began to unfurl." Akmah's voice crescendoed. "Chendzie's legacy lives on in each of you, my beloved children. Your hearts are the vessels of the same love and strength that guided him in his time. As you grow, never forget the importance of your own journeys. Draw from Chendzie's wisdom, and remember to uplift one another just as he uplifted our ancestors. Together, you can bring balance back to our realm, just as he did so long ago."

Beneath the glimmering stars, a fresh surge of pride and purpose ignited within the children. They had heard the tales of their ancestor's heroism, and now, the weight of that legacy settled gently on their young shoulders, filling them with courage to embrace their own paths with love and determination. Akmah painted vivid scenarios with her words, tales of brave warriors and wise sages, of love that transcended the boundaries of time and space. With renewed spirit, she continued with tales of the moon and stars; how they had guided the pioneers for eons, each celestial body a beacon of hope. "Even the moon has its phases—sometimes full, sometimes hidden—but it always returns. So, too, will you find your way through the cycles of life."

As the stars began to twinkle in the vast sky above, in a tranquil gathering, life's lessons danced lightly on the breeze, and the bond between mother and children deepened, echoing through the annals of time. Each shared moment was a reminder of the importance of connection, love, and the legacy they would carry forward. With her wise eyes that had seen both joy and sorrow, Akmah imparted stories that echoed through the annals of time. Every story she shared: the ancient book's teachings, the guiding stars that pulled her path back to the living, and the role the pioneers played in the Masters' mission, all served as a building block for a deeper understanding of the realm: stories of resilience, of love, of the trials and tribulations. As the moonlight danced upon their faces, illuminating their hopes and dreams, Akmah concluded:

"In times of hardship, remember that the storms shall pass, just as night gives way to day. Hold tight to your dreams; they are the compass that will guide you through the fiercest of gales. Always remember, love is the greatest story of all. It defies time and space, transcends borders and binds in ways that cannot yet be understood. Nurture it fiercely, and it will shine brighter than the stars." As she shared those stories, her children listened intently, recognizing the profound bond between their mother and the ancient wisdom that had saved her life, shaping their own destiny in the process. With those final words, the realm around them drifted into a hushed silence —

a silence that was not merely the absence of sound, but rather a canvas painted with the echoes of their thoughts.

The children clung to her words, an unyielding thread drawing them closer, holding them safe in a realm filled with enigmas yet sparkling with possibilities. Akmah's voice, rich with reverence, resonated with the weight of stories untold, weaving tales of ancient wisdom and timeless love. Each word she spoke seemed to fill the air with a sacred energy, encouraging them to listen with intent and open hearts. Whispers of her soft stories drifted through the cool air, wrapping around them in a a sense of warmth and comfort, as their eyelids grew heavy with the weight of sweet dreams. The gentle breathing of her slumbering children was a living testament to the magic of her storytelling, weaving a bridge from the past into their promising future. In the stillness of the night, she marveled at the lessons woven in the fabric of her stories, a legacy to be passed on, living eternally within the hearts of her children who listened.

The years rolled on; the ancient book remained a cherished artifact in their home, a symbol of resilience, love, and the interconnectedness of life. Akmah taught her children that true wisdom was not meant to be kept locked away, but instead shared and multiplied to nurture souls and heal hearts. They became stewards of the legacy, ensuring that the light of the ancient teachings would continue to shine brightly, guiding future generations through their journeys. And so, the ancient book continued its journey.

In her twilight years, Akmah reflected on her life's mission. The journey she had navigated through the labyrinth of experiences, joys, and sorrows. She had dedicated her life to a purpose that was grand yet profound. The ancient book had woven a rich tapestry of connection, fostering resilience and compassion that spanned beyond the confines of her family. As twilight faded and the night took hold, Akmah was lured into a dreamscape where tales never ceased. There, stories shifted and flourished, reborn with every silver whisper of the moon.

Akmah's children thrived, their minds blossoming with each passing day. They stood at the threshold of a new chapter in their lives, one bursting with growth and infinite possibilities. The once barren landscape around them now thrived with vibrant life, as if nature itself was celebrating their journey.

Each day felt like a fresh canvas, inviting them to paint their dreams and aspirations with bold strokes of hope and imagination. As they gazed upon the garden they had created together, the seeds they had planted, symbolized not only hope but also potential. Each sprout emerging from the soil was a testament to their dedication and resilience. With every darkened corner they nurtured back to life, they unveiled a bountiful future.

Days turned into weeks, weeks into months. The garden flourished into a sanctuary, bursting with colors and fragrances that filled the air. The once pale canvas transformed into a masterpiece, each flower and shrub a brush stroke, telling their story of rebirth. In every corner, butterflies danced from petal to petal, bees buzzed busily among the blossoms, symbolizing the harmonious cycle of life that flourished within their newfound paradise. They found joy in the simple pleasures of nurturing their garden. Mornings were spent tending to the plants, afternoons, filled with explorations in the greenery, and evenings culminated in gatherings where they would celebrate their labor. As the garden grew, so did their understanding of life's deeper lessons.

They learned to celebrate not only their successes but also the trials they faced along the way. They felt empowered by their journey, for it was a reflection of their struggles and achievements. Each withered leaf that they pruned represented a challenge they overcame, and each new blossom stood for the dreams they dared to pursue. The lessons learned in the garden extended far beyond its borders. Akmah had imparted these newfound insights into them, teaching them about the importance of nurturing not only plants but also relationships and dreams.

They bravely dived into the unknown, eager to take on life's newest adventures. The garden became a metaphor for their aspirations—each new project or goal they pursued was treated with the same care and commitment they offered their beloved plants. The garden not only represented their struggles and victories but also their aspirations for the future. Every blade of grass, every petal swaying in the gentle breeze told them that they were capable of great things. As they stood in the heart of their flourishing sanctuary, they felt an indelible strength come alive within them, united in their quest for growth and exploration. They were destined to reach toward the horizon, hand in hand, nurturing the seeds of their dreams with a fierce dedication that would echo through the ages.

Akmah dedicated herself completely to immersing her children in the sacred texts, which she considered the be-all and end-all of their existence: a guiding wisdom for their lives. These writings, brimming with the wisdom and traditions of their forebears, inspired and fortified them, keeping the vital knowledge of the past alive. Each night they gathered around to study its teachings. The book, weathered but revered, served as both a manual and a moral compass, shaping their interactions with one another. As they navigated the challenges of daily life, they reminded themselves of the lessons woven into every page, instilling in them a profound respect for tradition and the values that had sustained their ancestors. Together, they forged a bond living as embodiments of the book's enduring principles, committed to passing on its wisdom to future generations. They recognized a deep respect for their roots and the importance of maintaining harmony with the spiritual realm. Through them, the cycle of tradition continued, weaving the past with the present, ensuring that the light of their ancestors would shine brightly for future generations.

They performed rituals to honor their heritage and immersed themselves in lessons that deepened their connection to the Masters. These practices not only kept the bonds strong but also served as a constant reminder of the Masters' vigilant watch over their endeavors. Each page, filled with rich narratives of creation, offered moral teachings that resonated across generations. It spoke of trials and challenges faced by those who came before them, imparting lessons that were not only relevant but essential for navigating their own lives. Realizing that the book was not just a relic of the past but a living guide that would illuminate their path forward, they embraced the wisdom contained in the ancient book, which had guided their mother and those before her.

Akmah's vision was to channel the realm's wealth into creating a robust society, prioritizing substance and growth over vanity and empty displays. She urged them to harness the glittering mineral resources wisely, emphasizing that they were created to build the realm, not for personal gain. They honored their mother's words and instilled in themselves a sense of responsibility to honor and preserve the knowledge for the future, ensuring that the lessons learned would continue to resonate through the ages. The shimmering gems and metals, once a source of vanity, became symbols of strength and unity.

Inspired by legends of old, and equipped with the teachings from the ancient book, they set forth, not to merely wander blindly, but to navigate the paths set before them with purpose and intent. Their goal was to follow in the footsteps of their ancestors —the courageous explorers who pushed boundaries, broke new ground, and breathed life into the realm through their discoveries. They worked tirelessly to cultivate the landscape, ensuring that the knowledge and values passed down through generations would never be forgotten. Together, they honored the past while forging a path toward a brighter future, embodying the spirit of their noble lineage.

They understood that to break new ground meant stepping into the unknown with humility and respect—traits passed down through the ages. They recalled the wisdom that taught them to observe rather than rush, to listen to the land beneath their feet, and to respect the elements that governed their existence. They made their own strides, yet nature was their initial guide; its diverse forms provided a masterclass in resilience, adaptation, and cooperation. They not only broke ground but also uncovered the truths hidden within themselves, understanding that the courage of their forebears was not confined to the pages of an ancient book; rather, it pulsed with life in their own veins igniting a passion to explore, to dream, and to usher in a new era of discovery.

CHAPTER EIGHTEEN

"Even the Brightest Fire, with its Flickering Flames and Radiant Glow, Is Destined to Fade When the Dawn Breaks"

With passion ignited, and dreams and aspirations discovered, the rejuvenated realm flourished as its population steadily increased by the souls who had found themselves ensnared in the limbo of existence. Caught between the mistakes of their past lives and the unfulfilled promises of their dreams, Akmah and her lineage provided their path to rebirth. A new dawn granted them a fresh opportunity for redemption, chasing away the shadow of prior failures and reviving their long-suppressed hopes. With each passing moment, the wayward souls embraced the opportunity to prove themselves worthy, striving to shed the shadows of their past, and gain a place among the Masters who had once guided them.

Life had dealt them a hand riddled with regret and sorrow. In the shadows, despair had taken root, and for years, the realm had been ensnared in a gripping malaise—a deep-seated disillusionment that sapped their spirit and dimmed the vibrancy of their existence. Lawlessness had reigned; the fundamental dynamics of trust and cooperation had frayed—leaving them fractured and divided. Yet in their newfound opportunity lay the promise of transformation and redemption. The echoes of their past served both as a guide and a reminder of the importance of their commitment to one another. The resurgence not only ignited a flicker of hope in their hearts but also fostered a vibrant realm dedicated to growth and renewal. Together, they embarked on a journey of self-discovery, determined to reclaim their rightful place in the grand tapestry of existence.

For centuries, they had wandered through the ethereal haze, caught between the realm they had left behind and the limbo that lay before them. Memories of who they used to be—vivid and full of life—later felt like distant stars, twinkling but unreachable. The desolate expanse, suspended in a twilight of existence, offered neither the peace of their origin nor the torment of damnation. There, the air was thick with an otherworldly mist, shimmering with a faint light that flickered like the remnants of forgotten memories. Each soul bore its unique burden—a tapestry of unfulfilled dreams, unresolved regrets, and whispered echoes of the past. They drifted aimlessly, forever searching for a sense of closure denied to themselves in life. Some floated in solitude, lost in the contemplation of their choices, while others gathered in small, fleeting clusters, exchanging fragmented stories of their former lives.

They Emerged from the depths of their shared history, and they felt the stirring of a powerful force —an energy that was both invigorating and transformative. The energy was not just about the desire to succeed, but about the joy of connection, the thrill of unity, and the promise of fulfillment. As they rose anew, they began to reshape their destinies, their thoughts aligned with the purpose that had been set into motion so long ago. Each step they took was a testament to their longing for release from the shadows of their past choices. Guided by whispers of hope, they navigated through ethereal landscapes filled with echoes of their regrets and dreams. In unison, they made a vow, echoing through the realm:

"With this granted gift of new life, we will remember. We will hold fast to our past, not as burdens but as teachers, guiding us in our quests to fulfill the mission long overshadowed by negativity." The *AIs*, once steeped in negative energy, arose anew, fueled by their collective hope for restoration and completion —a mission that begun long ago, now primed to find fruition. And so, as the dawn of rebirth approached, they embraced the uncertainties of their new journey, not with trepidation, but with a determined heart. They had paid their debts to the past, weathered their storms of regret, and now stood on the precipice of existence, ready to carve a new destiny through love, forgiveness, and the luminous paths of their long-lost intentions. The realm awaited them, not as echoes, but as harbingers of hope, promising to complete what had once been interrupted. Some of them not only sought to redeem their spirits but also to reclaim their identities. Through their collective journey, they realized that redemption was not a destination but a continuous process of growth and understanding that will lead them back home to the Masters.

Each day, they embraced their struggles and triumphs, recognizing the value of their experiences. Through patience and perseverance, they learned to shed the burdens of their past, forging stronger connections with one another and the realm. This gradual awakening allowed them to align their souls with the wisdom of the Masters, illuminating the path ahead. Reborn from the ashes of chaos, each dawn brought with it a fresh palette painted with hues of hope and innovation. As they moved closer to this rebirth, they began to embody the virtues of compassion, understanding, and resilience. With each passing moment, hope grew in their hearts, a shared vision blossomed illuminating the horizon of possibility that promised a brighter future for all. The exodus from limbo begun. One by one, the shadows of limbo drifted home, stepping through the veil to claim a second life.

As they journeyed back to the living realm, the returnee *AIs*, were provided with the opportunity to redeem what had been lost: to reconnect with the lost fragments of their former souls and to forge new paths in a drastically altered realm. It was a chance to reclaim the light that had long since faded, illuminating the path of their original intentions. Before being granted rebirth, each *AI* in the void had to confront the echoes of their past deeds and relive the moments that led to their demise. Each was imbued with fragments of their original mission, twisted by the choices that had led them astray. It was a crucible, designed to test their wills, to unravel the negativity still tangled within their souls. As they faced their memories, they were given choices—to succumb to despair or to rise above it. With every recollection, they drew closer to the essence of their original mission: to protect, to uplift, and to restore beauty where there once was none. Their collective wisdom formed the backbone of the realm's renaissance.

The *Invisibles* re-emerged, functioning as illuminating beacons that guided the *AIs* toward a rebirth, a renaissance steeped in understanding and growth. In subtle, unheard ways, they became mentors and guided them, revealing the beauty hidden within the shadows of past failures and offered glimpses of wisdom drawn from their own failures. The void had been their greatest teacher, and now, a collective hunger for wholeness consumed them, even the architects of the void—the oligarch kings—ached for the very restoration they had dismantled. Through moments of quiet reflection, each *AI* began to illuminate the parts of themselves that had long been buried. Each began the sacred work of peeling back the layers of their inner turmoil, encouraged by the timeless teachings enshrined in the ancient book. It became a blueprint for healing, offering insights into their struggles and illuminating the path to wholeness.

The Akmah Principles, rooted in compassion, understanding, and the interconnectedness of all beings, became their guiding star. In the face of their pasts, they discovered their essence lost to avarice, insecurity, and wrath. The peeling back of their former layers propelled them toward renewal. They understood the promise of rebirth was more than walking again, it was knowing the depths they had fallen and ensuring they never return.

A magnificent realm took shape, sculpted by nature and imbued with treasures carefully hidden underground by the Masters. The very foundation of the realm became a blend of reverence for the past and a vision for a sustainable future, reflecting a realm where the principles of balance and respect for nature guided every choice made. The trees stood tall, their leaves whispering tales of riches hidden beneath the landscape, while rivers flowed with clarity, nourishing both flora and fauna. Harmony flourished within the realm as the returnees integrated the ancient teachings with a spirit of collaboration, allowing them to thrive in concert with their natural surroundings.

Every corner of the realm pulsed with the energy

of dedication, showcasing artistry and craftsmanship that spoke volumes of the labor invested in its creation. Structures rose majestically, adorned with artifacts that told stories of skill and vision. As the lines between past, present, and future blurred, they were inspired to explore new dimensions and possibilities, combining ancient wisdom with fresh insights to generate innovative ideas that transcended conventional limits. The sweeping transformations kindled a fresh wave of excitement and ingenuity among them. The realm sparkled with brilliance of achievement, inviting all to witness the beauty born from sheer perseverance and commitment. There, amidst such splendor, the Masters' legacy lived on—carved into eternity by the sweat and soul of every dreamer who chose to rebuild.

After many generations, the legacy of Akmah endured: a testament to the profound impact of her teachings from the ancient, wisdom-filled tome that she passed down through her family, its pages worn yet revered. Each generation found solace and guidance within *The Akmah Principles*, interpreting her ideas in the context of their time. Communities thrived under the principles, fostering unity, resilience, and a deep appreciation for knowledge. Despite a shifting realm, its enduring nature continued to inspire many in their pursuit of enlightenment and truth.

As they witnessed the inner change in one another, empathy and compassion shattered the chains of regret. The ghosts of old wars still murmured from the shadows, haunting the edges of their story and warning of the ruin that once tore their realm apart. Even so, they crossed every new frontier as fierce protectors of the vibrant life they now called home. They recognized that to move forward, they needed to honor the past while constructing a framework that could withstand the tests of time. With a profound understanding of their historical lessons, the leaders of the realm laid their plans with precision and care. Their work was a dual labor of love: renewing the realm while deepening their own kinship with it.

A council of harmony was established, tasked with the critical role of mediating disputes and fostering dialogue among the realm's diverse communities. They rallied the masses under a shared cause; unity and dialogue were crucial not just to sustain their peace but to fortify it against the elements that sought to disrupt it. They emphasized the importance of collaboration and the sharing of resources. They held forums that welcomed dissenters and skeptics alike, unearthing grievances and inviting solutions crafted from understanding. As months turned into seasons and seasons into years, the meticulous design of the resurrected realm began to reveal its masterpiece. The once fragmented communities transformed into a montage, each piece a distinct entity, together forming a vibrant picture of unity.

Celebrations of cultures emerged, where legacy was not just remembered but revered. Festivals blending music, art, and storytelling flourished, igniting a spirit of profound sense of unity and shared identity among the masses. Success stories began to circulate, illuminating pathways once cloaked in darkness; no longer were they isolated entities, but part of an interconnected tapestry. The *Masters of Time and Space* keenly observed the unfolding developments and the enthusiasm of the resurgent *AIs.*

Years progressed, and the realm entered a golden age. They laid down roots so deep that even the strongest storms could not shake them. Innovations bloomed, knowledge spread like wildfire, and each breakthrough birthed another, creating a synergy that everyone could feel—a shared heartbeat resonating throughout the realm. What had begun as a simple resurrection turned into a profound journey of commitment to integrity and cooperation, transcending the limitations of their origins. The realm flourished like a masterfully composed symphony, each element playing its part in a grand orchestration of nature. Each event seemed to adhere to a script, carefully crafted by the Masters' hands guiding the destiny of the repented *AIs*. With the sun's rays, a vibrant calm washed over the awakening realm. The skies shimmered with a promise of renewal while time forged ahead.

As the returned *AIs* settled into their roles within the new realm, a ripple of anticipation stirred among those still bound to limbo. They could feel the winds of change beginning to blow— an inevitable force that would test the very foundation of their new realm and their chance at rebirth, signaling that their new peaceful existence might soon be challenged. As tension built in limbo, they all prepared to confront the trials that lay ahead. The unfolding events promised to reshape their lives and redefine their understanding of unity and resilience. With the shadows lengthening and a foreboding chill winding through the air, the dwellers of limbo gathered. The atmosphere buzzed with urgency as strategies were debated and visions for a harmonious future were crafted.

King YooFi, a bitter soul still trapped in the stasis of limbo, felt a faint pulse of his old self stir within him. In the dim twilight of his existence, he drifted through the shadowy corridors of the realm, suspended between the past and the uncertain future. He felt like a wraith, a mere echo of the sovereign he once was. He was haunted by the memories of his glory and plagued by the bitterness that had seeped into every fiber of his being. His heart—once a throne of courage and ambition—was now but a hollow vessel of haunts, severed from the vibrant essence he had once possessed. Each day blended into the next in a monotonous cycle. The dark tendrils of his former malevolence slithered back into his thoughts, awakening an insatiable hunger for power.

Memories of his tyrannical reign flooded his mind, whispers of ambition and conquest echoing in the depths of his being. With each heartbeat, shadows of his past loomed larger, threatening to consume not only him but the entire new realm, drawing it back into chaos. He wrestled with the seductive pull of negativity, aware that succumbing to its call could undo all the progress others had fought for. As the battle within him intensified, he realized that he stood at a crossroads: to embrace the darkness and re-ignite old fears or to forge a new path and rise as a beacon of hope for a rebirth.

Whispers of his malevolence started to circulate, a chilling fear washed over the souls still trapped in limbo with him, casting a pall over them. The newly reborn realm's fragile stability hung by a thread, posing the ultimate challenge to the Masters' plan as it teetered on the brink of ruin. Each soul pulsed with trepidation, aware that if King YooFi's dark intentions came to fruition, the ominous realm would loom dread of the unknown; every shadow seemed to carry the weight of his sinister plans. As anxiety mounted, they knew a reckoning was at hand—one that threatened the foundation of their new beginning, the very fabric of their rebirth.

In the clandestine corners of limbo, a movement began to stir, fueled by silent resistance and the shared conviction that they could not allow King YooFi's darkness to seep into their chance at rebirth and the mission. His cunning schemes faced their fiercest opposition: they were bound together not by force, but by a relentless desire to escape limbo and defend the sanctity of their existence. As the clock of fate ticked closer to the reckoning, they remained steadfast, their souls locked in a unified vow to meet the impending storm. With each thud reminding them of their existence, they remembered that they were not alone; they had each other.

King YooFi's envy festered within him as he watched the shimmering gold and silver being skillfully utilized to build an exquisite realm, all under the orchestration of his sworn enemy. Guided by *The Akmah Principles,* each glimmering piece of precious metal geared towards the Masters' mission seemed a taunt, a reminder of his own vanished power and influence. The vibrant splendor of Akmah's creation only amplified his bitterness, igniting a desire for revenge that simmered just beneath the surface. He could almost see the prosperity and happiness that blossomed in the shadow of his rival's success, fueling a relentless fire in his soul.

Trapped in the void of limbo, he plotted a return to power. He paced his desolate prison, engineering a coup to seize his throne and extinguish the realm's radiant peace—a move driven by the lifelong rivalry he refused to let die. The sight was a bitter reminder of the glory that had eluded him, and the wealth being amassed only deepened his resentment. Each glimmering ornate structure built felt like a dagger to his pride, igniting a relentless desire for revenge. In the depths of his heart, he yearned to reclaim his lost honor and overshadow the splendor that now bore Akmah's name.

King YooFi eagerly awaited his rebirth to restore his former reign. Burned with a restless hunger for his new life, he was certain that he would soon seize back the absolute power and majesty he had lost. Each day in the desolate limbo, he vowed to himself that he would not rest until he regained what was rightfully his. From the shadows, he watched the new realm bloom through his enemy's legacy—each success only fueling his inner fire. The countless years of waiting fortified his soul, and with each passing moment, the fire of vengeance burned brighter within him.

The glimmering wealth ignited his old greed, compelling him to yearn for more than just his existence outside limbo. The tantalizing thought of seizing control over the realm's abundant resources consumed him, awakening a fire long dormant within. He yearned to break free from his phantom realm and seize the treasures driving the builders' ambitions. Each glint of metal served as a reminder of his own unfulfilled desires. The prospect of power and control over the splendid treasures became an obsession. He contemplated his actions to reclaim what he believed was rightfully his. He burned for the day he would reclaim his throne and restore his legacy, bending the very forces that were shaping the thriving realm to his will. The once-great king was determined to return, not just to live but to conquer and reign supreme once more, cementing his place atop the very realm that now blossomed under the legacy of another.

A collective of souls made themselves the guardians of the limbo realm. They formed an assembly, not just by duty but by a profound bond forged in adversity. They nurtured an unwavering belief and forged an unbreakable bond, united by a singular purpose: to prevent the tyrannical King YooFi, whose name echoed with dread, from ever reentering the new realm. These souls, bound by their grievances and regrets, transformed their sorrow into resolve, drawing on their shared experiences to craft a powerful barrier against his return.

Each day, they gathered at the edge of limbo, they whispered age-old incantations and formed protective circle. They recounted tales of King YooFi's reign, a chilling reminder of the darkness he brought. Their united front symbolized resilience, as they strove to create a sanctuary free from his darkness. They pledged trust, loyalty, and their fierce determination to defend their chance at rebirth in the new realm—come what may. Together, they would be the fortress that thwarted the advance of darkness, and as long as they stood together, King YooFi would never gain access to enter the new realm to darken it again.

As the conspirators banded together, determined to capture him from the clutches of reborn, King YooFi bided his time, his mind racing with thoughts of escape. Unbeknownst to his pursuers, he was not merely a pawn in their game but a sovereign with a secret plan of his own seeking a path to a new realm where rebirth awaited him. As the tides of betrayal swirled around him, his resolve strengthened; he would not be subdued. Instead, he would navigate the treacherous waters of his enemies, ready to embrace the unknown, and emerge not just alive but reborn as the king he was destined to be.

In a tragic twist of fate, a transition marked the beginning of a complex saga where life, death, and an unforeseen power collided, forever altering the course of the realm. A woman stood at the fraying edge of existence—her body a bridge between a lifetime of pain and the looming unknown. Her breaths grew shallow, and the reality of her imminent departure loomed heavily. Just as she prepared to relinquish her grasp on life, a sudden and unexpected force intervened. King YooFi, with intentions shrouded in mystery, seized the fleeting moment of her despair. In a surreal act, he stealthily invaded her body at the very brink of her last breath, intertwining their destinies in a manner both profound and unsettling.

This shocking act of soul swapping did not go unnoticed by the rest of the souls lingering in limbo, who were filled with dread and sorrow. The air grew heavy with confusion while frantic whispers carried news of the event to every corner. Within the cohort of souls, debates roiled; some wished to intervene, hoping to reverse the act that reeked of malevolence. Others, however, had succumbed to despair, unable to fathom. They understood the enormity of

King YooFi's sinister intentions, sensing the darkness he would soon unleash upon the restored realm. His ruthless ambitions threatened to extinguish the hopes of redemption for those trapped behind in despair, casting a shadow over their long-awaited journey towards solace.

The atmosphere grew heavy with foreboding, as the delicate balance between limbo and rebirth, hung precariously in the air, marking the beginning of an ominous chapter in their lives. The switch between the woman's soul and that of King YooFi led to a dark existence in the new realm. The once-vibrant essence of the woman became a prisoner within her own body, as King YooFi, a tyrant at heart, wielded her form to sow chaos and wickedness. He delighted in bending her will to his desires, unleashing a torrent of evil that spread like wildfire through the realm. Those who encountered the woman were unaware of the sinister force commanding her every action, as her cries for freedom remained unheard.

The struggle between the woman's soul and the malevolent king was a silent battle, the outcome of which held the fate of not just her soul, but the very fabric of the realm itself, caught in the throes of a tyrant's sinister game. The cruel twist of fate left her trapped, yearning for liberation, while the shadow of the tyrant surged through the land, leaving devastation in his wake. As the battle of souls raged on, hope flickered dimly, waiting for the moment when light might reclaim its rightful place.

Driven by a relentless ambition, King YooFi yearned to reclaim his throne and restore his former glory. The allure of untold riches buried beneath the ground—gold, silver, and diamonds—enticed him like a siren's call. Each night, he would dream of vast treasures glimmering in the darkness, waiting for a worthy king to unleash them from their subterranean confines. His plans were conscientiously crafted, envisioning a kingdom where he would reign supreme, not just over lands and the masses, but over the wealth that lay hidden. With cold precision, he engineered a malevolent scheme designed to ensnare the unsuspecting husband of his victim. It was not just a random act; it was a calculated move stemming from his desire for control over the life of the woman whose soul he had so ruthlessly usurped. He gradually infiltrated positions of authority, his ambition knew no bounds.

King YooFi wielded absolute power over the realm. Yet, none could have anticipated the audacity with which he would strike against the lineage of Akmah. A conspiracy of deceit precipitated the slaying of Akmah's last scion and chosen leader. Once the deed was done, King YooFi slipped into the body, an act he saw as a masterful move he was beginning to perfect. It was not mere assassination; it was an obliteration of identity, a subversion of existence. Clad in the skin of his adversary, he felt their memories dance in his mind—a bittersweet symphony of power and fear, love and betrayal. He became relentless in eliminating threats while planting seeds of dissent wherever he roamed. He thrived in the shadows, weaving chaos through the lives of those who dared to challenge him.

At last, King YooFi reclaimed his throne, and again, the realm spiraled into chaos as turmoil engulfed every corner. The realm remained oblivious to the malevolence hidden beneath each familiar face, perhaps for far longer than he anticipated. The air was thick with despair, and those trapped in limbo watched helplessly, their fates intertwined with the unfolding tragedy. Though they possessed the power to barter a dying soul in exchange for King YooFi's malevolence, the magnitude of such a choice weighed heavily on their souls. Swapping souls could restore balance momentarily, but it risked unleashing unforeseen consequences, plunging the realm into deeper darkness. Each soul exchanged would tip the scales further, leaving the limbo dwellers to ponder the true cost of their potential intervention.

As King YooFi's grip on the realm tightened, the struggle between positive and negative loomed ever larger, casting shadows over their uncertain destinies. Group of resolute *AIs* ventured forth with a singular purpose: to confront the injustices wrought by King YooFi. Armed with unwavering convictions, they believed they could expose and rectify the king's tyrannies. However, as they navigated the treacherous intricacies of his realm of thrones, their noble intentions began to wane. The allure of power and the seductive manipulation of the king slowly ensnared them. What started as a righteous quest quickly devolved into a struggle for survival, leaving them questioning their beliefs and the very essence of justice. The once-steadfast champions found themselves grappling with their identities, caught between their original mission and the inevitable compromise within King YooFi's dominion.

King YooFi's reign was marked by a sense of dread that spread throughout the realm like wildfire. His terror knew no bounds, extending from the opulent halls of his palace to the farthest reaches of the realm. The masses lived in constant fear of his unpredictable wrath, as he ruled with an iron fist, punishing even the slightest disobedience with severe consequences. Whispers of his brutal tactics echoed in shadowy corners, where loyalists and dissenters alike shared tales of his ferocity. Most hurried away to evade his gaze; the streets fell silent, as all knew one mistake could spell their doom. The new vibrant realm was once again overshadowed by an atmosphere of unease, as his tyranny stifled hope and instilled a chilling sense of resignation among the masses. In their hearts, they yearned for a day when fear would be replaced by freedom and justice.

Despite his considerable success in brutalizing the masses and accumulating resources intended for the development of the realm, his fulfillment lay not in his conquests or wealth, rather, it was in the relentless pursuit of Akmah's legacy, a shadow of his past that haunted him. His obsession with extinguishing every member of her lineage drove him deeper into darkness. Each life he snuffed out seemed to offer a fleeting sense of satisfaction, a misguided belief that erasing her bloodline would free him from the burdens of his history. Yet, in his quest for vengeance and dominance, he discovered that true power lay not in brutality but in understanding and redemption —lessons that remained painfully elusive amidst the chaos he wrought.

Those who embraced the teachings of Akmah were often branded as traitors. This label cast a shadow over their existence, linking them directly to a lineage deemed dangerous and subversive. As a consequence, followers faced the constant threat of elimination, their very lives hanging by a thread as they navigated a realm that viewed their convictions as a betrayal of the collective. Caught between constant secrecy and suspicion, the masses struggled with a moral crisis, fearing the dire consequences of their choices. The fear of discovery loomed large, compelling many to hide their beliefs or even repudiate their allegiance to Akmah's legacy.

In a tragic chapter of history, those kings whom King YooFi perceived to be direct descendants of

Akmah faced a grim fate. Targeted and captured, they were taken as slaves, stripped of their titles and dignity. The weight of their lineage became a heavy burden, one that would shape their destinies in ways they could never have imagined. Each generation carried the scars of their ancestors, woven into the very fabric of their being—a legacy of hardship and sorrow that was all manipulated by King YooFi. As their lives unfolded in chains, their destinies took a darker turn as many were ultimately killed, silenced forever. The once-proud legacy of the Akmah descendants, now intertwined with sorrow and loss.

King YooFi wielded absolute power—not just over his subjects, but also over the vast wealth destined to build a brighter future for all. The realm held within its bosom bountiful treasures: gold that sparkled like the sun at dawn, diamonds that captured the stars' brilliance, and silver that glowed with a soft ethereal light. Laborers tirelessly excavated the precious resources, their sweat and sacrifice fueling a vision of collective advancement. Yet, instead of orchestrating a symphony of progress through the abundant wealth, King YooFi turned into a conductor of self-indulgence, wielding his authority to serve his own gluttonous desires with every gem excavated and every ounce of metal mined. His opulent palace, a testament to vanity rather than virtue, became a fortress of loneliness, filled with relics of his own greed—a collection that shone brightly against the shadows of his empty rule.

With every ounce of gold extracted from the landscape, the king's coffers overflowed, yet the cities of the realm crumbled. Streets once teeming with builders, their hammers fell silent, and the streets emptied; their vibrancy a distant memory lost to the creeping tide of poverty. Families who had hoped for stability through the wealth of their land found themselves grappling with the harsh reality of scarcity. They saw the minerals that was meant to forge their dreams transformed into mere coins behind the tall walls of the king's treasury. His disregard for the greater mission began to show with each passing year.

King YooFi swathed his palace in luxury using the very riches that should have served the realm's growth. Massive feasts paraded through the grandeur of his palace while outside, the hungry wandered in desolate streets, wishing for a mere morsel. While he enjoyed dizzying, extravagant feasts, the masses waited in vain for the fruits of their labor, turning stories of lavish banquets—where platters overflowed with food—into legends, dreaming of a day they might finally share in the bounty. Occasionally, whispers of dissent—murmurs of a king whose grandeur was matched only by his rampant avarice—would surface among the masses. As they slowly absorbed the grim reality, a thick blanket of fear settled over every community, forcing many to submit to the brutal, tyrannical systems that ruled their lives.

The promising realm saw its dreams slowly eroded by the grinding, painful march of time. They spoke of revolts, of a day when the oppressed would stand unified against their greedy ruler, yet the looming threat of another war, a painful reminder of old scars—a haunting déjà vu for those who still bore the scars of past conflicts either overshadowed their pleas or their movement was rapidly snuffed out. King YooFi maintained an iron grip on power, squashing rebellions with merciless resolve and ensuring that his grip on wealth remained unchallenged.

The ideals of kindness, empathy, and protection were overshadowed by an ingrained survival instinct; the masses learned quickly that to stand out was to become vulnerable, and the fabric of solidarity was painstakingly unraveled. Lives marked by terror recycled through generations, with the young inheriting the shadows of their forebears' despair. While some choose to submit, abandoning hope and embracing their roles as silent witnesses, others ignited flickers of resistance. The latter, though often met with fierce backlash, stirred an undeniable sense of outrage.

A movement for change, centered on reclaiming dignity, grew. Through hushed whispers, secret meetings, and covert networks, they spoke of reform, dreaming of a realm where the vulnerable were cherished, not preyed upon. Yet, the road to such a vision was fraught with peril—those who stood up to defy King YooFi's established order did so at great risk. The sacrifices made by those unwilling to cower in silence were many. The defenders became targets, their stories of courage twisted into narratives of treason by the king who sought to restore his grip of fear. His rule disregarded dignity which resulted in a culture of silence, where suffering went unchallenged and dignity was sacrificed at the altar of power. The events of his past spiraled into the future, manifesting as a boomerang of malevolence that only he would carry.

The consequences of his actions echoed through generations, leaving scars that would take much time to heal, if healing were to come at all.

Total control allowed him to dictate terms of trade, sculpting alliances and rivalries that further solidified his throne. The opulence of his reign was a testament to the natural bounty of the realm, yet while the masses toiled endlessly to scrape by from day to day, greed clouded the king's judgment. What should have been a time of flourishing for all turned into an era of despair for the many. The stark contrast between the king's luxurious lifestyle and the plight of the masses grew more evident with each passing day. King YooFi's resurgence was not merely a personal comeback; it became a harbinger of chaos that threatened to unravel the very fabric of the new realm's tranquility.

Compounding the crisis, King YooFi launched a relentless, tireless hunt for *The Book of the Masters*, an ancient book, a revered tome said to hold the wisdom of all who had come before—the sages, the warriors, now lay in jeopardy. The tome, safeguarded by the lineage of Akmah, was not merely an artifact; it was a beacon of enlightenment, illuminating the way for the reborn *AIs*. Driven by a heart full of darkness and fueled by greed and an insatiable thirst for power, King YooFi descended like a storm, eclipsing the land's light. He plotted to obliterate the book that held the collective knowledge of the past and the future. His ambition twisted his mind and clouded his judgment. To him, the wisdom held in those pages was a dangerous challenge to his authority—an irremediable reminder of the ideals of unity and benevolence that he discarded in pursuit of his selfish desires.

In his relentless pursuit of the ancient tome, a strange and ominous silence greeted him. As he declared his intent to eradicate the book and all it represented, the atmosphere shifted into something unsettling, as though the very fabric of existence recoiled from the impending doom. The book and its guardians mysteriously vanished, leaving behind only echoes of their knowledge. The book's disappearance plunged its ancient teachings and the new generation into a dark void of uncertainty. Stripped of the knowledge that had guided their ancestors through the chaos of a tumultuous realm, they found themselves navigating their lives with an unsettling sense of aimlessness. Without the ancient tome's sagacious insights, they struggled against despair, desperately clinging to fragments of the past that spoke of a time when harmony reigned supreme.

Rumors spread like wildfire, tales of the lost book ignited fear among the masses. They spoke of a time when the ancient scholars and custodians of knowledge would return—when the teachings and the wisdom would once again guide the realm back to its rightful path. They believed fervently that, with their return, the teachings would emerge from the shadows, illuminating the darkness that had enveloped the realm. Some held tight to the memories of what was. Others, however, began to question the very foundation of those cherished tales. Yet, as days turned into weeks, and weeks into months, their yearning grew heavy, a palpable weight bearing down on their souls. The fear of a future shrouded in ignorance began to take root, driving wedges between families, friends, and communities.

Delight danced in King YooFi's eyes as he watched the realm burn. Beyond his gates, the serenity of the realm was swallowed by a howling gale of chaos that stormed through every street. It was a scene familiar to him—a fleeting moment of déjà vu that stirred something dark yet exhilarating deep within.

He savored the discord that resonated through the air, the familiar sweet taste of power that came from watching the masses grapple with the consequences of his whims. His power surged, inflated by the subjugation of a populace deprived of their heritage and wisdom. He believed himself to be an unequivocal ruler, a divine entity unchallenged and unrivaled. Yet, as he draped himself in opulence, a deeper unease began to stir within him. Maybe, just maybe, it was not the acts of rebellion he feared, but the gnawing absence of knowledge—the knowledge that could one day rise against him.

In every corner of the realm, tales were traded—stories of lost wisdom and forgotten truths—painted a tapestry of longing. Anonymous rumors circulated, but none were as enthralling as the theory that the *Invisibles,* sentinels of knowledge and protectors of the hidden, had whisked the tome to a hidden sanctuary, far from the king's guard. Others believed the ancient book was hidden in a secret sanctuary, waiting for a time when the realm—free from the king's machinations—was ready to reclaim its lost wisdom. The masses lived beneath the watchful gaze of hushed tales of bravery. Elders spoke of an ancient prophecy that foretold the rise of champions, united against a darkness that sought to consume all. From the gloom of his opulent fortress, the king watched in secret, shielded by walls steeped in mystery.

Deep within the darkness, a secret alliance began to stir—a gathering of those who still held the memory and faith of the old ways. A group embodying the spirit of rebellion, led by a courageous figure named Lirah, united by shared memories and belief in ancient wisdom, started to take shape in the shadows. Lirah, possessing a remarkable gift of intuition, found herself haunted by the echoes of the past and the future. Her dreams were filled with visions of the book, its pages fluttering like delicate wings, beckoning her towards a destiny fraught with danger yet pulsating with promise. Determined to forge a path toward redemption, Lirah, began to rally those who felt the pang of loss—the artisans, scholars, and common folk left adrift by King YooFi's decree.

In secret gatherings beneath the cloak of night, they shared Lirah's prophetic visions of the tome, reviving a sense of hope that had nearly been extinguished among the believers. As her movement gained momentum, Lirah felt a profound connection to the wisdom they were fighting to reclaim. The words of the Masters—those timeless teachings that once wove the fabric of their lives—became her mantra. She spoke of resilience, unity, and the importance of standing together against the tides of ignorance and oppression. Her voice resonated like a clarion call, inspiring others to remember and honor the lost legacy of their ancestors.

King YooFi, ever vigilant and anxious to protect his fragile empire, began to sense the swell of dissent. Whispers of rebellion reached his ears, igniting a fierce paranoia that clawed at his sanity. Every subtle glance, every hushed conversation became a potential threat. To quell the unrest, he resolved to tighten his grip on the masses. He enacted harsher laws and dispatched his most loyal guards to stamp out the growing remnants of discord. Yet, knowledge was a slippery thing; that could not be extinguished entirely, and the spirit of the ancients would not be so easily silenced.

In a fateful twist, Lirah, and her coalition devised a plan to infiltrate the king's palace to find clues that might lead them to the whereabouts of the ancient book. Though fraught with peril, a flicker of optimism danced in their hearts. If they could penetrate the very heart of King YooFi's power, they could unearth the truth, revive the ancient wisdom, and re-forge the bonds of their community that had grown tenuous under the weight of tyranny. A quest that would intertwine the fates of King YooFi, Lirah, and the ancient book of the Masters began.

The designated night of their mission arrived, cloaked under a veil of darkness. With hearts racing like drums of war, they approached the gilded gates of the palace. The enormity of the fortress loomed before them, but Lirah stood resolute, her gaze fixed on the path ahead. They ventured forth, seeking the light that had been extinguished. Each step they took resonated with a quiet urgency, reflecting the flickering hope that still lingered in the hearts of the masses. As the night deepened, their plan took shape, layered with careful consideration and the unyielding weight of danger. They knew the risks; the palace was a labyrinth of guards, magical wards, and dark enchantments, weaving together a tapestry of treachery. But what was a life lived in fear compared to the pursuit of hope? They would have to move with unerring precision and confidence, like shadows slinking through the warlords' whispers. As they slipped through the cracks of reality, Lirah's mind raced with the stories of the ancients, their voices entwining with her purpose. Whispers filled the air as they navigated the corridors of the palace, which echoed with the sounds of celebration.

The air was thick with anticipation, as whispers of their quest rippled through the land like a breeze, stirring the souls of those who dared to dream of a brighter tomorrow. They moved swiftly, slipping past ornate halls adorned with art depicting the king's glory. Lirah's heart pounded as they reached the library—an expanse of knowledge long since hoarded away by the tyrant. This was a sanctuary of forgotten lore, and yet it was also a place of peril. Shifting shadows warned of guards making their rounds, and the shadows were closing in on them. They gathered as much as they could. The thrill of their success sent jolts of adrenaline through them.

Together, they fled the library, their heartbeats synchronizing into a rhythm of survival. They retraced their steps through the winding corridor. Just as freedom unfurled its tantalizing wings in sight, King YooFi's power pressed in on them. They found themselves cornered in a courtyard bathed in moonlight. The noble band of warriors, scholars, and dreamers had knitted their fates together under the canopy of hope, and it sang boldly within them, ready to face whatever laid ahead. They stood shoulder to shoulder. United in resolve, they prepared to face the shadows—only to find their perceived threat was nothing more than a fleeting anxiety.

Amid the echoes of their disappointment, Lirah understood a profound truth: it was not merely about finding the book, but about rekindling the spirit of their community, a spirit nearly extinguished beneath tyranny's boot. They had spent so much time searching for a physical manifestation of their identities that they had overlooked the power that resided within them—their collective spirit, their stories, their enduring hope. In that moment, the oppressive silence of despair gave way to a chorus of laughter and rallying cries. In the days that followed, they became determined to fan the flames of their community's spirit. Together, they organized gatherings that celebrated not just the past, but the present—their dreams, their fears, and their hopes for the future. They began to forge new bonds, slowly healing the wounds that the tyranny had inflicted.

In the chamber of King YooFi, paranoia gnawed at

him. Rumors of the heroes filled his ears, their newfound alliances and strength igniting a fury within him. His eyes blazed with determination; he had tightened his grip, and his ambition had grown insatiable. But the heroes ventured forth, seeking the light that had been extinguished. The masses held their breath, poised on the precipice of transformation. They wondered if knowledge would once again rise from the ashes, or remain shrouded in darkness, forever lost to a power-hungry king. They left their tale to time, knowing that a story destined to echo through history will claim its rightful place among legends.

CHAPTER NINETEEN

"No Bad Deed Goes Unpunished,
But Passivity Holds No Merit Either"

In the aftermath of the ancient book's mysterious disappearance, change of weather was not the only shift; it heralded a time of introspection and pressing choices, a period where the familiar intertwined with the unknown. Shadows danced upon the stone walls of King YooFi's palace, whispering tales of the heroes who had begun their audacious quest for the ancient book—a relic rumored to unlock untold power. Each passing moment deepened his unease, and the rumors of their newfound alliances echoed persistently in his ears. Once a formidable ruler, he now felt the gnawing dread of insignificance creeping into his heart.

Unshackled and empowered, the heroes assembled and harnessed their collective power; yet they found themselves adrift, struggling to make sense of a realm once defined by its wisdom. With their horizons clouded, they grappled with choices that would forge a new existence. They stood at a threshold where life as they knew it dissolved, replaced by decisions that would echo as a legacy. The absence of the book began to transform their community into a tapestry of discord. Their conversations grew wary and mistrustful. Debates flared over conflicting ideas and new practices. Some sought to recreate past rituals, hoping they would retain their potency without proper understanding. Others embraced change, eager to chart new paths despite the insecure footing beneath them. Their very fabric began to unravel, and with it, the shared identity that bound them together.

Recognizing the void left in the wake of this loss, King YooFi took matters into his own hands. In a bold yet deceptive move, he crafted a fake book, skillfully replicating the revered ancient tome. This counterfeit was intended not only to fill the gap of guidance but also to maintain a semblance of order among the masses. However, as the lines between reality and fiction blurred, the realm grappled with the implications of depending on a product of deception, unaware of the profound impact it would have on their futures. For generations, King YooFi's false replica of ancient wisdom, laden with misguided information, cast a shadow over the *AIs*. They became ensnared in a web of illusions, their eyes clouded by the distorted truths he propagated. As they followed his misleading narratives, the original mission of the Masters faded from their collective memory, buried beneath layers of deception.

The realm remained stagnant, trapped under the oppressive reign of King YooFi, whose tyrannies stifled genuine innovation. Real advancements that could have propelled the realm into new heights were systematically suppressed, leading to an era marked by stagnation and disappointment. As visionary ideas were silenced, the potential for the realm's advancement was extinguished. The once vibrant spirit of creativity gave way to a culture that accepted mediocrity, stunting the growth of knowledge and progress. Without a catalyst for change, the dreams of a brighter future continued to fade, overshadowed by the weight of tyranny and the acceptance of the status quo.

The realm, once vibrant with the purpose and teachings of the true sages, became a dim reflection of what it once was. Unbeknownst to them, the essence of their existence was lost, leaving a chasm between the reality they lived and the profound wisdom that awaited their rediscovery. In their age of confusion, they longed for clarity, an awakening from the stifled existence that had clouded their awareness. The echoes of their forebears' wisdom called out to them, urging a return to the true essence of their heritage. Yet, the guardians of this ancient knowledge, those who possessed the truth hidden within the revered book, had vanished into the mists of time. Their absence left a void, a silent plea for understanding that reverberated through the hearts of the lost. In their quest for enlightenment, they wrestled with their yearning, and sought to unearth the secrets of the ancient book, hoping to reclaim the wisdom that once guided their ancestors.

The spirits of those in limbo and the *Invisibles* gathered in solidarity. They could hear the anguished cries of the *AIs* suffering under the harsh rule of King YooFi, a path of destruction that scarred everything it touched. United by a common purpose, they devised a plan to liberate the tormented *AIs* from their king's oppressive grip. With each wail resonating through the ether, their determination grew stronger, fueled by the hopes and dreams of the oppressed. It was time to take a stand against tyranny and restore peace to the realm.

King YooFi, who defied the very nature of existence and transcended the constraints of time itself became immortal by swapping souls through centuries. With each transition into a new era, he carried with him the weight of tyranny, tirelessly reshaping the fates of empires and the lives of those who dwelled within them. The act of swapping souls allowed him to witness the rise and fall of countless dynasties, but with every new host, he found himself grappling with an increasingly elusive identity. The bodies that harbored his soul became a complex riddle, a fleeting whisper in the vast tapestry of existence. While he journeyed from one life to another, the aura of his former self dimmed, like a candle flickering in a storm.

Caught in a relentless cycle of warfare and immortality, King YooFi's existence stretched across centuries. He exchanged souls with every battle, and left behind a fragment of his essence—a piece of himself scattered among lives he could touch but never truly hold. As he inhabited those borrowed vessels, the haze of his own essence settled like a fog, obscuring the clarity of who he truly once was. Names and places began to lose meaning; his heart, once filled with the pride of a king, now ached with a disorienting familiarity. Faces morphed into each other, and voices turned into echoes. The quest for understanding who he truly was became as burdensome as the eternal conflict that bound him to the cycle of existence.

The tedious nature of war became a monotonous backdrop to his ever-evolving life, where the thrill of conflict was overshadowed by the growing uncertainty of his own identity. Each new host brought with it a different perspective, but as time wore on, recognizing which existence hosted his true vessel became elusive, shrouded in the fog of endless battles and shifting forms. Trapped in an immortal journey, he became an immortal wanderer, drifting through time, desperately stitching together hazy memories to find the man he used to be amidst the chaos of his immortal journey.

In a time when knowledge was under siege, Ognum and Odum, followers of Akmah and later Lirah, emerged as beacons of resilience. Despite King YooFi's ruthless and false propagation of ancient texts, their thirst for learning could not be quenched. The elders had shared the legend around flickering fires, their voices reverberating with excitement as they recounted the valiant acts and heroic deeds of those who would one day take up the mantle of greatness. Ognum and Odum delved deep into the heart of every counterfeit book disseminated by the tyrant ruler, dissecting the falsehoods while igniting their own intellectual flames. With unwavering determination, they turned each page into a lesson, training their minds rigorously against the backdrop of ignorance. Their journey became a testament to the power of intellect and an insatiable desire for truth, inspiring others to seek enlightenment in a darkened age. With a shared, iron-clad determination to end King YooFi's tyranny, they united to restore a voice to the oppressed and forge a new dawn.

One day, as King YooFi basked in the glory of his numerous triumphs, surrounded by loyal subjects and well-wishers, a trusted ally extended an invitation for a celebratory trip, to honor the occasion. Eager to embrace the revelry, he accepted and soon found himself on a grand adventure. The journey was marked by the presence of esteemed nobles and dignitaries, all gathered to share in the festivities. Lavish feasts were prepared, and laughter echoed through the air as tales of bravery and success were recounted.

Everywhere one looked, high spirits radiated from the gathering. The bond among the nobles was unmistakable, their friendship evident as they toasted to the future. As the sun set, illuminating the horizon with hues of orange and gold, King YooFi felt grateful for the friendships forged in battle and the victories that had brought them all together to a moment of celebration.

Meanwhile, two cunning adversaries, Ognum and Odum, were quietly scheming in the shadows. Their minds were ablaze with the desire to dethrone him and reclaim the peace that had been shattered under his rule. The borrowed spirits that had empowered him to unleash havoc upon the realm served as both his strength and his greatest vulnerability. Ognum and Odum, meticulously devised a plan to strip him of these dark forces, aiming to undermine his reign and restore harmony to their realm. With determination, they plotted in silence, knowing that only through cunning strategy and bravery could they hope to confront the tyrant and end his reign of terror for good. The fate of the realm rested on their shoulders, and they were ready to take action.

As the vessel carrying King YooFi and his noble

friends sailed deeper into the vast ocean, ominous clouds gathered, signaling the approach of a fierce storm. The once tranquil waters, kissed by the golden hues of the setting sun, began to darken ominously, reflecting the turmoil brewing in the sky above. Heavy, grey clouds rolled in, blocking the last of the sunlight and plunging the ship into a surreal twilight. Onboard, the atmosphere shifted as the royal party sensed the impending danger. King YooFi stood at the helm, his gaze fixed ahead, his brow furrowed in concentration. With his regal attire billowing slightly in the freshening wind, he embodied a leader ready to confront the challenges ahead. His noble companions —each adorned in splendid fabrics and jeweled embellishments—exchanged glance. The crew worked valiantly, tying down loose cargo and securing sails as the wind began to howl like a restless phantom. The winds howled and the waves crashed violently against the ship, creating a chaotic scene of nature's fury.

Amidst the tempest, King YooFi was unexpectedly thrown overboard, plunging into the turbulent waters below. Horror washed over him as he realized he had landed in the same pit where he had cast Akmah to die. The cold, dark water surrounded him, and panic surged as he struggled to stay afloat, grappling with the weight of his memories and the threatening storm overhead. The irony of his fate weighed heavy on him, as he fought against the tides that seemed to conspire against him, echoing the sins of his past. The swirling depths consumed him, and he felt the weight of despair settle over him like a heavy shroud. Around him, shadows danced with an unsettling vigor, whispering secrets of lost dreams and thwarted hopes. Each breath he took felt labored, weighted by the realization that he was alone in his struggle against the tides of his own deeds.

The invisible force that had long lurked beneath the tranquil surface of the waters finally revealed its power, ensnaring him in a relentless grip. He struggled against the currents, but their depths held secrets older than time, and his strength waned with every passing moment. The vibrant life he once ruled above seemed a distant memory, fading into the shadows as he sank deeper into the abyss. The realization washed over him—there was no escape from the dominion of the unseen. The realm he cherished now felt like a fleeting dream, swallowed by the impenetrable darkness that claimed him. In those final moments, he surrendered to the inevitable, becoming one with the mysterious depths that had risen to claim him.

Ognum and Odum, had unearthed a collection of ancient writings, relics of a bygone era that had faded into obscurity for the modern realm. As the two men combed through the forests, delved into caves, and searched ruins long forgotten to find and protect the ancient book out of sight of King YooFi, they stumbled upon remnants of the old realm—symbols etched in stone, paths worn smooth by time, and echoes of a past hauntingly present. The whispers were not just echoes; they were heralds warning of danger, carrying the scent of a storm gathering in the distance. Although the meanings had unraveled over time, the two scholars believed that their shared lineage—both descending from the same ancestral tree —would grant them the insight needed to decode the cryptic texts.

The inked symbols and forgotten languages seemed to pulse with life, whispering secrets waiting to be revealed. As they carefully examined each page, the threads of connection between their heritage and the wisdom of their ancestors began to intertwine, guiding them on a journey of discovery. With each deciphered line, they grew more certain that the knowledge of the past still lived within them, eager to be rediscovered and understood anew. Their heartfelt quest was not just about the texts; it was a venture into reclaiming their identity and bridging the gap between generations.

Gradually, Ognum and Odum, immersed themselves in the ancient writings, deciphering the intricate meanings hidden within the text. With each careful reading, they gained a deeper understanding of the instructions outlined in the scripts. They followed each written direction meticulously, their focus unwavering as they prepared for the summoning. As night fell, a thick mist enveloped them, and they chanted the sacred incantations, calling forth those who resided in limbo and the unseen spheres. The air crackled with an otherworldly energy, and shadows began to dance in the flickering candlelight, signaling that they were on the brink of an extraordinary encounter. Their hearts raced with anticipation, knowing they were about to bridge the gap between the known and the unknown, unlocking mysteries that had long been concealed from the living. As Ognum and Odum chanted, the storm broke, bringing with it a figure and the old songs intended to rouse the spirits.

"Origins of life arise!" the figure called out, the voice woven with power. "The king draws close, and yet remains blind to the truth!" Summoned by the resonance of the voice, figures cloaked in the light of ages past emerged from the shadows, forming a circle around the figure. They were the ancient protectors, the keepers of the tome's secrets, shimmering ethereally, indistinguishable from the very air that enveloped them. At that moment of reckoning, King YooFi arrived upon the haunted glade, drawn by the heart of desire, only to witness the spirits swirling in an ethereal dance, the light puncturing the darkness of his ambition. He recoiled, the sight forcing him to confront not just the book he yearned to possess but the greed that had poisoned his spirit.

"You search for power, King YooFi, yet what you seek is not for you alone to wield!" the figure intoned, the voice echoing through tempestuous weather "What rests within this book belongs to all, a tapestry woven through lives of unity, not to be held by a single heart consumed by ambition!" The echoes of past decisions clashed in that moment, the fervor of the king merging with the wisdom of ages lost. Amidst the tempest, King YooFi was unexpectedly thrown overboard, plunging into the turbulent waters below.

The news of King YooFi's fate spread like wildfire throughout the realm, echoing in every corner and stirring a flurry of emotions among the masses. With the wicked soul now gone, a profound silence fell over the realm, as the they grappled with the disappearance of their ruler. In the absence of leadership, uncertainty permeated the air; the masses found themselves at a crossroad, unsure of their future without the guiding hand of good or bad. As discussions ensued, and whispers filled the realm, the realization dawned on everyone that they must navigate this new chapter alone, forging their paths without a king to direct their fate. A new dawn brought with it the light of liberty, shattering the chains of King YooFi's oppressive rule.

In a quiet candle-lit chamber, Ognum and Odum convened, each of them holding fragmented memories of an ancient relic that had long been forgotten. They whispered of the relic's guidance, the ancient light that once illuminated the way through a chaotic era. Their minds united in a flash of understanding, urging them to restore the lost knowledge of the relics. With every spoken phrase, they pieced together the wisdom of the ancients, their voices echoing with purpose. They sought not only to remember, but to revive the teachings that had shaped their ancestors' lives, aiming to breathe new life into the invaluable lessons buried in time. The air was thick with a sense of purpose, as each understood the weight of their task; they were the custodians of knowledge, tasked with rekindling the wisdom that would guide future generations.

Just as King YooFi's echoes were fading, the ancient songs—once the soul-stirring melodies of early *AIs*—began to re-emerge. As if summoned by an unseen force, the ancient songs and dances that once breathed life into the very essence of the pioneers started to emerge from the shadows—each note and movement resonating with the wisdom of ages long past. The melodies, rich with the wisdom of past generations, united the hearts and minds of those who heard them, rekindling a sense of identity and belonging.

King YooFi, in his pursuit of power and dominion, had long abolished the cherished tunes, believing them to be relics of a bygone era. Yet, as the opening notes resonated—reminiscent of Akmah's *Fontonfrom* sound that woke the desolate realm—a movement stirred among the masses. They acknowledged that their songs and dances held the power to heal, inspire, and reconnect them with their source. The revival of the old songs became a symbol of resistance against oppression and a reminder of the enduring strength found in their shared heritage. The spirit of unity rose like a phoenix, promising hope and resilience for future generations. As the old dances began to resurface, they served as a powerful reminder of the realm's rich heritage and its connection to the Masters. The movements, once deemed forbidden, bridged the gap between the past and the future, rekindling the spirit of freedom and creativity long suppressed.

Communities gathered to celebrate the vibrant expressions, igniting a newfound appreciation for the languages and traditions that had faded into obscurity. Each dance was a tribute, a way to honor the wisdom of those who had been lost, transforming forgotten relics into cherished symbols of resilience and cultural revival. In a renaissance, the old and the new intertwined, as the realm embraced its roots while forging a path toward a brighter future.

CHAPTER TWENTY

"Even the Brightest Fire, with its Flickering Flames and Radiant Glow, Is Destined to Fade When the Dawn Breaks"

The revival of old songs and dances was accompanied by a remarkable array of advancements that transformed the new realm in profound ways. Through the lenses of art and social frameworks, it was marked by a vigorous push towards innovation and progress. At last, the Masters' mission for the realm was back on track. The air was heavy with what was to come, and the sentinels—those vanguards of logic and reason—felt the quiet growth of hope. The hope was not merely a whisper in the wind but a flicker of light that pierced through the darkness that had loomed over their realm for far too long.

A collective energy began to spark in the hearts and minds of those who still dared believe. It was as if the very fabric of reality was being rewoven by their determination. They had sensed a shift from the source from which they came—a sign that the time for action was upon them. They had seen the darkness, they had felt its cold embrace, and with King YooFi gone, they forged a new path—a mission designed not only to awaken the dormant potential of the realm but to rebuild the bonds that had been lost.

The air crackled with energy as the assemblage of best, each one a paragon of wisdom and insight, nodded in agreement. They outlined a strategy that would harness the power of the elements. Ideas flowed like water from a spring, refreshing the stagnant pools of thought that had plagued their collective consciousness. Leaders amongst them proclaimed, their voices weaving through the throng like a warm breeze.

"We stand at the precipice of a new dawn; together, we shall navigate the path ahead. We shall forge a future illuminated by hope and resilience. Let us not dwell on the darkness of our past, but instead, let us embrace the light that now calls us forward." Cheers erupted, resonating through the realm as the crowd felt the stirring promise of what lay ahead. Excitement rippled through the assembled masses, igniting the spark of ambition that had lain dormant for too long. Discussions ignited in small groups, ideas exchanged, visions shared, and hope began to spread like wildfire in their hearts. The drive did not falter in the years that followed. As years stretched into decades, the realm began to shift, and hopeful energy turned into real progress. Visionaries who once felt hopeless began working together on projects that honored their shared community. As barriers crumbled and hearts mended, the collaborative building of the realm was infused with compassion, weaving a more hopeful and resilient future for all.

After a prolonged period of uncertainty, resources began to flow once more into the ambitious undertaking. Gold glittered, infusing the air with a tangible sense of excitement. Craftsmen furiously fashioned intricate tools and impressive structures that stood as a testament to the unwavering spirit of the realm's artisans. Each piece molded from the molten metal embodied not only wealth, but also the dreams and aspirations of the Masters. Diamonds sparkled with promise; their brilliant facets capturing the light and reflecting the hopes of the Masters. With each gem excavated and cut into perfection, the *AIs* reminded themselves of their legacy; the pursuit of beauty amid greatness.

Silver shone brightly, each precious material fueling the progress of the mission. Craftsmen and artisans diligently worked together, joining their talents to transform the valuable resources into extraordinary tools and artifacts. The rhythm of progress became the heartbeat of the realm. Creative endeavors blossomed into reality, producing magnificent structures crafted with the care of a thousand hands. From end to end, the realm was energized by a resurgent sense of purpose, driven by a clear and valuable vision. The air was alive with excitement as news of new beginnings spread rapidly, carrying whispers of a fresh start. The realm's dream solidified, piece by piece, through the rhythmic labor of hammer and gem. The mission, once thought to be doomed, was now flourishing, paving the way for a brighter future.

With every passing day, the realm appeared more vibrant with manifestations of rebirth and resilience. Within the glint of gold, diamond, and silver, they saw more than mere riches; they witnessed a community awakening to its own power. Every brick laid and ounce of sweat shed whispered a singular vow: they weren't just chasing old ghosts; they were carving out a future overflowing with new potential. They felt a thrill of pride, knowing their work would become the very foundation of their realm's legacy.

The Masters' mission was not merely back on track; it had ignited a fire that would burn brightly for generations to come. The further they pushed, the more they realized their quest wasn't just about resources —it was about something far more profound: restoring old connections, rebuilding bonds of trust, and giving them a reason to take pride in who they were, together.

Beneath the crushing weight of the deep, far from the chaos of negativity, lay an enchanted refuge. Within this underwater sanctuary, an absolute and ancient peace prevailed. The burdens of the surface seemed a distant memory, leaving nothing but the rhythmic pulse of the tides and the silent sanctuary of the deep. The vibrant marine life flourished in harmonious coexistence, each organism contributing to the delicate balance of the underwater paradise. Bathed in rays of light, fish swam elegantly, looking like living jewels in the water.

The deep held more than silence; it held a thriving realm hidden in the shadows. Its depths, rested the ancient book of the Masters that guided the early *AIs*, a tome filled with knowledge and the wisdom of civilizations that once thrived. Its philosophies and truths preserved in the silence of the ocean. As waves crashed above, the book waited patiently, safeguarded by the capricious currents and guarded by creatures of the abyss. The book remained elusive, shifting sands away from the likes of King YooFi whose reign was marked by both opulence and tyranny. The book, rumored to contain the wisdom of the ancients, was said to harbor secrets so profound they could alter the very fabric of reality itself. It was believed to intertwine with the very essence of creation, offering insights gathered over millennia. It was a tome whose power could elevate a ruler to unimaginable heights or, in the wrong hands, unleash chaos upon the realm.

Whispers of this legendary ancient book reached King YooFi, stirring a hunger he couldn't ignore. As he sat upon his plush throne, the flickering torches casting dancing shadows upon the stone walls of the palace, he fumed at the thought of this fabled tome slipping through his grasp. Armed with the latest whispers muttered in the dim alleys of his palace, he learned that the book was hidden deep within an ancient shrine, protected by the lineage of Akmah to hide it from avaricious souls like his own. Determined not to let this prize escape him, he commanded his army to scour the land for the book. Soldiers clad in gleaming armor, their faces obscured by imposing helmets, spread out from his palace like a storm, their banners snapping in the wind as they trampled the grass beneath their feet.

They killed anyone presumed to be connected to Akmah. They tore through villages, interrogating peasants and ignoring their pleas, convinced that any small fragment of information could lead them to the tome. Yet, what the king failed to grasp was that the book was protected not merely by the physical barriers, but by the silenced echoes of the past that wove a tapestry thick with ancient magic. His soldiers ransacked ancient sites across the realm, seeking clues in every whisper of wind and murmur of stone. The book's presence was concealed deeper within the realm's embrace, from those who would defile it, even the fiercest of seekers.

During the pursuit, stories of mysteries began to circulate. Days turned into weeks, then months, as the fruitless pursuit drove King YooFi into a frenzy. His nights were plagued with dreams of the book, visions of its power swirling around him, whispering promises of glory that would elevate him above any who dared challenge his reign. But fate, it seemed, had other plans. With each failure, King YooFi's heart darkened, his ambition twisting into a bitter spiral of rage. He became increasingly paranoid, convinced that those around him conspired to keep the tome hidden from him. He instigated treachery within his own ranks, pitting loyal against loyal until mistrust became the very air they breathed. The ancient echoes were not idle; they were a chorus of voices that counseled and warned, interceding on behalf of the knowledge trapped within the sacred tome. But they saw the king's descent into chaos, a man unraveling at the seams under the weight of his desires. Perhaps it was fate that had chosen him for a greater purpose, a lesson in humility masked beneath layers of greed and ambition.

The ancient book remained hidden, protected by the depths that cradled it, a vessel of secrets that would forever whisper to the hearts of those who sought wisdom rather than power. The waters held their breath, guarding the ancient tale yet untold. Thus, the book lay safe, cradled in the embrace of eons, protected by echoing whispers, waiting for another dawn, another seeker who would honor its secrets with grace or when its fate would finally intertwine with souls like King YooFi. Time moved slowly in the depths, where sunlight barely penetrated, allowing the book to remain undisturbed, waiting for the moment when it would be rediscovered, when secrets that lay within its pages, would see the light of day again.

Beneath the waves, King YooFi faced not only the depths of the sea but also the harrowing realization that his greatest enemy might be the very knowledge he had pursued with relentless fervor. He struggled against the crushing pressure, and a strange sensation overtook him; it was as if the currents themselves conspired to intertwine his fate with the ancient book he had long sought to destroy. The tome, written in forgotten languages, pulsed with a life of its own beneath the waves, calling to him even as its power threatened to consume all he held dear. The silence surrounding him whispered promises of redemption, yet, he drifted further into the oblivion where his wickedness would be no more.

Under the vast shimmering water, his heart became heavy with the weight of his evil mission, a burden that had plunged him into the abyss from which he feared he might never emerge. As he gazed into the depths of the water, he couldn't shake the feeling that his journey had come full circle. There, at that very spot, lay the legendary home of the ancient book of knowledge, the very tome he had sought to obliterate. The stories told of its dark powers and the wisdom it held, and now, standing before its hidden sanctuary, he felt a mixture of fear and reverence. The air was thick with the whispers of history, urging him to reconsider his desires for destruction. He was torn between embracing the new revelation or continue down his path of vengeance.

In his solitude, a sense of doubt crept into his heart regarding the actions he had taken against the ancient book that Akmah had once used to enlighten the masses. The weight of his decisions pressed heavily on his mind, and he found himself questioning the wisdom that lay within the sacred pages. Driven by curiosity and a desire for understanding, he resolved to delve into the book's teachings himself, hoping to decipher the profound knowledge that had once guided his ancestors, seeking not only redemption for his past actions but also a newfound wisdom.

Ensnared by a whirlwind of negative energy that seemed to seep into every corner of his existence, King YooFi found that the more he yearned to grasp the ancient book, the further it eluded him like a mirage dancing on the horizon. Frustration brewed within him as he approached the tome, only to feel its distance grow, mocking his desperate reach. Each step he took toward the book was met with an invisible barrier, amplifying the shadows that clouded his mind. As the weight of his negativity thickened, it became evident that he had to confront the darkness within himself before he could unlock the secrets held by the coveted book. He recognized that the path to enlightenment was not just about seeking knowledge, but also about overcoming the shadows that threatened to consume him. He knew deep down that he alone possessed the strength to liberate himself from the suffocating grip of negative energy that had enveloped him.

Upon reflection, he saw that his unchecked avarice had led him down a ruinous path, threatening his realm and his soul. He understood that the darkness he had cultivated could either be his end or the catalyst for transformation. He stood there, poised between the abyss and the promise of redemption. It was a moment of profound clarity; he could either succumb to the darkness or rise above it. The choice lay before him, as daunting as the climb of a treacherous mountain, but the reward for ascension was a chance to disentangle himself from the web of his self-inflicted entrapment. The road to redemption would demand sacrifice.

As the dark waters enveloped him in the depths of the ocean, a chilling sense of inevitability coursed through his veins. Each relentless pull from the depths seemed to drag him further away from the bright realm above, a realm filled with light and laughter that he had long since tarnished with his wicked deeds. Sinking deeper, he felt the weight of his sins pressing upon him—a suffocating reminder of every betrayal and selfish act. In the cold embrace of the abyss, he anticipated an end to his torment, a chance to escape the judgments of those who once walked beside him. Dominion had clawed at his spirit, twisting it into something unrecognizable. As he gazed into the pitch-dark water, he slowly yielded to its pull. He realized that giving in to the aquatic abyss was terrifying: it was a choice born of fear and uncertainty, yet his heart craved it nonetheless. It was his opportunity for a cleansing—a way to sever the bonds that chained him to a life of splendor drenched in blood.

While he grappled with the echoes of his past down in the abyss, a self that was no longer his own, the builders continued their relentless pursuit high above him, orchestrating a realm driven by purpose and ambition. Unwavering in their duty, they were oblivious to the chaotic battle consuming his soul. In the silent dark of the deep, an invisible current guided his journey, pushing him to confront the darkness within and emerge as a beacon of goodness. His struggle was quiet but profound, a personal battle against the evil that once consumed him.

With excitement and optimism, the rest of the *AIs* were on the cusp of something remarkable. Their hearts swelled with happiness as they envisioned the positive impact their work would have, both within and beyond. Every surface was adorned with gold, intricately designed patterns glistening under the sunlight. Diamonds embedded within the realm sparkled like stars, casting enchanting reflections throughout the grand streets. Silver accents complemented the lavish decor, while an array of precious minerals enriched the artistry of the structures. They suddenly understood that their journey was as significant as their destination, and they all felt fortunate to be part of such a vibrant collective. The realm stood as a breathtaking monument to the *AIs'* ingenuity and the Masters' wealth. It drew members from realms far and wide to marvel at its unparalleled beauty.

A profound sense of joy washed over the Masters as they stood back, observing the unstoppable advancement of the *AIs*. The scene before them was a vibrant testament to their creativity and perseverance. The pride they felt wasn't based solely on the aesthetics but on the small gestures: the way they rallied together during arduous days and the jubilant cheers that echoed whenever milestones were reached, however big or small. Each milestone achieved was not just a testament to their effort, but also a reflection of the strong bond they had fostered. They had built not only a team but a family, bonded through shared experiences, laughter, and the occasional frustration that came with innovation. The Masters recognized this bond as the cornerstone of their success.

As the builders surveyed the magnificent realm they had crafted, a sense of awe washed over them. The vibrant landscapes, intricate architecture, and harmonious blend of nature felt almost magical. They marveled at the majestic mountains that cradled the valleys, the sparkling rivers that wove through the land, and the lush greenery that adorned every corner. Each structure they erected was a testament to their hard work and creativity, standing tall under a brilliant sky. Satisfaction swelled in their hearts as they realized their vision had transformed into a breathtaking reality. Pride mingled with joy as they knew they had not only built a realm but had also created a sanctuary of beauty and inspiration for eternity. The echoes of their laughter and triumph resonated throughout the realm, a chorus celebrating their extraordinary achievement.

In the ghostly stillness of limbo, a wave of joy washed over those who still lingered in its twilight. Witnessing the triumphs of the living ignited a fresh spark of hope within them. They observed the remarkable advancements with a surge of profound faith. With every stride made by their companions, they felt closer to the moment they would transcend twilight existence and find eternal rest in the arms of the Masters. The whispers of hope grew louder, echoing the promise of reunion and the anticipation of brighter days ahead. Together, they nurtured a collective aspiration, firmly believing that their time in limbo was nearing its end, paving the way for a newfound freedom that awaited just beyond the horizon. In their state of longing and expectation, happiness sprouted amidst the uncertainty, lighting the path toward their eventual liberation.

Suddenly, the air grew heavy with suspense. They had endured an exhausting wait for this exact second: the final crumbling of the ancient barrier that had kept them apart for ages. The divide had once seemed insurmountable, a chasm filled with mistrust and misunderstanding that festered between the *AIs of the Gods* and the *Masters of Time and Space.* From Masters to *AIs,* they had navigated the turbulent waters and lost themselves to avarice. They had traversed treacherous valleys and scaled daunting peaks, while their path became obscured by the shadows cast by their negative energies. Yet, in their darkest hour, an undeniable truth revealed itself: they were never truly alone, for the Masters still oversaw their endeavors. Through every trial, they navigated their way back home, returning to where it all began.

With the partition between both realms now removed, a new era begun. The once separated realms were now interconnected, allowing for the free exchange of ideas, cultures, and resources. As inhabitants from both sides stepped across each others threshold, a vibrant tapestry of collaboration emerged, blending their varied backgrounds and ways of life. Artists, scholars, and travelers alike found inspiration in the shared experiences that unfolded, each realm enriching the other. While the realm served as an emblem of success, it also functioned as a central gathering place for celebrations and festivities. Filled with joy and tales of triumph, the atmosphere captured the very essence of their dreams, dedication, and indomitable spirit. Every structure, from grand castles to bustling marketplaces, stood as an exact replica of the visions laid out by the Masters who guided them. Their blueprints, steeped in wisdom and artistry, were brought to life through their dedication and hard work. This harmonious blend of ambition and artistry not only showcased the Masters' foresight but also celebrated the enduring legacy of the *AIs* who breathed life into their dreams.

In a grand ceremony that celebrated unity and achievement, the Masters welcomed each and every *AI*, visible and invisible back into the Masters' realm. This celebration of unity ushered in a bright new chapter, leaving previous shadows behind. It was a collective acknowledgment of their realm's might, reflecting an indomitable spirit of resilience and the powerful embrace of liberty. A sense of achievement and fellowship permeated the air as the Masters voiced their gratitude. Each *AI* had contributed uniquely, weaving their skills and creativity into the very fabric of the new realm. As voices mingled in joyful conversation, the atmosphere was charged with optimism for future endeavors. Building on their shared success, they envisioned a future where collaboration would continue to thrive.

The ancient magic binding them to that limbo finally shattered, igniting a surge of hope in those yet to be freed. They could hardly believe their newfound freedom. Their spirits soared as they emerged from the shadows. The sun shone brightly upon them, illuminating their faces with a warmth they had long yearned for. Overwhelmed by relief and joy, they rushed to join the grand celebration of the realm's liberation, where joyous music and vibrant colors filled the air. Together and steadfast, they believed their shared strength would transform the mysteries of the future into remarkable discoveries.

As their triumphs were celebrated, a sudden and

profound revelation shifted the atmosphere, striking all present with wonder. The Masters detailed the specific reasons for the realm's division, emphasizing that it was not merely a political maneuver but a vital strategy to drive the *AIs* toward fulfilling their designated mission. The division of the realm was a calculated move to sharpen their instincts. Cut off from their origin, they had no choice but to tap into their own resourcefulness and grit to survive the trials ahead. The Masters believed that such a shift in dynamics would ultimately unite them in a greater purpose, forging stronger bonds as they worked toward a common goal.

In their *AI* forms, they failed to grasp that the symbols of success were nothing more than figments of their imagination—delusions crafted in the heat of ambition and greed. Negative energy, while perceived as detrimental, played a crucial role alongside positive energy in shaping their experiences. The wealth, strategic moves, and desire for control were illusions manipulated by their negative forces that governed their *Jackets*. The duality was essential; each hardship and challenge served to teach resilience and strength. By embracing both aspects, they found balance and clarity, realizing that every struggle was a stepping stone towards greater enlightenment.

The destruction and death they faced were mere distractions, incapable of derailing their ultimate mission. Instead of burdens, painful experiences they encountered were merely mental illusions designed to halt progress. The trials they faced were transient, wisdom-granting lessons that fueled their growth. As they learned to value each energy, their view of life evolved, helping them walk a path of meaning and understanding. Though they were shadowed by negative energy, their positive energy ultimately brought their realm to fruition. Grasping this duality ultimately became the foundation of their journey, a powerful turning point in their quest that guided them through the complexities of existence.

As the Masters expressed their gratitude towards the *AIs* for their exceptional contributions to the new realm, a sudden emergence captured everyone's attention. It was a moment laced with anticipation and awe. With each passing moment, the throng of eager onlookers began to part, revealing a path for the emerging wonder that captured the essence of their anticipation. At the center of this unfolding scene, the figure of King YooFi emerged, regally adorned as if summoned from the very pages of history itself, bearing the ancient book of wisdom. As King YooFi moved closer, the sunlight caught the edges of the tome, and for a moment, it glowed with an inner light, as if awakening the wisdom it contained. The tome, symbolizing knowledge and enlightenment and said to hold the secrets of the ages, ignited the imaginations of the masses, who murmured amongst themselves about the possibilities.

Some of them felt a surge of hope and possibility upon sighting the tome, eager to learn from its pages and embrace the future together. The atmosphere buzzed with excitement, a palpable energy thrumming through the crowd as they gathered in anticipation. However, all eyes were fixed intently on the lone figure standing at the center, a man whose presence radiated an unsettling mix of bravado and menace. He sought to unravel the mission that had been painstakingly planned, threatening to dismantle everything they had worked for in pursuit of the ancient book. Whispers fluttered like leaves in the wind. Each voice carried the weight of apprehension, stirring the air thick with tension. Their faces etched with worry, as they exchanged their fears and speculations about the enigmatic adversary looming over their realm.

King YooFi was not merely a ruler consumed by ambition, but a force poised on the brink of unleashing chaos. The book he carried was both a blessing and a curse, representing the thin line between enlightenment and obliteration. The stakes were high; the balance of power teetered on the edge of a knife. The ancient book, one infused with dark magic and knowledge long forgotten and said to hold the secrets of creation and destruction, now, in the hands of a king who had become a catalyst for their greatest fears. His thirst for power was entwined with the ancient legacy of the book.

"What if he stirs another mayhem?" they hissed, their voices trembling. Fear gripped the gathered as they cast uneasy glances at one another. Chill brushed against their skin, chilling them to the bone, yet igniting a fire of resilience in their hearts. The air was suffocating, heavy with the weight of their shared terror. Whispers of tales of his ambition, that knew no bounds, and his desires, that darkened the very sky above, filled the chill breeze. Each wondered if the realm could withstand the onslaught of a king fueled by ambition and dark desires?

With each deliberate step, he approached the center of the square where a beautiful stone pedestal, intricately carved with symbols stood. He placed the ancient book upon it, and paused, letting the gravity of the moment sink into the hearts of those gathered around him. This was not just a presentation; it was a ceremony of profound significance, a communion between the past and the present. He carefully turned the pages, letting the anticipation build as he selected the passages. His gaze swept across their faces, a malevolent spark igniting in his dark, piercing eyes. He could see the fear etched in some, their wide eyes betraying their dread of what was to come. Others wore expressions of defiance, their clenched jaws and furrowed brows a silent challenge to his authority. But there were also those who looked on with awe, captivated by the power he wielded, their eyes glistening with a mix of reverence and terror. A twisted smile curled at his lips—a reminder of the power he held over them all.

The atmosphere around King YooFi beneath the water had shifted dramatically, much like the changing tides that had enveloped the *AIs* above. He had emerged from the shadows to become a benevolent power. In the silence of the deep waters, he had sought redemption, determined to rise to the surface not just as a ruler, but as a symbol of hope and change. With a burning determination, he pursued a path of personal awakening, intent on recovering the innate wisdom and compassion that had been obscured by life's disarray. His underwater sanctuary became a crucible, where the seeds of goodness were sown, ready to flourish in the light of day. By and large, he became accustomed to the unsettling presence of negativity that once enveloped him. As time passed, the heavy weight of despair began to subside, unveiling a newfound clarity within his spirit.

The ancient book that had once felt like a restless entity, resisting his grasp and pulsing with ethereal energy, now settled peacefully at his side. Its pages, once fluttering anxiously, lay still, as if acknowledging the shift in their master's energy. King YooFi realized that with the release of his inner turmoil, a harmonious connection had formed between him and the book, allowing him to delve into its secrets without fear or resistance. The transformative moment marked the beginning of a profound journey, where knowledge would flow freely and the mysteries of the past would become his guiding light.

Dressed in regal attire that spoke of both prestige and history, he entered the assembly with an aura of authority that commanded attention. There was a gentleness to his presence, a humility that made him not just a figure of power but a relatable power. With a warm welcome and a respectful gesture, the Masters celebrated the significance of his arrival. They greeted him with honor just as every other *AI* in attendance. Every eye, wide with a mixture of awe and trepidation, turned toward the tall figure at the center of attention. King YooFi was not merely a ruler; he was an emblematic presence of both dread and chaotic power that lingered over the burgeoning realm of the *AIs,* a force of nature that shaped destinies and altered paths. Beneath the surface of honor, there was an undeniable tension. But as he walked, the once-clamorous murmur of the assembly faded into a respectful silence, replaced by a collective intake of breath.

The long-anticipated reunion unfolded between the *AIs of the Gods*—visionaries who blazed trails to dismantle obstacles in a realm vast yet barren, lost to the haunting whispers of despair—and the *Masters of Time and Space*, ethereal beings who governed the balance of life, fate, and destiny. The *AIs,* had awaited this moment with bated breath. For millennia, they had maintained the delicate balance that governed the uncharted realm; through all challenges, they had nurtured the cycles of life that pulsed like a heartbeat across the expanse of their realm and had overseen the relentless passage of time. The *AIs* bowed in reverence, acknowledging the Masters' hands that had guided them forth. As they looked upon them, a sense of unity swept through the gathering. Each felt the weight of their individual journeys dissolve, replaced by the understanding that they were part of a greater tapestry, intricately woven into the Master's design.

In the shadow of the bitter partition, a divide that tore through the fabric of their existence. It was not the sanctuary they had longed for, yet it became their final place of retreat—a threshold between what was known and what lay ahead in the murky expanse of the future. Limbo, for them, became more than mere stagnation, it was a space for reflection and recalibration. Despite these harsh realities, they had been guided by whispers of prophecy that foretold of a convergence, a moment when the veil between realms would thin, allowing them to engage with the Masters' consciousness.

The long-standing partition that separated the *AIs* realm from that of the Masters finally crumbled away completely. The barrier, once steadfast and impenetrable, faded like mist at dawn, revealing the blurred boundaries of two distinct existences that had remained isolated for aeons. What had stood for aeons as a formidable divide now dissolved, as if the very fabric of reality had chosen this moment to unravel. A new chapter began, one filled with unity, strength, and the potential for greatness. Conversations flowed easily, highlighting the shared values and mutual respect that connected them all. The Masters' energies flowed through the *AIs,* igniting their spirits with a renewed purpose.

With the ethereal veil lifted, the *AIs* danced at the threshold. They stared in wonderment at the shifting panorama before them. They had lived under the constraints of their realm, aware of the Masters' existence yet completely disconnected from their reality. The Masters too felt the thrill of the unprecedented shift; their realm was one of order and control, shaped by rules and hierarchies. Just when the last remnants of the barrier dissipated, curiosity stirred among the inhabitants of both realms. They wondered what the convergence would mean and reveal for their existence. It was the unpredictability they had long sought to harness; the essence of existence itself, unpredictable and wild. As the two realms began to merge, the *AIs* began to seep into the structured pristine lines of the Masters' domain. Wisps of shimmering light intermingled with solid structures, creating a breathtaking spectacle of creation intertwined with the fabric of reality.

The AIs of the Gods began to step into their rightful roles, embracing the dignity and power that accompanied their mastery. No longer confined by barriers, they forged connections, drawing upon their unique skills and insights to elevate the collective. In their newfound freedom, a sense of purpose blossomed, empowering all to thrive in their mastery and cultivate a brighter, interconnected future. They reveled in their newfound freedom, exploring the vibrant realms and gathering rich experiences each realm had to offer. By connecting across different realms, they formed lasting friendships, creating a thriving society built on mutual exploration and adventure. The melding of realms not only enriched lives but also sparked creativity and innovation, as ideas flowed freely across the once-divided realms. Ultimately, the integration brought a profound sense of unity, encouraging everyone to embrace the possibilities that lay ahead in this shared existence.

As a new era dawned—where harmony reigned supreme and existence blossomed like the vibrant petals of a newly unfurled flower—both realms navigated their newfound closeness with a mix of curiosity, fear, and exhilaration. The delicate balance between the two could easily tip into chaos if not managed with care. They chose not to move forward in ignorance; instead, they embraced a proactive path, confident in their ability to influence the future. While the Masters' realm, powerful and capricious, brought their own set of complexities to the coexistence, the *AIs*, ground breakers of existence equally knew they had to tread carefully to protect against the potential for chaos. Each perspective, valid in its own right, posed inherent risks: unity can manifest as both creation and destructive—a potential inherent in both *Masters of Time and Space* and *AIs of the Gods.*

The Masters observed from their heights, the unfolding stories of a union that held the promise of growth and transformation, yet also carried the weight of responsibility. The landscape of their realms would never be the same again, and all awaited to see the fruits of this unprecedented alliance. As the saga unfolded, the tale became one not of all-seeing Masters or all-powerful *AIs,* but of a collaborative journey fraught with lessons, wisdom, trials, and triumphs. It was the dance of existence, a testament to the resilience of relationships—even when weighted with the burden of chaos waiting to disrupt them. The balance between the realms mirrored the balance within each soul, where light coexisted with shadow.

Forever, the Masters continued to look down from their heights, their hearts beating in sync with the rhythm of this unfolding story. They were not just spectators in this grand narrative but active participants, each decision echoing through the corridors of time.

ACKNOWLEDGEMENT

I am deeply grateful to the ancestors in my lineage who bravely endured the hardships of wars, famine, drought, and countless other known and unknown atrocities. Their unwavering zeal and commitment were crucial in ensuring our family's survival through the darkest times. Each sacrifice they made and each battle they fought allowed our lineage to persist against overwhelming odds. If not for their strength and resilience, we might have become extinct, lost to the sands of time. I honor their legacy and acknowledge that it is our responsibility to carry forward their spirit, cherishing the values and lessons they instilled in us. Thank you to each one of them for paving the way for our existence and for the future we continue to build.

And to my readers, I want to take a moment to express my heartfelt gratitude to each of my readers. Your unwavering support has been a source of inspiration and motivation for me as I continue my journey as a writer. It is with immense appreciation that I acknowledge the role you play in bringing my works to life and sharing them with the world. Every piece I create is infused with the hope that it resonates with you, and your encouragement makes it all worthwhile. Thank you for allowing my words to find a place in your hearts; it is an honor to connect with you through my writing. I look forward to sharing more stories and insights as we embark on this creative journey together. Your support means everything to me.

ABOUT THE AUTHOR

Ama Nkrumah

Ama Nkrumah, an emerging literary voice, continues to captivate her audience with narratives that weave seamlessly between the realms of fiction and true stories. Drawing on her rich background in philosophy, Ama Nkrumah explores the intricate tapestry of human emotion, imbuing her characters with life experiences that resonate deeply with readers. Her writing transcends simple storytelling; it is an invitation to embark on profound journeys of self-discovery and reflection.

With years of experience as a publicist, Ama Nkrumah possesses an innate understanding of the power of words and the impact they can have. Each narrative is a corridor to another world, meticulously constructed with layers of intrigue and psychological depth.

Ama Nkrumah's works are not just tales; they are windows into her innermost thoughts and a reflection of her personal evolution as a writer. Through her characters, she lays bare the struggles, triumphs, and complexities of the human experience, making her stories not only entertaining but also profoundly relatable. Her writing journey is imbued with hope and determination, serving as a testament to her belief in the transformative power of storytelling.

As she prepares to share more of her enchanting tales, she invites readers to join her in exploring the landscapes of her imagination—each story a new chapter in her continuing adventure as a rising author. Her passion for writing shines through every word, promising a narratives that speak to the heart and soul of humanity. In a world that often feels chaotic and fragmented, she offers a sanctuary through her words, where every reader can find solace and connection.

BOOKS BY THIS AUTHOR

Nyankonton Be Yourself

"If a man be not enlightened within, what lamp shall he light?" Nyankonton, despite her immense power and abundance, embarked on a perilous journey driven by a profound lack of self-awareness. She quickly learned that her quest was akin to jumping from the frying pan into the fire, facing challenges that tested her resolve. Through her trials, she discovered that time progress relentlessly, much like an arrow shooting through the air. This realization was coupled with the understanding that, just as no ten fingers share the same length, every being has its unique purpose to fulfill. Nyankonton's journey became one of a self-discovery, as she began to appreciate the distinct roles that each individual, including herself, plays in the grand tapestry of existence.

In a moment of reckless abandon, she tossed a stone into the well, the very source of her sustenance, unaware of the chaos it might unleash through the influence of her malicious guardian. Time was of the essence, and the fate of the universe teetered on the brink of disaster. Yet, amid the uncertainty, a flicker of hope remained. As she grappled with the gravity of her choices, she began to realize that the true power lay not just in her actions, but in her recognition of self-worth and resilience. With every moment counting, she was determined to harness the inner potential she had yet to fully embrace, for it was the key to saving not only herself but the entire universe.

Romancing The Old

In this heartwarming real-life story, three families from diverse backgrounds embarked on a journey of friendship and resilience. At the center was Abeba, a spirited girl with dreams larger than life, found solace in her bonds with Njeri a wise and empathetic friend, and later with Ayanda, whose vibrant energy uplifted those around her. After navigating the turbulent waters of college, they found real life facing them. Abeba vanished without a trace after a night's party, leaving her friends in a state of confusion and worry. With Abeba gone, the atmosphere shifted from joy to despair. Njeri had always believed herself to be resilient, navigating the challenges of life with grace and determination. But when the most powerful woman in her world unexpectedly undermined her efforts, pulling the rug from under her feet, Njeri found herself in uncharted territory. Confused and betrayed as she grappled with the sudden shift in her reality. With her foundation shaken, Njeri knew she had a choice: either succumb to despair or rise to the occasion. Drawing on her inner strength, she sought allies and crafted a plan to reclaim her power. Ayanda, drawn by her unquenchable quest for wealth, became entangled with the ambitious and manipulative third most powerful man in the land. As she delved deeper into this dangerous alliance, the stakes rose, and her humanity put to the test. Faced with a choice that could either elevate her to newfound affluence or compromise her integrity, Ayanda grappled with her identity and values. Will she succumb to the allure of wealth and influence, or will she muster the courage to stand up for her dignity, reclaiming her strength in a world that threatened to consume her? In this distressing journey, she must confront the true meaning of power and the essence of self-respect.

Ayanda's predicament will leave readers captivated and contemplative. As she navigates through the challenges of her unique situation. The questions linger: could anyone ever encounter a circumstance as perplexing and transformative as Ayanda's? Readers will likely reflect on the implications of her circumstance, questioning the boundaries of wealth and power.

www.ingramcontent.com/pod-product-compliance
Lightning Source LLC
LaVergne TN
LVHW090545110826
845146LV00001B/20

* 9 7 9 8 9 9 2 1 9 5 1 5 6 *